M000188691

WHEN THE THE WORLD TIPS OVER

JANDY NELSON

Dial Books

DIAL BOOKS

An imprint of Penguin Random House LLC
1745 Broadway, New York, New York 10019

First published in the United States of America by Dial Books,
an imprint of Penguin Random House LLC, 2024
Copyright © 2024 by Jandy Nelson

Dial & colophon are registered trademarks of Penguin Random House LLC.
The Penguin colophon is a registered trademark of Penguin Books Limited.
Visit us online at PenguinRandomHouse.com.

Library of Congress Cataloging-in-Publication Data is available.
Printed in the United States of America
ISBN 9780525429098
1st Printing
LSCH

Interior illustrations copyright © 2024 by Jessica Cruickshank
This book was edited by Jessica Dandino Garrison, copyedited by Regina Castillo,
proofread by Kenny Young, and designed by Jennifer Kelly.
The production was supervised by Jayne Ziemba, Nicole Kiser, and Vanessa Robles.
Text set in Calisto MT Pro

Epigraphs quoted from
Margaret Atwood's *Moral Disorder and Other Stories*
John Steinbeck's *The Grapes of Wrath*
Oscar Wilde's *Vera; or, The Nihilists*
Walt Whitman's *Leaves of Grass*
Paul Éluard's *Ouevres complètes, vol. 1*
Kabir's *Ecstatic Poems*, translated by Robert Bly
and used here with thanks.

For my family,
who double as the very best friends,
and
for my friends,
who double as the most amazing family

In the end, we'll all become stories.
—Margaret Atwood

*How can we live without our lives? How will we
know it's us without our past?*
—John Steinbeck

*One can live sometimes without living at all, then
all life comes crowding into a single hour.*
—Oscar Wilde

*Day by day and night by night we were together—
all else has long been forgotten by me.*
—Walt Whitman

There is another world, but it's in this one.
—Paul Éluard

*Are you looking for me?
I am in the next seat.*
—Kabir

FANTASIA (NOUN)

fan·ta·sia | \ fan-ˈtā-zhə

1: a composition, often musical, with an improvisational style

1b: a literary work composed of a mixture of different forms or styles

2: a work in which fancy roves unrestricted

3: something possessing fantastical, bizarre, or unreal qualities

DIZZY

Encounter #1 with the Rainbow-Haired Girl

The morning of the day twelve-year-old Dizzy Fall walked into the path of the speeding eighteen-wheeler and encountered the rainbow-haired girl, everything was going wrong. In the divorce with her best friend, Lizard, who now went by his real name, Tristan, Lizard-now-Tristan had been granted popularity, a cool haircut, and a girlfriend named Melinda.

Dizzy had been granted nothing.

They'd been a twosome since first grade, wandering around in each other's innermost secrets, baking through the list of *Pastry Magazine*'s most ambitious desserts as well as their mutual favorite activity: surfing the internet for pertinent information regarding existence. Lizard's area of expertise was weather and natural disasters while Dizzy's was all cool things.

Lately those cool things had been stories about saints who rose into the air in fits of ecstasy, Himalayan yogis who could turn their bodies into stone, Buddha, who'd made duplicates of himself and shot fire from his fingers (yes!). Reading about these woo-woo things made Dizzy's soul buzz and Dizzy wanted a buzzy soul. A buzzy *everything*.

Also, recently, pre-divorce, Dizzy and Lizard had kissed for three seconds to see if they'd feel the endorphins Lizard learned about online or the spontaneous internal explosions Dizzy read about in the romance novels her mother kept behind the literary ones on the shelf, particularly *Live Forever Now* starring Samantha Brooksweather, which was Dizzy's favorite. Lizard thought romance novels were totally useless, but Dizzy learned so much from them. She wanted the door of her wild femininity to swing open already, her fiery furnace to ignite, her passion-moistened depths to awaken, and, although, unlike Samantha Brooksweather, she'd never seen a real live penis, from these books she knew an absolute ton about stiff members, turgid shafts, and throbbing spears. Unfortunately, however, during the three-second kiss with Lizard, neither of them had felt endorphins nor spontaneous internal explosions.

Anyway, all that morning of the telltale day of the first encounter, Dizzy sat in class and watched ex–best friend Lizard-now-Tristan stealthily texting with awful new girlfriend Melinda, probably about all the spontaneous internal explosions they experienced when they kissed each other at the dance three weeks before. Dizzy had watched it happen, her throat knotting up as Lizard's hand reached behind Melinda's neck right before their lips met. Since that moment, Dizzy, a renowned motormouth, hardly spoke at school and when she did, she felt like her voice was coming out of her feet.

But what was there for Dizzy to say anymore? Her mother had told her once that the great loves of one's life weren't necessarily romantic. Dizzy had thought she had three great loves already, then: her best friend, Lizard; her mom, Chef Mom; and her oldest brother Wynton who was so awesome he gave off sparks. But what now? She didn't know people could stop loving you. She'd thought friendship was permanent, like matter.

After lunch—which Dizzy spent in the computer room learning about a group of people in Eastern Europe who believed someone or something was psychically stealing their tongues—she walked halfway across school to the bathroom no one used. She was trying to avoid passing Lizard-now-Tristan and Melinda, who were always camped out together lately by the water fountain outside the closer bathroom with their hands and souls glued together. Only when she swung open the door, there was Lizard at the sink of the school's one all-gender bathroom.

He was alone at the mirror putting some kind of gel in his new hair, looking like all the other boys now, not like the Lizard of a month ago with cyclone hair like hers and geek-kid-at-the-science-fair personal style, also like hers. He'd even gotten contacts, so their black ten-ton Clark Kent eyeglasses no longer matched. She wanted the old Lizard back, the boy who'd told her about sun pillars, fog bows, and said, "So dope, Diz," at least five hundred times a day.

The fluorescent lights in the slug-colored bathroom flickered. They hadn't been alone in what felt like ages and Dizzy's chest felt hollow. Lizard glanced at her in the mirror, his expression unreadable, then returned his attention to his hair, which was the color of butternut squash. He had pale skin with scattered freckles on his cheeks, not galaxies of them like Dizzy. Once in fifth grade when lifelong Dizzy tormentor Tony Spencer had called Dizzy an ugly freckle farm, Lizard had come to school the next day with galaxies of his own that he'd drawn onto his cheeks.

Dizzy glimpsed her reflection in the mirror and had the same sinking reaction she always did to her appearance because she looked exactly like a frog in a wig. She couldn't believe this was what people had to see when they looked at her. She wished they got to see something better, like Samantha Brooksweather's head, for instance. Samantha Brooksweather set men's hearts on fire with her soft silken locks, pouty pillowy lips, and glittering sapphire eyes.

Dizzy settled her plain old unglittering brown eyes back on her ex–best friend, the real version, not the mirror one. She wanted to hold his hand, like they had secretly for years under tables. She wanted to remind him how she used to braid their hair into a single braid so they could pretend they were one person. She wanted to ask him why he wouldn't return her texts or calls or come to his bedroom window even after she threw thirty-seven pebbles in a row at it. Instead, she went into the stall and held her breath for as long as she could and when she came out, he was gone.

On the mirror in black marker was written: *Leave Me Alone.*

Dizzy felt like she was going to blow away.

Then came gym. Dodgeball. Hour of terror and dread. She was sweating through her shirt on the broiling field, practicing invisibility, pretending not to notice Lizard huddled with Tony Spencer. Ack. Ick. Lizard the Traitor. Dizzy wanted to burrow into the ground. Why hadn't she thought to make more than one friend in life? But she had no time to contemplate this because Tony Spencer had broken away from Lizard and was charging at her with the ball and a gleaming, cartoon-y knife of a smile. Plus homicidal intent. Her insides plunged. She tried to psychically steal his tongue then cancelled the order because: ew.

A weird embarrassing yip of a noise came from her lips as Tony lifted the ball into the air and then pummeled it into her gut, knocking the breath out of her, the dignity out of her. Then when she was lying on the ground like a gulping, gasping fish, holding her belly where he'd reamed her, he turned around, squatted over her, shoved his sweaty, gym-shorted butt in her face, and farted.

Dizzy's mind froze. No, she begged, make it so this did not just happen to her. Let her hit delete. Hit escape. Power off.

"What color is it, Dizzy?" Tony said with glee because Lizard must've told him about her synesthesia, how she saw scents as colors.

Everyone laughed and laughed but Dizzy focused only on Lizard's horse-neigh of a laugh, laughing like Dizzy wouldn't have eaten a tub of spiders to spare him a second of sadness.

That was what had made Dizzy cry. That was what had made her command her bare, bony stick-legs to run across the athletic field, climb over the fence of Paradise Springs Middle School, and peel through vineyard after vineyard, so that now here she was in a deserted part of town in her gym clothes in the middle of the school day, in a heatwave, wanting to just jump out of her stupid sweaty body and leave it behind.

Because Tony Spencer had done that in her face! In front of everyone!

And Lizard had laughed! At her! God! She'd need a disguise from here on out, a whole new identity. She could never go back to school, that was certain. She'd have to steal her mother's credit card and book a flight to South America. Live in the savannah with the capybaras because Dizzy had learned in one of her online research marathons that capybaras were the nicest of all mammals.

Not hateful like seventh-grade people.

And hello? Synesthesia wasn't even something Dizzy was embarrassed about, like she was her frog-in-a-wig looks, or her nuclear mushroom hair, or her freckles, which colonized every inch of her including her toes, including her fiery furnace. Or the everything. Like how small and concave she was and how she had no hair anywhere exciting yet and how she often felt like a dust particle. Not to mention how scared she was to die or to go to sleep or to lie there in the dark or to leave a room if her mom was in it or to be ugly forever. Or even how much time she *really* spent surfing the internet for pertinent information regarding existence or so many, many things that made Dizzy feel like life was hopping from one private or public humiliation to the next.

She careened down the empty sweltering sidewalk, lost in her mind, not registering the burnt amber scent of the air, nor the shops closed because of the infernal temperatures, nor the sun-scorched hills in the distance, nor the strange creaking quiet because all four streams that ran through Paradise Springs had run dry. She didn't even register the sky, empty of birds who couldn't be bothered to fly with The Devil Winds roving down the valley, causing the worst heatwave in recent memory.

She stepped blindly into the street.

Then, a screeching like the world was splitting in half.

The ground beneath her shook, the air rattled. Dizzy had no idea what was happening.

She turned around and saw the massive metal face of a truck barreling toward her. *Oh no oh no oh no oh no.* She couldn't move or scream or think. She couldn't do anything. Her feet were encased in concrete as time slowed, then seemed to suspend entirely with the revelation: This was it.

It it.

The End.

Oh, she hoped she'd get to be a ghost. A ghost who baked all day beside Chef Mom at her restaurant, The Blue Spoonful. "I want to come back immediately, please," Dizzy said urgently, out loud, to God. "A ghost who can talk, sir," she added. "Not one of the mute ones, please."

She swallowed, flooding with sorrow, with *so* not-ready. She was going to die only having used up three seconds of the two weeks the average person spent kissing in their lifetime. She was going to die before she fell in love and merged souls like Samantha Brooksweather and Jericho Blane. Before she rose up to meet someone's urgent thrust or was burnt to cinders from the frenzy of simultaneous eruptions or any of the other epic sex stuff in *Live Forever Now*. Worse, she was going to die before she ever even had an orgasm on her own—she couldn't figure it out or was malformed; she wasn't sure which.

And this was even worse than all of that: She was going to die before the father she never met—because she was in the womb the night he left— returned. She knew he wasn't dead like some people said though, because she'd seen him once up on the ridge in his cowboy hat, looking like he did in all the photos, except no one believed her about this (except Wynton and Lizard) on account of how she regularly saw those mute ghosts in the vineyard, and no one (except Wynton and Lizard) believed her about that either. Oh Wynton. And her other brother Perfect Miles. Her mother! Panic seized her. How could she leave them? Leave the world? She didn't even like leaving the breakfast table. How could she die before they— Wynton, Perfect Miles, Chef Mom, Un-disappeared Dad, Weird Drunk Uncle Clive—could squeeze together on the ancient red velvet couch in the living room, a happy people-pile with Dizzy smack in the middle, all of them watching *Harold and Maude* or *Babette's Feast* (her mom's favorite old movies and now hers too). Oh, she hoped everyone would watch those two movies in her memory, in lieu of flowers.

Not that her family had ever watched anything in a happy people-pile or been that happy, period. But now there was no chance of it.

She was going to die before all the chances.

And the really awful part wasn't even that the last thing that happened to her before death was being face-farted by Tony Spencer and betrayed by Lizard. (Actually, forget the old movies—in lieu of flowers, please egg and toilet paper both their houses.) The worst part was she was going to die before anything truly miraculous happened to her in life.

And then something truly miraculous happened to her in life.

Two hands planted themselves hard and strong on her hips. She turned and saw a girl. A bright and shining, shooting star of a girl.

Dizzy lifted her hand to touch the face that was framed by rainbow curls tumbling to the girl's waist, fairy-tale tresses of every color, but before Dizzy could touch the light-struck cheek, the girl spoke, bopped Dizzy's nose with her finger, then shoved Dizzy mightily, and up Dizzy went. Up, up, up. The sky tipping as Dizzy hurled forward out of all thought, out of time and place, landing finally in a splatter of limbs and bewilderment on the hot pavement.

Holy holy holy.

Dizzy didn't move for a moment. Um. What had just happened? Her heart was a wild animal in her chest, her face pressed into burning gravel. Was she a ghost? She touched two fingers together. No, still flesh. She tried to lift her head and was met by blur—where were her glasses? She rolled onto her back and a figure, a man, she could tell even without her glasses, not the girl she expected to see, was towering over her, blocking the sun, offering her a hand, and talking a blue streak.

"Close call. Close call. Oh Jesus God. But look at you. Like new. Not a scratch. Thank the lord." He helped Dizzy to shaky feet with shaky arms. Despite the gravel in her cheeks and palms, the pavement burns on her knees, the pounding in her chest, she was okay. Dizzy wasn't so sure about this man, though, who she thought might be on the road to hyperventilation. He was sweating through his shirt in stained patches, his scent staggering, a pumpkin-orange smell, the color Dizzy associated with men, with men-sweat. Girls and women smelled mostly green. Except not all of them, she now knew. The rainbow-haired girl who'd just saved her life had smelled magenta, like flowers did. "Oh jeez. Oh lord. Oh God," the man said. "What are you, nine, ten? I got a grandbaby your age. Built like a feather just like you."

"I'm a *twelve*-year-old feather," Dizzy said defensively. Because yes, it was annoying to still be asked to be an elf in the Paradise Springs summer parade, thank you very much. She bent down to feel for her glasses, only to realize they were stuck in her hair, which doubled as her personal lost and found. She disentangled them and put them on to see that the man, with his big sweaty friendly mustached face, was, for all intents and purposes, a talking walrus.

The girl, however, was nowhere in sight.

"Okay then, twelve. Stand corrected," the man said. "Whew-y. So glad you're all right. Thought you were a goner."

"Me too," said Dizzy, her mind revving. "I hoped I'd get to come back as a ghost, but I didn't want to be one of the mute ones, you know?" She could feel words, words, words, a tidal wave of them, straining to break out of her like they used to in the good old pre-divorce days. Sure, some people who shall remain nameless thought Dizzy talked too much and should get her vocal cords removed, but those people weren't here, so on she went. "That would be awful. There, watching everything and everyone but unable to talk, to tell people anything, even your name. Like the ones in our vineyard."

"I think you'd be terrible as a mute ghost," the walrus-man said.

"Yes. Exactly." She looked around. "I have to thank the girl, sir. Where'd she go?"

The man made a face that caused his bushy eyebrows to bunch up. "Where'd who go? All I seen is sun, then you standing in it, frozen, looking up to the heavens like some religious statue. And then I'm slamming on the brakes, riding 'em for my life, but the next second you were flying outa the way. You must be some kind athlete, 'cause you really flew. It was a sight."

"*So* not an athlete. That's my brother Perfect Miles. I hate sports. All of them. I don't even like being outside." She took a breath to slow down her thoughts, which loved to avalanche. "I flew like that because a girl pushed me. Hard too, just shoved me into the air. You didn't see her?" Dizzy looked up and down the street again. No one was anywhere. No tourists. No cars even. The Devil Winds had turned Paradise Springs into a dry, dusty ghost town. "She had all these colorful tattoos of words"— Dizzy touched her arm where the tattoo of the word *destiny* had been on the girl—"and she was *so* beautiful, her face—"

"Just us here, honey. Must be the heat. No one's thinking straight."

Walking home through the vineyards under the burning sun, her sweat-soaked clothes stuck to her, Dizzy couldn't get the girl out of her mind. That magenta smell. The way she'd looked right at Dizzy, eye to eye. "Don't worry. You're okay," the girl had said in a strange husky voice before touching Dizzy's nose with her finger—*bop*. All Dizzy's panic about the oncoming truck had vanished. All Dizzy's panic and uncertainty about *everything* had vanished. Light had been everywhere on the girl, streaming around her head, around those endless rainbow-colored curls, like a halo.

Like a halo.

And then she'd pushed Dizzy into the air.

DIZZY

The next morning, Dizzy was at the breakfast table—alive and breathing air and thinking thoughts and *touched by an angel*! She could barely contain her news, wanted to shout it at Perfect Miles sitting across from her but he had a Keep Out sign up, meaning he was huddled over some novel, like always, his raven ringlets ringletting ravenly around his princely face.

Dizzy and her oldest brother Wynton had no clue where Perfect Miles came from. He was on an athletic scholarship at a fancy prep school three towns away (Wynton, like Dizzy, regularly walked into walls). He was quiet, serious, and scary-beautiful (Wynton, like Dizzy, looked like a frog in a wig and engaged in unserious pillow fights and unquiet screaming contests). He loved to go for runs in nature (Wynton, like Dizzy, loved walls, roofs, snacks in front of the TV).

Also, Perfect Miles was *good,* spent his free time walking three-legged dogs and brushing blind horses at the animal refuge (Wynton was always bad, even got himself thrown in jail a couple weeks ago, and Dizzy specialized in ugly thoughts about her peers). And the cherry on the sundae Perfect Miles would never eat because he didn't indulge in sweets (no comment): He was voted both Class Hottie and Most Likely to Succeed in the yearbook two years running.

Perfect Miles made Dizzy feel especially warty.

She poked his arm. "I saw an angel yesterday."

He didn't take his eyes off his book.

"She saved my life."

Nothing.

"By bopping my nose, maybe."

Nothing.

"Miles!"

"Reading," he said, not lifting his head.

Because Dizzy was the youngest and so small and was now a friend-less girl who'd been face-farted, certain family members like Perfect here thought it fine to act like she didn't exist.

"An angel, like, for real, Miles. A super cool one who had tats and everything."

He turned the page.

Dizzy studied his lashy eyes, his stupid Cupid's-bow mouth, his loose, lazy curls that shined and never frizzed (like Samantha Brooksweath-er's!). The rest of his Class Hottie features. Seriously, how was it she, the face-farted, and Perfect here were part of the same species, let alone the same family?

"The thing is, Miles," she said. "You don't know if today's going to be your last day alive. You could get hit by a truck or an asteroid or a sink-hole could open up right under your feet. It's so harrowing that you have absolutely no control over when you'll die, don't you think? Don't you think it's so hard being mortal?"

Miles started choking on his dry brown rice toast (no comment), then recovered, all without lifting his head from his book.

Argh.

We should all try to be more like Miles, her mother always said. *He never wastes a minute.* Dizzy wasted all the minutes. This was because time went faster for her than other people. How else to explain what happened when she went online? Or looked out a window? Or whatever. She often snoop-read the little note pads Perfect Miles kept in his back pocket and stored in the bottom drawer in his dresser. They used to be full of To-Do lists but recently they'd gone off the rails. A recent item said: *Find someone to trade heads with.*

"I don't want to die at all," Dizzy continued, undeterred. "I mean at all at all at all. I want to be immortal. Lots of people say they'd get bored living for millennia or too depressed seeing everyone they love die again and again. Not me. How about you?"

Dizzy looked at Miles expectantly.

He turned the page.

She watched his skin gleam.

She watched his lashes flutter.

She watched him get more perfect.

This sibling thing between them wasn't working out. They were terrible breakfast companions. Really, she hadn't spent much time alone with Miles until recently. He never used to come down for breakfast (or dinner, or movies, or spontaneous dance parties, or baking marathons, or screaming contests, or pillow wars) when Wynton was around, which was every day until a couple weeks ago when Mom kicked Wynton out and changed the locks. (Except right this minute Wynton was crashed in the attic because Dizzy had illegally left out keys for him.)

Dizzy knew she was annoying Perfect Miles, figured on a scale of one to ten she was at a seven, but hello? It was annoying to be ignored too. Very annoying. "So, guess what?" she said, giving it one last go. She did have a couple things in her arsenal that could start a conversation with a rock. "You won't believe this, Miles, but there's a woman in Pennsylvania who has orgasms from brushing her teeth." This was from a site she found last night while trying to figure out what she was doing wrong with the whole masturbating thing. Dizzy pretended to brush her teeth with a nearby fork for dramatic effect, wishing it was Lizard she was telling this awesome tidbit. If only.

At a solid annoyance-level of ten, Miles stood—he was so tall now, like having a telephone pole in the family—grabbed his book, and headed out the front door to the porch to brave the heat. The toothbrush orgasmer hadn't had the desired effect. Perfect's fun thermometer was surely broken. Still, Dizzy rose to follow him because she couldn't help herself, but then she heard the dog stampede and decided to stay in the air-conditioned house.

Miles was a cross-species sensation. If they didn't close the front door, his bedroom turned into a dog park. She suspected he talked to them like St. Francis did. Dizzy didn't like dogs. Like why in the world did they put their noses in her fiery furnace? She preferred grazing cows and horses, reasonable animals in distant fields who weren't perverts. She sat back down, sliced into the warm gingerbread she'd made last night and had now reheated. Steam rose out of it, along with a mingling of cloves and molasses—a cornflower blue that misted into Dizzy's field of vision as she inhaled deeply and thought some more about Perfect Miles.

When she was little, she used to sleepwalk, even once into Mrs. Bell's house next door, but Miles's room was the favorite in-house destination. Night after night, she'd sleepwalk into his bedroom and curl up on the brown beanbag chair under the window. This was how she learned that Perfect Miles cried in his sleep. The sniffling would wake her, and then she'd walk over to him and touch his arm. Her touch always stopped it. But what was strange, stranger even than that, was no matter how dark it was in the room, she could always see him. He never woke up and she never said anything to anyone about it—neither about the crying nor that he kind of glowed in the dark—but often she felt like the real Miles was the boy weeping in darkness, giving off some kind of strange dream-light, not this perfect one who was more like a boarder than a brother.

Sometimes, honestly, Dizzy forgot Miles existed. For her, having a brother was all about her oldest brother Wynton. And Wynton said Perfect Miles was a snob or had a stick up his tight ass or thought he was better than them or was a fucking phony or a ton of other mean things that made Dizzy feel queasy.

She cut into the lavender butter (from Chef Mom's restaurant) and started spreading it on her gingerbread, watching it melt into the crevices. "Are you here?" she asked the room, not sure if angels had the ability to go invisible, which would mean her angel could be in the next seat. "If you are, beautiful angel, thank you for finding me yesterday, for saving me. I'd really love to—"

"Dizzy!" she heard, and jumped out of her chair. It was a gruff voice, a man's voice, but that didn't mean anything, did it? Angels probably switched genders and ages at will. Or maybe a new one got sent down to her.

"Yes," she said, putting down the gingerbread. "I can't see you today."

"Over here. It's me."

Dizzy turned around and saw Uncle Clive at the window motioning for her to come to him. Oh, for Pete's sake. His head was sideways to better talk to her through the narrow opening of the window that they never could get to completely shut—the house was over a hundred years old—even when the air-con was blasting. "I thought you were an angel," she said.

"That's a first. Now listen, I had a dream about Wynton."

Dizzy walked to the window, opened it wider, and her uncle straightened out. A blast of hot oven air infused with his smell—a cigarettes, sweat, and alcohol combo, the color of rust—assaulted her. His look was Sasquatch. He had a sagging face, and his blond hair and beard were long and straggly, his clothes mismatched and worn, his girth expanding hourly it seemed. He wore a flannel shirt and mud-caked jeans despite the heat. His flushed face glistened with perspiration. Rumor had it, a long time ago he'd been a playboy, but this was hard to imagine. Mom repeatedly warned them to steer clear of their uncle when he'd been drinking, which happened to be always. She said sometimes people break and can't be put back together, but Dizzy didn't agree with that. She thought all people could be put back together. Her uncle was lonely. Dizzy could feel it like an undertow when she was around him. And she never told her mother or anyone that she often spied him slipping into their house at night to sleep, curling up night after night on the red velvet sofa like a sad old mountain lion.

Uncle Clive leaned in and said, "In the dream, Wynton was playing violin, except no sound was coming out of it. Then he opened his mouth to sing and nothing. Then he started stomping his feet and no stomping sound. You see?"

Dizzy nodded. "There was no more music in him."

"Exactly. Knew you'd get it, sweet-pie. It's a portent. He needs to be careful."

"I'll tell him," she said.

Uncle Clive stroked his beard, searching Dizzy's face with bleary solemn eyes. "Okay. Good. Come visit soon so we can catch up." He turned to go. Of course, Dizzy never told her mom that she visited her uncle in the brown house on the hill either. She loved to listen to him play piano and occasionally the trumpet, loved looking at his drawings and photos of cows, loved hearing about his dreams and David Bowie. But mostly she loved when he talked about her missing father, his big brother Theo, which he would do until he invariably got upset and made her leave. Dizzy knew Perfect Miles visited Uncle Clive too. But Wynton never did. Wynton said Uncle Clive had loser-mojo and loser-mojo was highly contagious.

Dizzy watched her uncle tromp across the now dried-up creek that divided the property between his and theirs, then up the hill, making his way willy-nilly through the scorched vineyards he long ago began renting out to other winemakers. Apparently, once, the Fall vineyards and Fall wines were celebrated as some of the best in the valley, but that was before her dad rose from the dead in the hospital morgue (yes!) and then disappeared into the night. Or ran away. Or who knows what happened to him. Dizzy missed him, even though she'd never met him—it was like being thirsty, but always.

She wanted a real father so she could stop secretly pretending Wynton was her dad.

She put her hands on the window, watched as her uncle got smaller and smaller, trying to think of Wynton with no more music inside him, but she couldn't. It wasn't possible. Other people played music; Wynton *was* music. She dismissed the portent as she watched her uncle disappear over the hill. Then she squinted her eyes, tilted her head, and relaxed her mind in the way she did to see the less sentient inhabitants of the Fall vineyards, using her soul sight.

And . . . voilà.

There above the sauvignon blanc vineyard were the kissing ghosts. Two glimmering older men, one dark, one fair, flickering in and out of the morning light. These ghosts were in love and whenever they kissed, they rose into the air. Dizzy wished she wasn't the only one who could see them but long ago stopped mentioning them to anyone (besides Wynton and Lizard). She was sick of hearing about her overactive imagination, which really was a nice way for people to call her a liar or a nut.

Dizzy had long suspected the ghost with dark hair was her great-grandfather Alonso Fall because he looked like the statue on the town square. The only thing was, the plaque on the statue said Alonso Fall had been married to a woman, so Dizzy didn't understand why he was always kissing this other guy in his afterlife.

Still, she was crazy about these two flickering men and wanted to be just like them with someone, except alive and not mute, though perhaps they spoke ghost-language to each other, and she couldn't hear it. She also loved their best friend, an older female ghost who wore men's clothes and ran barefoot through the vineyards, her red hair spun with flowers and billowing behind her like a red river of fresh blooms.

"Hey guys," she called out to the floating men. "Do you know anything about angels?" But of course she got no answer. They were mid-kiss, midair, entwined and enraptured as always.

Their eternity was only each other.

The Resurrection of Winemaker Theo Fall

Paradise Springs—Was it a miracle or a failure of medical equipment at Paradise Springs Hospital this past Monday? That's what residents of Paradise Springs are asking themselves about the apparent resurrection from the dead of acclaimed winemaker Theo Fall. Fall fell ill suddenly with a viral pneumonia and slipped into a coma last Thursday. He died four days later. The time of death was recorded as 6:45PM. A few hours later, however, Theo Fall was drinking tequila with Jose Rodriguez in the hospital morgue. The two men can be seen below in the date-and-time-stamped photograph. Rodriguez tells the *Gazette* that he was playing chess with fellow hospital worker Tom Stead on their break when they started hearing shrieks coming from inside from the body bag on the table. According to Rodriquez, Stead ran screaming from the morgue, believing the dead man had come back to life. Stead informed the *Gazette* he will not be returning to his job. Rodriguez unzipped the body bag and welcomed Theo Fall back to the land of the living with a shot of tequila. The County Clinic has retired the heart monitor that hadn't been able to detect Fall's heartbeat and is now asking for donations for a new one.

The Disappearance of Winemaker Theo Fall

Paradise Springs—Beloved winemaker Theo Fall, who recently recovered from a viral pneumonia or rose from the dead (depending with whom in town you talk), appears to have driven away from his family, his home, his town, his award-winning vineyard. According to a source close to the family, Theo Fall's wife, Bernadette, the chef and owner of The Blue Spoonful, pregnant with their third child, is at wit's end. She revealed to our source that her husband left a note. While she wouldn't share the contents, she did say she was quite certain the winemaker would not be returning to Paradise Springs. The plot thickens, as they say.

The Town Tried to Keep Winemaker Theo Fall

Paradise Springs—Most longtime residents will confirm that entering and leaving Paradise Springs can be a challenge at times. Since their invention, cars have been breaking down for no mechanical reason at the town's edge as if Paradise Springs itself doesn't want certain people to enter and others to leave. Before that, it was horses, refusing to cross hooves over the border, stranding carriages and frustrated riders at the roadside motel and bar, the aptly named Better Luck Next Time. An eyewitness is now reporting that all four wheels of Theo Fall's truck blew out as he crossed out of town a week ago, shortly after being proclaimed dead of a viral pneumonia. "He just kept driving, seemed like nothing could've stopped him," said local Dylan Jackson, who was on the shoulder changing his tire, suffering a similar fate. "All the world's bad weather was in the man's face. Had a flare going so I saw right into his cab as he flew by. Never seen Theo look like that. He ain't never coming back if you ask me."

DIZZY

Dizzy was back at the breakfast table, mid-bite, thinking how if the angel hadn't saved her yesterday, she wouldn't be here now eating lavender butter on hot gingerbread. Her mother entered the kitchen. "Morning chouchou," Chef Mom said, like she did every morning.

"I don't ever want to die," Dizzy told her mother. "Like ever, so you never have to worry that I'll kill myself."

"Dizzy!" Her mother said her name like this often, like it was an expletive. "The thought never occurred to me." She shook her head as if to shake away the idea. "Until now." Her mother's face was as plastered in freckles as Dizzy's and she also had a frizz bomb on her head, but she didn't resemble a frog and wasn't built like a feather.

Her mom put her bag on the counter. Dizzy could see the notebook in it. It was her mom's bizarro version of a diary, full of letters she never sent. She said she started doing it after her brother Christophe died when she was Dizzy's age because she needed to talk to him so badly. At first, she only wrote to Christophe, but over time she started writing to everyone, including her dead parents, Dizzy's missing father, and even Dizzy herself. Dizzy acquired this specific intel because she might have snooped looking for her own name once. It was mostly gooey stuff about how much she loved Dizzy even though she was such an oddball and talked too much. She also saw a letter to an apple. And one to a meal Chef Mom had in San Francisco. It was from this notebook Dizzy also learned that Chef Mom made dinner for Dizzy's long-gone father and left it in the restaurant under a heat lamp. Every. Single. Night. Like a total weirdo.

"You know what's occurred to me?" Dizzy said to the weirdo. "Never leaving the house again so nothing too bad can happen to me. I wouldn't get bored. I could bake and watch movies and shows and do my research. Basically, what I do anyway but without the threat of catastrophic accidents or humiliation by my peers—"

"Humiliation by—? Did something happen? Is that why you really took off during gym yesterday?" After Dizzy's dramatic exit, the school had called Chef Mom at the restaurant, and Chef Mom had called Dizzy. She'd told her mother the heat had gotten to her, but she was fine now that she was home making gingerbread.

"No," Dizzy lied. "Nothing happened. It was just so hot and . . ." Dizzy blah-blahed until her mother's eyes glazed over. It wasn't the first time Dizzy had broken out of school.

"You can't run off like that, honey," she said. "Next time go to the nurse, okay?"

Dizzy nodded and scooted her chair around so she could better see Chef Mom. Her mother was big and flashy. She wore flowery dresses and high heels when not working. She liked to say she was smashing the patriarchy by not conforming to socio-cultural standards of skeletal female beauty and she had the refrigerator magnets to prove it: *Riots not diets*; *Never trust a skinny cook*; *I'm a feminist, what's your superpower?* Dizzy thought her mom was beautiful. Everyone did.

Well-known fact: Dizzy had never, not even for one minute of life, been beautiful and never would be. She had not won the looks lottery. The only people who said looks didn't matter, she noticed, were the beautiful ones like Perfect Miles and Mom. Looks mattered. Hello? What could be more obvious than this? Dizzy figured she'd have to find a mystical, inward-looking boy to merge souls with, one who'd see only her good heart.

Her mother hadn't gotten home until late last night, after Dizzy went to bed, so she didn't know yet. Dizzy hadn't wanted to share such a momentous life event over the phone. "Mom, I have breaking news, amazing news—"

And . . . her mother was calling someone, because, seriously, Dizzy did not exist for these people. She wasn't even a dust particle, she was an atom inside a dust particle. "Glad we hired that kid for sauté, what was his name . . . Right, Felix Rivera," Mom said into the phone in her chef voice. "That dish he made—brilliant. I liked everything about him . . . Yes, especially the fedora." Dizzy could tell it was Finn, her sous chef. "Okay, let's do this. . . . No, no, get chicory or puntarella instead. Wait, they actually have squash blossoms already? Get 'em. . . . No, not halibut! Coming out my ears! Go for the trout. We'll do . . ." Dizzy tuned out her mother. She got up and was now standing at the counter making it very clear with her most dramatic facial gestures that she really needed to talk. To no avail. The long-distance shopping trip with Finn went on and on. Dizzy began waving her hands in front of her mother's face, which only succeeded in making her mother turn her back on Dizzy and continue the conversation facing the stove. "A cold soup, not gazpacho. How about the chilled cucumber and avocado. Okay, yes, good idea, we'll do a crudo too. Fine, halibut—"

Dizzy hollered, "Mother, I'm pregnant!"

Her mom whipped around, dropping the phone. "What?" Her face had lost all color. Ack. Dizzy backtracked. "No, no. Not really, of course not, saw that in a movie, but I really have to tell you something."

"Dizzy, how could you do that to me? Seriously, my heart stopped." Both of her hands were now pressed to her chest. "Please don't ever do that again. Promise me?"

"I promise."

Her mother bent down to pick up the phone. "And we've already agreed no sex ever. Remember?" She checked the phone, sighed, placed it on the counter. "I'm assuming the chastity belt is still a good fit? Not too cumbersome under your jeans?" This made Dizzy laugh, which made her mother smile so that her already squinty eyes got even more squinty. She and Chef Mom were laugh partners. "Okay, so what's so important, my not-pregnant child? You have my undivided."

"I saw an angel yesterday." Dizzy brought her hands to her heart like her mother had, to show how serious this was. "For real, Mom. An angel came to me." She skipped the part about almost getting run over by a truck and the angel actually saving her life because her mother was always giving her grief about how she didn't pay attention to the world around her, especially when crossing the street. "I felt something very profound, feel it still, something—"

"You've got to be kidding me." Her mother's hands took to the air. "It's the mute ghosts all over again. Then what was it, God himself in your closet?" Dizzy had made the mistake of telling her mom she suspected this one night. "Now an angel. This is what you got me off the call for—Dizzy!" She picked up her cell, punched a number, put it to her ear. "Finn, sorry, my daughter has lost her marbles, runs in the family. . . . Seriously, who the hell needs marbles anyway?" She gave Dizzy a look, said into the phone, "Okay, go on. You know what? I'll just come. See you at the Lady Luck farm stand in fifteen."

She ended the call and then wagged her finger at Dizzy. "Do not under any circumstances let your brother in this house, you hear me?"

"I hear you." Dizzy walked over to the front door, opened it a crack, yelled out to Perfect Miles on the front porch, "Mom says you're not allowed back in the house! Sorry!"

"Very funny." She buttoned her chef's coat. "I mean it."

Dizzy didn't like to lie, so she said, "You changed the locks, remember?" A true statement but omitting the detail that Wynton was already in the house, thanks to Dizzy. "Mom, if I die in some fluke accident before we see each other again, know that I don't forgive you for how you're treating him. Wyn says he didn't even take the ring. And anyone can get in a car crash."

"What's with you today? You're not going to die in a fluke accident," her mother said, obviously not wanting to get into it with Dizzy about the night Wynton totaled her truck, drove it drunk as a skunk into the statue of Alonso Fall, their great-grandfather, now beheaded on the town square. The bill from the city was twenty thousand dollars, and Wynton had ended up in jail.

"Well, if I do die, there's my last will and testament," Dizzy said, pointing to a note she'd left on the fridge this morning. "I thought it important for you to have."

Chef Mom gave Dizzy a what-planet-are-you-from look, but an amused version. "Chouchou, were you always this odd?"

"Yes," Dizzy said. "And well-known fact, Mom: Jews totally believe in angels. Your spiritual tradition. Your people." They didn't go to temple, but Mom did make Passover seders and on Yom Kippur, she closed the restaurant and fasted. Dizzy always stayed home with her on the highest holy day, waiting for God to arrive, and pretending to fast, but really, hiding behind the refrigerator door when necessary and shoveling in her mouth whatever was available.

Chef Mom rolled her eyes. "Please. No, we don't. We're a practical lot."

"Actually, the Jewish religion is jam-packed with angels," Dizzy insisted. "I looked it up last night after my encounter—"

"Your encounter!" Her mother laughed. "Dizzy! C'mon. C'est folle!" Only occasionally did French words fly out of her mom's mouth.

"It's not folle—" Dizzy stopped speaking because stomping down the steps in his motorcycle boots was Wynton. He had his shades on and his face was broken open in a cockeyed smile showcasing the chipped tooth he got in some fight while in juvie. He had on ripped black jeans and a black T-shirt with the insignia for his band on it: The Hatchets. Hanging from his mouth was an unlit cigarette. He was carrying his beat-up violin case under his arm. He looked like he belonged on an album cover. He always did. The frog-in-a-wig look worked way better on him, on guys generally, especially musicians.

Well-known fact: Boys got to be sexy-ugly, not just ugly.

"Did I overhear a heavenly messenger visited my Frizzy?" he said, and delight spread through Dizzy like flames.

"Yes, you did!" Dizzy cried. At least one person in this family listened to her, believed her, appreciated her!

"Love it," he said, putting down his case, tucking the cigarette behind his ear. Then in quick succession, he bear-hugged Dizzy, lifted her like she was made of air, twirled her around singing the Beatles song "Dizzy Miss Lizzy" (her theme music, according to him). In equally quick succession, Dizzy flushed, squealed, cracked up, and then was light-years away from the sad, boring, face-farting, Lizard-less world. One hundred percent Wyntonized in five seconds flat.

Her mother—with whom Dizzy was currently avoiding eye contact because of the whole leaving-out-the-keys-for-Wynton thing—once told Dizzy that it used to be believed a white truffle was made when lightning hit and entered an ordinary mushroom. That's how Dizzy thought of Wynton—unlike the rest of the ordinary mushrooms like her, he had lightning inside him.

"All right, then," he said in his rasp as he lowered her to the ground. "'Bout time we made some inroads with the Almighty." He mussed Dizzy's hair. "Be sure to send this angel my way. I need some divine intervention." He smiled at Dizzy with his whole face, every tooth and freckle and crease. "Been missing you, Frizzy," he said, and her heart grew a size.

"The angel has long curly rainbow hair and tats everywhere," she told him. "You can't miss her."

Wynton opened his violin case and pulled out some wilted wildflowers. Dizzy could see ants on the petals. Wynton collected flowers as he walked. When he lived at home, there were always hand-picked bouquets dying all over the furniture.

Wynton exhaled, turning his attention to Chef Mom, who was standing at the counter, her cheeks flushed, her eyes burning holes in his head. She was trembling. This was real anger, Dizzy thought, rare for her mother, who kept her cool daily in a chaotic restaurant kitchen. Wynton walked toward her, arms up in a gesture of surrender, the dying flowers in one hand, their spines broken.

Chef Mom looked at Dizzy with a hard expression. "You let him in?" Dizzy pretended she was struck with deafness. Chef Mom turned her attention back to Wynton. "Please stop using your sister's big heart to get to me. I don't want you here when I come back from the farmer's market." Dizzy tried not to smile. She didn't know her mother thought she had a big heart. *She* didn't know she had a big heart.

"I hear you," Wynton said, reaching into his pocket and pulling something out. Dizzy stood on her toes to see. It was the sapphire and diamond engagement ring! Uh-oh. He *had* stolen it. "I'm sorry," he said, putting it in Chef Mom's hand. "Forgive me, okay? I needed a new bow for this gig tonight. I really am sorry, Mom." Dizzy watched her mom swallow as she gazed at the ring in her hand. She looked like she might start crying. He said, "You were right. I took it but I sold my motorcycle yesterday so I could buy it back from the pawn shop." Dizzy's shock was reflected on her mother's face. His beloved motorcycle?

"Okay," said her mom, drawing out the word.

"I wasn't thinking right when I took it."

"You're never thinking right—that's the problem!"

"Everything's about to change for me, Mom. I've been trying to tell you. There's this guy coming to hear me tonight—"

"Have you heard all this before, Dizzy? Because I sure have. There's this guy. There's that guy. There's a gig. Then there's my totaled truck. Police at my door—"

"I'll pay you back for everything. You'll see. This time it's different." He paused, then smiled the smile that made girls' heads explode.

Her mother sighed in a tired way. "You've gotten away with far too much in life because of that grin, Wynton. There's nothing funny about any of this. I don't want you ending up—"

"Like Uncle Clive?" Wynton said.

"I was going to say I don't want you ending up a vagrant." She began the daily search for her keys. Dizzy saw them on the counter but said nothing. She didn't like when her mother left. She wished her mother had a kangaroo pouch she could just chill inside all day long.

"You fired me, remember?" Wynton said.

"You stole from my restaurant, remember?"

"I needed the money to make a demo."

"And where is that demo?"

"He'll do it," Dizzy said. "He will."

Wynton smiled at Dizzy like a deranged scarecrow. "You see? Frizzy still believes in me."

"I believe in you, Wynton," said Mom. "You could've asked me for the money instead of—"

"Oh!" Dizzy blurted, interrupting. "Uncle Clive wanted me to tell you. He dreamt you were playing violin, but no sound was coming out."

"What?" Wynton's face darkened.

"He dreamt there was no more music inside you. He said it was a portent . . ." Dizzy's voice trailed off. She realized she shouldn't have mentioned it. Her mother often told her she had to learn to read a room before blurting things out. It was clear the room didn't want to hear about this portent.

Wynton's eyebrows furrowed. "I hate that. Don't tell me that. God, I hate when he dreams about me." He rubbed his eyes with his hands. "The last thing I need today is a hex."

"There's no such thing as hexes. Hexes *or* angels. What's wrong with you both? Really, why can't you two be more rational?" Chef Mom said, not adding *like your perfect brother Miles* but Dizzy heard it anyway. She assumed Wynton did too. It was amazing how many things people said to you without actually saying them. "And Dizzy, I told you to steer clear of your uncle Clive when he's not on the wagon, and he certainly isn't these days." Her mother spotted the keys hiding behind the espresso maker, grabbed them and her bag with the notebook in it.

"You'll see, Mom," Wynton said, returning to the table where he'd left his violin case and opening it. "You'll see this time." He lifted the instrument out. The violin gleamed. He held up a bow for them. "My whole damn motorcycle for this guy. Listen." He swiped it across the strings. "Have you ever heard tone like that?" He played some more. "Did your angel talk sweeter than that? No, she didn't."

"You sold your motorcycle for that bow?" It was Perfect Miles. He stood at the front door, looking different than he had earlier. His eyes were cold, his jaw tight, his body tense.

"I did." Wynton looked at the bow admiringly and started polishing it with his shirt.

"Excellent," Miles said, and before any of them knew what was happening, he jumped the red velvet couch and leaped over the coffee table. He was heading straight for Wynton like a mad bull.

"Miles!" Chef Mom shouted.

Dizzy hollered, "Angel! Come now!"

That made Wynton laugh as he put his arms up over his head to shield himself from Miles's assault until he realized that Miles wasn't coming for him but for the bow in his hand. "No fucking way," Wynton said, maneuvering the bow behind his back to protect it, but he was too slow.

Miles grabbed the end of the bow right out of Wynton's hands, breaking skin as he did so. Dizzy saw blood pearl in a line on Wynton's palm.

Miles hopped back, graceful as a gazelle, bow in hand, and without hesitating, Perfect Miles broke the bow in half over his knee like it was a twig, then dangled it in the air, before dropping it on the floor as he bolted out the door.

At the far window where Uncle Clive had been, Dizzy saw the three ghosts. The two men (no longer kissing) and the redheaded woman. They had woeful worried expressions on their dead faces.

Dizzy would wonder later what might've been different had she not left a key out for Wynton, had he not been in the house that day.

She'd always wonder if everything that happened to him next was her fault.

To Whom It May Concern,

In the event of my unforeseen death, please serve at my memorial: mini black truffle soufflés, thyme gougères, butternut squash tartlets with fried sage, and brioche toasts with gravlax, crème fraîche, and caviar (don't skimp on the caviar, Chef Mom).

For dessert: mini chocolate-raspberry soufflés so everyone falls in deep endless love, like Samantha Brooksweather and Jericho Blane in *Live Forever Now*.

I want Wynton to play calypso music on the violin and everyone to dance in the vineyard in the moonlight. After that, please watch *Babette's Feast* on the red velvet couch in a happy people-pile.

Good luck, world. I will try to come back as a ghost who talks.

Sincerely yours,
Dizzy Fall

From Bernadette Fall's Notebook of Unsent Letters:

Dear Dizzy,

It's been so hard keeping this secret from you, but all will finally be revealed next week. Okay, my chouchou, are you ready? Drumroll . . . I'm putting the dessert you made for me on the menu! (I remember my first dish that went on my parents' café menu. It was a sour grape and taleggio galette. A life-changing moment for me.) They'll be called "Dizzy's Pansy Petal Crêpes with Lavender Cream" unless you have something else you prefer. I already told Finn to track down a half pound of fresh pansies.

Only question: Is Paradise Springs ready? The other day you were going on (and on and on and on and on, dear girl) about the history of airborne people (as one does!) and mid-spiel you started calling them air-walkers. Ha! Well, that's what your dessert did to me, turned me into an air-walker. I'll expect nothing less than the whole dining room levitating off their chairs upon finishing your crêpes.

Cannot wait until next week. You are my favorite child on earth.

Chef Mom

Dear Theo,

Dreamt of you again last night. We were spooning, your arms tight around me. I could feel your breath on my neck, your hand on my hip. Your thoughts in my head. Your soul in my body. Love ripping through me all night like a storm. Desperate heartache ever since. Been telling everyone at the restaurant I have allergies to explain the tears.

When I made your nightly meal this evening, my goal was to get the dream on the plate:

Starter: Steak Tartare with a Smoked Quail Egg and Tamarind Dressing—ecstasy

Main: Duck Confit with Roasted Garlic Sauce and Pommes de Terre Sarladaises—safety

Dessert: a Gâteau Marjolaine—my new recipe, the almond meringue is light and crisp, the dark chocolate ganache robust, the hazelnut buttercream, preposterously rich and velvety, then the fountain of sauce anglaise poured over it—it will kiss every inch of your mouth

Paring: Sage Farms Private Reserve Cabernet—pure joy, you lucky duck

Miss you like the earth misses rain.

Bernie

MILES

Encounter #2 with the Rainbow-Haired Girl

No one would ever suspect it, but Miles Fall could see the souls of dogs.

He kept this to himself.

Along with the part about how he communicated with one dog telepathically, a black Lab named Sandro from the Bell Ranch next door, who was barking now as he peeled through the grapevines toward Miles. Sandro always found Miles when he hid in the vineyards, which was what he was doing instead of going to school, because . . . well, that was the question.

An answer: He was hiding from Wynton, who surely wanted to kill him now for breaking that bow. (For the record: Wynton deserved it and more.)

Another answer: There was this guy. His mother called him her voice of reason, her steady Freddy. Teachers called him their prize, coaches their star, teammates their bro. His siblings called him Perfect. Girls sent hot pics to his phone. Unsigned love notes found their way into his backpack, were posted on social media, scribbled on bathroom walls. When he arrived at school—always late to avoid the morning melee where he'd have to pretend to be a person who said person things—he'd have leaves in his hair from running in nearby woods and girls named Emma or Demi or Morgan would pick them off of him. *Here let me get that for you, Miles,* they'd say, then keep the leaves until they were ashes in their pockets.

There was this guy who glided down the hallways of Western Catholic Preparatory High School, talking and partaking little or not at all but no one seemed to notice that or care. No one seemed to notice that he was always trying to get away, that he ducked out of rooms, out of conversations, that he ran so fast at practice because, out there in front of the pack, he could be alone. This was why he climbed walls too—literally. Often, he was halfway up the brick façade of the school the moment after the bell rang, which made him weird, but also cool.

He *was* weird. He knew this. He suspected he was in the wrong body, family, town, species, that there'd been some big cosmic mix-up. Like maybe he was supposed to be a tree or a barn owl or a prime number. He only found himself, his real self, in novels, not even in the stories and characters, but in the sentences, the lone words.

He also never cried, and this made him feel even less human. Not once that he could remember in his whole life. Though sometimes when he woke his pillow was damp and he'd wonder if he'd cried in a dream.

Early on, Miles had figured out how to be by himself and with people at the same time. There and not there when he sat with the track/cross country teams at lunch, there and not there when he made out with girls at dances or parties. Mostly not there.

Once this all worked fine.

But: Not. Any. More.

His mother didn't know yet. Not that he quit track, the math club, the animal refuge, the academic decathlon. That the grades that were supposed to get him into Stanford were tanking.

That he couldn't get out of The Gloom Room.

She didn't know that two weeks ago at an away track meet (right after the suck upon fucksuck night with Wynton), on having the baton slapped into his palm, an entirely newfangled kind of frantic came over Miles, and he'd taken the baton and then he'd run the hell off the track and jumped the fence and then kept on going. And going. And going going going. He'd hitchhiked home and hadn't been back to school since.

No one knew *anything*. He'd made sure of it, erasing all email messages and voicemails from his school to his mother. Oh—

Here was Sandro! The black furry fella in a yapping yipping wiggling frenzy despite his advanced age. In human years: eighty-seven. Luckily it was decided by Miles long ago that Sandro would be the first dog to never die.

You don't look good, Miles, Sandro remarked right away. *Like crap actually*. This was no surprise. Miles had hardly been sleeping or eating. *Like bugly-mahfugly,* Sandro added. The old dog loved slang. He picked it up everywhere.

Yeah, tell me something I don't know, Miles said to Sandro, though really, he didn't know. He never looked in mirrors if he could help it.

Okay, here's something you don't know, Sandro said, his tail stilling. He looked up at Miles so forlornly, it made Miles's heart skip. Miles kneeled down so he was face to snout with the dog.

What is it? Miles asked. Sandro put both paws on Miles's thigh.

I've been having dark thoughts, Sandro told him. *Sometimes I don't want to be here anymore, here as in Here, as in anywhere.*

Miles put an arm around the dog and stared into his plaintive eyes. *No, you're okay, we're okay, we're in this together, two bugly-mahfuglys.*

Sandro wriggled out of Miles's touch, stuck his nose in the dirt. *I couldn't get out of my bed this morning. Even getting to my water bowl overwhelms me. I feel so alone all the time. I'm way too anxious to go to the dog park. I curl up into a ball and pretend I'm sick, so I don't have to go.* He picked up his paw and waved it in the direction of their houses. *The other dogs don't get me. No one does. Ever since Beauty left, my life is empty.*

Beauty was the love of Sandro's life who ran away years ago. *I do, Sandro, I get you,* Miles told him, rubbing him behind his ears until the dog lifted his snout high into the air and met Miles's eyes. *I understand how much you miss Beauty.* Miles stroked beneath Sandro's chin. *And getting to the water bowl overwhelms me too, Sandro. Everything overwhelms me. I just want to curl up into a ball too. Don't worry. You can always talk to me. We have each other.*

Sandro nuzzled his snout into Miles's face, his cold nose touching Miles's warm one. Miles felt his body relax. Sandro was the only one who took the doom out of him. The dog bopped Miles's cheek with his paw. *Maybe I was being a little overdramatic.*

"What else is new?" Miles said aloud, standing. "You're the biggest drama queen in Paradise Springs."

Takes a queen to know a queen, Sandro quipped.

Miles laughed. Sandro had known Miles was gay since Miles knew, which was pretty much always, though nothing exciting had ever happened about it outside the privacy of Miles's mind until a few months ago when a cook at The Blue Spoonful followed Miles into the walk-in refrigerator at a restaurant party his mother made him go to and kissed him until his mind reconfigured into a bonfire.

Until that moment, Miles's religion had been: imagining boys lying beside him, imagining boys walking beside him, imagining boys running beside him, imagining boys naked, imagining boys clothed, imagining boys who imagine boys who imagine boys, and then suddenly there was a way better religion: making out with a boy in a restaurant refrigerator in secret in a hurry.

Even though Miles never felt at ease with anyone, not truly, he had certain ideas about love because he'd been devouring his mother's stash of romance novels since he was ten, particularly *Live Forever Now,* which he secretly reread every few months. He wanted to drown in love like Samantha Brooksweather. Really, he wanted to *be* Samantha Brooksweather.

And suddenly in the walk-in refrigerator that night, he was!

For weeks he replayed the kiss, this *Get Out of The Gloom Room Free* card. He replayed it while eating tacos with the track team. He replayed it while brushing old horses at the refuge. He replayed it when Amy Cho surprise-kissed him at the dance. He replayed it to get out of bed the mornings when he felt like mold and could barely move.

The night of the restaurant party, he'd been on a lime run for the bartender. He'd had a white plastic container in one hand and was heading into the walk-in refrigerator when someone came up behind him. Miles felt a hand fall on his shoulder, saw another on the walk-in handle in front of him. "Can I join you in there?" he heard. Miles knew who it was right away, not the name of the sauté cook, but the velvet voice that went with a tall lanky body that went with black straight hair that fell into dark sleepy eyes, eyes that had been tracking Miles around the party all night long, making Miles's neck hot. Miles had sucked in air at the words—*Can I join you in there?*—wanting to holler yes! Scared to. Stunned that something he'd imagined—he was an expert on these kind of imaginings—was really and truly happening.

Miles looked left and right. It was just them, two shadows in the shadowy back corner of the kitchen. Miles nodded, nervous as hell, like before a race nervous, and then he felt the guy's chest press against his back as he gently guided Miles backward, pulling open the door and then releasing Miles into the chilly air.

The heavy door thudded behind them, cutting off the music, cutting off the rest of the world. They were alone in the cold with stacks and stacks of eggs, sacks of onions, trays of marinating grass-fed beef filets, crates of zucchini, sheets of fresh herbs. It smelled like chives. It smelled like meat, like blood and bleach. And now hope, excitement, sweat. Miles's heart pounded through to his fingers as he turned around, his hands damp despite the chill, his breathing quick, his erection straining. He smelled alcohol on the guy's breath as he approached Miles (the scent familiar from his uncle, his brother). He heard the words: *beautiful boy* (normally words Miles would've unheard immediately, but here now they were flying embers) and then it happened: the collision of their mouths, this guy's skin so much rougher than the handful of girls he'd kissed in his life, sending currents of *yes* to his heart, to his head, to his groin, to his former self and to his future one, until they were interrupted by the expediter, a guy named Pete with tattoo sleeves who said, "What the hell? Hands off or I'll tell his mother and you'll be out of a job, Nico."

Nico.

A name that was turquoise because of Miles's kind of synesthesia—words came in colors. (When he was little, he'd play this game where he'd pick out the yellow words on a page and rearrange them to make a purely yellow sentence. Or an orange one. Or a striped one. He loved words that didn't belong together. Like him.)

Anyway, Miles hadn't known how to make it happen with Nico again—he couldn't find him online—so he wandered into the restaurant after school daily and stared at the guy like it was an Olympic sport. He was too shy and uncertain to do anything reasonable like talk to him, so staring it was, but Nico, when not drunk, seemed to keep his sleepy eyes on anything but Miles. Still, Miles stared. While he was helping out (Mom: *Even with your volunteer work you find time to help out, thank you, always so thoughtful*) doing roll-ups or garnishing soufflés or bussing half-eaten plates of coq au vin, he stared. While marrying bottles of home-made aioli and ramekins of lavender butter, he stared and stared and stared like a psychopath. And when he wasn't staring, he'd go into the walk-in alone and wait, re-enacting the kiss, pressing his hot lips to the cold refrigerator door. He even wrote a poem about it and submitted it to his school's literary journal. It was called "Finding Religion in a Walk-in Refrigerator" and they'd accepted it. Everyone, including Hot AP English Teacher Mr. Gelman, thought it was about God, not a hot, sleepy-looking sauté cook, probably the only other young gay dude in the whole stupid town where Miles lived—a town that was mostly all yokel with some wine and hippie thrown in. This was why, long ago, Miles made Sandro an honorary member of the human queer community.

I love communities! the dog had told Miles that day. Miles had been ten.

Another walk-in encounter never happened, and soon after, Nico was fired for drinking on the job, but that was the kiss that changed everything.

Meaning: The Season of Porn—Miles not only devouring it whole but stopping and starting, rewinding and replaying, again and again, trying to figure it all out.

Meaning: He couldn't get through a run in the woods without ducking behind trees, his hands plunging into his shorts as he dive-bombed into all that would've could've should've happened in that refrigerator, had expediter Pete not barged in.

Meaning: He felt guilty all the time of some unspecified crime, and like he was lying even when he wasn't.

Meaning: He feared that instead of saying "Please pass the salt," or "Nice race, dude," he might, by accident, say "I'm gay. I mean, super-gay. Like you have no idea how gay."

Meaning: the dating app Lookn. (More on this later.)

Meaning: He began studying other boys like he was an anthropologist. This was how close they stood to each other. This was when they said "yo" or "bro." This was the pitch they laughed and talked at. This was what they did with their faces instead of swooning like Samantha Brooksweather.

Miles bent down and buried his face in Sandro's fur.

At least you love me, he said to Sandro.

Oh, I do! I love you so much! You're my best friend! You smell so good!

Miles and Sandro began the trek back to the house through the vineyard, through the stifling heat. Miles would have to remember to erase today's messages from the dean and his coach, both on the house phone voicemail and on his mother's computer. Thank God the school didn't have her new cell phone number. Though he supposed eventually they'd call the restaurant. Maybe they already had and couldn't get through? Would they show up at the house or restaurant? He figured eventually they would.

I broke Wynton's new bow, he told Sandro. *He'd sold his motorcycle to buy it.*

Good. He deserves it after what he did to you that night.

Yeah.

Wish you'd let me bite him already. Me and the other dogs are sick of just growling at him all the time. How about a nip on the leg?

I'll think about it.

Well?

Yeah okay.

The air was blazing and breathless even this early because of The Devil Winds. The whole valley felt like it was one spark away from bursting into flames. Miles had already sweated through his shirt.

Hey, did you know women have orgasms from brushing their teeth?

Human dude, are you high? That is redonkulous, a soup sandwich, shit-bat mad whack, insane in the membrane.

My thoughts exactly, totally wing-a-ling.

Miles, I think you need a checkup from the neck up.

Ah, good one.

Miles learned a ton of slang from Sandro. Slang he hardly ever used except with the dog.

When Sandro and Miles crested the hill, Miles saw some kind of vehicle by the side of the utility road, which was weird. Uncle Clive was vigilant about overnight trespassers (after years of waking to naked tripping hippies). But indeed, there was a vintage orange pickup in mint condition.

He walked over to the driver's-side window and saw that fanned across the double seat was a sleeping girl with a waterfall of multicolored curls. Green glitter swept across her eyelids. Words were tattooed all over her skin, which shined with perspiration.

Whoa. Sleeping Beauty. For real, he told Sandro.

Pick me up. I want to see. Pick me up!

Despite a persuasive bout of head-twisting and tail-wagging, Miles didn't pick Sandro up. He gave his honorary queer, suicidal, psychic companion a love tap with his foot while he focused on the girl, who seemed to be around his age, maybe a little older. She looked like she should be spinning straw into gold in a forest or locked in a tower or sleeping like this until some prince swooped in and—

Such a hopeless romantic, human dude.

Like you said, takes one to know one. Beauty, Beauty, Beauty.

Miles checked out the avalanche of books all over the girl's seat, seeing how many he'd read, seeing how many he'd want to. There were some books on California history, on winemakers of Northern California, but there were also novels. There was even one—*East of Eden,* a novel Miles mostly detested—upright in the girl's hand as if she could sleep-read. Why was she here? Why was she sleeping in her truck? Why so many books?

Miles tried to decipher some of the words tattooed on the girl's arms. There was *true love* and *hummingbird* and *destiny.* And then a bunch of words he didn't know, maybe in different languages? A cool sentence: *We were together, I forget the rest.* And another: *If the path before you is clear . . .* but the rest of that one wrapped around her arm and was hidden.

Miles was in contortions trying to see the other half of the sentence when he noticed the light was on in the cab. She must've fallen asleep reading that awful Steinbeck book. Miles reached his hand through the half-open window and turned off the overhead, so she didn't wake to a dead battery. As he was carefully pulling his arm out of the open window, the girl bolted upright, gasped, looked at Miles with fright, then shock, then cried out, "Oh no! Sorry, I'm going." Her voice startled him. She sounded nothing like she looked. If they were on the phone, he'd bet she was a two-pack-a-day, whisky-swilling guy.

"It's okay," he said, unable to take his eyes off her. Her large, pale blue eyes were almost translucent, making her look otherworldly.

She was searching for her keys, first in her pockets, then running her hands all over the seat, in the creases. He watched her, having an overwhelming urge to get in the truck.

"It's really fine that you're here," he said, leaning into the window and getting hit with a powerful blast of flowers—lilacs maybe, roses? He breathed in and then scanned around the truck, expecting a blossoming bush somewhere, but there were just sun-scorched vineyards in all directions. He searched the cab of the truck but the only flowers he saw were sewn-on daisy patches all over her jeans. "My uncle owns this land. He won't care," he told her, noting also the ankle bracelet, the toe rings, the skull on her T-shirt, the extensive metal in her ears, the leather motorcycle jacket on the seat. Hippie meets punk meets biker.

The urge to get in the truck with her was so powerful he had to put his hands in his pockets. His words had done nothing to curb the frantic key search. She was bending over the passenger seat now feeling for the keys under it, and although he was trying, he still couldn't make out the rest of that sentence she loved enough to tattoo on her triceps. She straightened up, keys in her shaking hand, struggling to get one into the ignition. "Are you okay?" he asked. She did not seem okay. Had she run away? "Are you hungry? I live over there." He pointed down the hill at his house engulfed in morning sunlight, looking like Oz. "We have excellent pastries. Lavender butter too." What was he doing? Why was he being so insistent? Lately he'd rather climb out a window than make conversation. "Or maybe you need a better novel?"

Somehow this broke through her frenzy to flee. She looked down at the novel still on her lap. Her brow creased. "What? This one? I love Steinbeck."

"I'll forgive the lapse in literary judgment if you tell me the rest of that sentence." He touched his upper arm in the spot where her tattoo was. "Can only see half of it. Total torture."

Her mouth twisted like she was about to smile but then didn't. She started the engine.

"Wait," he said. "Please, just one more minute."

Creepy, said Sandro. *What's with you?*

She shook her head. "Sorry. Places to be, people to see." She put a hand over her face. Her hand was still trembling. She groaned. "That was *so* cringe."

She turned to Miles and their eyes met—it jarred him. Then she smiled and that jarred him further, not only because she had one of those bring-the-dead-back-to-life smiles, but because, well, he didn't know why, he just knew he couldn't look away, didn't want to, *never* wanted to, and this was making his stomach shift and his heart speed up.

Years passed.

Better, happier years.

"My parting gift," she said finally in her gravelly old man's voice, breaking the epic eye lock. "'If the path before you is clear'"—she did a ta-da with her hands—"'you're probably on someone else's.' Joseph Campbell."

Then Miles was watching her drive away, wondering what had just happened to him. Had he seen her soul? He felt like he had. But he'd never seen a person's soul before, only dogs'. She was driving slowly, and he could tell by the angle of her neck that she was looking at him in the rearview mirror.

He felt a tugging at the center of his chest.

She looked sad too, didn't she, Sandro?

Wouldn't know. Someone wouldn't pick me up.

Who is she?

I'm going to bite you.

God, talk about gorgeous.

I thought you only liked boys.

Miles didn't reply. He didn't know how to. He never reacted to girls like this. He wanted to run after her. He wanted to drive all night with her through the empty desert and then read together in some noisy diner.

He wanted to tell her everything.

Human dude, have you turned into a country song? Or one of those romance novels you read?

I don't read romance novels.

Sure you don't, Samantha Brooksweather.

Miles ignored Sandro and pulled his pad out to write down the Joseph Campbell sentence. *If the path before you is clear, you're probably on someone else's.* It was a good one. Especially because the path before him, which used to be fairly clear, was now an effing thicket. He could barely move. And when he did, he went the wrong way. He then wrote down the one that was on her forearm: *We were together, I forget the rest.*

"Come back," he said aloud.

Right before the turnoff onto the main highway, the orange truck stopped, and the passenger door swung open. A big fat balloon of hope swelled in Miles's chest and then he was running like it was a prison break, Sandro at his heels, toward the open door.

 From Miles's Pocket Pad:

Miles can't come to the phone, to school, to your party, to practice, to existence. He has a terrible case of doorknobs. He has a terrible case of sludge, of dead birds, of what have I done, of keep out. He has a terrible case of fuck off already all of you. He'll get back to you when he's found someone to trade heads with. Thanks for being in touch.

Miles Pretending to Be a Person Conversing with an Actual Person at School:

Real Person: *Yo, Miles, what's good, didn't see you at Julie's this weekend.*

Perfect Miles: *Was there for a bit, it totally raged, man.*

(He wasn't there for any bits, he was home reading Charlotte Brontë, he was in a field with some warblers and daffodils, he was talking to a dog named Sandro.)

Real Person: *Yeah it did. McKenzie and Conner—*

(Yada, yada, yada.)

Perfect Miles: *So dope / Count me in / What a joke / Yeah / Who knew? / Whatever with that / I feel you / Got you / So down.*

(Words, words, words coming out of his face on his body, which was a combination of carbon molecules on a rock hurtling through space.)

Real Person: *Miles, want to come—*

Perfect Miles: *Hey, gotta go, man, talk at lunch.*

(At lunch Miles will tear-ass to the creek, collapse onto his back, look up at pieces of blue sky through green canopy, glide his fingers along hot river stones, breathe in, breathe out, try to keep his spirit from falling out of his body.)

Miles Conversing with the lady on the Depression Hotline:

Lady: *To put it as simply as possible, depression is grief not in proportion with an individual's circumstances. Did something happen to make you feel this way? Or—*

Miles: *Yes, something happened.*

(However, not how Miles would describe depression. He'd go with something more along the lines of waking up to find you've turned into a cockroach like in that story Hot AP English Teacher Mr. Gelman had them read by Kafka.)

Lady: *When was this event?*

Miles: *A couple weeks ago but I don't know maybe it isn't that . . . maybe what happened wasn't that big a deal.*

(Because did this all really start after that night with Wynton? No. But Miles never used to think he was *depressed* depressed, he just thought he was one of the sad solitary people. Like if he were in a Victorian novel, he'd be the melancholic who constantly fainted and took to her bed.)

Lady: *Would you like to share what happened? I think it would help.*

Miles:

Lady: *Well, do you think the level of heartbreak you're experiencing is commensurate with what happened?*

Miles: *I don't know.*

(Was heartbreak what he was experiencing? And how do you quantify losing your shit anyway? He guessed there was an amount of unraveling that was acceptable. He felt like the sun was slowly being extinguished inside of him—was that acceptable?)

Lady: *Can you describe how you're feeling?*

Miles:

(He was afraid to tell her.)

Lady: *You can tell me anything. This is a safe space. I want to help you.*

Miles:

Lady: *Is there someone in your life you can talk to? A parent? A teacher? A priest? A guidance counselor at school? An older sibling?*

(An older sibling. His fucking older sibling. He hung up.)

Dear Miles,

When you stopped eating my lemon bars recently, I decided it must be the recipe. Worked on it all last weekend. Added more butter to the shortbread crust, only used Meyer lemons, and after much trial and error stumbled on an ingredient that changed everything: apricot preserves!

After I cracked the code, I waited for you to come home, felt like a kid I was so excited. These new bars were incredible: tangy, rich, bright pulpy perfection, like eating sunshine. But when I offered up the plate, you said, "Not hungry," and went upstairs. Um, excuse me? "What does hunger have to do with perfection?" I cried out, following you up with the plate. I couldn't get you to take a bite. Or to talk to me. You said you needed to do homework.

Something's wrong, Miles, I know it. You seem so alone even with your phone blowing up all the time. It's like you can't shake out of some deep sadness you think no one sees. I see it but find it impossible to communicate with you except with stupid lemon bars and now that's off the table. Wynton and Dizzy make me nuts and I make them nuts.

I wish you made me nuts.

Maybe it's my fault. Maybe it's been too easy not to worry about you. My pillar. So much like Theo. (And wow do you look like him now. Sometimes when you come around the corner, I gasp and have to pretend I'm coughing.) But now I'm worried. Maybe I should take you somewhere, just us? To the city for a book signing? Of course, I'm glad you read so much (also like Theo), but sometimes I think it's your way of shutting us all out.

I think you need your father.

You are the best child, my favorite,

Mom

Dear Chef Finn,

Only going to say this here so it doesn't inflate your already massive ego: You were right! It was worth the wait and the endless string of interviews and tryouts. The new sauté cook Felix is a find. So passionate about everything. Love his French-Mex ideas—got me going. Jalapeno souffles? Duck confit tacos with honey chipotle sauce? Pork tenderloin stuffed with green chiles and cheese?

He's way more talented than that derelict Nico ever was.

Now, please, take this new cook Felix to the farmer's market all week so I can sleep in. Also, as always, promise me you'll never ever quit. I could not operate this restaurant for one day without you.

Chef B

MILES

"I'm Miles," he said, leaning into the cab. "And this is Sandro." The girl brushed books off the seat with her free hand to make a place for them. Sandro jumped onto the seat. "He's suicidal."

How dare you? Sandro said to Miles, aghast.

"Well, we better keep our eye on you, then," the girl said to the dog, scratching behind his ears. This pleased Sandro. A lot, though he was not pleased with Miles and the betrayal of his confidence. He was standing on the seat with his butt in Miles's face, hogging the whole passenger side. Miles gently slid him onto the floor despite a growl, as Miles hopped into the miracle of air-conditioning and closed the door.

"So, what's your problem with Steinbeck?" she asked in the great rumble that was her voice, acting like they were English class study partners and had this plan to cram together for weeks. Now that Miles was inside the cab, the floral aroma was overwhelming.

"Do you smell flowers?" he asked.

She peeled out, dismissing his question with a shake of her head, and continued on. " 'Cause I think Steinbeck *is* California. You see California when you're reading him, smell it, hear it, right?" She was patting the steering wheel with her hand for emphasis. Each fingernail was a different color. "And oh my God, I love how evil the mother is in this one! Every time she appears on the page, I start sweating. *Actually* sweating." She looked at Miles expectantly.

I'm not speaking to you, Miles, Sandro said, *but she's familiar. I've smelled her before.*

The flowers? You smell them too?

It's her. That's the way she smells.

No one smells like this. Are you sure?

I'm a dog!

"Well? You don't agree?" she said, clearly wanting to get into it about Steinbeck.

This was so weird, but what the hell? No one he knew read like he did, like his life depended on it. The only one he talked to about literature was Hot AP English Teacher Mr. Gelman. (And it was hard to pay attention because Miles was always imagining him naked, etc. Lots and lots of etcetera.) Miles was the only junior in the AP class, but his sophomore English teacher had insisted, saying Miles was a gifted reader and writer, that his papers were at a college level.

"I agree the characterization of the mother is incredible," he said.

She smiled close-mouthed, smugly, and it made Miles want to laugh.

"But it bugs me how didactic Steinbeck is. He's always inserting his opinions into the story, like he knows everything, and the reader is this imbecile, but, that said, okay, really, *The Grapes of Wrath* is fine, good even, possibly great. I give you that one." Miles thought for a second. "Maybe it's just the brothers in *East of Eden* that bug me so much. Maybe it's a personal thing." He bent down to pet Sandro, who scooted away from his hands like they were on fire. "I guess they remind me of my older brother and me."

Her brow crinkled. "I think they're modeled on Cain and Abel."

"Exactly," he said.

She stared at him, her eyes wide, questioning. "All ears here. Greatest hits. Go." The sadness he saw or sensed before seemed to have evaporated right off of her. And oddly, he felt the same. The sun was coming over the mountain, spraying rays across the valley, and they were driving straight into it, into brightness. The girl visored her eyes in defense, but he was used to the way light fountained in the valley. Somehow, he no longer felt like he had a ticking time bomb in his chest either. Or like he was in The Gloom Room. He glanced at the speedometer. Driving straight into brightness at eighty-five miles an hour. This girl. Miles leaned back, put his knee on the dash. "Okay," he said, even though he didn't talk about family stuff. Not to anyone. But when had he ever driven off with a strange, tattooed girl who smelled like a flower garden in a vintage orange truck?

"When I was six," he told her, "and my older brother was eight, he tried to *sell* me."

She cracked up and her laugh was as unexpected as her voice, rolling and loud. It had a contagiousness too, and Miles felt an unfamiliar sound escape his lips: laughter. "Yeah," he went on, "my mom even kept the ad. I quote: *Little brother for sale. He has dimpulls.* Spelled *d-i-m-p-u-l-l-s. Everyone says he is so cute. $3 or best offer.* One of our neighbors saw it on the supermarket bulletin board, recognized the phone number, and hand-delivered it to our mother."

"Three dollars! Christ, didn't think you were worth very much, did he?"

"No." Miles looked out the window. That was the crux of everything right there. Never has, never will.

"I'm sorry. I—"

"It's fine." She was turning onto Hidden Highway, a two-laner that went deep into the mountains. Miles was committed to entertaining her. He was trying to think of the minor assaults on his dignity, not the soul-crushing ones. And certainly, no need to mention the night two weeks ago.

"Go on," she said. "Hit me. What other injustices did you suffer?"

"Okay. The first day of high school—a new school with all new people—I woke up, went to the bathroom, and looked in the mirror. He'd taken a black permanent marker to my teeth while I was sleeping."

The laugh again. It filled Miles up. "Oh shit!" she cried. "That's awful! The worst!" Sandro was looking up at her with a moony expression and Miles realized he was as well. He tried to snap his face out of it.

"He also filled my track spikes with horse manure before State last year."

She was laughing now full stop, banging the wheel with her hand, and he made a decision: He never wanted to be less than three feet from this girl. "What an asshole," she cried.

"And two weeks ago, he left me for dead in a Dumpster. I woke up in total darkness covered in vomit and garbage. I thought I was in a coffin at first. There were rats everywhere. The smell—It was—" Oh man, he was there again, in the terror. Blood rushed to his cheeks. He hadn't intended to tell her this! He hadn't intended to ever tell anyone this.

All light went out of her face. She looked at Miles, incredulous.

"Yeah," he said, and once again, he was choking from the stench, his head reeling and disoriented, rotting garbage in his hair, slime on his skin, the stink coating his nostrils, vomit in his mouth, not knowing where he was or if he was alive, if he could escape, banging on the sides of the metal Dumpster like a crazed animal. Panic unlike he'd ever experienced.

And Wynton did that to him.

If he could've broken Wynton's neck this morning instead of the bow, he would have.

That night two weeks ago, Miles had been minding his beeswax on the town square, using his great-grandfather Alonso Fall's massive stone leg as a backrest, writing in his pad. It was dusk, the square deserted. He was sweaty from practice and feeling chilled, but he didn't want to go home. He was tired of decaying in his room all night doing homework while Dizzy and Wynton threw popcorn at the television, flopped together like puppies on the red couch.

When he'd heard the familiar honk, he had turned, expecting his mother on her way home from the restaurant, but it was Wynton in his mother's work truck with two girls Miles didn't recognize. "Perfect Miles!" Wynton yelled, leaning—no, careening out the window, looking like his facial features were thrown together by a madman. He was clearly blotto, his grin lopsided, his eyes bleary and bloodshot, his blond hair electrified. Wynton was someone anyone with a brain would cross the street to avoid, even in daylight. "Why aren't you on some field breaking records?" he asked, the words sloshing out of his mouth. "Or walking blind dogs? Or winning the Nobel Prize? Or figuring out climate change?"

A girl with black hair cut like a bowl and long fake eyelashes stretched over Wynton and gawked at Miles. Her lipstick was smudged, making her mouth huge, ghastly. "Finally, I get to meet the perfect brother," she said. "And he *is* perfect!" Miles glimpsed the other girl leaning forward with pink spiky hair. "I want to see him," she said, like Miles was a zoo animal.

Normally, he would've taken off to the other side of the known universe as quickly as possible, but for some reason when Wynton said, "For once in your life, surprise me. Get in, man," Miles did. For whatever the hell reason, he squeezed himself into the cab of the truck.

The girl with spiky pink hair smelled like coconut lotion and had a silver dolphin nose ring. Miles knew both these things because she was half on his lap. "You looked sad sitting there," she said to him. He tried not to recoil from her alcoholic breath. "Didn't he look sad, Bettina?" She squeezed Miles's arm, didn't let go of it. Girls often invaded his space like this, assuming he was straight, like they had a right to touch him. "But we got you now," she exclaimed, then whooped about nothing as far as Miles could tell, before swigging from a bottle. She turned toward him and before Miles knew what was happening, her lips were on his and the liquid in her mouth was dribbling into his. Um? Gross. He pulled away and spit the liquid out in a spray, then started apologizing and trying to wipe it off her shoulder and the dashboard.

"Perfect Miles doesn't drink," Wynton said. "Perfect Miles is no fun."

It was true. Perfect Miles didn't drink and was no fun. He hated Perfect Miles. Fuck it, Miles thought, and took the bottle of tequila from the girl and chugged. "Wait," the girl said. "Not like that!" He felt his face pruning and puckering in rebellion, but he got the alcohol down. She took the bottle from him, said, "You want to sip tequila, like tea." She demonstrated, pinkie out, then handed it back to him. "I'm Madison."

"Bettina," the other girl said.

"I'm Perfect Miles," Miles said, and they all laughed. Even Wynton. Miles couldn't believe he'd made Wynton laugh. He peered around Bettina to make sure Wynton wasn't ridiculing him, picking Miles off the sole of his shoe like usual. But no. Miles had legit made his brother laugh. This was a first and it lifted him. The tequila was warming him too, uncoiling him, making him feel better, livelier. Miles and Madison passed the bottle back and forth.

"Now one of these," Madison said, popping something into Miles's mouth. At first, he thought it was a breath mint because he was that dumb. He bit into it, expecting peppermint, but bitterness filled his mouth, aspirin maybe, he thought stupidly. He should've spit it out, but not thinking and wanting the bitterness gone, he took a swig off the bottle and swallowed it.

These were the last things Miles remembered clearly, well, fairly clearly, from that night:

1) Busting through the door of a party with Wynton's arm around him like they were best friends. Wynton introducing him to everyone, saying, "This is my little brother Miles! This is my little brother Miles!" *His little brother Miles.* Wynton had never called him that before. Not once. He remembered feeling effervescent, mighty, *elated,* all new to him. (Maybe this was the drug.)

2) Trying not to gag as beer funneled down his throat through a beer bong.

3) Jumping up and down in what felt like slow motion on a crowded sweaty dance floor with Wynton, Madison, and Bettina, all of them— including him!—shouting to each other, "I love you guys so much!"

4) Sitting on a bed as Madison undid his jeans, then Madison on top of him, swarming him like an octopus, then Madison actually turning into an octopus.

Then nothing nothing nothing nothing.

Until he woke covered in vomit and slime in the rank, rat-infested Dumpster in an alley in the center of town with his jeans half-buttoned, his shirt on inside out.

So.

Yeah.

He'd blacked out and Wynton had thrown him away. Literally. And Miles probably had sex with a girl for the first time (but couldn't remember any of it) before he'd ever even had sex with a boy.

The next morning, Miles found words in his own handwriting in his pocket pad that he didn't remember writing: *The wind has blown my face off*

And: *Hurricane is an emotion*

And: *Easier to choose what to wear when all your clothes aren't on fire*

That afternoon Miles took the baton at the track meet and ran out of the race, out of his head, out of his perfect life.

"Jesus. Why does he have it out for you like this?" the girl asked Miles, snapping him back to the truck.

"I don't know," Miles said. He tried to unclench his fists, his jaw. God, he wished he could remember what happened in the blackout; it gnawed at him not knowing. And how did Wynton even get him in the Dumpster? Miles was so much bigger than his brother. Did the girls help? Ugh. Did they hold his feet? All three of them laughing at him while they did it? The humiliation was unbearable. "He hates me. Always has." His voice cracked. God, why did he care so much? "I worshiped him when I was younger. Despite everything he did to me." Miles sighed, shame creeping up his spine. "He's this amazing violinist. Like however amazing you're thinking, he's more amazing. I used to sit outside his room and listen to him practice for hours. And he's cool, in this human grenade kind of way. You want him to have your back. You want him—when I was little, I just wanted—"

Miles clammed up. Why couldn't he stop talking? When had he ever talked this much?

"What did you want?" she asked gently.

He exhaled. Something about her voice, so curious, so caring, and them roaring down Hidden Highway at this scandalous speed, and before he knew it, he was saying, "I just wanted him to love me. Like. So. Fucking. Bad. But he didn't. He doesn't. Obviously." He cringed at himself. Then because it was already all out, he added, "No dad or anything. So, he was it. He was everything." Miles felt himself flushing. He knew he sounded like a kid. He felt like one, the same sad kid who spied on Wynton and Dizzy from the stairs while they baked or watched movies, knowing if he joined them, they'd go silent, or worse, Wynton would turn mean as acid.

The same sad kid who imagined his father in the doorway of his room saying good night, who wrote emails to him (never sent, no address) begging for him to come back and rescue him. And he still wrote emails to his dad, even though he could hardly remember the man, keeping the drafts, the pleas, in a folder on his computer called *Help Me!*

He searched for his father too, mostly late at night, on his computer. He had this idea that he'd be able to find him by reading wine reviews. He looked for wine notes that were similar to ones written about his dad's famous pinot: *deep garnet color, hints of cherries, roses, has you talking to the moon and the moon talking right back, pairs well with heartbreak, makes you feel so in love you might ask strangers to marry.* Or this one: *With his new Pinot Noir, Theo Fall has done the impossible—he has concocted true love out of grapes. With hints of black cherry, forest floor, and pure zingy bliss, you can pair this juicy wine with game birds, fatty fish, and the one who got away because this wine is sure to bring them back. It is a dance you didn't know you knew until the music came on.* From actual reviews of his father's wine! A few times he did find wacko enough wine notes for a pinot that he was certain the wine had to have been made by his dad under a pseudonym, but when he googled the winemaker, it was never the man in old family photos.

Sandro was curled up contentedly on the floor, that swoony expression still on his face except when he'd turn his head and give Miles the stink-eye, still peeved about the *suicidal* comment.

Sorry! Miles told him, but the dog rebuffed his apology with a head roll and a yawn.

She, on the other hand, kept catching Miles staring at her, and he her, and when they did, they'd both turn and smile foolishly out the window until it'd happen again. And again.

"You have a nice smile," she said one of these times.

"Me? You've got to be kidding. If the grid goes out . . ." He pointed to her grin.

Sandro lifted his head, made eye contact with Miles. *Miles, that was embarrassing. I thought you had better game than that.*

Why would you think that? I have no game whatsoever. And it's true. Look at her. Look how she catches the light. I think I see an aura.

I don't believe in New Age things like auras. Maybe it's a halo, though? I certainly believe in halos.

Miles took a deep breath of the flower-filled air, wondering if maybe he was dreaming. Something didn't feel real. He'd get a similar feeling sometimes when reading became more like breathing and he knew he'd left real life and his soul had transferred from his body into the story. But he'd never felt this way with another person—*because of* another person.

She looked at him and said, "I'm just driving nowhere." He took out his pad to write that down and she laughed and pulled a similar pad out of her own back pocket, smiled, and said, "Write it in there too."

WTAF?

Had they blown away on a gale into another world?

After a while, the road narrowed and turned to dirt and the trees got even taller. She turned off the air-con and opened her window; Miles did the same. The air was a little cooler here. The smell of eucalyptus filled the cab, mingling with the flower garden. Neither of them mentioned the fact that they should be in school. Unless she was already out, he thought, or she could be in college. He was about to ask when she spoke.

"Any other siblings?" she asked.

"There's Dizzy," he said. "My little sister."

"You guys close?"

He shook his head. "Not at all." Miles stuck his arm out the window, felt the air whip against his open hand. "I don't matter to either of them. I'm like this unperson around the house." He couldn't believe he'd said this aloud, just like that. Neither could Sandro, who hopped up on the seat and put his head in Miles's lap, finally forgiving him out of pity. Miles pet the dog, stared out the window.

Even though Dizzy had chosen Wynton from the get-go, he loved his little wingnut sister. How herself she was at all costs. And there were costs he never suspected. He'd walked her home from a dance recently (always Wynton's job until he got kicked out) and Miles couldn't believe the wisp of a girl standing all alone—hair in her face, shoulders hunched, clothes from the wrong column—was Dizzy. Precocious, chatterbox Dizzy who at home filled up every room at once. He'd watched her for a while, wondering where her friends were, where *she* was. How could it be that someone like her was standing there all alone and someone like him, ridiculously closed off and fake, was always surrounded by "friends" at school. When she saw Miles, she rushed across the room like a gangly bird unaccustomed to walking. He wanted to pick her up and put her on his shoulders and make her fifteen feet tall. On the walk home, she turned back into her at-home self, prattling on about who knows what, but he'd seen it, her secret daily torment, and it had made his heart sink.

They were almost at the turnoff for Jeremiah Falls, one of his favorite spots. Uncle Clive had shown it to him, said he used to go swimming there with Miles's dad and mom when they were all in high school. Miles gave the girl directions.

"Why'd you change your mind?" he asked her as the road grew even darker, the air cooler in the shade of the giant redwoods, and the river roared because they were so close to the falls. "Before. Why'd you stop the truck?"

"Had to." She pressed her lips together. "I saw you in my rearview mirror and you looked—I don't know. It's like I had no choice—"

Without thinking, he reached across the seat and touched her cheek. She raised her shoulder to catch his fingers. Again, that same tugging in his chest. He had the strongest urge to write something down but didn't have the words. He was being crushed by tenderness. He couldn't believe he was feeling this way about a girl.

Sandro's eyes were on him, two question marks.

I know, he told him. *Don't know what's going on.*

"There's this German word," she said to him. "I have a tattoo of it on my shoulder. *Sehnsucht.* They say it doesn't translate well to English but the closest we get is: inconsolable longing." Their eyes met. Miles swallowed. "That's what I saw in your face." She gazed upward at her own reflection in the rearview mirror. "Me too."

Sandro? Are we dreaming?

I don't dream in human language. In my dreams, you bark.

Really? You've never told me that before.

You never asked.

When they pulled into the turnout to park for the falls, he realized he was better. No, that was an understatement. He felt transformed, like light was seeping into him instead of out of him. This must be happy, he thought.

After they parked, she started filling a backpack with books. Like a dozen of them. "Who knows what we'll feel like reading," she said, continuing to sort through the books, adding one or two more to the pack, tossing others aside, making it very clear why there were so many books in this cab. "At the risk of sounding weird, I'm pretty sure my spirit or soul or whatever is a pile of words. Sometimes I don't even read in order, just read some from one book, some from another, whatever, all night long. Like all—and I mean all of everything—is just one really long story."

He wanted to yell out, *Me too!*

All around them the forest leaves glinted like tiny mirrors in the sun.

Their eyes held. For centuries this time. Something that had been long balled up, left for dead even, his spirit, began to rise inside him. His body was vibrating. What was going on? How could it suddenly feel so easy to be human? Why had he confessed so much to her? Was he falling in love? Was she real? Just an hour ago he'd stood in misery and spite with Wynton's broken bow dangling in his hand. A perpetual resident of The Gloom Room. Mourning a months-old kiss with a stranger. Now he was his own horizon. "What's happening?" he asked her.

Her smile was slow, beautiful. "We are."

He was for sure dreaming—only possibility. "Who was together?" he asked, pointing to the tattoo on her forearm: *We were together, I forget the rest.*

"Everyone!" she said joyfully. "That's life!"

Yes. He felt it too in this moment, part of, not apart from. But why? How? What was going on?

Minutes later they'd walked the short path through the old oaks and arrived at Jeremiah Falls. Water cascaded down the mountainside. "Gorgeous!" she said, and raised her arms in the air.

Miles was thinking the same thing looking at her.

Oh brother, said Sandro.

C'mon. You can't take your eyes off her either.

I know. I almost feel like I'm betraying my long-lost Beauty.

She kicked off her sandals, pointed to a word on her ankle. "Nemophilist," she said to Miles. "One who loves forests, trees in number. A haunter of woods. From the ancient Greek. Kickass word, right?"

"Right," Miles said, thinking he might die of happiness from learning this word.

She bent down and picked up a large black-and-orange caterpillar. "Soon to be a crescent butterfly." She glanced at Miles. "You like bugs?"

"Indifferent," he said, not wanting to admit he *hated* all manner of creepy-crawlies. He did not see their souls, nor did he ever want to. Spotting a spider made his head swim and stomach turn liquid. Seeing two required immediate evacuation.

She put the caterpillar back down on the rock where she found it. "I'm going in." Without any self-consciousness, she slipped her T-shirt over her head, then half hopped to pull off her daisy jeans, until she was in a blue lace bra and tight green underwear. She was amazing head to toe. He watched her walk to the edge of the massive blue pool, thinking she looked like Venus in the Botticelli print on the wall in the bathroom at The Blue Spoonful, thinking also that he wasn't feeling it, not in *that* way, not at all, nothing, rien du tout, rien de rien. And if he ever was going to feel it for a girl, it would be now, here, with her.

Sandro was at Miles's feet, wagging his tail. *Case closed then,* the dog said after a moment.

Miles nodded. *Yeah, I like her so much, just not like that, I guess.*

Then, right inside his head, he heard her unmistakable husky voice, heard it loud and clear: *You know I can hear you numbskulls talking, right?*

Sandro and Miles stared at each other speechless with WTAF, then looked at her in shock. She smiled at them, winked, then pivoted around and dove into the water.

MILES

Minutes after Miles and Sandro were dropped off, the morning with the girl began slipping away, just like dreams do the moment feet touch the floor.

You heard when she called us numbskulls, right? Miles again asked Sandro.
Sure did.

Miles hadn't questioned her about it. What would he have said? "So, this dog here and I communicate telepathically, and we could've sworn you just jumped onto our channel—did you?" Ah, no. And it was only that once. The rest of the time, they'd swum in the pool, floated on their backs, and read her books in the shade. He'd read about the California gold rush, how San Francisco was ninety-five percent men back then, which sounded to him like paradise.

Sandro was circling Miles, wagging and panting and raving: *I feel so much better! I have a new lease on life. I'm going to rid myself of old patterns. I'm going to join a support group. No, no support group. I'm going to become a bon vivant! I'm going to try new things: Camembert cheese and rock climbing and polyamory and . . . I'll set out to find Beauty!*

Miles zoned Sandro out. It was only after he closed the truck door behind them that he realized he'd asked her nothing. Not one thing. Not her name. Or age. Or where she lived. Or what she was doing in Paradise Springs. He'd told her everything, more than he'd ever shared with anyone in his life, and she hadn't revealed a thing. The opposite of *every* previous encounter in his life. Maybe she'd hypnotized him? Or put a spell on him?

Miles studied Sandro, suicidal just hours ago, now frolicking at Miles's feet, blathering gleefully about Camembert cheese and finding the love of his life, Beauty. And what was up with the flower scent? And that voice that didn't seem to belong to her? And all those books? And who on this earth was so radiant?

I think I like her more than you, human dude.

Ouch, though I don't blame you.

He head-butted Miles's leg. Hard. *How could you have not gotten her number?*

I didn't even get her name!

Miles had jumped out of the truck like they'd all be seeing each other again in an hour. Like the tattoo: They were together! He'd forgotten the rest!

Well, at least she knows where we live, Sandro said. *She'll come back for us. We'll wait, right?*

Miles reached down and rubbed Sandro's head, then belly, as the dog flipped onto his back and shimmied in delight. Miles thought of the word she'd had on the small of her back: *hiraeth*. She'd said it was a Welsh word that meant homesickness for a home you can never return to or that never was.

He'd told her he always felt that way.

What he didn't say was: Until now.

Until her.

Yes, he told Sandro, petting his exposed belly, *we'll wait.*

Paradise Springs is strange.

Let's start with the grapes, so many fermenting at any given time that the townspeople get inebriated just from breathing the air.

Then there's the light, so bright, newcomers unused to the glare are easily spotted shielding their eyes with their hands and sometimes walking into trees and other passersby. Crepuscular rays, those thick beams of sunlight that break through clouds forcing you to momentarily believe in God or magic, are ever-present in the flower-frenzied town. Not uncommon are thirty-foot-tall sunflowers swaying like fools in the breeze, clarkias glowing in the night like pink moons, and orange poppies so animate, they might even tap you on the shoulder as you pass.

The surrounding forest is lush, primordial, and changes so much day to day that it's believed groves of trees swap places and creeks reroute themselves in the night. It's quite possible to walk into this forest one person and out of it another.

Then there's the waterfall tumbling right into the square, the town's endless hourglass.

Lastly, there's the fog. When it descends, the town disappears, the whole valley does. Completely. As in: No trace.

Not even on maps. Not even in history books. Poof, gone.

In these times, no one can find the town, not even those living in it.

The Devil Winds Are Back

Paradise Springs—Rumors abound in Paradise Springs about The Devil Winds. We've all heard the stories. How the attorney of Priscilla Jones, accused of murdering her husband Gabriel Jones, used The Devil Winds defense to keep his client out of jail. How Charlie Holmes stripped down to his birthday suit one blisteringly hot day, and with only The Devil Winds at his back, walked across the surface of the Paradise River like Jesus Christ himself in plain sight of several local fisherman, who snapped the now famous photograph. And most notoriously, how the sweltering winds drove one of Paradise Spring's most beloved residents, Theo Fall, from the environs, never to be heard from again. Well friends, they're back. We expect temperatures well over 105 degrees for the coming days and flame-hot winds. We advise keeping your ice trays full, your air conditioners blasting (except between 4PM and 8PM), and your heads on your shoulders.

Miles's Emails to His Missing Father in the Help Me! Folder on His Computer:

Dear Dad,

For two millennia the violin has been associated with Satan. The greatest violinist of all time Paganini supposedly sold his soul to the devil for his gift. Rumor has it, he used the guts of murdered women to make his strings. Draw what conclusions you will from this about your genius violinist son Wynton.

Miles

Dear Dad,

The house talks to me at night. It doesn't say nice things.

Miles

PS. I'm gay. No one knows except the black Labrador next door. Not because I think anyone will really care or whatever. It's just that no one except this dog knows ANYTHING about me. I feel like a human off switch. Are you like this? I did try to tell Mom I was gay once, got some words out, but then Wynton barged in, and I vanished. If Wynton or Dizzy are in a mile radius of me, Mom doesn't register my existence. I don't know why.

Dear Dad,

Where are you? How could you leave me with these people?

Miles

Dear Chocolate Cake at Annie's Paradise Deli,

You make me want to hop on a motorcycle and ride like a banshee out of all my responsibilities.

I. Love. You.

I thought I had it this time. Was certain the secret ingredient was lemon juice. Went to Annie's yesterday with a slice of my latest attempt to do yet another side-by-side tasting. I didn't have it. It wasn't lemon juice. If only Annie would just tell me what's in the freaking recipe, but alas, she's having too much fun with my obsession.

It's been three months, dear chocolate cake, since I first had you. Still, you do not have a chance. I will figure out what you're made of.

Bernie

PS. Wait, is it vinegar? Annie! Omg, it's vinegar!

WYNTON

Encounter #3 with the Rainbow-Haired Girl

What no one knew (except Dizzy) was that Wynton Fall still heard his father's trumpet. In the distance, just out of full earshot. Not all the time, but enough for Wynton to think, however illogically, that his father's music stayed when the man himself left, that it got caught in treetops, in the wind. People in town thought it was strange how Wynton played his violin outside, a fiddler not only on roofs, but by creeks, on hilltops, in meadows, but he had no choice.

He went wherever his father's ghost-music took him.

Once, years ago when he was thirteen, it took him to a meadow reeling with sunflowers and buzzing with yellow jackets where he found a girl crying. They'd sat back-to-back, he and this girl, that's what he remembered, his back to hers, the perfect fit of it, the perfect feel of it. And her smell, like all the flowers in the world blooming at once. (This being the reason he was so flower-crazy to this day.) That afternoon in the meadow, he'd closed his eyes and tried with all his supernatural might to take the sadness from this girl, to pull it out of her, like he sometimes did with Dizzy, and it had worked. Soon she was happy and chatting with him in a big, deep, froggy voice—weird coming out of such a slight girl—and this had turned him into a new boy (for that moment anyway), one without the bad parts.

To this day, when anyone asked him if he'd ever been in love, he thought of this girl who smelled like flowers, this moment in the meadow, thought of how he'd asked her to marry him (at thirteen!), and she'd said yes. (Just like that book of his mom's that was in the can for a while, *Live Forever Now* with Samantha Brooks-something and Jericho-something-else who decided at thirteen they'd marry one day.) Except unlike that pair, he never saw this girl again, never was called to that meadow again by his dad's spectral music, but he went back anyway to play there when he was the most lost and alone, when he heard nothing in the wind but wind.

The night his father left and disappeared like smoke, he came into Wynton's room and placed his trumpet next to him on the bed. (Wynton still needed it beside him to sleep, which was embarrassing but whatever.) He was seven years old and awake, but he pretended to be asleep because he knew his father died that night, and so this replica had to be a ghost, and Wynton was scared of ghosts then. The look-alike said, "For you, Wynton, music is another body part like hands or knees. Never stop playing." It was the rightest thing anyone had ever said to him. A decree. An oath. Just thinking it—even all these years later—felt like religion. It made him hold his breath.

So that was why Wynton was repeating it now, like a mantra, a prayer, as he had a smoke outside the Paradise Lounge in the mad heat—the whole stupid world had a fever—before heading in for his first solo show, the night he'd been waiting for his whole useless life. Because tonight he was going to meet Destiny. Tonight would be his farewell to this Podunk town and all the Podunk people in it. Goodbye to The Devil Winds too, to this stifling heat that made him feel even more trapped in his skin than usual. Sweat ran down his face, his neck, his arms. He was melting probably.

He took a sip of vodka from his flask. He had the perfect high going, the kind of galactic high that took away all the soul-ick, the heart-ick, the mind-ick, all the ick-ing ick. He just had to sustain it until showtime. Hell Hyena and the Furniture, one of his favorite bands and one of the only ones that showcased an electric rock violinist, was coming from Los Angeles to scout him. Him! All this, thanks to the universe sending that rock critic to Paradise Springs for a wine-tasting holiday months ago. The dude waltzed into the local dive Better Luck Next Time and caught Wynton's band The Hatchets doing their regular gig. After, he wrote on his blog: *"Wynton Fall plays violin like it's his last night on earth, and if it were mine, this would be the way I'd choose to go out: listening to him. The kid is astonishing."*

The kid is astonishing!

Him, the *astonishing* kid!

Wynton had printed out the review, folded it up, and kept it in his pocket ever since. He even slept with it inside his dad's trumpet, right by his head. He'd admit to no one how many times a day he read it—probably around eighty, so on average five times each waking hour, and when he wasn't reading it, he was touching it to remind himself he wasn't a colossal waste of space.

Four months after the critic posted on his blog, Hell Hyena and the Furniture saw it, then found Wynton's YouTube video, which had a whopping thirty-one views (that he suspected were mostly Dizzy), and tracked Wynton down.

The first thing Wynton did when he got the voicemail from Sylvester Dennis, the lead singer of Hell Hyena, was go to The Blue Spoonful to play the message for his mother ("See, Mom!? See?! I told you!"), but she was too angry on account of her totaled truck and the money she was out for the statue of Alonso Fall (20K!) and of course the subsequent jail misunderstanding and the booze he stole from the restaurant and the pièce de résistance: the heist of the sapphire engagement ring, which he'd pawned so he could buy the bow he needed for this gig that was going to change his life, selling his motorcycle (like pulling his heart out of his chest) to buy the ring back, only to have Perfect Fucking Miles break the bow.

Or whoever was possessing his brother's body this morning. Jesus.

Anyway, that day Wynton had tried to play the message from Sylvester Dennis for his mother over her tirade and her face turning devil red and all the tears, but she just took his phone and threw it into a simmering pot of onion soup.

So again, this morning he'd tried to explain to her the importance of tonight's gig but to no avail. He was still kicked out of the house which was a bummer because his sort-of girlfriend Chelsea also kicked him out because he'd accidentally fooled around with her hot roommate Bettina and then his best friend Max kicked him out because he found out about hot roommate Bettina, who happened to be Max's hot fiancée Bettina. Yeah. He was a dumb prick. Chelsea had called him a human wrecking ball, which had made him prouder than it probably should have. He also thought it'd be a good name for a band.

He tried not to be a dick in life, he really did, but he never got very far with it. When he wasn't playing violin, he'd get bored. Like pour-gasoline-down-his-mouth-and-light-a-match bored. And he'd get this hungry feeling too, life-hungry, life-*ravenous*. Then he'd do all the things he shouldn't. Really, he didn't understand how everyone else remained so calm when they too were alive for such a finite amount of time. Why wasn't everyone else coming apart? Shaking up the snow globe? Trying to lick out every pot? They were all just paper people in a burning world, weren't they? Dizzy once told him about these foot-long snails in Africa that eat houses. He wanted to eat houses! He wanted to eat *everything*.

The only problem Wynton foresaw for tonight was that he'd already been triple-hexed today. First by Miles when he broke his new bow. (WTFF, yes, but also: Props to Perfect Miles. First time he did anything shocking in his seventeen years.) That said, still, a most serious kind of hex. And it had forced Wynton to "borrow" a bow from his ex-violin teacher Mr. Bliss, who was away in Europe. He'd had to break into Mr. Bliss's house, additional bad mojo. He knew he should've "borrowed" an old cruddy bow Mr. Bliss wouldn't have missed, but then he saw the CodaBow Marquise. And well, dude. That was that. He was going to bring it back after the gig anyway, and so no one would be the wiser. And he figured Mr. Bliss would want him to play with the Marquise tonight, even if he hadn't spoken to Wynton since the recital incident five years ago. However, the new replacement bow, though awesome, might, in and of itself, be bad luck. But the third hex by Uncle Clive was the most upsetting. What the hell kind of dream was that to have? That Wynton no longer had any music inside him? The night before the biggest gig of his life! He hated to think of Uncle Clive dreaming of him. He hated to think of Uncle Clive, period.

He touched the lucky blue horse tattooed on his wrist—it was glistening with sweat. He whispered, "I need your help, blue buddy." Like he always did. Then he shook a pill from the container he'd swiped, broke it in half, and popped it into his mouth, swallowing it with his saliva. This shit was a big score, a gift from the universe, well, from Miles, anyway, who'd probably had a wisdom tooth pulled or something and had never taken the painkillers. Twenty effing pills! He'd found them stashed in Miles's sock drawer. Most likely their mother had told Miles to hide them from him. What dummy hid anything in a sock drawer? It was the first place people like Wynton looked for anything. His mom had hidden the engagement ring in a button box in her sewing kit. That was a pretty good spot. It had taken him a whole day to find it. He was very good at finding, at stealing. Sometimes he felt like he turned invisible the way he could lift items off store shelves, money out of wallets, the way he used to pocket everyone's cash tips at the restaurant before his mother canned him for stealing a $400 bottle of Cabernet.

Wynton flicked the cigarette, stamped it out, lit another one. Man. He'd expected a thank-you at least from Miles after that bonkers night a couple weeks ago. Or sainthood even. Instead, he'd broken his goddamn bow.

Well, he probably deserved it for everything else he'd done to Miles over the years. If he were Miles, forget the bow, he would've snuck some glass into his own food by now.

Wynton sighed, guilt at the front door of his mind, banging on it with both fists. But he wouldn't let it in. No, he wouldn't let himself think about Perfect Miles today.

Ah, too late.

He took a good hard drag off his cig. It hadn't always been so messed up between them. When they were little, before their father left and everything changed, Wynton had been *so* into Miles. Thought the kid had magic in him. Thing is, he still kind of did. Like, get this: If Miles stayed in one place in their mother's garden for a bit, the flowers all started to turn toward him like he was the goddamn sun. Yes. Wynton tried it multiple times, staying in the garden for hours. Nothing moved his way but flies. Very disappointing because of his thing for flowers, especially those teeny-tiny purple-and-yellow petal-heads that smelled the most like the girl from the meadow.

Hello? If Wynton had Miles's looks, brains, athleticism, plus some weird-ass ability to make flowers turn their heads, he'd rule the universe. People were physically unable to peel their eyes off the oblivious kid too. Total strangers went gooey and catatonic just to see Miles walk across the street. Lucky fuck. Dizzy was plain on the outside, like Wynton was, but unlike him, she was a geode, had a sparkling kingdom of glory within. He had a rodent farm inside.

But that wasn't why Wynton couldn't stand his brother—

The growling of two dogs snapped him back. They were straining toward him on their leashes like they wanted to rip him to shreds. A harried woman with short hair in a white tennis outfit cried, "They're never like this! They're golden retrievers! Therapy dogs! I don't know what's gotten into them," as she jerked the dogs away, crossing the street.

Wynton sighed. He'd gotten used to canine hate, couldn't remember a time when a dog walked by him in town without letting him know they could see all the way to his ugly soul.

Unfortunately, this counted as another hex, which made four.

Things were not looking good.

He realized he was hugging his violin case like someone was trying to steal it, noticed that next to him now was a guy with long gray hair in a ponytail also having a smoke, leaning against the wall on the other side of the door. He was watching Wynton, wearing doctor scrubs. There were damp patches under his arms. "You okay?" he asked as their eyes met.

"A-okay, Doc," Wynton said, unspooling and getting up quickly, wiping his brow of sweat, trying to unfreakify himself. How long had this guy been studying him like this? He stamped out his smoke.

The doctor cracked a smile, offered his hand. "Everyone calls me Doc Larry." He had a baritone voice, kind of like a tuba, that Wynton liked right away. Liked him right away too, the irony of him—a hippie doctor sucking on a kill stick—until he said, "What you taking there?"

"What? Oh, nothing, aspirin. Headache."

Doc Larry's face did not seem to believe him. "Ah, I see, well, if you need help with . . . Well, we have a clinic at the hospital—"

He gave Doc Larry The Glare. The Wynton Fall Glare was epic. He used to silence the whole cafeteria at Paradise Springs High with it. It worked less well in juvie but was still pretty effective one-on-one with people like the doc here, who presumably wasn't a violent offender or a sociopath.

The doctor put up his hand. "Fine, fine. Good luck with that headache. Stay hydrated."

"Shouldn't smoke, Doc Larry, bad for your health," Wynton said, and headed into the club, the blast of cold-conditioned air like bliss.

Carlos the bartender, who had the body of a sumo wrestler and a gold front tooth, called out, "The man of the hour. Make us proud tonight."

Wynton flipped his shades up, then let them fall back down because the bar in the light of day was all wrong, too exposed and vulnerable, like seeing someone naked you're never supposed to see naked, like your grandma. An assortment of fossilized daytime drunks was lined up, all of them fellow oblivion-seekers, fellow members of The Ravenous Tribe, spinning through days on barstools, waiting for nighttime, when the train that was real life finally pulled up to the station.

Wynton scanned each and every one of them.

You might think if your dad rode off in his truck and vanished twelve years ago, you'd stop looking for him after a while. You'd be wrong. No one on this small blue planet got by Wynton without a good hard glance. He was always on it.

There were sightings too, and not just by Dizzy:

Could've sworn I saw Theo Fall down by the river today. Had that same walk, slow and lazy, like he had all the time in the world, same black cowboy hat tipped low. Lordy, what a handsome man he was, solid as a tree, and remember his pinot noir, tried it once and it had me dancing with my shadow.

Wynton listened to the out-to-lunchers especially, the ones who thought because his dad "rose from the dead" he was some kind of messiah, who was going to come back and save them all. Wynton believed this too. Always had. He still waited by the window, sometimes all day, staring down the long, tree-lined driveway. It was more than a habit, more like a spiritual practice. Looking off. Waiting. Hearing music played by no one.

It wasn't the same for Dizzy and Miles as it was for him. How could it be? He was the only one who was old enough when their father left to actually remember the earthy, humid scent he had that made hugging him like putting your face in a pile of leaves. The only one who remembered him wrapping his arms around their mother one night when she was washing a white plate and saying in the low lilting way he spoke, "Look at you, baby. Holding the moon in your hands." The only one who remembered him moaning theatrically at each bite he took of a soufflé she'd made and her laughing at his moaning and then him laughing at her laughing until they both fell off their chairs.

But Wynton remembered.

He remembered *everything,* which was probably why he was so screwed-up, truth be told. If his siblings knew half of what he knew about their parents . . .

One of the fossils at the bar spun on his stool and lumbered off of it. "Well if it isn't trouble."

"It is indeed," Wynton said, and walked over to Dave Caputo, a sad old guy who somehow lost his family and looked it.

"Up for it?" he asked Wynton. He and Wynton played chess in the town square most days, where Dave regaled Wynton with stories that never quite added up, but Wynton didn't care. He was used to liars.

"Not today. I'm playing here tonight. Solo."

Dave put a hand on Wynton's shoulder. "Way to go." He nodded toward the guy next to him. "Tommy here was just saying he could've sworn he saw your old man last night at the Better Luck. Must've been a ghost, I told him."

"Must've been," Wynton said, hope filling his chest, thinking that maybe, just maybe, his father had come back to hear him play tonight on this night of nights.

Crime Report

Paradise Springs—The statue of Paradise Springs's founding father, Alonso Fall, one of the greatest winemakers this town has called its own, was beheaded tonight by his great-grandson Wynton Fall, who drove into the statue while under the influence. He has been released from the county jail and will be subject to a fine of twenty thousand dollars. By no means is this the first time the Fall boy has fallen afoul of the law. A year ago . . .

From Bernadette's Notebook of Unsent Letters:

Dear Wynton,

My favorite son, my human minefield, now my employee, I don't know what to do with you. You raise the temperature of my restaurant just by being in it. And that grin is making my unsuspecting servers and cooks trip over their own feet. The other day, I overheard the bartender Bridgette say, "Dude can change the weather with a swipe of his bow, I've seen it." She's lost her head, along with half the staff.

Please keep it together.

Mom

Dear Wyn,

It's too much. My engagement ring! My totaled truck! Jail! The beheaded statue of Alonso Fall! Stealing from the register! Stealing other servers' tips! Stealing the bottle of Silver Oak!

And still, you so squeeze at my heart. Everyone sees your talent or your growing criminal record, I see your fragility. I see the way, to this day, you sleep curled around Theo's old trumpet, the way you stare out windows. The way you search Theo's face in photos. It makes me so sad.

I heard on the radio today that magpies sometimes use cigarette butts to make their nests, occasionally snagging a lit one as building material because they're attracted to the glittering ember. Then they burn up their whole nest. Which burns up the tree the nest is in. Which burns down the whole forest. Wynton, you are this magpie.

And so am I.

Mom

Dear Clive,

You have to stop drinking. It pained me to tell you to stay away from the kids again last night, but I'm too scared of the dark places alcohol takes you. Same dark places it took your father until it killed him. I wish you would try rehab again. Try something. Make music. Make a life.

—Bernie

Happy birthday mon frère Christophe!

You'd be officially middle-aged. Ha! You would not like it, big brother. The gray. The pooch. The regrets. The lives still unlived. I remember us looking in the mirror together. All four of our teenage eyes always on you.

Dizzy worships Wynton exactly the way I once did you. I can't believe I was only one year older than she is when I lost you.

I've written you letters now for over three decades. Funny how what began as this need to communicate with you after you were gone has become the way I privately communicate with everyone and everything. Maybe when I'm dead and gone too, I'll let the kids read these notebooks. But not until then. Actually no. Into the fire they'll go with all my secrets.

I made you a 12-layer caramel cake with caramel icing because I was thinking of us eating caramels behind our prayer books in temple when we were supposed to be fasting—remember?

I read somewhere recently that losing a sibling is like losing part of your soul. I'm certain that's true. And then, I lost the rest of my soul when I lost Theo.

Even my bones are lonely.

Bon anniversaire, Christophe, from your little sis, forever and always your little sis, no matter how damn old I'm getting.

WYNTON

Two hours later, under the hot stage lights, midway through his second set, Wynton unplugged. He did it super metal, putting the instrument right up to the amp, letting the feedback blow out ears and electrocute the room before he pulled the cord, picked up his acoustic and his hexed-but-still-totally-awesome bow. He wanted to play Eugène Ysaÿe's Sonata #3. Yeah, not club fare, but he didn't care. He was going to play like it was his last night on earth, like that critic said, and this is what he'd play if it were.

He'd lick out the last pot.

The first note was a bell ringing. All went silent. The bartenders stopped mid-shake, mid-pour, and looked up. Everyone else lowered their drinks, their defenses. There was hardly a breath, a murmur, a heartbeat, and then Wynton became unaware of his surroundings, unaware of the space-time continuum, all out of his skin, tears running down his face under the shades (he wore them because this always happened when he played; told people there was something wrong with his eyes, but really, he had no idea what the deal was) until he finished, and drenched in sweat, he raised the bow and violin into the air . . . but no one clapped, not one person, and he didn't understand what happened, thought he must've really bit it.

He wiped his wet face with his arm, with his lucky blue horse, then lifted his sunglasses to see the damage he'd inflicted on the room. What he saw were startled faces, what he heard was nothing, the silence lasting one, two, three, four nervous seconds until the room erupted, exploded right along with his head, and the sitting people in the audience stood and the standing people started jumping and hollering and the applause was a rocket, and he was on that rocket blasting into the stratosphere.

After, people were saying *awesome,* saying *what the hell, man, best ever,* and everyone was slipping him beers, and that was combining with the pills he'd taken earlier, so he was feeling wow, and there was no Dad, but there was Doc Larry saying in his baritone tuba voice that he never heard anyone play that hard in his life and maybe Paganini didn't sell his soul to the devil after all, but to you, Wynton Fall, which was a sick thing to say, and there was Max, who hated him because of ex-fiancée Bettina but was now fist-bumping him and looking at him like he was a deity, saying, "You killed it, Wyn."

But where were the guys from Hell Hyena and the Furniture? When they didn't come backstage beforehand, he figured there was some kind of protocol and he'd meet them after the set. Sylvester Duncan was the lead guitarist's name, right? Or was that the donkey in the story he used to read to Dizzy, the one where Sylvester the donkey got trapped inside a rock, holy shit, the most terrifying story ever written and the saddest and he couldn't believe it was meant for children and good thing he wore his sunglasses each and every time he read it to Dizzy because man did he lose it when Sylvester turned back into a donkey and got reunited with his donkey parents.

Sylvester Dennis maybe? His stomach dropped as he scanned and scanned the room from his barstool and still did not see him, except then his gaze smacked into Dawn someone he knew from somewhere, whose hair was long and light, like straw, whose eyes were green, whose fingers kept running under the hem of her short yellow skirt. And then she was right there, standing beside him, and her hair smelled like candy, and the next thing he knew, he was in some back room with her and her long bare legs were so long and bare and the two of them were laughing, Dawn someone from somewhere saying he was as crazy as everyone said and he hollered, "I am a crazy man!" and she laughed and he inched up her skirt and his fingers were unsnapping her bra and her hands were on his arms, his neck, and music was cracking open his head—orchestral music, God he was so high, whoa, maybe too high, he couldn't remember how many of Miles's pills he'd taken either, four? Four thousand? And there were legs wrapped around him and he was in love in love in love even if he kept forgetting who he was with, still he could feel it, could feel love banging around in his chest, against his ribs trying to get out, banging so hard, so loud, no not love it was *life*, life mic-ed up and blasting inside him, amped to the max, and they were both sweating so much because: heatwave, tidal wave, slippery as seals they were, and Dawn was saying in his ear how amazing he played, and how amazing it was that he cried when he played and how amazing how amazing how amazing and that it made her feel so much and she wanted to feel so much and he did too, that's all he wanted, to feel so much and they were, they were feeling so much, they were so much, and then it was over

And he was alone

WYNTON

Wynton was alone in the black night heading home, except he didn't have a home anymore and he didn't have a dream anymore because Sylvester the donkey hadn't come and he didn't have friends anymore because he was such a prick and so he was walking to a rusted-out car by the river where he was going to sleep. Like a rat.

He put his hand in front of his face and couldn't see it. Because he was turning into the dark. He touched his face, okay, he was still there, but ouch, and why were his fingers wet? He put his hands to his mouth, tasted metal, blood, because oh yeah, that guy had punched him, kicked him in the ribs too, oh right, that was why he'd left. He'd been in the alley behind the bar. He could see himself on the ground now like it was a movie, curled on the pavement like a dirty rind getting kicked again and again. How was he supposed to remember he knew Dawn someone from somewhere because she was the girlfriend of that neckless Brian Fuckmutt from juvie?

He took a swig of the bottle he'd swiped—what was it? Gin maybe? Who cared? He was at the point in the night when the alcohol began drinking him.

It was so hot still, oven-living, he thought, staggering left and right, unable to go straight even when he tried, unable to stand totally upright either. Who needs upright anyway? He'll be a bat. Bats are cool. No eyes, right? They navigate by sound, like him really.

But the thing was: Sometimes when he was messed up like this, he got to see his dad. Theo Fall would appear out of nowhere, and he'd put his arm around Wynton, and he'd talk to him about music, jazz mostly, his dad was so into jazz, as he walked Wynton home.

But Wynton couldn't seem to make his father come out of time tonight and he had no home to walk to . . .

So.

He was remembering something now, how when he was on the ground in the alley he looked up at the neckless Brian Fuckmutt, and in his mind, Fuckmutt became Miles and so it was Miles—who never fought with anyone, who walked dying dogs and captured spiders in the house and set them free even though he despised spiders—who was beating the living hell out of him, kicking him again and again, ribs, gut, ribs, gut, Miles paying him back finally *for everything,* and he'd wanted each blow then, each burst of pain, each blast of hate from his brother. He didn't even try to run away. He let that neckless reckless monster beat the crap out of him for Miles. For Miles.

How idiotic was that?

He stopped in the middle of the road needing to play, needing to get away from the suck and yuck of it all. He managed to get his violin out of the case but couldn't control the bow, kept striking the air. He used it to scratch his back, then swiped it across his arm. He was under a yellow streetlight that looked like a tiny sun. Okay, he was playing now under the sun, sound was happening, noise more like, oh the noise was him crying.

He had to quit the middle school orchestra because of the crying. It was then he learned to wear sunglasses when he played—it became the only way. Usually, the tears rolled down his cheeks not bothering him but sometimes when he was playing by himself, he cried so hard, he'd get afraid he was going to warp his violin.

He gave up trying to play, sat down, wiped his face with his arm, tucked his head between his knees. There was him and there was the really bad person inside him. The poison-person the dogs growled at. He didn't know what was wrong with him. He never had.

He was just in the wrong tempo, the wrong key.

Oh man, he was coming down. Hard. Like being buried alive hard. But then he remembered. More pills! There had been TWENTY! He reached for them in his back pocket but then forgot.

Then the dark itself started making a racket.

"Dad? Dad, is that you? Hey, come out," he said, but he sounded like he was speaking another language. He sat up, tried hard to say the words: "I hear you, now I see you too." But the words were sound blobs and burbles, mouth-chaos. There was a shadow in the road that didn't seem attached to a person. "Is that you, Dad?" No, not Dad, too small, and no hat. And also, real, unlike his dad. "What's that on your head?" It looked like an octopus. "Or is your head just shaped like that?"

"You need to get out of the road," the shadow said. Under the tiny sun, he could see now it was a girl shadow but one with a very deep raspy voice.

"Is that your real voice?" he asked. He'd never heard a girl with such a deep voice. Or maybe he had. He didn't know. "Talk again."

The shadow was getting closer. "You need to get home."

"Home," he repeated. "Your voice is tremendous."

"Can't understand what you're saying." The shadow was coming at him. It was pointing a phone-light at him. "Let me help you out of the road."

"Let me see you better," he said.

"Got that." She pointed the light at herself. The shadow was a girl with tons and tons of curls, all different colors.

He started laughing. "Dizzy's angel with the rainbow hair! She said she'd send you to me and she did."

"Look, going to help you into my truck," she said. He hadn't heard a truck, had he? Maybe that had been the racket? He looked around and saw a few yards away, there was indeed a truck, orange, like a lit-up pumpkin under the streetlight. "I'm going to take you home."

"To your cloud house?" Wynton asked. The rainbow-haired girl was trying to get him to his feet. "Doesn't each angel get her own cloud house? Let's go there instead. Let's go up."

She laughed under her breath, and it sobered him for a second. Her laugh was fantastic too. Rumbling and wild. And familiar. "Understood that," she said. "Sounds good, we'll go up. Taking you to my cloud house."

"You sing, right? Your voice is wow." He stumbled around so he was face-to-face with her. They were under the small sun and he could see her clearly. "Holy shit, you're pretty. No wonder she thought you were an angel."

She touched his face. He pulled back not because it hurt but because he wasn't used to being touched so tenderly. "Your eye," she said. "We need to clean that."

"I'm totally in love with you." He said it slowly, wishing his words would stop coming out all at once. In some other language.

She laughed again. She'd understood. Thank God. "C'mon, Casanova. You won't remember this or me in the morning." She'd gotten her arm around his side, but he maneuvered around so he could face her again. She was waking him up.

"I will remember you. I mean it. I'll remember you." Love was falling out of him, not fake sex-love like earlier with Dawn-someone, but real love, like music. "Marry me," he said. "Will you marry me?"

She didn't answer, instead asked, "Why do you cry when you play?"

"You were there? You heard me tonight?" Joy went off like a geyser inside him. This girl saw the best performance of his life. It suddenly felt more important than Sylvester the donkey seeing him. Or even his father.

"I've never heard anything so extraordinary," she said. "You were incredible."

"It was incredible," he said, then added slowly so she was sure to understand, "I was eye to eye with God."

She smiled at him, and his heart opened. He smelled flowers. "What's your name?"

"Cassidy," she said.

That voice. The timbre. He'd heard it before, he was certain. But when? Where? They stared at each other in the glow of the streetlight. The human-maker must have had a whole lot of extra beauty lying around when it was her turn. The moon broke through clouds lighting them up further. He felt so awake suddenly, like he'd been plugged into his amp.

"Cassidy," he said under his breath, trying it out. He'd never met anyone named Cassidy, he didn't think, but as the word stayed in the air, and her scent filled the night with invisible blooms, it hit him. "It's you." Adrenaline tore through his body, further sobering him. He thought of that day so long ago, the two of them sitting in the long grass while he tried to play away her sadness with his violin. He'd never known her name. "You came back."

"For you," she said.

For him? So many times since their meeting, he'd returned to the meadow dreaming of this. But his dreams never came true.

"No one comes back for me," he whispered.

"I did."

Was he hallucinating? He must be. Did he care? No, just as long as it continued.

There was the heat pulsing in the air, on their skin. The moonlight spilling through trees now, splashing onto the road. There was the way she was looking at him like he had the answer or *was* the answer, even. A part of Wynton that was forever folded, began unfolding. Bitterness and drunkenness and hopelessness drained from him as the night sounds sang out: the creaking trees, the bird calls, the rush of the river. The forest was playing music for them. A ballad, he thought, no, it was a waltz. He opened his arms, and she glided into them, their bodies snapping together as if the puzzle had finally been solved.

The world began to tip as they swayed together under their private sun in the middle of the night standing on a speck of dirt on the tiny spinning blue planet.

He decided this would have to be the one slow dance in the history of humankind that never ended. No matter if asteroids careened down, wars broke out, earthquakes toppled cities, the two of them would still, in a thousand years, be here by this river, in starlight, under the redwood trees, swaying together, more one than two, because he suddenly somehow knew deep in his heart that this girl was the kingdom, and for once in his stupid screwed-up life, he was the one who had the keys.

"I've never felt this happy," she whispered into his ear. "I've been thinking about you my whole life."

He had to look down to confirm they hadn't floated into the air.

But the eternal dance was shorter than anticipated. Before he could put his hands in her hair, before he could kiss her, before their blood could catch fire, Cassidy disentwined herself. Her face was lit with joy. She took a step, reached out for him, saying, "C'mon, let's get out of the road."

Before Wynton could take her hand and never ever let go of it, a car screeched around the bend and the girl he met in the meadow all those years ago, the only girl he'd ever loved, screamed so loud, the stars vanished from the sky and all went black for Wynton Fall.

Cassidy: There's been an accident, it's bad, Wyn—a boy, a man, he's nineteen, was hit by a car, a hit and run, please send someone to, oh no, I don't know where we are . . . I think he's—I'm not sure he's—

Dispatcher: Can you see a street sign? My name is Jean and I'm going to help you.

Cassidy: No, it's—There's—I can hear the river, there's a lot of redwoods. Oh, I remember—it's Old River Road. Please. I'm scared he's not moving—he was drunk and maybe on narcotics too.

Dispatcher: I'm tracing this phone. Please tell me your name. Give me a second . . . Got it. I've sent an ambulance to your location. Are you still there?

Cassidy: Yes, don't think he's breathing, I'm trying to do CPR . . . I know how. Cassidy. I'm Cassidy.

Dispatcher: Cassidy, is there a pulse?

Cassidy: I'm not sure. Oh my God. I'm really not sure. If so, it's faint. His arm is—his hand, oh God, it's awful. He's a violinist! I'm doing the compressions! Then the two breaths.

Dispatcher: Okay, very good. Please continue, help is on the way.

Cassidy:

Dispatcher: I'm with you, Cassidy. Assuming you're doing CPR now.

Cassidy: I'm trying. I can't tell if it's working—

Dispatcher: Thirty compressions followed by two rescue breaths. Keep at it.

Cassidy: He can't die. He can't. I just got here.

Dispatcher: He won't. You're keeping him alive until help arrives. What's your relationship?

Cassidy: He's—he's—so important to me, please, hurry.

PART
TWO

WYNTON

You know you're in a hospital. You listen to the buzzing lights, the staccato beeps of the heart monitors, the sorry shuffling feet, back and forth. You listen to the sighing, so much sighing, the discordant breaths.

You're calling it: *Fucked in D Minor.*

The doctor said it quietly so you wouldn't hear, but he has a baritone voice (a familiar one you can't place) and you heard.

You will never play violin again.

If you could talk while in this coma, you'd ask someone to kindly suffocate you with a pillow.

If you could move, you'd do it yourself.

You vaguely remember someone in your arms. The scent of flowers. A beautiful girl saying she came back for you. A feeling of home. Was it a dream? Must've been.

You leave the hospital room with all the people in it and swim through time to find your father. Then you do. It's the year before he left, and you live on his shoulders as he walks the vineyard north to south, east to west, sunlight cracking through the sky so that you both have to squint. The game is you keep your mouth wide open, and he blindly pops grapes back up at you with his free hand, trying to get one inside your pie-hole. Only happens once and you both are so happy, maybe that's the happiest you've ever been in your whole life. That moment of victory after with him holding you in his arms over his head and twirling you, tart warm grape nectar in your throat, both of you laughing and hooting and hollering, "Score!"

You swim through time, wanting to say sorry to someone (you don't know who) about something (you don't know what).

And there's your dad again. It's your sixth birthday and you wake to him sitting in the rocking chair across the room, waiting for you to open your eyes. On his head is his black cowboy hat, his occasion one, cocked real low like always and on his lap is a present. He says, "Know I'm supposed to wait until the party later, but I just can't. Your mom got you something else. This is from me."

You are a heat-seeking missile as you throw off the covers and launch yourself across the room and into Dad's lap, where you rip open that box. You're not sure if your heart has ever beat this fast as you take out the gleaming instrument. Right away you know the bow is a magic wand. He says, "The violin is the instrument of instruments. I wish I could play it, but I can't, 'cause to really play it, you have to start when you're your age. Got you lessons too. John from The Fiddleheads is going to come around every other day until you're as good as he is. Swore to me."

You stay on your dad's lap all morning, bowing the thing, making screeching cat sounds while he hums along like you're Yo-Yo Ma.

On second thought, maybe *that's* the happiest moment of your life.

You remember. It's Miles you need to apologize to. You remember why too.

A day. The day. You and Miles on swings. Your father pushing one son with one hand, the other son with the other hand. You and Miles catch each other's eyes as you pump higher and higher into the sky. Neither of you can stop laughing. You have never loved anyone as much as your little brother.

But that was before.

Before, before, before.

This day on the swings was the day everything changed.

You see as you swim through time that your whole life has been about your father's absence, about skin growing over a wound that never heals.

What no one knows, and will probably never know now, is that it was your fault. Yeah, that's right. Now that you're half out of the world, just admit it. It's your fault your father left.

Admit it.

Admit everything already.

You're fourteen, skinny and rangy and trouble. You know now the world is not made for people like you but for people like your perfect little brother Miles, whom you despise.

All you think about is the Viper, the love child of Jimi Hendrix's Flying V electric guitar and a violin. The sound it makes is a haunted house, a head-banging sledge-hammering metal show, a high tea, the saddest love story never told, a bluegrass festival, all of everything all in one. You need its amplification, its sixth string, the High E, which is the transcendent one. Oh, the Viper can do anything. It's all you think about.

You get kicked out of school and sent to juvie for dealing, dealing so you could buy the Viper—

Wait. You smell flowers.

Her. Maybe you didn't dream up the girl, that moment under both sun and moon. Is she here? In the hospital room with you? If only you could open your eyes. Then you hear her unmistakable voice say your name. She *is* here! You remember now. She's the girl from the meadow! Dizzy's angel. Cassidy, she said. Her name is Cassidy. And she came back for you, just like Samantha Brook—what the hell was her last name in that romance book?

You're so glad no one suffocated you with a pillow.

She's telling you that you can't die because she has to tell you something. "No," she says. "I have to tell you *everything*, Wynton."

If you weren't already in a coma you'd faint from happiness. You want to know *everything*. You don't even know why she was crying in the meadow that day so long ago.

She must've waited to come into your room until the others left because it's so quiet now. You suspect it's the middle of the night. Or that time stopped. If only you could see her. Hold her. Dance with her again into the air. You guess, because the door didn't squeak like it does when everyone else comes and goes, that she either just materialized (is she actually an angel?) or climbed in through the window.

Oh, who cares how she got here, she's here, she's come back, she's found you again.

And now she's saying someone named Felix, who drove with her down to Paradise Springs, had called her Scheherazade, the Persian queen in *A Thousand and One Nights* who saved her own life by telling stories. She says she plans on keeping you alive in the same way—by telling you her story. You hope that means her story is a long one and she'll stay by your side forever.

You also hope this Felix person is not her boyfriend.

"In the end, we'll all become stories." This is her favorite quote by an author, she tells you, and that it's tattooed on her hip.

You want to see her hip.

Then the world becomes only her voice saying: *When you don't have a house, a bike, a sibling, a mailbox, a phone, a friend, a father, an address, neighbors, grandparents, a front stoop, a back porch, a bedroom, a street that you live on . . .*

CASSIDY

When you don't have a house, a bike, a sibling, a mailbox, a phone, a friend, a father, an address, neighbors, grandparents, a front stoop, a back porch, a bedroom, a street that you live on. When you don't go to school or ballet or soccer or the mall. When you've never had a sleepover, a classroom, a school locker, a playdate. When you've never logged onto anything. Or streamed anything. Or called anyone. When you've never watched a TV show. When you've never had a last name.

You hold on to what you do have, and Wynton, I had a mother named Marigold.

Had.

I'll start here:

Mom's twenty-six and I'm eight and we live in a canary-yellow mini-RV named Sadie Mae, parked now on a bluff over the ocean at the furthest edge of Northern California. We haven't talked to anyone but each other in weeks.

Sadie Mae has huge flower decals all over her. She looks like the Summer of Love exploded into a recreational vehicle and Janis Joplin and Jimi Hendrix are alive and living inside it, not us. Not some turbulent young mother looking for a town she saw in a dream (yup) and her weird bug-collecting daughter. Especially not me, the weird bug collector. But Sadie's one of us and we love her and buy her funky beaded necklaces that we hang around the rearview mirror like we do our own necks.

Mom says we're on The Great Adventure and that California is our religion. She calls us modern pioneers mostly but sometimes road scholars or nature mystics or dream chasers and our mission, according to her, is enlightenment. She says The Divine Force is going to gobble us up like two tacos. I tell her I most certainly don't want to be gobbled up like a taco, which makes her laugh and chase me around Sadie trying to gobble me up like a taco.

Plus, in the process of achieving enlightenment, she says, we're going to find The Town from her dream where we'll settle down. Apparently, we were really happy there in her dream.

At this point, we've crossed 141 California towns that aren't The Town off our map.

There's 341 to go.

Tell me about The Town, I ask her before going to bed, on waking up, on endless beach walks, during hot desert drives. And tell me she does, until it begins to feel like it was me and not she who dreamed of The Town in the first place.

Can you guess where The Town is, Wynton? I bet you can.

Here's a photograph of us around this time. No idea who took it. You can see Sadie Mae in the background. And the granite peaks of pine-covered mountains, so we're probably way north. We're usually in the northern part of the state because that's where Mom thinks The Town is.

Please take note of our clothes. We'd just played our thrift store game where we'd see who could make the most clashing outfit. The winner got to buy it in its entirety. We declared a tie that day, so both of us are in our winning looks, though I think my mom is hard to beat in the purple paisley jumpsuit with bell bottoms and red and green polka dot jacket. Agree? Also take note of our bare feet, ankle bracelets, toe rings. The dirt streaks on our skin. The lady and her son to our left looking at us like we're off our rockers as we perform a parking lot runway show, me mimicking Mom, who's doing an exaggerated model walk, both of us mid-strut, hands on hips, a psychedelic mother and daughter gone runway, gone rogue.

Mom says, because of savings, if we live frugally, we can live like this forever.

Finally, note the look on our faces, bliss somehow, right? Often that was what being around my mother was like. People would catch it like an illness.

After Sadie Mae came another mini-RV we called Purple Rain. The Purple Rain years are harder to talk about, but I'll get there. Like I said, Wynton, I need to tell you everything.

Some important things to know about my mother when I'm eight:

She's in pieces to me. There's: Happy Mom, Teacher Mom, Story Mom, Mean Mom, Sad Mom, Silent Mom, Gone Mom.

She gets enormous. Like: When we go on our science walks, her head keeps bumping the sky, so she has to keep her neck bent. *That* enormous. Unlike me. I get surprised when I look in the mirror and see that I'm there, that I'm actually a me and not a part of her. What part? A freckle maybe.

She's always forgetting me, driving away from rest stops, gas stations, roadside diners, thinking I'm in Sadie with her and then doubling back when she realizes I'm not. This is because I don't make enough noise. She's always telling me to speak up. "I can't hear you, Cassidy!" To walk heavier. "Stop sneaking up on me!" She's always looking for me when I'm right in front of her. "Oh, there you are!" Always telling me to look up instead of at the ground where most of the cool bugs are. "Will you just look at this view, Cassidy!"

Last thing about her when I'm eight. She looks exactly like a rosy maple moth. Promise me you'll google this bug when you wake up, Wynton. She doesn't think this is a compliment because there's something wrong with her and she hates insects, even fuzzy flying pink-and-yellow ones.

Okay, I'm going to tell you my story in three betrayals.

There is a fourth betrayal as well. That is the one that involves you, Wynton. Yes, you. We'll get there.

The day of the first betrayal, I wake to sunlight and seagulls cawing. I pop my head out of my bunk to see Mom already sitting like a triangle on her meditation mat below me. I watch her. I'm always watching her, even when all she's doing is nothing. It's not just me. Everyone does it, especially the men at RV camps and supermarkets and gas stations and everywhere, all looking at her like they want to drop a net on her. Yes, she's pretty. As I said, she looks like a rosy maple moth, the most beautiful insect on earth. She has long blond beachy chaos hair, sea eyes, and pink legs as long as me.

Finally, I tear my eyes from her, roll over, and quietly greet my bug family.

In my care are: a cobalt milkweed beetle named Beetle Bob, a dark Jerusalem cricket named Crackle, a California rose-winged grasshopper named Harold the Hopper, a praying mantis called Barney, and a wooly bear caterpillar named Awesome Creature who is a girl like me. Each lives in its own jar-house with air-holes at the top, plenty of food, and a comfy grassy place to sleep. Despite what Mean Mom says about captivity, they are happy bugs. I let them hop and crawl around and be friends with each other in a shoe box terrarium that has rocks, moss, dirt, and a bowl-lake that even has algae in it. I sleep with the jars lined up on the shelf in my bunk except for Awesome Creature, whom I keep right by my pillow because she's afraid of many things, including the dark and my mother because she's so big. She's also afraid to turn into a tiger moth, which is her destiny.

That morning like all the previous mornings since I found Awesome Creature, I whisper into the holes to calm her for the day. I tell the beautiful red-and-black-striped caterpillar how much I love her and how lucky she is to be so furry and how I'd so rather turn into a tiger moth than a grown woman like Mom and how cool it is that she'll get to fly one day and how grateful I am that she and I are sisters.

I carefully pull out the shoebox terrarium so as not to spill the lake and place it on my bed, then take out Beetle Bob, Crackle, Barney, and Awesome Creature and place them inside for their morning social hour. I put in Harold the Hopper last, so he doesn't jump out before I get the slatted plastic cover on. I watch them all cavorting until I hear Mom start chanting, which means her morning meditation is coming to an end.

"Morning peach," I hear after the last chant.

"Morning plum," I say, and start to put my bug family back into their jar-houses.

"Morning blueberry."

"Morning watermelon."

And then Mom's head's right there because she's standing up. "Returning the prisoners to their cells, I see."

I quickly put my hand over the top of Awesome Creature's jar-house so she doesn't hear, then turn my back on Mom and whisper into the holes, "Don't listen to her. She doesn't understand how much we love each other."

I pretend I don't hear Mom saying, "The whole point of us, of The Great Adventure, is freedom, and we have a maximum-security prison going on up there. It's wrong, Cassidy." I don't see what the difference is between a bug living in a jar-house and us living in Sadie Mae, but I don't say that. I want her to move on. "It really upsets me," she says, not moving on. I listen to her banging around below me, knowing exactly what she's doing just from the sounds. Water in kettle. Granola in two bowls. Yogurt on table. Berries in strainer under faucet. "Are you saying something up there? Because I can't hear you if you are." Then over the running water she says again, "You need to speak up, honey, I can't hear you."

I open my mouth and make my hands into fists and vibrate my head as I silent-scream at the top of my lungs. I do this all the time. Then I pop my head over the edge and say loud and clear, "Morning tangelo." I add an arms-only version of our Monkey Dance.

She looks up from the faucet, her pick-on-Cassidy face melting into delight. In her hands is a strainer full of strawberries. She reaches up and touches my nose with her wet index finger—*bop*. This is how small it is inside Sadie Mae—we are never more than an arm's length from each other. "Morning, my monkey-dancing strawberry," she says, smiling like a goof and I'm happy to report Mean Mom or at least Irritable Mom has been eighty-sixed. (I learned this term the last time we were at an RV hookup. That's where I learn all the good words like *butthuffer* and *assclown*.)

After breakfast we swim in the ocean in our wet suits pretending to be dolphins. "Be the dolphin, Cassidy! Really be it!"

"How?" I ask her as I bob like a buoy, which makes her swim away from me in frustration. I'm bad at her kind of pretend. I know I'm not a dolphin. Still, we stay in the water, me as me, she as a dolphin, until our fingers are pruned, and our feet are ice, and we're both shivering with blue lips. It never occurs to either of us to get out until we're icicles. (It does occur to me much later, of course, that another mother might've known when it was time for an eight-year-old to get out of the frigid ocean.)

Anyway, after we use the blow-dryer to de-ice ourselves and are back in our dresses, we fluff auras. I love fluffing Mom's aura because I can get real close to her without her calling me a leech. We find a sunny spot and make a circle in the dirt. I pull over one of our chairs and stand on it, and with my hands, I start at her waist and fluff fluff fluff around her all the way up while she stands there with her eyes closed. Sometimes I only pretend I'm fluffing and just look at her.

Then it's my turn.

After that we do five straight minutes of primal screaming, which is a very long time to scream about nothing in particular. I do primal listening instead.

Then school.

At eight, I'm already three years ahead in the curriculum we use, so we do a lot of side studies. Our current one is California history because Teacher Mom's obsessed with it. We alternate topics, though, so next is my pick, which is bees and their waggle dances.

Mom's already begun today's lesson and is pacing around Sadie, arms in the air, voice high and excited. Teacher Mom's my second-favorite mother. "Pay attention, honey," she says to me because I'm preoccupied with Awesome Creature, who I see crawling under a leaf. Mom can tell I'm preoccupied because she has the power to break into my mind. I wish I could break into hers, but I can't, even though I try all the time. There are so many things I need to know in there.

"I'm paying attention," I say.

"Okay, good." She pushes some hair behind her ear that frees itself instantly. "It's a certain kind of person who chose to come to California in the nineteenth and early twentieth century," she says. "And honey, it's also a certain kind of person who chooses to live here now, at the edge of a continent"—she points out the window at the endless blue ocean— "where the ground beneath your feet is always quaking, where one spark sets the whole caboodle on fire, where you can't take another step west without falling into the sea. Going west, being a pioneer, happens now in the mind." She taps my head. "It's all in here—that daring journey into the unknown. California is a religion as much as a place, and we are practitioners, you see that, Cassidy?"

I nod but I don't have a clue what she's talking about even though she's always talking about it. I prefer when we study California's shifting tectonic plates rather than the stupid people like us who choose to live on top of them. But Mom can't get enough of this idea. She sits on the counter by the sink and gathers her hair into a ponytail, then ties it in a knot. I put down my pen and do the same with mine, so it looks like hers, like we're two soft-serve ice-cream cones.

She continues. "Sure, maybe it was greed that lured the vast majority of settlers out here in 1849 during the gold rush, but avarice aside, you had to be daring to make that journey, right?" *Avarice?* I write it down to look it up later. I love words. I have a list of ones that describe my mother. It's a very long list. And a very short list of words that describe me. Mom's getting super animated. "From every continent across the globe, the wild ones came here. Risk takers, desperadoes, greedy bastards, adventurers, misfits, outcasts, grifters, free spirits. The population went from eight hundred people to *three hundred thousand* people in a few years—just imagine that, Cassidy. Largest mass migration in the history of the western hemisphere, one that absolutely devastated Native communities, which we've talked about and will continue to study, but for today let's think about that pioneer."

She hops down, takes a step, and is at the table with me, looking down at the open books and maps spread out before us. She points to a map that shows a few huts on a beach and then the same beach a few years later turned into the city of San Francisco and behind it a horizon full of ships. "Three hundred thousand people came practically overnight!" Pretty cool, I admit. I follow her with my eyes as she goes to the window and peers out again at the waves rolling into the rocky shore. I'm amazed once again how much she looks like a rosy maple moth.

Mom must get one of her creepy story ideas then, because she takes the pencil from behind her ear and rips a scrap of paper out of my notebook and writes something down, then folds it and puts it in the pocket of her dress. I make a mental note to find that piece of paper later. I secretly collect the words she writes on napkins, receipts, movie stubs, scraps of paper, and keep them in a bag of words under my mattress.

She also writes in a journal. When I ask her what she's writing, she says she's trying to crash into infinity with words. I don't know what this means. I admit that I read the journal too because I have no choice. I'm trying to find out things about my grandparents, my dead father, about us, about anything that happened before The Great Adventure began. I don't remember anything before Sadie Mae, and she won't talk about it.

But her journal is just full of the same creepo stories she tells me at night around the fire: *In the time of forever,* they all begin. Stories of people whose sadness makes them go invisible, of girls born with wings that fall off, of whole towns that wake up blind, of bolts of lightning that become boys, of mothers and daughters, who, when they hold hands, freeze over like glaciers. Not to mention the shadow-man who leaves gifts in the night, the sad drunk giant who takes apart the world looking for his lost love, and finally, the singing dead woman who lures women into The Silent World next door. That last one is my least favorite story because my mother is one of these women who gets lured by the singing, and The Silent World is where she goes and loses the ability to speak or hear, where she becomes first Silent Mom, and then Gone Mom, my least favorite mother times a billion.

When she's Gone Mom in The Silent World, I can scream butthuffer and assclown over and over right in her face and get no response. I can cry or do The Monkey Dance or let my bug family out on her skin or draw giant beetles on the walls with markers or pull my hair out strand by strand, and still: nothing. I just have to wait until she "gets back" and make my own food and talk to no one for thousands of years while she stays in bed or curls up by a tree.

"Are you listening, Cassidy?" I nod, tuning back into the lesson. "Let's remember, ninety-five percent who landed on the shores in those years were young men. A city that was ninety-five percent men—can you imagine such a nightmare? Thankfully some were gay men who'd come to escape oppression around the world." She pops a cashew into her mouth from the bowl on the table. I pop one in my mouth too. "There were thirty brothels—you know what that is, right? Okay good—so, thirty brothels for every church in San Francisco. More champagne was drunk in a week in San Francisco than in a year in Boston. Cross-dressing was common, men as women and women men. Sexual experimentation and permissiveness were the norm. Lawlessness and decadence reigned." I write down *decadence*. "So that's who's building this new society, this new city: the wild ones who left—you get that?" She's so excited, her face is ladybug-red and her voice is shaking. "Free spirits like us, Cassidy. We left too!" She raises her arms. "We are California, do you see that!? Do you?"

I nod because she's so happy about this, about how *We are California!* "Groundbreaking, ground-shaking ideas that change the world are born here again and again decade after decade. And you can feel it, can't you? How it's always vibrating outside." She's at the window again. "Look how bright the light is! Look how tall those redwoods are—they touch the sky! Look at that ocean! I mean, there's got to be something in the air, right?" She sticks her head out the window and her hair whips every which way in the wind. "Breathe it in, Cassidy. Breathe it in. Can you feel it? Can you?" She looks back at me. There's a wildness in her eyes that both scares and excites me and I get up and stick my head out the window too, wanting to breathe it in with her and then when she asks me again if I feel it, I hear myself saying, "I do, Mom! I feel it too!"

She puts her arm around me, squeezes, and I feel like I'm lifting off. "Then let's go skinny-dipping," she says. "Last one in is a—"

But I don't hear *rotten egg* because she's dancing her way out of her clothes as she flies out the door and I'm barreling forward, out of Sadie Mae, lifting my dress over my head and then running naked down the bluff after her.

Later, we're back in our dresses and walking along the cliff on a trail that overlooks the ocean. She calls it sky-bathing, but really, it's just walking. The afternoon sun is low, creating the endless glittering path of light on water that goes all the way to the horizon. We're yakking away. She says we're like two mockingbirds on a branch with no one else to sing to.

I skip ahead of her and squat to check out a hammerhead worm squirming across the trail. I pick it up and run back to show Mom.

"Cassidy, please! Gross. Put it down. C'mon. Get it away from me."

"Tell me about your parents then," I say, wiggling the worm at her like she hates.

"Put that thing down!"

"Tell me!"

"Let's get back," she says, picking up the pace. "Please leave the worm here where it belongs. Don't even think of keeping it in Sadie with your other hostages."

I put the worm down and quickly say goodbye and tell him I wish he could be part of my family and that I'll love him for the rest of my life. Then I scramble after Mom because I can't let her get too far ahead. She might get in Sadie and drive away without me. On purpose, not by accident. I have nightmares where this happens, but I don't tell her because I don't want to give her the idea if she hasn't already thought of it on her own. "Why won't you ever tell me about your parents?" I say when I catch up. She pretends she doesn't hear me. She says she wants me to speak up, but really, she only wants me to speak up about things she wants to hear.

When we get back to Sadie, Mom goes straight up to her bunk. I climb the ladder after her. "Please don't go to The Silent World," I say, but she's already there. I can tell because she's in a ball facing the wall like a pill bug. Also, because the air is colder, and my heartbeat is so loud, I have to cover my ears.

I jump down, then quickly climb the ladder to my bunk and take out

Awesome Creature and the others, all except Harold the Hopper. We make a circle, and they all tell me how much they love me and that they will never ever die like my dead dad or drive away and leave me all alone. Then we tell each other our most secret secrets.

Finally, I put them away because I'm hungry. I go downstairs and open the peanut butter and stick my finger in and eat until my stomach feels bad. Outside, the sun's setting and the sky's full of red and orange and purple, like a bruise.

I want my mother.

I wait.

And wait.

And wait and wait and wait and wait and wait and wait and wait and wait and wait.

I try to count all the hairs on my head.

I go up her ladder. "Mom," I say. Then louder: "Mom!" Then as loud as I can: "MOM!"

I sit next to her and watch her breathe. This means she's converting oxygen to carbon dioxide. The trees do the opposite. I like science but not as much as I like words.

I start counting the hairs on her head.

The last thing I remember is asking the dusk-time moon out the window for help and the moon telling me he can't help because he's 240,000 miles away from me and to get a clue, Cassidy. I hug myself and pretend it's not me doing the hugging and that's the last thing I remember.

When I wake up, only a few minutes later because it's still dusk, Mom's looking at me with her here-blue-eyes not her gone-blue-eyes. She's back. So soon this time. I'm so relieved, I can't even speak. I snuggle into her, and she wraps an arm around me and all I smell is her jasmine oil and I'm so toasty and happy.

(I'm going to interrupt myself for a second, Wynton. It's hard for me to really know how long my mother's trips to The Silent World were. I remember them lasting days, weeks at times, but maybe it just felt like days or weeks. I wish I could ask her. I wish I could ask her so many things because I only trust my memory so far when I'm this young. But The Silent World was as real a place to me then as the town square might be for you. It's very hard to unbelieve stuff from when you were little, isn't it? So hard to shake off the stories we were raised on. Even now at nineteen, my mother's stories, those strange fables, cling to me. I still look at girls and wonder when their wings fell off. I pass through towns and imagine soon all the people I see will wake up blind. I always pray my own sadness won't make me disappear, always listen for the dead woman singing, always think of the sad drunk giant taking apart the world looking for his lost love. And every day, I look for a guy who was once a lightning bolt—is that you, Wynton? So often, I've thought it was. Plus, I write in a notebook now too and make up my own *In the Time of Forever* stories, and I think I might finally know what it means to want to crash into infinity with words.)

Anyway, back to the day of the first betrayal.

"Okay, I'll tell you about my parents," Mom says to my great surprise as we cuddle in her bed in the *gloaming,* a word I just learned that means twilight. "Remember how Moses's parents sent him down the river in a basket?"

Uh-oh. "Your parents did that?"

"Lots of parents do that."

My stomach tightens. I did not know this. "Well, who found you in the basket, then?"

"The bears, honey, you know that part of the story."

I sigh. I don't want the bear story. I want her parents to be like the grandparents in the books we read and in the movies we watch, not like Moses's parents and definitely not like bears. I want to know if my grandparents had a dog and where they lived and what color their house was and if they loved me. I want to know more about my father than his name, Jimmy, and that he's dead as the deer Mom hit and killed because she was practicing something called Fervent Gratitude while driving one night and lost control of Sadie. All the time, I think about how my dead dad is decomposing like that dead deer, but more slowly, because he's in a coffin and the carrion beetles can't get in. He died in a surfing accident, which means he drowned, which is why Mom taught me CPR and the Heimlich maneuver so I can save her if she's drowning too or if her heart stops or if she chokes on a grape.

I reach behind her and twist the fabric of her yellow dress around my fingers. I do this a lot, hold on to her without her realizing. When she does realize, that's when she calls me her little leech. It's a horrible nickname. I know a lot about leeches from my bug books. They release a chemical so the host doesn't feel them sucking their blood, and then they secrete an anti-clotting agent. This means they can suck the blood of the host, in some cases until the host dies like the deer and Jimmy the Dead Drowned Dad.

"So, besides the bears, you were all alone," I ask, going along. "When you were my age?"

She's looking my way, her eyes dancing. "Yes, except when I was with a lovely family of bullfrogs for a time, they taught me to do this—" She bleats out a *ribbit* sound so loud and funny, my fear and frustration with her vanish, just poof it goes, and then it's Happy Mom, the best Mom, and she's tickling my stomach and making the frog noise in my belly button until I'm all stretched out squirming and shrieking and laughing and trying to fend her off as she looks down on me, smiling like daybreak, her hair falling around my face like it's my hair, and it could be because we have the same endless wrecked hair, seaweed hair, mermaid hair, and then she's saying the things that make me turn into a sun. "Don't worry, baby. I'll never leave you. It's you and me. Always and forever. My love for you is so big, Cassidy, it hardly fits in here." She touches her chest.

I touch my chest back at her and she leans down to press foreheads and noses. I love Forehead-Noses. We close our eyes and breathe together, nestled in our hair curtain.

There is no one but us for miles and miles.

"We don't need anything or anyone else," she whispers, our faces still together. "We're free." This is the longest Forehead-Noses we've ever had.

(Mom had a digital camera and we took pictures with it constantly, especially during these Sadie Mae years when things were still pretty good with us. She'd set up the tripod and then we'd run in front of the lens and jump as high as we could. I look at these pictures now the most: our arms up, faces exhilarated, wearing our dirty dresses, suspended like that in the air. That's mostly how I think of these early years now, Wynton. Like we were not on earth.)

That evening, I go up to my bunk feeling cheery as the fat full moon, which is now beaming out of the night sky and into the window by my bed. Mom's writing in her journal at the table and there's a cozy feeling in Sadie Mae. Before I go to sleep, I whisper into the holes of each of the jar-houses. When it's Awesome Creature's turn, I hug her jar to my chest and tell her not to be afraid of the dark and how we're both going to wake up to so much sunlight tomorrow and how our dreams won't be the ones where we're completely alone on a beach that goes on forever in both directions and the sand is so deep, we can hardly move.

But instead of waking to sunlight, I wake a few hours later to Mom climbing down the ladder of my bunk with one of her arms pressing the bug jars to her chest. "What are you doing?" I ask, panic coursing through me, immediately dissipating any remains of sleep. "What are you doing, Mom?" I repeat. My voice is shaking like my hands are, like my legs are, like my heart is. I push off the covers and drop down the ladder, then grab the back of her powder-blue robe and pull, trying to turn her around or make her stop. Instead, I get dragged across the floor and then we're at the door, which is open to the balmy night. "What're you doing?" I say again, my words full of crying now, because I know exactly what she's doing as she puts the jars one by one on the shelf over the door so I can't reach them.

"It's not right," she says. "They need their freedom." I jump, trying to reach the jars, but they're too high. I pull at her robe, at her hands, but she shakes me off. I can see Beetle Bob up against the glass, looking at me, terrified, asking me to stop Mom. I rush for the rocking chair and drag it across the floor and stand on it, but I still can't reach.

"I'm sorry, Cassidy," she says, taking Beetle Bob's jar in her hands. I grab at her as she maneuvers the jar away from me. Beetle Bob backslides down the glass landing upside down on his back. My heart falls out of my body.

"He can die on his back! You're murdering Beetle Bob!"

"No, I'm not." She shakes the jar and Beetle Bob turns over. "I'm saving him. I can't bear witness to this anymore. Every living thing deserves to be free."

"He doesn't want to be free! He wants to be with me! Look at him. He's begging me to help him."

"You have to learn to let go of those you love."

"Why?" I'm crying now. "Why can't I just love them?"

"You can't keep living things in cages, Cassidy. It's wrong. They'll die in those jars and then how will you feel? They need air, leaves, rain—"

"They need me!" I cry, pulling at her robe, though I know it's the other way around, that I need them. My throat's hot, tight, full of pain.

With me hanging on her, begging her, Mom unscrews the cap and shakes out the jar into the night. She doesn't even let Beetle Bob crawl out onto the ground. I squeeze around her legs, tumbling into the dark to see if he survived the fall. I'm crawling around on the dirt looking for him, mistaking a pebble or a piece of a stick for Beetle Bob again and again. Then she walks past me with the three other jars in her arms. "Please Mom," I beg. She doesn't turn around, stops a few feet away and shakes them out one by one. I sit on the ground, feel the cold on my bare legs. I'm crying so hard, I can barely get words out. "They're my family. They're my only friends."

She turns around. "I'm your family. We're best friends."

I want to say I need other family, other friends, ones that don't go to The Silent World.

"It's captivity," she says.

"It's not if they want to be there."

"And how do you know they want to be there?"

"Because I speak Bug!"

I notice then there are only three empty jars in her arms. Just three. Plus Beetle Bob's jar, which she opened first. Hope replaces despair. My heart starts to race. Awesome Creature must still be next to my pillow, safe and sound!

"I'm going to bed," I say, wiping my face. Is Awesome Creature still up there? My sister? Could it be?

"I am sorry, honey, but it was the right thing to do."

The right thing to do! Something snaps in me, years of "Speak up!" and "Stop sneaking up on me!" Years of creepy stories and The Silent World and stupid stupid *We are California*. I open my mouth, squeeze my hands into fists, and scream as loud as I can, realizing I barely vocalize at all when we primal scream, realizing there is a scream in me as big as the entire world.

"Stop that!" my mother cries, putting her hands over her ears.

I don't stop. I need her to hear me, I need the moon 240,000 miles away to hear me.

When I return to my bunk, I see that Awesome Creature is indeed still there and it's like a parachute opening and saving me midair. I whisper into the holes in the jar telling her I will always take care of her and not to worry and nothing bad will ever happen to her like the others. I fall asleep with her jar-house in my arms.

After that, I keep Awesome Creature stowed under the covers 24/7 so Mom doesn't find and murder her. She dies a couple weeks later. I secretly bury her by a creek bed. It's so awful. I do not tell my mother.

I've never told anyone this until now, until you, Wynton Fall, the boy from the meadow, my very first friend who was not a bug.

This bug massacre was a starter-betrayal.

Just wait for two and three.

And then four. Yours.

In the time of forever, a woman couldn't sleep so she went outside, picked up the house in which she lived with her daughter, put it on her head, and began walking. "Look, a woman with a house on her head," passersby said one to the other when morning came.

The woman just kept walking.

In the house, the girl woke up, brushed her teeth, got dressed, and sat at the kitchen table, drinking some orange juice. She didn't notice that the landscape out the kitchen window kept changing.

Where is my mother? she wondered.

After some time, months, the daughter yelled out the window, "Where is my mother?" Then she saw the shadow of a woman and realized the house had been on her mother's head all these years. "Put the house down and come inside," the girl yelled out, but her mother just kept walking.

Years passed.

Gradually, the daughter started to look out the window at the passing landscapes, started to enjoy the fleeting pictures, started to enjoy the fleeting. One day, the girl hopped out a window and walked with her mother beneath the house for a while, sharing the weight.

Not too long after that, they dropped the house on some street somewhere and mother and daughter kept on walking without it.

DIZZY

Dizzy and her mother burst through the doors of Paradise Springs Hospital at two forty-five a.m. More country clinic than hospital, it was as bustling as the town diner during the day but eerie and deserted at night. A pale spidery woman Dizzy didn't recognize rose from her desk as if she'd been expecting them. She looked like she slept in a coffin, Dizzy thought, hearing only bits and pieces of what she was saying: *Hit by a car, lucky to be alive, broken bones, potential internal injuries.* Dizzy's chest collapsed. This woman was under the impression that Wynton was bones and organs, not the guy who plugged in the world.

Dizzy tried to breathe, heard herself say, "What about his arms, his hands?"

Words: *Multiple fractures, crushed hand.*

"Right or left?" she asked, then added, "He's a violinist. I mean, that's all he is. Most people are lots of things. He's only one thing. He can't live without playing. He told me once that music was just another body part like—"

More words: *Right arm. Left hand. That isn't what you should be concerned about. He wasn't conscious when he went into exploratory surgery. Swelling in the brain. Possible coma—*

"But he's going to pull through, right?" Mom's voice was so high, it could break glass. Dizzy was the glass.

Don't ask that! she screamed at her mother, but only in her head. The spidery woman was talking and talking. Dizzy tried to focus. *One of the best surgeons in Paradise County, Dr. Larry Dwyer, very lucky he was on call, happened to be at your son's show, in fact.*

Dizzy put her hands together to pray, except she realized she didn't know how. Not officially. No one had ever taught her. She said to her mother, "I don't know how to pray."

Her mother shushed her and continued talking to the woman.

Right arm, left hand. That was not good. Not good at all. The worst for violin, Dizzy thought.

"Uncle Clive's dream predicted this," she said to her mom.

"Dizzy! Please, let me talk to—"

"Cynthia," the lady said.

"Cynthia, how long will he be in surgery?"

Dizzy didn't hear the answer. Her hearing wasn't working. Neither was anything. The floor felt like it was swinging. She could only breathe in gasps and her pulse was taking off, sprinting, breaking records as she tried to psychically contact her angel, to tell her to please come down right this minute. The angel had not shown again since the encounter. Maybe she'd had other people to watch over and didn't know yet what happened to Wynton. Dizzy had no idea how these things worked. Cynthia in her gray-tinted death skin escorted Dizzy and her mother, who were Velcroed together now, one terrified lump of mother and daughter, to a waiting area. Once there, Cynthia turned to Dizzy and said, "I'm an atheist but I meditate and it's a lot like praying. Want to know how I do it?"

Dizzy nodded.

She said, "I close my eyes." Cynthia closed her eyes. Dizzy closed her eyes. She heard Cynthia say, "And then I try to wrap my two puny arms around the whole world."

Dizzy sat down and tried to wrap her two puny arms around the whole world, even though she had no idea what this meant. She thought her mother was trying to do it too because they didn't move or say anything for an eternity. Ten minutes. Dizzy knew it had been ten minutes because she'd opened her eyes and was watching the clock as she tried to hug the whole world. She wished the world would hug her instead.

Mom called the house for Perfect Miles even though the note he'd left on the table next to his phone, said *Went camping for the night*. Which was something he did sometimes because he liked trees more than people. Mom had written on the note to come to the hospital. Dizzy was surprised how much she wanted Perfect there, how badly she needed him to huddle with them. She was pretty sure the bigger the huddle of humans in the waiting room the better. Also, Miles calmed Mom, and Mom calmed Dizzy.

Mom was not calm. Dizzy was not calm.

She gave up meditating. She gave up calling her angel. She was now in negotiations with the Almighty Himself. Major negotiations. She'd already promised she'd forgive Lizard and that she'd do all her homework even if it was so dull, it made her brain die. Then she added that she'd stop surfing the web for pertinent information regarding existence and stop being superficial and hating beautiful people and stop reading romance novels and stop trying to learn how to masturbate correctly and stop swearing and stop wishing she were someone else and then she'd gotten desperate, and before she knew it, she was promising she'd become a nun. This was when a doctor came in to tell them what Cynthia, the world-hugger, had already, that Wynton was in luck (in luck!) because their best surgeon had been on call, had been, funny enough (funny!), at Wynton's show earlier in the night. He also told her mother how much he loved her deconstructed coq au vin, how he proposed to his wife at The Blue Spoonful. He didn't seem to realize he was talking to two extraterrestrials from Planet Terror.

He then told them the surgery would be another few hours.

HOURS!

When the man had left and they were alone again, Dizzy lay down on the floor, stomach down, her arms spread-eagled.

"Dizzy, get off the floor. It's filthy. What are you doing?"

She'd seen a movie where the nuns did this. "I'm going to be a nun. I'm devoting my life to God. This is me prostrate before Him."

"We're Jewish!"

"I'm only half."

"The half that matters. It follows the mother. Now get up."

"No. And you really should join me down here. Prostrate yourself before God, Mom. Jews did it too until the Middle Ages. It came up in my research. C'mon. It's okay. Everyone does it: Buddhists, Christians, Muslims, Hindus—It feels good. It feels right."

Dizzy knew she was supposed to say prayers under her breath when she did this, but she didn't know any, so started reciting the only thing she could think of.

A strange sputtering noise interrupted her "prayer" and she lifted her head. Her mother's face was flushing, and her hand was over her mouth. She was shaking. Dizzy thought she was sobbing until the Olympic snort and then a wild peal of laughter escaped her mother's mouth. "Oh my God, Dizzy! Are you reciting Ms. Mary Mack? That's your prayer?" Dizzy was. *Ms. Mary Mack, Mack, Mack, all dressed in black, black, black, with silver buttons, buttons, buttons, all down her back, back, back* . . . It was all she'd had. Her mother was cackling now, and it was setting Dizzy off too. This was how it worked with them. If one went, the other followed. Dizzy could feel the hilarity taking over her prostrate body until they were both gasping for air. "I'm going to pee," her mother shrieked. "Oh God, this is so bad! I'm going to have to be a nun too."

Which set them off again.

Cynthia, who must've heard the ruckus, was at the doorway looking at them like they were a carnival act. They tried to stifle the hysteria, tuck it back into pockets of propriety, but Cynthia's ghoulish face only provoked another bout. She shook her head and as she left said, "The best medicine."

Another hour passed.

Her mother walked over to the window and opened it despite the air-con. "My father always said you had to pray with the windows open so God would feel invited in."

"He did? You never told me that." How come her mother never mentioned this pertinent info regarding existence before? Just because her mother no longer believed in God didn't mean Dizzy didn't feel His presence in her closet on occasion. Her mother always said after her brother Christophe died, she stopped believing in God and after her parents moved back to France, she never set foot in a temple again. "What kind of God could let him die?" she often said to Dizzy, but her mother still lit the Yahrzeit candle and said the Kaddish for her brother and her parents on their birthdays and on Yom Kippur. Dizzy wanted to set her feet in a temple but there wasn't one for almost a hundred miles. They were practically the only Jews or half-Jews in Paradise Springs.

"And my mother said she heard God's voice in running water. She used to put her head to the faucet and say to my father, "Benoît Fournier, God is telling me that he wants me to go to Mexico en vacance."

Dizzy loved knowing this. "Did they teach you how to pray?"

She shook her head. "They wanted us to go to Hebrew school and get bar and bat mitzvahed but neither Christophe nor I wanted to go. I do know some of the Hebrew prayers, though. Want to recite them with me?"

Dizzy nodded and put her hands in a prayer position while still sitting on the floor.

"Let's put our palms together," her mother said.

"Is that how your dad and mom used to do it?"

"No, but let's anyway."

Dizzy rose and put her hands against her mother's and her mother began speaking in Hebrew. It made Dizzy feel better. That she didn't understand the words didn't matter. They filled her and when she started repeating them, she felt even better yet. Like someone somewhere might hear these ancient words and come help them.

"We're praying Jews."

Her mother smiled. "We are."

"I think it's going to work, Mom."

"Me too."

And then she pulled Dizzy into her arms.

It wasn't possible to love another person more than Dizzy loved Wynton. "He has lightning inside him," she whispered, into her mother's neck. "Like the white truffle."

"I know," her mom whispered back.

"That means something," Dizzy said.

"It means he'll be okay," her mother said. Her voice was tiny. Dizzy looked at her, saw the despair. She knew her mom hated hospitals because Christophe had died in one when she was around Dizzy's age. In an operating room. And then there was what happened to Dizzy's father here.

"Are you thinking of Christophe?" Dizzy asked. Her mother nodded. "You loved him so much?"

"Like you love Wynton."

Dizzy often studied the photograph Chef Mom kept by her bed. In it, her mother looked like a miniature version of her older brother— same leather jacket, same clunky black boots, same riot of dark curly hair. They were bent over, laughing all out of control, like they were laugh partners too.

Sometime during the third hour, Dizzy declumped herself from her mother and moved across the room. A fury had taken root in her chest. A red-hot one directed at her mother, who must've been having a mind-meld with Dizzy, because she said, "I never should have kicked him out. You were right."

She wanted to say, "It's not your fault." Instead, she said, "I told you." Her mother clammed up.

Sheriff Ortiz arrived at dawn. Dizzy and her mother were once again lumped together, terror having trumped Dizzy's anger. This was pretty much how they were last time they saw the sheriff too, when she came to the door with Alonso Fall's stone head in the passenger seat of her patrol car to tell them Wynton was in jail for driving drunk into the statue. Then, the sheriff had been livid. This time, she took Mom's hand and said, "We'll find out who did this." Then she asked them if they knew the young woman Cassidy who'd witnessed the hit and run. Sheriff Ortiz told them this Cassidy person had called the ambulance, done CPR, and rode with Wynton to the hospital, where she checked him in.

Dizzy and her mother both shook their heads. They didn't know anyone named Cassidy.

"The on-duty nurse said she had all different colored hair, and very curly, to here." She touched her own back above the waist. "About eighteen or nineteen, maybe twenty. She said she was a friend of your son's but had vanished when the nurse returned to her station."

"Was she tall, with tattoos of words on her arms, and really pretty?" Dizzy asked.

"The nurse did mention tattoos, and yes, she said she was a beautiful girl."

Dizzy jumped up, relief slamming into her. "That's the angel! The one who saved my life! Oh! Everything's going to be okay, now I know it!" The angel had found Wynton like Dizzy had asked her to. The angel had listened to her. And done CPR! Probably some magic celestial kind, Dizzy supposed. The sheriff was looking at Dizzy with a furrowed brow. Dizzy told her, "She pushed me out of the way of a speeding truck the other day. I sent her to Wynton."

Her mother turned to Dizzy also with a creased brow, this near-death information about Dizzy's angel encounter being new.

Sheriff Ortiz nodded. "Okay," she said. "Sometimes angels walk among us. I don't want to imagine what would've happened if this girl hadn't been there to call an ambulance and do CPR. So, yes, I'm with you, Dizzy. An angel in my book. We'll find her. Hopefully she can help us figure out who did this. She told the nurse that Wynton was inebriated and thought he'd taken pills as well. He had Vicodin on him, a prescription that was for your other son, Miles."

This sunk in slowly. Did Wynton steal the Vicodin that morning? Because Dizzy let him in the house? Her stomach turned over. If she hadn't let him in, he wouldn't have had his bow snapped, wouldn't have found pills, been so wasted, wouldn't have gotten hit by the car.

This wasn't her mother's fault, it was hers.

Her mother burst into tears. Then Dizzy did too. Sheriff Ortiz looked like she was about to join them. "I'm so sorry." She then became the third person to tell them how lucky Wynton was that Dr. Larry Dwyer was the surgeon on call when this happened.

When she left, her mother took Dizzy's hand and squeezed it. "Who is this Cassidy who saved the life of two of my kids in two days? Who's this angel walking among us?"

Dear Maman,

I need you. Wynton's in surgery. I wish it were me on that table, my brain, my hand, my life in the balance. Dizzy's asleep in my lap. I feel like I can hear her heart breaking. Miles is still in a world where he doesn't know what's happened.

It's been déjà vu sitting in the waiting room with Dizzy. The same spiky terror as when you and I and Dad waited for Christophe to come out of surgery after the aneurism. I wish I'd been funnier for you and Dad. My girl somehow had me laughing despite everything. How I wish you could've met her. All the kids.

I keep thinking of how you stopped speaking when Christophe died. I finally get it, Maman. There were no more words, right? How could there be without Christophe? The story had ended mid-sentence.

I can't bear the idea of Dizzy sitting on Wynton's bed like I sat on Christophe's, staring at his posters of Tupac and Ani DiFranco, obsessing on all the music he'd never hear now, the people he wouldn't love, the meals he wouldn't eat, the rivers he would never swim in. I never want Dizzy to feel like that, like the world is made of ashes. Like she's a shadow that has been detached from its person.

I never want her to know that a life is an abandoned unfinished story.

Crying now too hard to write. How did you ever recover, Maman? How? How did you ever cook another meal? Bake a cake? How can there even be cakes in a world that takes children from their mothers?

I left a message for Finn to close the restaurant until further notice. I wish I could close my heart until further notice.

I don't believe in God anymore, but I still can't shake the feeling that He's punishing me for the things I've done.

Bernadette

MILES

Miles woke before dawn in the vineyard, face down in the dirt, half in, half out of his sleeping bag. Enough light was creeping up the mountain for him to see there was no orange truck. He sighed, rolled onto his back. The idea had been to crash by the spot where the rainbowed-haired girl parked the night before, hoping she'd return again to sleep. The need to see her, to hear her rumbling voice, to feel the way he'd felt around her— like himself—had so overwhelmed him last night that instead of getting in bed, he'd grabbed his sleeping bag and took off to stand vigil, or sleep vigil.

He also hadn't wanted to risk seeing Wynton after the bow fiasco. Obviously.

Really, he never wanted to see Wynton again. He registered he was making fists and shook out his hands, tried to release the rage. It was always with him now—this inner tantrum. It had become elemental, along with the humiliation, which made his insides feel like they were curdling. How could Wynton have left him for dead in that Dumpster? He'd never get over it. What had Miles ever done but need him? And how it rattled Miles not to be able to remember so much of the Dumpster night, all he might've done, all that might've been done to him . . .

He sat up, still in his sleeping bag, and brushed off the dirt clinging to his face. He breathed in the river, watched the stars vanish one by one, trying not to clench his jaw, trying not to hate his brother, trying not to feel abandoned by the rainbow-haired girl, trying not to get sucked into The Gloom Room.

All around him, the birds called to each other mournfully, the dawn air already full of heat. He could feel sweat beading on the back of his neck.

One time, when Miles and Uncle Clive were out canopying the vines, before Uncle Clive gave up on winemaking and leased out the vineyard, his uncle had popped a grape into his mouth, then placed one, still warm from the sun, on Miles's tongue, and said, "You can taste it, can't you? You can smell it in the air." Uncle Clive had reached down then, grabbing a fistful of dirt. "In the earth too," he said, burying his nose in his hand and inhaling. "When people drink our wine, what they're tasting, what breaks their heart a little more with every sip, is *regret*." Uncle Clive brought the handful of earth under Miles's nose. "Can you smell it?"

Miles didn't then, but today maybe he did—regret. Heartache. Everywhere on their property. Clive was drunk a lot, talked out loud to no one, drew cows, thought his dreams were prophesies, played piano and sometimes trumpet until dawn, and said weird things all day long, but yes. Yes. There was something different about the Fall vineyards, and it wasn't just the way the grapes tasted or the way the earth and air smelled either. It was sad here. The birds sang too loudly, and the river slowed down for no reason Miles could ever figure out. Even before the drought, it ached by. And no matter where Miles went on the property, he felt certain someone was behind him, yet when he turned around, no one was ever there.

His thoughts were getting thicker, dreamier, so he lay back down, rolled onto his side . . . and the next thing he knew, a familiar wet tongue was licking his cheeks and he opened his eyes to Sandro in the morning light.

Why didn't you get me if you were going to come out here and wait for her?

Miles sat up so he could pet Sandro properly with both hands. *Last-minute decision.*

Sandro looked around. *Wonder where she is.*

Me too.

How could she abandon us like this?

Don't know.

They both sighed.

In the old days, he told Sandro, touching his finger to the dog's cold nose, *they would've called us melancholics.*

Except when we were with her. Yesterday we were joyholics.

This was true. When Miles had been with the rainbow-haired girl for those hours, he'd felt like anything he touched would hold on to his glow. Now he once again felt like anything he touched would hold on to his darkness.

He pressed his head into Sandro's sun-warmed coat. *Probably I'm to blame for your depression, doggo dude. Sorry.*

What you feel, I feel. What I feel, you feel. Just the way it is when you're best friends.

Yeah. Miles shimmied out of his sleeping bag, which was damp with sweat, as was he, and stood up, looking toward home, where Dizzy and Mom were most likely getting up. The white house sparkled gemlike in sunlight. There was none of the morning fog that often made it look like it was rising out of a cloud at this hour. Was Wynton crashed in the attic again? No way was Miles going home; not even the air-con could tempt him, so he ditched the bag and started walking in the opposite direction toward town, hoping he might spot the orange truck.

Sandro followed along quietly in the feverish air, panting already. Neither of them was particularly chatty. When Miles tuned in to Sandro's thoughts he heard: *Oh! Yum dirt, oh a fire hydrant! Cow paddies oh so much better, horse manure yum! Hot so hot too hot out! If only Beauty were here! I miss Beauty so much. Oh, where has Beauty gone?* Miles zoned him out, trying to curb the panic as he thought about how he hadn't been to school in over two weeks now. It was epic how much trouble he was going to be in.

For as long as he could remember, he'd been "Perfect Miles." It had been his only option after seeing the terror in the face of his kindergarten teacher, Mrs. Michaels, when he and his mother walked in for his first-ever day of school. Miles had been acutely aware how her voice, which had been cheerily welcoming kids, had deadened when she said to Miles, "I had your brother." His mother had calmly replied, "You'll see they're very different boys."

Miles made sure of it. He raised his hand if he had a question. He used his inside voice. He never ran down the halls. He colored in the lines. He was nice to everyone, even Stevie Stanford, who smelled like fish. He was every minute of every day the anti-Wynton, proving it again in first grade when Mr. Painter blanched at his arrival, then second grade, on and on, at home as well, becoming for his mother what Wynton could never be: The one she didn't have to worry about or even think about because he'd always do the right thing, the smart thing, the expected thing, and in this way, year after year, Miles Fall, whoever that was, whoever he might have been, began to disappear, to secretly unbloom. Finally, becoming so exemplary he was encouraged to apply to the prestigious Western Catholic Preparatory High School, which he got into with a scholarship.

There, where the bathrooms weren't graffitied with Wynton's name (*Need Weed, call Wynton: 555-0516*), where the roof hadn't been blown off by the sound of his brother's violin, where there were no singe marks from the time he nearly burned down the chem lab (on purpose), where there were no legends of his brother's bad behavior or his musical genius, Miles thought he'd finally be able to be his own person, plant his own flag, come out even, but it was too late. By that time, he didn't know how to be anyone but the anti-Wynton. He didn't know how to be himself, or who that was, and even if he figured it out, he was afraid he'd be rejected, as he had been by his siblings. He was an actor who'd become his character. He was Dr. Frankenstein and his monster in one. Yes, that was exactly it. He'd become a nice, good, smart, athletic, straight, reliable monster.

Perfect Miles, the perfect monster.

The rattle of an old vehicle behind Miles, and Sandro's accompanying bark, shook him out of his thoughts. Could it be? He turned around, wishing with everything in him to see the rainbow-haired girl's orange truck, but it was Uncle Clive in his beat-up Jeep. Miles lifted his arm to wave, hoping his uncle would drive by so Miles wouldn't have to talk. His uncle's face, normally ruddy from alcohol, was devoid of color, even with the windows down in this heat. He slowed, then stopped, took off his shades. His eyes were wide, his mouth rigid, his neck coated in sweat. His hand white-knuckled the wheel. Miles knew immediately that something was wrong.

"Get in," his uncle said. "It's your brother and it's bad."

CASSIDY

Okay, here we go, betrayal #2. Wynton, it's a biggie.

It's four years after The Bug Massacre and I'm twelve years old. We pull up to Sister Falls, one of our favorite spots to boondock in Northern California, unaware that everything's about to change forever. (Boondocking, what we mostly did then, entails finding a remote place, then winging it, storing sewage and limiting water and battery usage as much as possible.)

It's pouring as we arrive and another ragtag RV's parked where we usually set up. We've been coming to Sister Falls every spring since the beginning of The Great Adventure and we've never encountered anyone here before. It's one of our secret spots and I feel instantly, spectacularly irritated. To be fair, everything irritates me during this period of my life, including sunlight, rainbows, fairies, laughter, and especially my mother. She says it's hormones, which, of course, irritates me.

"Bummer," Mom says. "Bummer, bummer, bummer. Hope they keep to themselves."

"Probably a stupid dick weasel," I grumble. "A fuck trumpet, cocknose, arse badger."

Mom's brows rise. "She speaks and seems to have acquired Tourette's syndrome."

I'm barely talking to her. It's been a long, silent, crabby drive. Mom's eyes fix on me, full of amusement, not taking my dark mood seriously. "Those English guys had a charming effect on you, Cassidy. Glad I do battle holding vocabulary cards in front of your face each night only to lose the war to two English drunks." The drunks had been parked next to us at the RV hookup, Malcolm and Matthew Michelson, brothers with hair like oil slicks who played poker and grilled hot dogs, which, by the way, are awesome—I'd previously only ever had tofu pups, which are decidedly unawesome. Malcolm and Matthew drank beer all day and called each other cock-noses and other fabulous bad words. Best bad words I ever heard. They taught me to play poker too. And how to smoke a cigar, though Mom doesn't know about that.

"English *blokes*," I say.

"Stand corrected, *mate*," she replies cheerily. "C'mon Cassidy, are you going to be impossible all day?"

"Yes." I'm my own kind of weather system at this point. Like mother, like daughter.

I pick up my novel. Reading had become an all-consuming obsession. It happened all of a sudden when I realized it was a way to have friends who weren't insects (though I still love bugs). Friends who don't have to meditate for two hours a day.

Or drink cleansing beet juice before breakfast (which turns your pee red) or detoxifying green drinks before dinner.

Or hug trees until they hug you back (which can be a VERY long time).

Or practice aura photography.

Or pretend to be a free spirit when you're demonstrably an unfree one, no matter how many hours a day you meditate or hug trees or drink beet juice.

"Well, the astrocartography's never wrong," Mom's saying. "So, unless Jack the Ripper's in that RV, we're staying for a few weeks."

(Okay, so, though not Jack the Ripper, we have no idea how dangerous the person in that RV will prove to be for us. Isn't it weird that you have no forewarning when your life is about to irreversibly change? Like that night, Wynton. If only I'd gotten you to the side of the road, to safety, right away. I'll never forgive myself. Never. But then I think how much worse it might've been if you'd been there all alone, sitting in the middle of the road, like how I found you.)

"Jupiter's right over our heads conjunct the sun," Mom adds. "What could be luckier? Nada."

That's mostly how we determined where to go in our perpetual search for The Town: astrocartography. One of Mom's passions along with: juicing, reciprocal tree-hugging, chakra balancing, aura photography, astral projection, tapping, communing with power animals, fervent gratitude, and many more. "Oh boy do we need a soul-recharge," she says. "I do, anyway." She shakes out her arms. "One week at the RV park and I feel absolutely covered in civilization. So gross. It's like a film on my skin."

This is the rub. Unlike Mom, I *love* civilization.

I love diners that have chocolate chip pancakes, grilled cheese, hash browns. I love going to movies all day (if there's only one theater in town, we see the same movie over and over) and to thrift stores, where I now refuse to play the clashing game (I don't want to clash, I don't want to be noticed at all), and to used bookstores, where we exchange our books, staying all day usually until we have the perfect collection. I love watching normal people do normal things like walking dogs (mom's allergic) and reading magazines (they rot the mind) and kissing (oh, I love watching normal people kiss, especially against walls; I practice on trees while I'm waiting for them to hug me back).

We still haven't found The Town, though not for lack of trying. By this point, we've crossed 201 Californian towns off the list. Mom says we'll feel it in our bones the moment we arrive in The Town. My bones feel it often. It's her unfeeling bones that are the problem.

Case in point:

"It's The Town!" I squealed a week ago between bites of chocolate chip pancakes on our first evening in Doe Creek, like I had so many times in so many towns over so many stacks of pancakes in so many diners, wanting so badly to have found The Town already, so I could live in a house and go to school and have a bicycle, a curfew, and a best friend to tell all my secrets to. Like in novels. Like in movies.

"Here? You've got to be kidding. Doe Creek? This is *so* not The Town. The town is . . . It's *The Town,* Cassidy!"

The good news is Mom's trips to The Silent World have gotten a little less frequent in the past few years (which I'll realize soon may have to do with medication) and I no longer think of her in pieces. Or think of her as being enormous. I no longer ask about her parents or about my father, aka Jimmy the Dead Drowned Dad, or about the time before The Great Adventure either, not because I'm not burning with curiosity, which I still am, but because I realized as I got older that it was those questions that were sending her off to The Silent World nine times out of ten.

Mom opens the driver's-side door of Sadie, and the balmy, stormy summer air fills my lungs. "I'm going under the falls," she says, kicking off her flip-flops. Her toenails are striped purple and yellow, as are mine. "You stay here and sulk and think about what a terrible mother I am, okay?"

"I will."

She smiles at me before she closes the door. I watch her run through the rain, missing her already. What has it been? Three seconds? I sigh. That's my dirtiest little secret. Despite the way I act—can't seem to help acting these days, like there's a mean little troll living inside me—I hate being apart from my mom even for three measly seconds.

Thanks to the week at the Doe Creek Hookup (an RV park with a store, electricity, and water) that left a film of civilization on my mother's skin, we're loaded with supplies, and not just staples like rice, beans, tofu, potatoes, cheese, but the good stuff that I'll go through in a day. I'm allowed five indulgences when we get supplies. This time, I chose Frosted

Flakes, salt and vinegar potato chips (I love these more than my mother and tell her so often), peanut butter cups, mint chocolate chip ice cream, and marshmallows. We also have two new boxes of books we spent half a day collecting at a used bookstore after selling most of ours back, some new duds, including a purple pair of overalls with painted flowers I will rarely take off for the next year, confirmed by countless photos. Then there's Mom's pills, which, until earlier that day, I thought were for a stomach problem that began shortly after the bug massacre of yore.

Mom knocks on the passenger window, and I startle. Her dress is plastered to her now, her hair darker and slick around her face. She looks like a mermaid. She puts her hand on the window, starts doing The Monkey Dance, which still mostly has the power to end our bad moods, but mine today has traction. She gives up when I roll my eyes, motions for me to lower the window. "C'mon, Cassidy. Did you really want to play with that girl so badly?"

I did. *So* badly. For the first time, I'd almost made a friend. Mom had needed space, so I'd been hiding under Sadie Mae to avoid stray kids— kids not in books or movies terrified me then, despite being desperate for their companionship. And then this girl joined me. She didn't say anything at first, just crouched down and looked at me hiding under the rig like a freak, then to my surprise, she shimmied under Sadie and lay on her belly beside me. "You look like a fairy," she said, touching my hair with her hand. I touched her hair back. It was black, soft, so shiny. My stomach buzzed with excitement. I thought of Frog and Toad, of Winnie-the-Pooh and Christopher Robin. She smiled at me, and said, "You're cool," before scuttling away like she'd come.

She'd said I was cool! Me? It was one of the most exciting things to ever happen to me.

About an hour after that meeting, when Mom and I, the newly anointed cool person, were doing road school, there was a knock at the door. Men knocked on our door all the time at RV parks. I put them in categories: Grizzlies were the big-bellied bearded ones, Eye-Bulgers were the meth heads, Butt-Crack Showers were obviously butt-crack showers; then there were the ones Mom liked the most so I hated passionately: Jesus Impersonators and Cowboys.

All category of male trespasser would lean into Sadie in the same way, one arm above their head, elbow on the doorframe. Then they'd proceed to ask Mom questions about our welfare, like we were damsels in distress, and she'd laugh in this fake way I despised and answer them in a fake voice I also despised. "We're doing just fine but will let you know if that changes." Or something. The problem was sometimes she'd venture out with one of the Jesus Impersonators or Cowboys. (She told me once you should only date a man who you could imagine on a horse.) When she'd leave with one of them, I'd spend the whole time in Sadie panicking she wasn't going to come back. My ever-persistent bugbear, n. *a thing that causes excessive fear or anxiety.* (I had a bad dictionary-addiction back then. Who am I kidding? I still do, Wynton.)

I hated when the doorknob jiggled in the middle of the night. We both slept with Mace next to our glasses of water because there were sometimes rumors of serial killers and rapists at RV parks. Mom also kept a machete under her mattress. But sometimes she'd rise at the sound of the doorknob jiggle and venture out and not come back for hours, during which I'd hold my breath in rounds or bite my fingers or take scissors to my favorite books or my hair. One time last year, I followed her and watched as she and a Jesus Impersonator got into another RV. I skulked under the window until I heard sex noises loud and clear (which I was familiar with from the movies), then ran back to Sadie in horror. She must've known I'd followed her, because the next morning, we had a cringe-y talk about how sex was part of her spirituality. "Plus," she said, "it's important the vag doesn't get all closed up with cobwebs," which I believed was a thing that could happen until she caught me contorted in my bunk recently. "Doing a self-exam?" she asked.

"Checking for cobwebs," I said seriously.

She shrieked with laughter. "Oh Cassidy, you take everything so literally!"

So, when I heard the knock at the Doe Creek RV park, that's who I assumed it was: a Jesus or Cowboy or Grizzly, not the girl with shiny black hair and a moon face. She was standing beside a woman with a coiffed beauty salon hairstyle, loads of makeup, and happy eyes. The woman said to me, "Tell me something. What's your name and how old are you?"

"Cassidy," I said, staring at the girl who had cards in her hand. I loved cards. "I'm twelve."

The woman said, "This is Maya, she's eleven, and I'm Haley. Do you play cards, Cassidy?"

I was so excited I might be able to hang out with someone my age who wasn't in a book and who didn't terrify me that I couldn't speak. I nodded and the girl Maya smiled. I thought I might start jumping up and down. My mother came up close behind me and put her hands on my shoulders.

"You full-timers?" the woman asked Mom. She was wearing a velvet off-white tracksuit. I wanted to touch it. We didn't wear comfy squishy things like that.

"We are indeed," my mom answered.

(I probably need to catch you up on this, Wynton. People who live like we did are called full-timers. Some are retired folks who want to see the country. Some are young couples out for an adventure. Some are families who want a cheaper lifestyle or an unplugged one. Some are criminals on the run. Some, like Mom, say they're on a spiritual path. And a handful are totally bonkers. Mom, of course, says full-timers are not too different from the kinds of pioneering people who arrived in California in the nineteenth and early twentieth centuries. Fellow practitioners of her religion.)

"Not us. We're weekenders," Haley said. "In other words, kidnap victims. My husband, he takes us against our will." She gently pushed a ribbon of Maya's hair behind her ear. "We prefer home, don't we, Maya? I like to bake on the weekends, a baking fool I am. Can't even fry an egg in our rig." She'd gotten my attention at that. I was obsessed with the idea of making pies since we saw the movie *Waitress* six times at an arthouse theater in a town that wasn't The Town a year earlier. Haley stepped into Sadie. "Oh! This place is adorable! It's like *Better Homes and Gardens* in here. All this beautiful painted wood. Wow. I might not mind so much if our jalopy looked like yours. Well done." Most people had this response when they came into Sadie because of the real wood floors that were painted white, the see-through purple curtains, the enormous funky chandelier made of all different colored sea glass, the rocking chair for two, the cool lamps everywhere, and of course, The Great Wall of Books. We were always going to craft fairs and farmer's markets in search of what Mom called "accoutrements for Sadie." Haley smiled and said, "Is it just you two?"

"It is indeed," said Mom.

"How brave of you. I'd be scared, just me and Maya. All these misfits always lurking around the parks, you noticed that?"

"I'm fond of misfits," Mom said, smiling in an unsmiling way.

"Right. I know, I'm so judgmental. You see? This is why I should be at home baking in the suburbs." Her eyes landed on our meditation mats. "Oh! Do you guys do yoga? I started with the Pilates. Life changer! Well, ass-changer anyway." She laughed and slapped her butt.

I giggled. So did Maya.

"We meditate," Mom said.

"Both of you?"

"Yup. Two hours a day."

"Two hours a day! My God. Cassidy, how do you like that?"

"It's very boring," I said, because it was.

Haley exploded in laughter. "Right? A girl after my own heart. Okay, here's the God-darn truth: I find yoga torture, just torture! All that woo woo and Savasana and posing like you're a dead man or a baby or doing that lion breathing"—she exhaled out her nose in short bursts—"all to get to know your own navel better, well thank you very much, I know my navel just fine." She was on a roll, half talking, half laughing, reveling in words that were surely souring in my mom's head, and I was loving it. "What's going on with all that wellness stuff anyway?" she continued. "I mean, I'm a nurse and I know sick people, and those yoga people are not sick, am I right?" This was addressed to me.

"You're right," I said.

"Exactly," she said. "Why look for wellness when for all intensive purposes you're already as well as well can be—"

"Intents and purposes," Mom said.

"What?"

"It's *intents and purposes*, not *intensive purposes*."

"Really? You're kidding me. Intensive purposes is intents and purposes? Who the hell knew that? How have I gone thirty-eight years of life without knowing that. Are you sure?"

"I'm sure," Mom said, and I thought: Haughty, adj. *arrogantly superior and disdainful.*

Haley didn't seem to notice. She slapped her thigh as if remembering why she was there and said, "So I was thinking while the girls played"— she took a bottle of wine out of a bag—"maybe the moms could have a wee drink?" She winked at my haughty mother but then Haley's eyes fell on the prescription bottles for my mother's stomach problem, which were lined up on the sill to her left. Her eyes darted to my mom and then back to the labels. My mother cleared her throat. Haley shook her head. "Oh sorry. How rude. It's the nurse in me. Can't help it. I'm definitely the person at parties who opens the medicine cabinet. Such a nosy Nellie. Anyhoo. Shall we break out the wine and let these girls play some Crazy Eights?"

I was confused at why she seemed flustered suddenly and got even more so when I glanced at Mom and saw that her face had closed up. In her most polite and formal voice, she said, "That's so kind of you about the wine, but I don't drink. Plus, we were about to blow this Popsicle stand."

We. Were. Not. About. To. Blow. This. Popsicle. Stand.

"I hope it isn't because—Oh, oh, what a shame, Maya was so looking forward to playing with Cassidy," Haley said. I looked down. Maya was wearing pink flip-flops. Mine were purple. I tapped her leg and quickly took off my right one and pushed it to her. She did the same so we'd each have a pink and a purple. Our mothers didn't notice.

When they were a few steps away from Sadie, I heard Haley say to Maya, "Never know who you're going to find when you knock on doors around these places, do you? That pretty lady may have the same condition as your uncle Billy, same drugs anyway. Don't envy her. Or the girl. I know firsthand how . . ." And then her voice faded away. When I turned back around, the prescription bottles were gone.

I remember this moment because it's the first time it dawned on me that maybe there was something wrong with my mother. How would I have known? We were the only people I knew. I still don't know what was in those bottles. She didn't leave them out after that and though I looked for them often, I was never able to find them.

"Okay, sorry, I was a fuck trumpet," Mom says now, reaching her hand through the window of Sadie to touch my arm, but I'm still not ready to forgive her, so I don't laugh even though I want to because she never swears. I know she's really trying. "I just felt like Haley was judging us. I don't like to be judged. I'll never do it again. I know how much you want a friend your own age. And now I'm really going under those falls and want you to come with."

I don't. I go back into our living space and open a bag of Doritos and shove Dorito after Dorito into my mouth (Mom's only indulgence, I don't even like them), letting the bright orange crumbs go all over the white floor against my every instinct for tidiness and order. Then I start to cry. This happens a lot lately. Sadness geysers, along with anger geysers, sullenness geysers, frustration geysers, pretty much every-emotion geysers. Mom says it's on account of me getting my period and our growing friction is because of the doubling of household hormones. "Hiding the knives, Cassidy, my terrible tweenager!" she jokes all too often.

Usually, she comes right away when I cry, no matter where she is, like she has superhuman mom-hearing attuned to my weeping, but she doesn't come, and soon I get bored and head out into the rain to find her. To my surprise, she's still close by, her dress soaked.

Even through the rain, I can tell she's crying too.

It's far worse for me when Mom cries than when I do because I fear it means she's headed to The Silent World. I fear she'll tell me she's tired of her words, tired of her own thoughts, tired of her own breath, tired of the taste in her mouth, tired of the air in her lungs, tired of the blood in her veins. I run to her and I'm about to say I'm sorry, certain I caused this bout of unhappiness, when I see the broken sparrow at her feet. I slip in under her arm.

"Did you kill it?" I ask. I know. What a horrible assumption for a girl to make about her mother, but I remember thinking it and asking. "Maybe I did," she says.

"But how?" I ask.

"Bad thoughts," she answers.

I know this can't be true, of course, and yet it disturbs me, and it's stayed with me too, like all her *In the Time of Forever* stories. To this day, against all rationality, I find myself trying to keep my thoughts positive around birds, expecting them to fall dead from the sky, right in my path, the moment I think anything sinister.

Mom starts laughing, softly at first, then with abandon. "Look at your face! My literal one. God, I'm a terrible mother. No! Bad thoughts don't kill birds! For such a practical girl, you're so gullible!" She takes me by the hand. "Next time you'll make a friend. I promise. Even if her mother's punishingly ordinary."

My cheeks get hot. "Am I punishingly ordinary?"

She pauses, puts a hand under my chin and lifts my face so we're eye to eye. "Far from it, but you shouldn't care so much what other people think. You've gotten so self-conscious."

"What other people? I don't know any other people," I say, but I get what she means. She doesn't care that people look at us like we're freaks when we hold hands and run into the water whooping all the way. She doesn't seem to even notice the looks we get. Maybe I didn't used to, but I sure do now. I used to love our days devoted to random acts of kindness where we'd hand out doughnuts on street corners or buy a bunch of umbrellas and rain ponchos and give them to unprepared passersby. The days when we'd fill the parking meters in a whole town with quarters or wash someone's dirty car while they're shopping and then hide in the bushes, watching their surprise and delight when they return to it.

Now I notice the side-eyes, the apprehension, the suspicion in others. I notice other mothers, especially, looking at my bare feet, my unbrushed hair, my dirty clothes. Mom never notices that people in the supermarket find it odd that she brings a peach to her nose and inhales its scent for a good three moaning minutes before putting it in our basket, that she rages when she sees dogs tied up and makes us wait with them, despite her allergy, until their people come back.

"That's what confuses me about you, Cassidy," she says. "Because basically you've been raised by wolves, or one wolf anyway. I'd expect you to be a wild child. So, I don't know where it comes from."

"Where what comes from?"

"This hesitancy, this *existential* hesitancy. A hesitancy to be—"

"To be like you?"

She laughs, lifting her face to the rain. "Yes! I admit it. How horrible of me! I want you to be like me. Or at least I want you to want to be like me." One of Mom's best traits is her honesty (not about the past but about the present), this blunt self-awareness.

What she doesn't understand is, I do want to be like her, though I don't tell her this. I don't have a clue who I am apart from her. All day long, I catch myself synching my breathing to hers and I still find myself secretly holding on to her clothes whenever I think I can get away with it.

(I wish she could know how much more like her I am today at nineteen.)

Mom kneels and starts digging a hole for the dead bird. I squat next to her and help, the rain, a benediction, now a drizzle. She places the bird in the hole we've dug with our hands and asks me if I want to say something. I don't. She nods, and to my surprise, she whispers over the little grave, "Little bird, please tell my mother and father I miss them."

"They're dead?" I say, so shocked, I can barely get the words out. "Your parents? How do you know, if they abandoned you? I thought they"—I make air quotes—"sent you down a river in a basket." This is how I've always interpreted it, that she was left, and whatever happened after that was ugly, and that's why she doesn't want to talk about it.

"They did send me down a river in a basket."

"When?"

"The year before you were born when they both died. I was seventeen."

I can tell this is the truth. And so, just like that, the mystery of her parents, my grandparents, is solved. Why that moment? I have no idea.

"How did they die?" I ask, taking advantage of this miraculous opening.

She's quiet so long that I think she's not going to tell me or that she's going to go into fairy-tale mode, but after ages, in maybe the most serious voice I've ever heard her use, she says, "Bad thoughts."

"What do you mean, Mom?"

"My mother killed herself. I haven't wanted to tell you. Especially because of your dad drowning. Too much death, you know?"

My stomach goes watery. "And my grandfather?" I whisper.

Her eyes meet mine. "Bad thoughts as well."

"He killed himself too?"

She looks up at the sky, lets raindrops moisten her face. "No." She sighs. "Well, in a matter of speaking. He drank his way to the grave. It's not a happy story."

I reach for Mom's hand and hold on and pledge I will never let it go, not ever. A small smile finds her lips. "I've wanted to tell you things, I don't know, stupid little things about my dad, like how he was so big, such a tall man. He'd tell me who in the neighborhood dusted the tops of their refrigerators and who didn't."

Something dawns on me then—not dawns, it's like a sudden cracking open in my mind, and knowledge falling in, irrefutable knowledge. "He's the sad giant who can't find his love?"

"Yes, he is."

We look at each other. Her face is naked, her expression open, vulnerable.

"I do want to be like you, Mom, more than anything," I blurt. "I'm just not."

She touches my hair with her hand and leaves it there. "It's lucky you're not like me. I see myself getting more and more like my mother. It's not a good thing."

Again, things are clarifying.

"Did your mother go to The Silent World?"

"Yes."

My mind whirs with understanding. "Is she the dead woman singing?"

"Yes."

"The mother and daughter who freeze over like glaciers when they hold hands are you and her?"

"Yes."

"Not us."

"Not us. Never us, honey."

I realize all this time she's been telling me everything I wanted to know about the past, just in code and I didn't realize I had the key.

In a land faraway in the time of forever . . .

The time of forever has always been now, been us. The creepy wondrous fairy tales are our heritage, our history, our life, our legacy.

"My father?" I ask. She doesn't like when I call him Jimmy the Dead Drowned Dad.

She smiles. "That's one of the only happy stories in the canon. The Shadow Who Leaves Gifts in the Night."

"And me?"

Her eyes soften, fill with emotion. "You're the gift, honey."

"Am I in any other of the stories?"

"No."

"Because I'm punishingly ordinary?" I say, knowing how punishingly ordinary it is to say this in this moment.

"Because you're remarkable, Cassidy. There are no words good enough, no stories worthy. I've tried. Maybe when you write your own stories, you'll—"

"I don't write stories."

"You will." She smiles. "All women write stories. It's just that only some transcribe them."

"And men?"

"Who cares!" she says, laughing in her way that makes me feel like I can fly. She crouches down and starts sprinkling dirt with her hand into the bird grave but then she stops and leans over the corpse. "What?" I ask.

She carefully picks up the bird, cups it in her hands. "Oh," she says. "Oh, Cassidy!"

"What?"

"Oh! Oh! Oh!" She lifts one hand off the other and the dead bird bursts from her palm in a frantic fluttering frenzy of life and then soars into the sky.

"That just happened!" she cries, jumping up and down.

I'm jumping too. "It did! It did!"

"It's a miracle!"

"It is!"

"It's my parents!" she says. "I know it! They're sending us a message! A message to keep soaring! Oh oh oh! Thank God. A good omen. C'mon!"

And then she's off and running in the rain to the falls. I take off my shirt and feel the drops and wind on my chest and back, in my hair. Mom runs back for me and grabs my hands and then we're spinning, both of us leaning back and looking up, letting rain fall on our faces. Jubilation, n. *a feeling of or expression of great happiness and triumph.*

"We're naked nymphs!" she cries.

"Naked *fairies!*" I shout, and there it is: the bursting obliterating happiness of being with my mother, of being two spinning suns in a rainstorm. "Cassidy the fairy!" she sings. Then pulls me to her and says, "I'm raising you this way because I want you to know how to be free." She touches my head. "In here. If you're free here, you're free anywhere, understand?"

I nod and she nods back, and we spin and spin until there are no more words, until there are no more stories, until there are no more selves.

CASSIDY

By the time we get back to Sadie, the rain's stopped and the sun's peeking around clouds in scattered rays. We change our clothes and hang the wet ones on the racks in the shower, never once bumping into each other, as if someone's choreographed us, so accustomed are we to maneuvering in a three-foot space. Then we start setting up camp like an ant colony of two. This includes taking out the reading chairs, hanging the hammock, opening the outside table, cranking the awning, putting out the stove (we prefer using our camping stove when possible). I clean up the Doritos, then come out of Sadie, arms loaded with ingredients for tacos, and join Mom at the table. She takes an onion and begins chopping it on a cutting board.

At this point, I've forgotten about the bugbear of a rig next door—Mom and I decided it was most likely empty, with its inhabitant in the woods camping—so when I hear, "Don't mean to be rude, but you're maltreating that vegetable," I startle, spinning around to see a man leaning in the doorway of the other RV. He's in a red plaid shirt that's unbuttoned all the way down and his arms are crossed against a strip of bare tan muscly chest. He doesn't fit into any of the man categories. His eyes are on my mother. "Did you know the ancient Egyptians worshipped the onion?" he says to her. "They believed when you bite into one"—he smiles and it's a blinding flash of white—"you are biting into eternity." The guy talks slowly, seems to stuff each word with many meanings. He has light brown hair, upended, like he just woke up, some scruffy facial hair, and his jeans are slung low so I can see the line of hair that goes you know where. A major dick weasel, I think. One who's still staring at Mom, which is normal, but what's not normal is that she's staring right back at him, her eyes lit with curiosity.

"Like biting into eternity, is that so?" Mom says, subtly shaking her head so her hair falls out of its loose knot. Uh-oh. The Dick Weasel registers the hair-tumble with a closed-mouth smile. I'm relieved, not wanting him to flash the glow-in-the-dark teeth at her again. Mom blushes and looks down like she's shy. *Hello?*

"It was believed onions allow us to taste time itself," he says. "So, you have to cut them properly or—"

"Or what?" Mom says, also speaking slowly and strangely now. "Or time stops?"

The dazzling smile again. "Possibly. Or flies forward and suddenly we're ninety years old. Life over, thinking of all the regrets, all the things we didn't do that we wanted to."

What are they talking about? It feels like they're speaking in a different language. Then I realize with alarm that they are and what's happening is FLIRTING. Just like in all the romantic comedies. Just like in Jane Austen. I study him. What is it about this cock trumpet that has gotten her attention? Sure, he's good-looking, but there've been plenty of good-looking men who've knocked on the door. None of them have put my mother in a trance like this. I want to pour ice water on her. Or give her an electric shock.

"One minute," he says, then ducks back into his RV. Mom dives into Sadie and when she returns, she has on lipstick and eyeliner, and it transforms her into a movie star. She never wears makeup. She resumes chopping the onion, her eyes on the arse badger's rig. When he returns a moment later, his shirt's buttoned and his hair's a little more organized. He also has an unlit cigarette hanging out of his mouth. Thank Jesus Muhammad Buddha Shiva and all Divine Forces. Deal breaker. Mom *hates* smoking. He walks up to her, says, "Allow me," and opens his hand for her to place the knife in it. She does! She hands him the knife. Our biggest, baddest knife except for the machete. I'll repeat that for you, Wynton: She hands this cock weasel a murder weapon!

"Mom!" I say, but neither of them acknowledges me. Who gives a strange man an enormous knife when you're in the middle of nowhere with your daughter?

This is the first sign of our impending doom.

"Like you're shaking hands with it," he tells her, gripping the knife. This is called mansplaining, which Mom loathes, but it doesn't seem to faze her coming from Dick Weasel. "It's important to handle knives with care, with . . . love." They exchange a glance.

Oh gross, oh brother.

He picks up an onion, throws it in the air, and slices it—*bam!*—in half right as it lands back on the table, then he cradles the fingers of his other hand around the half onion while chopping with the knife hand, and three seconds later the onion's in perfect tiny squares and both he and Mom are crying.

"Don't cry," he says to her softly, nudging her shoulder with his, like they're forever pals.

"You neither," she says, smiling at him. I can tell she's trying to un-smile but can't.

Cheeseballs, I think. Cheese Louise.

I grant him only that the onion-cutting trick was cool.

Mom says, "So my favorite sentence in literature reminds me of what you said about the onion. It's in *To the Lighthouse* by Virginia Woolf. Mrs. Ramsay is serving a piece of beef to a dinner guest but if you take out the comma in the sentence, she's actually serving the guest 'a tender piece of eternity.' It's brilliant."

I want to put my hand over the smile her words cause on this guy's face, so she doesn't keep talking in this way. "Name's Dave," he says.

Dazzling Dave the Knife-Wielding Dick Weasel.

"Marigold," my mother says.

"Marigold," he repeats, picking up another onion. "Where you guys coming from?" This is a question that Mom always answers, "Around," or "Everywhere and nowhere," which shuts down further conversation.

Instead, she says, "We hooked up for a week down near Doe Creek. Before that Mexico. Baja, a beautiful, deserted site we've been docking at for years in the winter. Hardly saw another soul for a month. Oysters barbecued on the beach every night."

Hello? Hello? Hello?

I walk over to Mom, whisper, "Why are you telling him so much? He's an arse badger." She brushes me away.

"Um, did you call me an arse badger?" he says to me in an English accent. His laugh is chaotic and loud, further evidence of his insanity and our imminent danger. "And with such a deep commanding voice to boot." I don't like when people comment on my voice, which is low and always hoarse. "That," he says, pointing the murder weapon at Mom, not waiting for an answer from me, "sounds like bliss. Barbecued oysters on the beach. Mm, mm, mm." He's moaning now. I give Mom a look that says, *See? He's crazy!*

But she's laughing. Wait, is he charming? I'm in too much of a dither to notice.

"And who's this arse badger?" He winks at me.

Never in the history of the world has there been a side-eye as nasty as the one I give Dazzling Dave the Winking Dick Weasel.

"This is my daughter, Cassidy. She collects bad words. That one's from these English"—she winks at me, why is everyone winking at me?—"*blokes* who were parked next to us. I don't encourage this. They also taught her to play poker and smoke cigars. Don't encourage that either." Ack. I guess she did know about the smoking lesson. "She's my little road warrior. We're full-timers. Twenty-first-century pioneers. Chasing enlightenment and other intangibles. Been at it for years."

For years where my mother has never been so forthcoming, so real, so *herself*, with anyone but me.

He whistles and shakes his head. "That's gutsy. With a kid. True adventurers. I'm impressed." He smiles at me like he thinks it's going to turn me into a talking fool too. Well, sorry, not happening. I side-eye him again. "So, Marigold and Cassidy, I can't top oysters on the beach, but I may have something that can come close. I'd like to formally invite you both to dinner tomorrow night at my restaurant about ten feet from here"—he points to his jalopy of a rig—"for an extravaganza of the morel."

"Morel?" Mom asks.

"Don't tell me you've never eaten a morel mushroom. Assumed you were fellow foragers and I'd have to share the spoils. Because out yonder there was a fire, and where there's burn, there's bonanza. Been waiting for the rain to hold." He looks up as if to gauge the weather. "Casual attire required. Seven o'clock tomorrow, sound good?"

I'm pulling on Mom's dress, whispering, "Can I talk to you in Sadie?"

"Not now, Cass."

Cass? She doesn't call me Cass. Ever. Not once in my whole life. She's forgotten my name.

"We'd love to," she says. "Thank you. That'll be fun."

I've had enough. I go into Sadie, then watch them interact from the window, like when we watch squirrels or birds interact during a science walk. I'm mesmerized at how Mom's hanging on this guy's words. I stare at him. What is it? This guy didn't even try to get her attention. He just had it. Maybe he cast a spell? Maybe that's why he was speaking so slowly at first about the onion holding all of time inside it.

I thought we'd talk about her parents tonight by the fire, that I'd finally get to know them. I thought I'd get to tell her how sad I was for her and how scared it made me that her parents died the way they did.

Instead, I'm exiled in Sadie.

Mom's excitedly talking with her hands now, probably about the history of California or about her philosophy of euphoric living. Or maybe she's telling him an *In the Time of Forever* story. Whatever it is, he's fascinated. She's doing that thing she does to me, turning him into brightness. Like I need sunglasses, that much brightness. But the strange thing is, it appears he's doing it to her as well. I feel like I'm watching two stars explode into supernovas.

(Do you believe in love at first sight, Wynton? I do because of this night. And, because it happened to me once. You might know when.)

My throat tightens as I watch Dick Weasel do my jobs: smashing the avocados, chopping the tomatoes and peppers, slicing the limes, warming the tortillas. When dinner's ready, no one calls me. Finally, my stomach's growling so loud, I open the door and walk out.

"Honey, grab a plate. We made tacos."

Like I don't know this. Like we aren't having tacos because it's my night to choose and I chose tacos! Like I wasn't about to starve to death in Sadie.

I give my mother the dirtiest look I can as I make a plate, but she doesn't notice. I hear her say, "I've always had these seeker tendencies, these spiritual yearnings. I was going to go to school there because of their divinity program but then my life changed very quickly, like I told you, my parents died and so I came up with this idea." I have to stop myself from folding like a chair, so shocked am I at these words. She told him about her parents? After one hour? It took her twelve years to tell me. I have a taste in my mouth like metal. I think I bit my cheek. And what divinity program? What is a divinity program?

I head back into Sadie with my plate, waiting for her to say, "Where you going? Come sit at the table with us, baby-cakes." Because we never eat apart unless she's in The Silent World, but she doesn't say a thing.

Inside Sadie, I sit at the table, take one bite of the cold cardboard taco and leave the rest. Then I climb into bed and curl into the position Mom gets in when she's in The Silent World, except the world is not silent. At all. They're outside the window laughing like fools. I get out of bed and watch them some more from behind the purple curtains.

It's a movie and Mom is being played by an actress that has a startling resemblance to her.

This role she's playing is so . . . I don't know what . . . so *her* is all I can think. Uber her. Now they've left the campsite and they're on their backs looking up at the waterfall. And then she's stripping, and while he's still taking off his clothes, she rushes into the falls in her underwear. He follows and then they're screaming into the falls at the top of their lungs, which is our thing.

I'm a popped balloon.

After the falls, Dave makes a fire, then he wraps Mom in a Mexican blanket he pulls from his rig. He sits on the table playing guitar and Mom watches him from her chair. Her face is like she's watching the ocean in the late afternoon.

For the first time in my life, when I wake up, my mother isn't there.

I leap down, not using the ladder—against the rules—landing on my ankle, feel the twinge of a twist, don't care, then bust out of Sadie and am relieved that Mom's dead body isn't by the embers still smoking in the fire pit (we see our share of gory horror movies), then I head over to Dave's RV. I'm about to knock when I hear sex noises.

I cover my ears and go to the outside table, count the cigarettes Dave smoked last night: twelve. The bottle that says *Wild Turkey* is half-empty. Mom hates drinking too, but not when Dick Weasel Cock-Nose Dave does it, apparently. Even with my ears covered I can still hear the sex noises, so I take my hands off my ears and repeat: gross, gross, gross, gross, gross as I stomp around camp like Rumpelstiltskin. I think about leaving, hiking to the lake, which is a mile away, to swim, but I'm not allowed to go into the woods alone.

When the disgusting noises finally stop, I bang on the door as hard as I can. I want to break it down. (Ire, n. *intense anger; wrath.*) Mom opens it in Dave's red plaid shirt from last night. It's misbuttoned. She's misbuttoned. She looks like she's been tumbling in a dryer. (Blowsy, adj. *disheveled in appearance, unkempt.*) "Morning, Cass," she says.

"Who is Cass?" I hiss at her, crossing my arms. "What about school?"

She squats down, looks in my eyes. "Do today's lessons on your own and in the afternoon we'll all go for a science walk and a swim." The betrayal of her words and the volcanic *ire* inside me leave me mute. My cheeks are fire. "I need some grown-up time with Dave, *Cass*. Just like you wanted to play with that girl Maya, remember?"

"But you didn't let me play with Maya!"

"Cass . . ."

"Who is Cass?" I holler it this time, storming off, not knowing who I am in this moment either as I once again stomp around camp in a fury before returning to Sadie Mae, where I eat marshmallow after marshmallow until I feel sick. I think about skipping school but don't because I like geometry and human biology, also European history and Spanish, and reading Zora Neale Hurston. This has been my favorite curriculum so far. I'm way ahead now—Mom says halfway through high school probably. After I study, I read the dictionary, my comfort, waiting as long as I possibly can and then knock on the door of Dave's RV again. No one answers. I knock harder. Still nothing. My stomach churns with panic. I pound the door with both fists and when I stop, I hear the muffled laughter. Oh my God. They're ignoring me, I realize. They're laughing at me. "You're both dick weasels!" I yell.

The laughter inside the rig gets out of control.

I step back horrified, mortified, and the next thing I know, I'm raging down the trail toward the lake, propelled by a betrayal I can taste in my mouth and feel in my bones. My vision's blurry, my skin's burning, my thoughts boiling up and over as I hurtle forward without seeing the narrowing trail in front of me, the trees looming all around me.

I realize, who knows how long later, that nothing's familiar, that I certainly don't remember the trail to the lake being so steep, so overgrown with brambles, so obstructed by fallen trees. I look around at the poison oak, with its shiny green-and-red leaves, blanketing the forest floor, riding up tree trunks, swarming onto the trail. There's squawking I don't recognize and rattling I do: snakes. Giant redwoods tower around me like an army. I look up unable to see their tops, not remembering them being this tall last year when we walked to the lake. I realize I don't remember any of this. Usually, I follow Mom along paths and trails and roads, just keep my eyes on her and that's how I know where to go. That's how I know where I am.

I've never been alone in a forest before.

I continue, recalling how mountain lions sleep in trees, realizing I can't remember if I'm supposed to run uphill or downhill if a bear's chasing me. Or what to do if a rattlesnake strikes. The sun must've gone behind a cloud, because in all directions the forest's grown gray, ashy. I hear my own heartbeat in my head and start to run only to trip over a root and land face down on the ground. Dirt fills my mouth. I get up, knees scraped and burning, whimpering now, forcing myself further down the path, certain I should be at the lake already. Why are there no flowers? I remember there were tiny purple and yellow ones last year, and Mom and I crouched over them, marveling. Where are they? Where is the lake?

And are the screeching birds warning me that something bad is about to happen?

I hear a new noise. A stick breaking? A woodpecker? Or is someone else in the woods too? Following me? I whip around and start running as fast as I can back the way I came, back toward camp, but nothing looks familiar even from a moment ago. Like where's the poison oak? The wind's picked up and is whistling through the trees, making the old growths creak eerily, sounding like doors opening and closing in the sky. My stomach starts to cramp as I plod forward, nausea making my mouth salivate.

Around each bend, there's just more woods and never the clearing with two RVs and a waterfall and a campfire pit. I arrive at a juncture with trails going off in three directions. I don't remember choosing a path before, but I must have. I must have chosen the wrong one. My heart's drumming so loud in my ears, I can't hear myself crying but know I am because I feel my cheeks getting wetter and wetter.

"Mom," I say, feeling pee run down my leg, splattering the ground as I choose a path and scramble down it. Except now, I'm going uphill, and I don't remember going downhill, so I return to the juncture and try another path, certain that my mother doesn't love me, that nobody does, that Mom and Dave have probably already left the camp together, happy to be free of me.

Because I've always known I'm a burden. You can feel things like that even if they're never said. But they are said! I'm a leech, she tells me when she catches me hanging on to her, and she wanted to go to a divinity program, whatever that is, but couldn't because of me. All she wants is to unscrew a jar and be rid of me like she was of my Beetle Bob all those years ago.

The new path is flat and there are those tiny flowers everywhere and shorter redwoods, so I get hopeful for a minute that it might take me back to camp, but it doesn't. I turn around, head back to the juncture thinking that the third trail has to be the right one, but I can't find the juncture this time and the sun's no longer hiding in the clouds but beating down on me. My shoulders and cheeks, even the part in my hair starts to burn. I stop to pick up a Jerusalem cricket and keep him cupped in one hand for company. I walk and walk, my stomach aching with hunger. I haven't eaten anything but marshmallows all day and I'm starving, but worse is the thirst. My tongue is sandpaper, my lips cracked open and bleeding. My legs already have poison oak bumps and I can't stop scratching them with my free hand so blood's streaked from my ankles to my thighs and there's so much blood and skin under my nails.

I'm getting so tired, wonder if there are still bones in my body.

The trees look like cadavers.

I accidentally squeeze the cricket to death.

I can't stop crying.

Until I do.

I think about my grandmother. I didn't even get to ask my mother what she was like. Did she look like me? Would she have loved me? Why did she kill herself? Is that why my mother is . . . is what? What did Haley say? *That pretty lady may have the same condition as your uncle Billy.* I want an uncle Billy. I want Haley to be my mother instead so I can wear squishy clothes. I want a mother who bakes and hates yoga. My legs feel so heavy, like I'm dragging them. I listen for my grandmother's song, wanting to hear the dead woman singing like Mom does and then I think I do.

I do! I hear it! And all the leaves in the forest are rustling along with her song and the wind is like a flute accompanying it and the birds are dancing in the sky to it and the cadaver trees are turning into forest girls like me. I follow the voice of the dead woman off the path where the ground is softer, like a bed.

I don't remember stopping or lying down.

I don't remember falling asleep or losing consciousness or whatever happens to me . . .

I wake up in the cold dark to a flashlight in my face and a man saying, "Thank God. Thank freaking God." I recognize his voice, remember vaguely who he is and that I don't like him. He blows a whistle and I hear a whistle sound from somewhere else. Then he squats beside me, puts water on his fingers and has me lick it off. I gag. He does it again and again until I stop gagging. Then he pours little sips of water from the bottle into my mouth. Between the moon and the flashlight strapped to his head, I can see him. "You're okay. You're okay," he's saying like he's trying to convince himself. "We're so sorry. So sorry, Cass."

I don't like the *we* in *we're*. "My name isn't Cass," I say, my voice unfamiliar, even more hoarse than usual, my throat tight, desert dry.

He laughs with relief hearing me speak, sounds giddy when he says, "What is it, darling?"

"Cassidy."

"Okay then, Cassidy it is. If you recall, I'm Arse Badger, also known as Dave Caputo." There's a whole lot of kindness in his voice and I don't hate him so much in this moment. I giggle but it comes out like coughing. He gently scoops me up in his arms. "The whistle around my neck, can you put it in my mouth?"

I do and he starts blowing and the other whistle responds and then he's running through the trees with me in his arms like I weigh nothing, moving so fast down the trail through the black night, blowing the whistle sometimes and getting a reply and soon we are back at camp and Mom's rushing to us, pressing into us, making a Cassidy sandwich, saying, "You're all right. You're all right. I'm so sorry. Forgive me. Never again."

Dave sets me on the table and Mom closes her arms around me, enveloping me in her warmth, her jasmine scent, and we do Forehead-Noses for decades while Dave watches us this time.

A line has been drawn. I drew it.

I. Come. First.

Wynton, if you think this was the second betrayal, you're wrong. Just wait.

WYNTON

You want to ask what your weekly chess partner Dave Caputo is doing in Cassidy's story—having sex with Cassidy's mother!—but of course you can't.

You want to tell her that, yes, you've betrayed many people in your life, sure, but you know you would never betray her. Ever. How could you be a part of some fourth betrayal?

Also, you need her to know if she hadn't been there that night, you'd have fallen asleep in the road and would be dead right now. It's because of her you're still alive.

It's because of her you still want to be.

Most importantly, you want her to please tell you again that she came back for you, that she's never been so happy as in your arms, that she's thought about you her whole life. Why hasn't she mentioned your dance in the moonlight? If you could talk, it would be all you'd speak about for the rest of your life.

Conversation Between Night Nurses at Paradise Springs Hospital:

Night Nurse #1: *Who's the girl with the rainbow hair in with the coma patient? Didn't see her come by the desk.*

Night Nurse #2: *She's been climbing through the window after the mother leaves. I told her no need for that, so now she brings me cookies. I think as hush money. I told her their secret—whatever it may be—is safe with me. It's better for him to not be alone. She always leaves at dawn before the family arrives. Couple of lovebirds. I call them Romeo and Juliet. Maybe a secret affair?*

Night Nurse #1: *How romantic. Love a good love story!*

Night Nurse #2: *She places her hand on his good one and tells him stories all night. I watch them from the door sometimes. I know it sounds weird, but his face is different when she's here. It's like he's hanging on her every word.*

Night Nurse #1: *With all their tattoos, they kind of look like one illustrated person, don't they?*

Night Nurse #2: *Like one of them graphic novels.*

CASSIDY

Things are different after I get lost and found in the woods. During school every morning, Dave joins in and raises his hand, asking irrelevant questions that make us laugh. Our science walks in the afternoons quickly become mushroom foraging sessions or swims in the lake with inner tubes and floats. I learn the art of the chicken fight. "You're little but mighty!" he tells me, beating his chest like a great ape when we vanquish imaginary Godzilla.

While on his shoulders, I tell him all about the Hercules beetle, the strongest creature on earth, and how it can carry 850 times its mass, which is like a person lugging around seven elephants. "That is fascinating, Cassidy!" he says to me, so I immediately tell him all the other cool insect stuff I keep to myself because Mom doesn't want to hear it anymore.

I also learn that dinner at Dave's restaurant is much better than dinner at our restaurant because he wears a chef's hat and blasts music while he makes meals that have many courses and take all night to eat. First, I decide Dave isn't so bad, then that he's the most fun person on earth or at least the most fun person I've ever met, which means he's more fun than Mom. He teaches me hide-and-seek, twenty questions, bloody knuckles, Ms. Mary Mack, hopscotch, cat's cradle, pick-up sticks, jump rope, Marco Polo, freeze tag, and how to burp the alphabet. He's flabbergasted that I don't know any games besides cards. I'm flabbergasted how much I love games.

One afternoon, I see him standing at the base of the waterfall looking up. "Shut off the faucet already, you cockbite!" he screams. I run to him, and he takes my hand, and I repeat, "Shut off the faucet already, you cockbite!" And we keep yelling that until I think I'm going to pee in my pants from laughing and calling God a cockbite so many times in a row.

New words I find: Jocundity, n. *uninhibited merriment.* Exultation, n. *lively or triumphant joy.*

I learn so much about my mother I never knew. For instance: Dave's funny and so I learn that my mother isn't funny. Dave can cook and so I learn my mother can't. Dave's patient and so I learn my mother's short-tempered. Dave's easygoing and so I learn my mother's a tyrant. Dave's stable emotionally and so I learn that my mother's a roller coaster (this I pretty much knew). The list goes on and on. Little daily revelations. But the biggest one is this: Dave is present. It's hard to explain the relief of this, of having someone around who's consistently reliably around, who's not in The Silent World. Someone who's not shushing me all day long or plugging me into a schedule so they can write or think or stare off. He lets me be with him. He lets me be myself. It's like he actually enjoys hanging around with me and seeing who can come up with worse bad words.

I don't need any key to understand his past either. He tells us he grew up in San Francisco, has a little brother named Alex, that he went to Berkeley for college and majored in architecture because he was supposed to be an architect like his father and his father's father. He says his family was one of the original San Francisco families who came after the gold rush, which of course interests Mom, but his ancestors were bankers and not the lawless Barbary Coast types Mom loves to talk about. He tells us after college he applied to the master's program in architecture also at Berkeley, but at orientation his life flashed before his eyes.

"Like what's supposed to happen before you die," Dave tells us one night between courses at his restaurant. "I saw it all and got sick, literally sick, nauseated, and dizzy, thought I was going to pass out. It was my father's life with me cast in the leading role that I saw, and I didn't want it. Pitch meetings with assholes. Drinks with assholes. Being cooped up with assholes in an office in a high-rise full of more assholes. Not. For. Me. I wanted to be free of my dad. He's—let's just say, he's difficult. No, let's say impossible. No, let's just say he's an asshole. No, he's the King of the Assholes. King Asshole. So, I hit it." I can't believe how many times he's saying *asshole*! Saying it like it's the most delicious word, making me want to say *asshole* too.

Then his voice takes on a dreamy quality. "Packed up my car that night and drove north. Didn't stop driving until I found paradise. Love it up here. Found work as a carpenter until I opened my own furniture shop. Bought a plot of land and slowly over the years built my dream shack. My dad still can't look me in the eye. Luckily my little brother started at the firm this year, so he has one of us to abuse. He's turning him into an asshole . . ."

Some nights he drinks too much (he seems to have an endless supply of Wild Turkey in his rig) and goes on and on about The Man and how he sucks out your soul. At first, I think this is an *In the Time of Forever* story and The Man is some kind of monster, but then I catch on that The Man is like society.

Mostly, though, Dave is delightful. There's really no other word for Dave the Dazzling Dick Weasel.

I start walking like him and talking like him. I co-opt his cowboy hat and his chef's hat and one of his plaid shirts and he makes me my own morel basket out of an old tin pot he finds in his rig. I never have to secretly hold on to him either. He's always picking me up and doing the helicopter, which means he spins me around over his head like I'm a propeller. He grabs my hand on walks or lifts me by my shoulders— "Whoopsy Daisy," he sings!—over fallen trees. Sometimes he holds me carelessly under his arm like I'm a surfboard.

Here's a picture of us, Wynton. Two peas. Two frickin' identical peas. I can't believe the joy on my face in this photo. On Dave's too.

Momma Bear, Poppa Bear, Baby Bear, I start thinking all the time, but I never say it aloud.

And then there are the cooking lessons—I'm the sous chef, which means I'm Dave's kitchen servant. I learn that you can love making food. I learn that adding milk and using a whisk, not a fork, is the key to fluffy scrambled eggs. I learn that an omelet must never brown or be flipped twice. I learn that not adding cream is the key to Alfredo sauce: "Butter, butter, butter!" says Dave. He tells me to never ever throw out the water I cook my pasta in because it's the elixir (n. *a magical potion*) for sauces. I learn that when making Dave's cacio e pepe I must make a thick paste of all the cheeses and press it around a bowl, then add the steaming hot pasta that's dripping wet with pasta water and stir until my arm feels like it's going to break ("You cannot stop until your arm's about to fall off your body, Cassidy!"), before adding the cracked pepper and shaved black truffle. To make a good Bolognese, I learn, you must start in the morning so it can simmer all day and that smelling it makes your soul crawl out from wherever it's hiding. I find out that Dave keeps one white truffle in his refrigerator at all times in case the world is about to end so he can shave it onto his tongue and die happy.

"What's the best thing you've ever eaten?" I ask him one day while we're making omelets for breakfast. He stops whisking the egg mixture and looks off, his mouth twisting while he thinks, and thinks, and thinks. He strokes his chin and thinks some more before noticing the look I'm giving him.

"What?" he says. "You asked me a question. I'm giving it serious consideration. Okay, got it. There's this little hole-in-the-wall place in the town I live in where a woman named Bernadette makes soufflés. According to town legend they make you fall in love. You know what a soufflé is, right?"

I shake my head and he goes into an endless monologue about what it's like eating a savory grape and blue cheese soufflé made by this woman

Bernadette. Then he goes back to whisking, only looking up a moment later to tell me I have the gift of gab, and this is a very important quality for a sous chef.

Dave teaches me that cookbooks can be read like novels with your feet up in a hammock if someone else is facing the other way in the hammock reading their own cookbook and nudging you every few minutes saying, "Oh, oh, oh! Imagine a chocolate vinegar cake! Vinegar in a cake, sounds bad but you know it has to be awesome, that bite of sharpness! Now that's a goddamn secret ingredient!"

And there's also Dave's effect on Mom. He makes her laugh all the time and loves when she talks about literature and spirituality and California history—he calls her Professor—and he shivers and shudders around the fire when she tells her stories about the drunken lovelorn giant and the dead woman who sings and the rest. I have the sense that if Mom went to The Silent World all he'd have to do to get her back would be to tap her shoulder and say, "Hey beautiful," like he does about a thousand times a day. They're always kissing slurpily, which is yuck and I get jealous when they leave me to go for a walk or to hang out in Dave's rig alone, but it's not too bad because I spend the whole time thinking of funny things to tell Dave when he gets back.

One night after dinner, he asks Mom, "So let's say you'd gone to divinity school—what would you have done after?"

"I don't know. Teach, write, preach on a street corner, drink myself to death, go to India and live in an ashram. This. Be a nomad." She glances at me. "When I was Cassidy's age, I wanted to be a monk."

"A monk! I would've guessed teacher with how advanced Cassidy is for her age."

Mom looks at him. "You have kids in your life?"

"You know, nieces, nephews," he says. "But a celibate monk? Now *that* I don't see." He winks at her, and she blushes because it's a dirty joke.

"How do you guys live, if I may ask, without you working?"

"Family money I inherited. Not a lot but enough to live like we do. We spend next to nothing. And my parents left a college fund for Cassidy, so we don't need to worry about that." This is the first I hear of this. College. Like people in books and movies. Normal people. I assumed I'd be full-timing with Mom forever.

"Do you miss having a home?"

"We have a home."

"Of course. I meant—I mean do you miss—"

"I don't miss anything."

Another week passes. Then another. Until Dave's been with us a whole month. One day, while Dave's out foraging morels on his own and Mom and I are in Sadie, she says, "I'm in love with him."

I'm brushing my hair in front of the mirror. "Like Lizzy Bennet and Mr. Darcy?" I ask.

"Yup."

"Jane Eyre and Mr. Rochester?"

"Yup."

"Frog and Toad?"

"Yup."

"Cathy and Heathcliff?"

"Oh God. Let's hope not like them!" She studies my face in the mirror. "I think you feel it too with Dave, don't you?"

"I wish he'd hold me like a surfboard for the rest of my life."

She puts her arms around me from behind. "Oh boy. We're in trouble." She's resting her head on my shoulder and it's as good as Forehead-Noses. She continues to look at us in the mirror. I do too. "Cassidy and Marigold," she whispers, and it's one of those moments where your heart hurts and you want to cry but you don't know why.

That night, I spy on them. Long after they think I'm sleeping, I hide behind the purple curtains and slide open the window and listen to them be in love. I hear Dave say, "I feel like my life began the moment we met. I wasn't alive before I met you. I wasn't anything before you, Marigold."

And Mom: "When we were in Mexico, I went to a palm reader. She told me I was about to meet my soul mate, my one true love. I told her that was impossible, that I was raising my daughter in a very particular way and there was no room for anyone else. She told me I'd make room. Then she smiled and said it would be a beautiful room. So, when I saw you, I knew who you were. I was expecting you." Mom starts to cry then. I peek through the curtain, see in the firelight, Dave kissing her wet cheeks as he tells her he didn't know a love like this existed outside of novels.

WYNTON

You need to wake the hell up. You need to speak to Cassidy. You try to squeeze her hand. You want to tell her that Bernadette, the soufflé-maker Dave just told her about, is your mother.

But mostly, you want to warn the little girl who Cassidy used to be about Dave Caputo.

You're putting things together too, how old she is now and how old you both were when you met in the meadow. Soon she will be in Paradise Springs. Soon you will enter her story and you can't wait.

How you love it when she says your name. It transforms you.

You don't need to go to a palm reader like Marigold. You know Cassidy is it.

When you had a life, you'd listen to people online singing at 963 Hz, called the frequency of divine harmony, aka "the God note," and when you did your heart would blow open and all the ick would fly out. This is how you felt with Cassidy in the meadow, with her when she was in your arms in the moonlight, the last moment of your ex-life.

This is how you feel right now as she tells you her story.

It's your luck that when you finally fall in love like that Samantha Brooks-whatever and Jericho-someone, you're in a coma for it.

You want to tell her you love her! And mean it for the first time in your life. With every ounce of strength in your body you attempt to move your lips, but you can't.

CASSIDY

The evening after Mom and Dave declare their love, Dave and I are on dinner duty while Mom swims. We're making crêpes, which I've never had before. Dave went to the farmer's market all the way in Jackson that morning, the town where he lives, an hour trip each way, and came back with loads of fruits and vegetables and a crêpe maker. Plus he filled up our water bags and returned with gas for our generators. We're using stoves in both RVs plus the camping stove to prepare the different fillings and so we've been running from rig to rig, wooden spoons in our hands. I've never had so much fun.

Finally, when we have all our fillings in what he calls mise en place, we start on the batter. While I'm cracking eggs, I ask, "Can we make a soufflé one day too? Like Bernadette from your town?" He said they were aphrodisiacal (which I looked up, of course), so I want him to eat it so he'll fall in love with us like Mom and I are with him.

"Most definitely," he says. He goes back to whisking, only looking up a moment later to say, "Wouldn't be so bad if we were a fearsome threesome from now on, would it?"

I don't know until this moment how big a heart can feel.

"This is the life I've always wanted," Dave says. "The life you two have." Then he smiles and kisses me hard on my forehead, making such a loud *mwah* noise I crack up.

"You're my second-favorite person on earth," I tell him, which is a lie because he's my favorite for sure, but it seems wrong to say that since I've known my mother so much longer.

"How many people do you know?"

"Two."

"That's a terrible compliment then. Try again."

"I love you," I blurt. I'd been feeling it for days. My whole body hurting from feeling it so much, like it's bruised on the inside.

His face breaks into the most dazzling of dick weasel smiles. "I love you too, sweetheart. Kind of nuts how much, actually."

"That means two people on earth love me now. Not just one." I go back to cracking eggs. "And you don't even go to The Silent World."

"What's that?"

"Where sad women go when they're tired of words and thoughts and the taste in their mouths and when they look in the mirror the person looking back won't even meet their eyes."

"Oh." He looks distressed but then surprises me by saying, "I go there too. They must admit some sad men into The Silent World."

"Can't imagine you there. You're too funny."

"I think what is being implied here is I'm not funny. Is that right?" Unbeknownst to either of us, Mom's back from the lake and right behind us.

"You're fun but not funny," I say. "Dave's both."

"I think you're funny," Dave says, kissing her forehead but not in a loud goofy way like he did mine. "And smart and deep and inspiring and beautiful—"

"Hey, what about me?"

"Now, you're *really* funny. One of the funniest I've come across. A veritable clown show."

I'm so happy in this moment, I can barely stay in my skin. I didn't know I was funny!

"Can we hook up next near Dave's town so we can have soufflés?"

"Fancy," Mom says. "Sure."

"Except that place closed down a year ago. We'll have to learn to make them on our own." He hadn't talked about Bernadette's soufflé shop like it had been closed, but I don't give it any thought.

Until later.

Mom gestures for me to follow her into Sadie. Once inside, she starts fishing in our closet. "I want to wear something special for the crêpe dinner."

"Me too."

She smiles at me. "Clashing game?" We've never dressed up for dinner or played the clashing game outside of a thrift store before.

"You're so different now," I say to her.

"So are you." She gently touches my hair. "Sometimes three is an easier amount of people than two."

I both agree with this and feel wounded by it, which she quickly picks up on. "Doesn't mean I don't love when it's just the two of us."

We shower together—the conservation kind, which means you stop the water when you're soaping. Then Mom does my hair in an updo so that I look like I have snakes on my head. We wear dangling earrings and all our beaded necklaces, including the ones we hang around Sadie's rearview mirror. When we walk out of the trailer, Dave exclaims, "Psychedelic princesses!" I look on the table for onions because I see tears on his face, which he quickly wipes away. No onions. I don't know if he was crying before we came out or if we caused it.

We eat the crêpes in the firelight and then instead of listening to him play guitar, we break out the stereo and have a dance party. We've only ever had dance parties just Mom and me, but Dave has moves and mostly we all just jump around for ages. When a slow song comes on, they don't exclude me. We three dance together in one swaying lump. And when the music stops, we continue swaying in the moonlight until Dave unhinges himself from us and takes one of Mom's hands and one of mine and looking at my mother says, "Will you marry me?"

"Yes!" I cry.

They laugh. "I think he may mean me," says Mom.

"Say yes, Mom!"

Then she is saying yes and we all are jumping up and down again and they are kissing and kissing, then I'm on Dave's shoulders and we're all getting baptized as a family under the falls beneath the stars on top of the world. We decide to crash outside in our sleeping bags because that's what fearsome threesome families do.

We fall asleep three spoons with Mom as the middle spoon.

When I wake up, Mom's arms are still around me, her steady breath on my neck. I keep my eyes closed, thinking about everything that's about to happen. A fearsome threesome with Dazzling Dave. A family. Will we all live in Sadie? Will we live in his dream shack in the woods of Jackson? Will we live on love-soufflés? Excitement is a butterfly party in my belly. I open my eyes, maneuver out of Mom's arms, but when I sit up, I see in the dawn light that Dave's gone. Not just Dave, but his rig too.

It's like finding the sky's been taken down.

I shake Mom's shoulder and her eyes open and her face breaks into a sunbeam of a smile. She reaches a hand behind her toward the ghost of Dave's spooning body. I think about this moment sometimes, her reaching backward for him, so certain that love is real. I gesture to where Dave's rig was. She turns, gasps, then rolls away from me. "Oh God. Not again."

"What do you mean *not again*?"

She doesn't answer, shimmies deep inside her sleeping bag until I can't see a single hair from her head.

When she finally emerges from the cocoon of her sleeping bag, she's decided that Dave went to Jackson to surprise us with beignets or soufflés or roses or something. "It's the morning after our engagement. He probably wanted it to be special. Maybe he went to buy a ring."

At lunchtime: "You know how it is, he probably got held up, saw people he knew."

I don't know how it is.

At dinnertime: "He'll be back, Cass. Don't worry. Knowing him, he went all the way to the farmer's market in Idaho to get some special mushrooms or whatever."

I let the *Cass* go.

For days, she keeps this up, Dave's whereabouts and plans getting more elaborate. "Well, he probably had to go restaurant to restaurant to sell his morels. And the farmer's markets. Maybe he stopped at his furniture shop and saw all the orders and realized he needed to do some work before coming back."

I believe her. I have to. Day night day night day night I repeat her explanations to myself, long after she stops making them.

Because she's entered The Silent World.

Dave left the crêpe maker, so sometimes I turn it on, put my hand on it, and wait to feel the burning, leaving it until I can't stand it, until I smell burning flesh. I never let myself cry out.

Mom doesn't notice the burns on my palms and fingers, of course. How could she, being in another world?

I don't know how much time passes. We run out of propane, the generators are tapped, our sewage tank is full. I go to the bathroom outside. I'm pretty sure my birthday comes and goes. I try everything to get Mom out of The Silent World, even pulling her out of bed, which is difficult when you're on a ladder. I even try a bucket of water. Nothing works.

I eat dry cereal and peanut butter sandwiches until the bread goes moldy.

I comb the dictionary for help, finally finding a word: Acedia, n. *a spiritual torpor.*

(Wynton, I remember my mother's retreat into herself this time lasting weeks, a month even. I wonder now if she took sleeping pills. I don't know. Maybe she did suffer from some mystery mental illness—there were those pills after all. Or maybe, and this is my inclination, I should take her at her word, that she heard her dead mother singing and had no choice but to follow the sound of her voice into The Silent World next door.)

Anyway, as the weeks pass, as the food dwindles and I get bone-skinny, I keep my eyes on the road, standing there sometimes for hours at a time like a sentinel, not even looking down for the good insects, believing Dave's going to come back for me.

Mom smells like an old sponge when I finally lie down next to her and whisper, "Let me come to The Silent World." Somehow after weeks of trying to break through to her, these are the abracadabra words that bring her back. She turns over and opens her eyes, which are pale and far away. "No, Cassidy. Never. It's not for you." Her voice sounds underwater.

"But you're there."

She puts her hand on my itchy head, combs through my greasy hair with trembling fingers. "I'm so sorry," she says. "God, I'm sorry, Cassidy. I'm keeping you from life."

"Isn't this life?" I say, and then because she looks so distraught, I add, "It's okay it's just the two of us again."

"Of course it is."

Except we both know it isn't okay. It's never been okay just the two of us. We're like-pole magnets with a force field between us that repels the other. Dave was an opposite-pole magnet from us and so we both rushed to him like ecstatic iron filings.

"I'm worried about us," she whispers.

"That we'll get so sad, we'll disappear?"

"Oh honey, listen to yourself. I'm not good for you. My stories aren't good for you." Her voice sounds panicky. "I saw the way you were with him. The way you came alive. You were so you, so beautifully you, all the time. It was like you finally met someone who spoke your same language." She props herself up on a shoulder. I can tell how difficult it is, like her head's a bowling ball. "He left me, not you. You know that, right?"

"It's the same thing. *We're* the same thing," I say, feeling something deep in the pit of my stomach in that moment and not knowing how else to articulate it.

Now I'd say this: There's an invisible artery joining the hearts of mothers and daughters through which pain is transferred from one generation to the next. Maybe it's the same for fathers and sons, I wouldn't know. But I don't have those words then, so I say the ones I do have again: "We're the same, Mom."

She closes her arms around me, and we weep together and there's no one to pull us out of this bottomless sorrow like there was never anyone to tell us to get out of the frigid sea, so we stay in it for a very long time.

Days or weeks later, again, no idea, I half wake in the middle of the night to see Mom's out of bed and at the table looking at a map, and when I wake again, it's light out and we're on the road, which means she broke down camp without me. A first. Also, Mom never drives if I'm not buckled in. I have to be in one of the three belted seats or the passenger seat. Clearly, I'm not in any of them. And we haven't consulted the astro-cartography books or anything.

"Where are we going?" I ask, maneuvering across Sadie and into the passenger seat despite the speed we must be traveling for Sadie to be shaking like this. "To hook up and for supplies?" We're almost out of drinking water.

Her eyes are alert, buggy. "To find him," she says. "It occurred to me maybe something happened to him. Why imagine the worst all the time, right? I mean, maybe he was on his way back to us with soufflés and a ring and he got in an accident and he's lying alone in a ditch or dying in a hospital bed." I don't point out that it's worse to imagine him alone in a ditch or dying in a hospital bed than not coming back to us with food. "Or maybe his rig broke down. Did you see how old it was? Or maybe he . . ." The words are a torrent that don't stop the whole way down the mountain. I put on my seat belt and hold on to the door handle so tightly, my knuckles go white.

Despite Mom's accelerated state and the accelerated speed she's driving, I'm so relieved to be on the road, to be going somewhere where there's food and toilets and hopefully Dave. I miss him in a way that's cataclysmic, adj. *of or relating to a violent upheaval.*

We arrive in Jackson, the town where Dave lives, at around noon. It has one of those main streets like a lot of the old mining towns we explored when we were studying the gold rush. In these towns, you can totally imagine tying up your horse and moseying into the saloon with gold nuggets in your pockets because the same hitching posts and saloons are still there. Mom pulls into a parking lot by a small farmer's market, finds a spot big enough for Sadie, and kills the engine. I unbuckle my seat belt and I'm about to open the door when she presses my chest with her palm. "Wait." I settle back in my seat, and we sit there for ten years with Mom scrutinizing each and every person that passes, like she's counting the buttons on their clothes.

"You think he's just going to walk by?" I say finally.

"Yeah, it's a small town. At some point. Where else is he going to go but the farmer's market?"

"You don't think he's in the hospital, then?"

"No."

"Or dying in a ditch?"

"No."

"What're you going to say to him?"

"Nothing. I just want to see him again."

"Just see him? Like through the window?"

"Yes. At first, then . . . I don't know yet."

"But you can't miss Sadie, Mom. He'll see her, and if he's avoiding—"

She looks at me, stopping me mid-sentence. "You're right. We'll have to be stealth." She starts the engine. "We need to find his furniture shop. We'll use the computer at the library—saw it on the road coming in."

We use library computers often to find doctors or dentists or information about my curriculum and that's how Mom does banking. I also use them when Mom's not sitting next to me to secretly search for information about Jimmy the Dead Drowned Dad. I type in "surfing accident" and "Jimmy" and "died." Or sometimes "dead dads." She says she was only with him that one time they made me and she was drunk as a skunk and high as a kite and that's why she stopped all that partying because she never learned his last name and can hardly remember his face and only found out about the accident because they'd exchanged numbers and when she called his phone to tell him about me, a girl answered who told her about the accident.

"Did you ask the girl anything more about him?" I questioned her one time. "How could you not keep the number? Maybe it was his sister. Maybe I have an aunt? Maybe I have cousins."

"You have me, baby," was her reply.

When we get to the library, we walk faster and faster through the sleepy space until we're sprinting for the computers because Dave is our opposite-pole magnet, and we must find him, and we can't help ourselves. After getting scolded for running like we're little kids, we fall into two chairs, giddy and hopeful. In a flash, Mom's typed "David Caputo" and "custom furniture" and "Jackson, CA" into a search engine. Nothing comes up.

"Bastard," Mom says. "What do you think he lied about? His name, his work, or his town?"

I'm shocked. Was Dave a liar? It never occurred to me to not believe him, or anyone, for that matter, but it's true this town isn't like the one he described. "He told me all about the town he's from and this one is different."

Mom expands her search: "David Caputo," "custom furniture," "River County."

I'm enjoying myself a little now. We're sleuths. But again, Mom finds no matches.

"I know," I say, remembering him talking about the town square with a waterfall on one side, a club with the best jazz music in a hundred miles, and the shop with soufflés that make you fall in love. "Search soufflé shop and the name Bernadette."

"Where?"

"Here. Or I guess: everywhere."

She laughs. She types in "soufflé shop" and "Bernadette" and "Northern California."

It's a bonanza! Listing after listing about a French chef Bernadette Fall and her soufflé shop *Christophe's* in a town called Paradise Springs.

"That's it, Mom!" I cry, getting a stern look from the librarian. "That's where he lives. It's got to be. He talked about Bernadette and how she made these soufflés in his town and if you eat them you fall in love!"

Mom types in "David Caputo" and "custom furniture" and "Paradise Springs," but still no custom furniture store comes up. There is, however, a Robert D. Caputo and an address. "Do you think the *D* stands for *David*?" she asks me.

"Dick Weasel," I say, which makes her laugh.

"So, where the hell is Paradise Springs?" she says. "Never even seen it on the map."

In the time of forever, there was a man and a woman who were in love but were forbidden to be together. Weeks of tireless scheming went into planning a single rendezvous. They were to meet in the woods at the darkest hour of night.

Each arrived at the designated spot and rushed into the other's arms. The moment their lips met, their mouths turned to snouts, their moans to grunts, their arms to legs, their hands to feet, and a coarse black hide covered their skin.

The lovers kept their consciousness and tried to make the best of the situation, but it just wasn't the same now that they were hogs. He had wanted to take his finger to her lovely mouth and watch it fall open. She had wanted to fold into his body as if she had no bones. They had wanted to whisper into each other's ears, not grunt and salivate like this.

Before they knew it, dawn was rising, and they had to get home. The unhappy hogs ran off in separate directions and with every step away from each other they became more and more their youthful, beautiful, ambulatory human selves.

Right before they were out of each other's eyesight, they turned around to see their true love as they remembered. This was their destiny, and that was the last time they ever saw each other.

DIZZY

Dizzy was certain Wynton's soul was still inside his body—she could feel it—and that was what kept her from screaming at the top of her lungs like she'd wanted to the first time she saw him post-surgery and every minute since. Her brother, the one who controlled the world's light switches and volume knobs, who made her *her* and life *life,* was connected to bags of fluids, his face swollen, bruised, and barely recognizable, his scalp stapled, his right arm and left foot in casts, his left wrist and hand also in a cast—with pins sticking out of it—but suspended, like he was a puppet, the only music around him that of the machines confirming he was still alive.

It had been four days of panic since the accident and two since the last surgery, after which Wynton was taken off the breathing machine (a good thing), and per Doc Larry's instructions, Dizzy and her mother had spent those two days on either side of Wynton, telling him stories, repeating how much they loved him and needed him to come back. Perhaps he could hear them, like the doctor suggested, but he remained gone. Not even a quiver of a lip. Though sometimes his eyes would open, which was another good thing, apparently, but also way creepy and didn't mean he was awake. That's when Doc Larry would touch Wyn's cornea with cotton to see if he'd blink.

It was all terrible, wrapped up in more terrible.

If only Dizzy had thought years earlier to lock Wynton in the house so nothing like this could've happened. When he woke, that was what she was going to do. Her mother too while she was at it. Even Perfect Miles. They could all live a fine life inside the house. Every day, she'd bake her top recipes like the pansy petal crêpes with lavender cream or the chocolava cake with coconut Chantilly and then they'd watch movies in a people-pile, search the internet for mind-bombs, and hit each other with pillows. She didn't understand the preoccupation with leaving home, where it was safe and everyone you loved was within earshot.

But for now, she and her mom kept at it, reminding Wynton of the time Dizzy dressed up as him and he her for Halloween or the Mother's Day when he'd snuck a piece of paper into Mom's coat pocket that listed all the things that made her awesome, or this time or that time, until so many times later, their heads were face down on the bed, out of memories, out of gas, out of tears. Dizzy had learned that not only were she and her mother laugh partners, they were also cry partners. She now knew her mother loved Wynton as much as she did and so she forgave her for how she'd treated him recently, kicking him out of the house and everything, and hoped her mother had forgiven her for leaving out the keys that let Wynton into the house so he could steal the drugs that led to this nightmare.

But Dizzy hadn't forgiven herself. She never would.

This was why she had to fix it.

Plan A was finding the angel whose name they'd learned was Cassidy because she'd given it to 911. Dizzy's running theory, which she stopped sharing—it made people look at her like she needed a nap, or worse, a bed in this hospital—was that Cassidy had somehow thought she'd already saved Wynton's life with the magic CPR she performed before she dropped him off at the hospital, so she went off to provide her angel services to the next person on her roster when in reality her work with Wynton wasn't finished. Dizzy didn't care one iota if no one believed her. She knew what she knew. She'd read enough about mystical experiences to know that her encounter with Cassidy had been one. (One time in a moment of frustration with Dizzy, her mother had said, "C'mon,

Dizzy. Grow up. Angels don't exist." Having done the research, Dizzy retorted, "Eight out of ten American adults believe in angels, Mother." To which Chef Mom replied, "Eight out of ten American adults are idiots.") Strangely, Miles was a fellow idiot, the only one remotely persuaded by her theory, probably because he met Cassidy too. He seemed to want to find her as much as Dizzy did and for a few hours yesterday she and Miles had even sat in the cleaning supply closet—Miles called it his office—like detectives, using their phones to try to search for her, but with such limited information, they'd come up with nothing.

Plan B was more complicated, more serious, and involved true sacrifice. Dizzy was still testing the waters on this front, which was why she was now walking around the hospital room with her arms clasped around her abdomen while she and her mother were on a break from their storytelling marathon.

"What's up with her?" Perfect asked Mom.

"Ask her," Mom said, not looking up from the notebook she was writing in.

"Dizzy, what's up with the weirdass pacing?" Miles asked.

"I'm not weirdass pacing. I'm doing a prayer walk. I learned about it from a nun. Sometimes she even does it on her knees." Neither lying prostrate nor the Jewish prayers her mother recited the night they arrived had worked. Nor had trying to hold the whole world in her arms like atheist Cynthia, the night administrator, had suggested. Today Dizzy had found a website called A Day in the Life of a Nun, and that was why she was gliding across the room, eyes cast inward on her capsizing soul, posture straight enough to balance a book on her head. "I'm thinking if I truly devote myself to a life of prayer, to God, in exchange He'll wake Wynton." These weren't empty words. Dizzy felt a fountaining of relief in her chest when she thought about committing to God like this. She wanted to leap into His open arms or jump onto His gargantuan shoulders. She'd whisper into His planet-sized ear, "Help us." And He would. Always. She wouldn't have to worry anymore about anything.

"Last I checked, we're Jewish," Miles said.

"Half, and we don't have nuns, so it's not the same sacrifice," said Dizzy. "I'll convert." Dizzy figured since there was only one God, what did it matter which religion you boarded to get to Him. She added, "I'm actually okay with the vow of poverty, but honestly, I'm worried about the vow of chastity."

"Dizzy!" her mother said, not lifting her pen or eyes from the page. Dizzy ignored her. It was true. The idea of her fiery furnace going cold and dark, of never being ravished breathlessly head to toe by someone burning with desire for her, of never loving another with the force of the sun (except Him), of not even enjoying the two measly weeks of kissing that everyone gets (on average) was troubling to say the least.

But Wynton waking was a necessity. She'd do anything.

After a few more minutes of prayer-walking, Dizzy got bored, upset, and so tired her bones felt like they were made of osmium—the heaviest material on earth, she knew from research—so she sat down in her chair and began stalking Lizard on social media (not only had he not come to the hospital yet, he and Melinda had gone out to a movie yesterday like they were Samantha Brooksweather and Jericho Blane, like *they* loved each other with the force of the sun). After that, she fake-ate a sandwich to appease her mother (she had no appetite), did some more research on people in comas, angels, nuns, and one-handed violin-playing while her mother continued to scribble away in her notebook, Miles continued to look at his phone or pretend to read (he never turned the page), and Wynton continued to not die, which she knew because every few seconds she checked the rise of his chest and the red numbers and lines on the machine that was attached to his heart. Just like she was.

Dizzy was about to ask her mother if she wanted to try to talk Wynton back to life again when she noticed tears were running down her mother's cheeks as she wrote. She tried not to cry in sympathy by pinching herself, then watched the ink blur on the page in her mom's notebook as words turned into blobs. Yesterday, she'd asked her mother what she was writing, and Chef Mom had replied, "A letter to your father." This had surprised Dizzy. Yes, she'd known about her mother's notebook of unsent letters, but she certainly didn't expect her mother to admit she wrote letters to their long-gone father in it. She'd assumed the letters to him would be a secret like the voicemails Dizzy left for Lizard every day since their divorce.

"Are you writing to our father about Wynton?" Dizzy asked her mother.

But before she could answer, Miles piped in with, "I write to him too."

She and her mom turned toward Perfect.

"Well, emails. I have a folder."

Dizzy was shocked at such a personal admission from her brother. Over the last two days, he'd sat in the corner blending into the wall or done who knows what in his office, i.e., the supply closet. He didn't look at Wynton or stand by his side or take his hand or talk to him at all.

Once when Miles and her mom were both gone from the room, she'd picked up his book. It was called *Giovanni's Room*. On the inside back cover, there were three sentences in Miles's handwriting: *The wind has blown my face off* and *What happened in the missing hours?* and *I have a brick in my mouth.*

"What kind of things do you write to your father about?" Mom asked Miles. Dizzy thought of those bizarro sentences.

"Just stuff," he said, signaling his daily allotment of words had been reached. Dizzy had been counting. Perfect uttered twenty-three words yesterday, thirty-two so far today.

"He should be here," Dizzy said, not knowing she felt this way until the words were out of her mouth. "Wynton would wake up if our father were here. He could play his trumpet." Miles peered at Chef Mom. They didn't really talk about their dad like this. In the present tense. Or in the past, for that matter. Whenever they asked her why he left or whatever, a curtain dropped over her face and she said something like, "I don't know" or "Who knows why anyone does anything?" after which, she'd leave the room.

Her mother closed the notebook, put it in her bag, sighing audibly.

"Come here, baby." She opened her arms and Dizzy got out of her chair, walked around the bed, and collapsed into the scent (kiwi green) and shelter of her mother's body. "You too," Mom said to Miles, beckoning him with the arm that wasn't cradling Dizzy.

"Come smush with us. It helps," Dizzy said to Miles, seeing something in Perfect's face that suggested he actually might want to join their people-pile. It did help Dizzy too, way more than prayer-walking. The only time she felt like her organs hadn't all switched places was when she and her mom were smushed together. To Dizzy's surprise, Miles rose from the chair, but then instead of joining them, he left the room.

Chef Mom whispered into Dizzy's hair, "Stay like this forever. Promise me."

"I promise."

She squeezed Dizzy with such force, Dizzy thought she might break, but she still wished her mother would squeeze harder.

A moment later, Uncle Clive appeared in the doorway looking like Father Time with his haggard face and long straggly beard that seemed to be graying by the minute. "Everything okay?" he asked. "Just saw Miles fly down the hall like a bat out of hell. I think he went into a supply closet?" Dizzy had gotten used to her uncle standing at the threshold of the hospital room, like a vampire (unable to enter a room unless invited) when Doc Larry or the nurses were imparting news or updates or doing tests (shining a light in Wynton's eyes, testing his reflexes, snapping and flicking fingers by his head), but he rarely appeared like this when it was just them. Mostly, when he was around, he camped out on the floor right outside the closed door like an inebriated sentinel. Sometimes he played the harmonica. Dizzy was happy her mother hadn't iced him out because of the drinking. He was the one who'd had the dream that foresaw all this, after all.

"I have an idea," Uncle Clive said to them. "Wynton's language is music. I talked to some people who were at his show that night. They said he played Eugène Ysaÿe's Sonata Number 3. I think we should play it for him."

"Yes! He'll hear the music and follow it back to us!" Dizzy said.

"Worth a try, Clive," said Mom.

He pressed a button on his phone and violin music filled the room along with all their hope.

But it didn't change a thing.

Dear Wynton,

I've never told you this but sometimes I'd pack myself a favorite sandwich (roast chicken with anchovy-olive tapenade and goat cheese on pan bagnat maybe) and follow you when you left for the river with your violin case tucked under your arm. I'd watch from afar—my skinny tattooed kid in ripped black clothes, picking wildflowers as he went.

When you'd start playing on the bank, I'd sit on a rock a distance away, eat my sandwich, then take off my shoes and socks, sink my feet in the cool river water, as your music filled the forest, the sky.

I hope there's music where you are. I hope I'm where you are, holding your hand.

I wish I told you more how much your music means to me.

Chef Finn has an idea that he and the new sauté cook Felix are going to cook gumbo at the hospital and the scent is going to lure you back. I think he's lost his mind.

Dear ~~Theo~~ Dizzy,

Did you know my mother stopped speaking when my brother Christophe died? I don't think I ever told you. I keep thinking about it, sitting here in this hospital room with you.

How every day after ninth grade, I'd put on an apron and join my mother by the ovens of our little San Francisco café and we'd communicate in silence by mixing flours, toasting nuts, glazing figs, the language of the kitchen becoming our language. When I come home to your baked creations, I think it's the same with us, my chouchou. What I wouldn't give for one afternoon with you, me, and my mother, all working shoulder to shoulder in a kitchen. How I wish she and my father were still alive . . . Life really becomes an accumulation of losses, but this is something I hope you never have to learn.

Okay, what's interesting, Dizzy, is that Paradise Springs— our town—brought my mother's voice back. It's the kind of memory you want to hang a hammock inside, so you can return to it in times like these and stretch out in it.

After a year of her muteness, my father took us for a drive up north, wanting her mind to wander across the vineyards, the fields of mustard and lavender that were so reminiscent of where he grew up in Southern France. We stopped in Paradise Springs for a bite and sat at a table on the square by the waterfall. Sunlight flooded out of the sky the way it does here and nowhere else. We were eating pastries (subpar, we noted) when my mother uttered her first words. "Let's stay here, Benoît," she said. "It feels like no one could ever die in this town." My father threw his arms around her, tears in his eyes, and said, "How I have missed your voice, mon ange."

"Me too!" I exclaimed, and the three of us hugged over the table.

My father was so excited by the prospect of a wife who talked, he bounced on his chair like a child, saying, "Yes. We will find a way to stay." And then, as we walked back to the car, we noticed a For Sale sign in a window of a vacant storefront with the words Sebastian's Spanish Bakery etched on the window. "It's kismet," my father said, writing down the number on the sign. "Beshert."

My mother said, "We'll call it Christophe's and we'll specialize in soufflés. Soufflés are about hope."

A month later, we'd sold our café in the city and packed up our stuff and moved into the apartment above Sebastian's Spanish Bakery, turning it into Christophe's Soufflé Shop. And two weeks after that, your father and Clive walked in.

How it seemed like sunlight attached itself to your father. I can't bear that he's not in your life. He is everything I'm not, Dizzy.

I keep looking at the door of this desperate room thinking he'll walk through it. I have never needed anyone as much as I need him right now.

You do too, but you don't know it.

Chef Mom

Miles's Emails to His Missing Father in the Help Me! Folder on His Computer:

Dear Dad,

It's easier to let Mom think I'm okay—*keep moving folks, nothing to see here.* You're the only one who knows I feel tapped like a tree for sap and all the light is pouring out of me.

Miles

Dear Dad,

I remember only one day clearly with you. You were pushing Wynton and me on swings. One hand, one son. The other hand, the other son. Again and again, pressing us into the sky, which was bluer that day than all my L words: Lonely, Liar, Left.

Miles

Dear Dad,

I used to tell the other kids that you died rushing into a burning house to save me.

Miles

WYNTON

You drift away from your mother's and sister's voices, nothing more than mouth-noise now. Because who is this person they're telling you stories about hour after hour?

How come they don't remember how useless you were?

Miles does. That's why he never talks to you even though you know he's in the room breathing in E minor.

Does he even remember what he said to you that night on the dance floor at the party: *On every single birthday candle, falling star, coin tossed into a fountain, he's only ever wished one thing—that he had a real brother instead of you.*

A knife to the chest.

That's why you did what you did that crazy night with him.

At least you know now that for one moment you acted like a real brother. Even if he was probably too wasted to remember.

It's getting hard to stay in the world. How tiny a moment is a whole life. If you still had one, you'd be sober as a rock. You'd savor *everything*.

Without a body, what are you, anyway? Longing, it seems.

And regret.

DIZZY

The next day, everything changed. The scent of gumbo—a beautiful violet color for Dizzy—overtook the hospital because Sous Chef Finn from The Blue Spoonful had commandeered the cafeteria, with the help of his sister, who happened to be on the hospital board. He told them he was going to cater this coma with a Cajun theme due to his belief that the scent of the Cajun spices of his youth—*jalapeño peppers, baby!*—could wake the dead, so certainly they'd be able to bring back Wynton from a measly coma.

Dizzy walked the hospital halls, where the smell of Chef Finn's gumbo was practically making everyone swoon, nurses, patients, and doctors alike. Not her. Her pants were getting baggier by the minute. Everyone, from her mother to Finn to the nursing staff, kept trying to get her to eat, but she couldn't.

She headed to the chapel, which was on the second floor. She needed to leave Lizard a voicemail and there was never anyone in there. Plus, that's where God might decide to show, despite how sad and gloomy the room was. It consisted of five rows of rickety wooden pews, a gray linoleum floor, and creepy peeling pink floral wallpaper. She stood at the door taking in the large grisly painting of Jesus bleeding from the crown of thorns that hung on the altar. Dizzy didn't know what to make of Jesus, whom she might be married to one day. "Hello husband," she said out loud as she walked down the aisle.

She sat down and had faint hope as the phone rang that Lizard might pick up this time, but then there was the familiar click and his recorded voice saying, "This is Tristan, leave a message." At that, her blood raged inside her. How could he go and change his name and become a different person at a time like this? How could he go to a movie with Melinda at a time like this? How could he not call or come to the hospital AT A TIME LIKE THIS?

After the beep, she said, "Hi Lizard. Maybe a sinkhole opened under your feet, and you're trapped deep in the earth and starving to death. If that's what's happened, I forgive you for not coming. If it's not, I'm never going to speak to you again. Not even if you draw freckles on every inch of your body . . ." She deflated, remembering how much he must've liked her once to have done that.

She ended the call and immediately punched the speed-dial number again: "Also, breaking news, Miles has only been pretending to be perfect all this time. He doesn't even go to school we just found out. Can you believe it? I can't." This morning, the dean of Miles's school had come to the hospital to talk to Mom, the gist being that Miles was actually a screwup like Dizzy and Wynton, only he'd been hiding it.

Then she called Lizard a third time and said, "You suck. I hate you." She put the phone down and curled into a ball on the pew. Lizard was as gone as Wynton. More gone. Even in a coma, Wynton loved her. She could feel it. But Lizard didn't. Not anymore. The problem was, even though she now hated Lizard with the force of the sun, she still loved him too. She didn't know what people were supposed to do with the leftover love that no one wanted anymore.

Well-known fact: Life was a soggy sock you can't take off.

Just then, the lights in the chapel began flashing. What the—Dizzy lifted herself up and turned around and there in the doorway was a sky-scraper of a guy in a chef's coat, but under it, were colorful, circus-y clothes. He was maybe Wynton's age and his hand—practically the size of a frying pan—was on the light switch. "Hello comrade!" he said enthusiastically. He wore mirrored movie-star sunglasses (inside?), had a squirrel of a mustache, and tangly dark brown curls mostly breaking out of a hair-tie. Who was *this*? Dizzy thought. In one of his hands was a plate of food. "Assuming you're Dizzy Fall, daughter of Chef Bernadette. Been looking for you. Was told you had hair like mine"—he gestured toward his hair-nest with his free hand—"and black nerd glasses. Tried the maternity ward first. That's where people usually go. In movies anyway." He slapped his head with his palm. "Then it hit me: chapel! Also a celluloid favorite. In how many scenes do we find our lead, our ingénue, in the hospital chapel?"

Dizzy felt something lighten in her as this enormous person walked down the aisle toward her. She didn't know she had any smiles left inside, but one seemed to be finding its way across her face. Had the angel sent a giant because she was busy elsewhere?

"I'm the lead in this movie?" Dizzy asked, then without thinking added, "And you're the giant?"

He laughed. "Yes, I'm the giant known as Felix Rivera from Denver, Colorado. And I've been sent to nourish you, small earthling. Apparently, you've not been eating." He bowed before Dizzy, presenting her with a paper plate of trinity gumbo, red beans, and collards. "Voilà," he said—and at that moment, thunder, the kind that sounded like someone had taken an ax and split the world, cracked explosively outside. Dizzy sucked in her breath and several seconds later, an ocean tipped over in the sky.

"You said voilà and then the rain . . ." This giant had powers.

He grinned. "Want a snowstorm next? Those are my specialty." A cool, welcome, wonderful wind that smelled like rain—a lovely coral color—breezed into the chapel through the window Dizzy had opened for God (and forgotten to close) the last time she was here.

Felix Rivera the Giant from Colorado lifted his sunglasses. His eyes were a super-light gray, same as Jericho Blane's, Dizzy thought, whose were described as *the color of mist*. They were awesome and she wished she could have them instead of her boring kind. "Listen," he said, pointing a finger in the air, "one: I'm new to this job and my first official task is to get you to eat, so do me a favor?"—two fingers—"two: People downstairs are legit freaking, it's *that* good"—three fingers—"and three . . ." He looked to the ceiling as if he might find the third thing up there. "Well, there is no three."

"I can't eat." Dizzy crossed her arms. Not even for this misty-eyed giant who might've single-handedly sent The Devil Winds away. "I'm sorry. I'm too . . ." She searched his face, having to bend her neck back to do so. His expression was kind as he peered down at her. So kind that . . . she had to drop her head in her hands because tears were threatening, her desperation rushing back. She didn't want the giant to see her face scrunch up. She tried to cry quietly, calmly, but failed as sob after sob broke free.

He sat down next to her and placed the steaming plate of food beside himself on the pew.

"Let's do potatoes," he said quietly.

"Potatoes?" she gasped out.

"Yeah. Potatoes. Got a problem with potatoes? We'll do potatoes."

She laughed a little, mid-blubber, and it caused her to hiccup. "I don't know what you mean though."

"I'll start. If I win, you eat. Ready? Three per round. Mashed. Hashed. Au Gratin. Go!"

Dizzy sniffled. "Oh. I get it." She wiped her eyes. "Okay, okay," she said. "Tartiflette. Dauphinois. Kugel. Go!"

"Aha! Daughter of a chef. Might be stiffer competition than I anticipated. Five per round."

He won with patatas bravas, pyttipanna, dum aloo, picadillo, and potatoes Anna, and so she forced in a few bites per the rules. It actually tasted delicious, so she had some more and soon found that she was feeling more energetic, which made her want to talk, and soon, she couldn't stop. "I read on my phone about this man," she told the giant, "an accountant, who was in a coma like Wynton, and when he woke up, he thought it was 1952 and that he was a race car driver. And there was another guy I researched who woke from a coma thinking he was his brother, like married to his brother's wife and everything. So, when Wyn wakes up he might not even be Wynton anymore. He might think he's Miles, who isn't actually perfect, we just found out from the dean of his school."

"Whoa, dude," he said. "That is some high-caliber information."

"Oh yes," Dizzy said, flattered. "I specialize in the highest."

"You know what I think?" Felix said. "I think—and I have connections on high—that despite that high-caliber info, when your brother wakes up, he'll still be himself and the first thing he'll do is tell you how much he missed you and thank you for being by his side while he was gone."

Connections on high? Changing the weather? "Did the angel send you?"

"Hmmm, sure." A smile took over his whole face. "And you to me."

Oh! Things were looking up. She needed to know everything about him. Between bites, she asked how old he was (nineteen), how tall (six feet, seven and a half inches), and if he knew that the tallest person who ever lived had died from a bug bite on his toe (he didn't) and if she could twirl his mustache (go ahead) and if he always wore such weird clothes under his chef's coat (his trademark). She asked when he got to town (a week ago) and how (got a ride in an orange truck with a cool, chatty girl), if he worked for God (difficult question, will consider and get back to her), and if he had secret powers (doesn't everyone?). Then she told him about Wynton being no ordinary mushroom, instead a white truffle with lightning inside it, about it being her fault he was in a coma and how she might have to become a nun even though she was mostly Jewish. Lastly, she filled him in about Lizard and their divorce.

He, in turn, somehow made Dizzy feel like everything was going to be okay, and so she went back to the hospital room assured, wanting to tell Imperfect Miles a giant had been sent to them now, it only registering when she was outside Wynton's door that Felix had said he got a ride to Paradise Springs a week before in *an orange truck with a girl* and Miles had told Dizzy the angel had driven him around in an orange truck—it had to be the same truck, the same girl/angel! And now, she was remembering that Felix had said the girl driving the orange truck had been chatty. What had the chatty angel told Felix? Dizzy had to find out.

She ran down to the cafeteria, but Chef Finn said Felix had left for the day. Then she returned to Wynton's room to tell Imperfect a giant had come to Paradise Springs *with* the angel Cassidy in the orange truck and so probably knew where she was, but her mother informed her that Miles had just left to go for a walk with the black dog from next door.

Dizzy took her seat by Wynton's side, unable to stop thinking about what secret information Cassidy might have shared with Felix.

Conversation Between Cassidy and Felix on the Way to Paradise Springs, a Week Earlier:

Felix: *Wait, so why are you writing about this guy again?*

Cassidy: *He actually founded The Town. It's for a class. On California history.*

Felix: *You say The Town like it's the only town on earth.*

Cassidy: *It kind of is. For me anyway. My mom and I looked for it when I was little without knowing the name.* (Rolling her eyes.) *Long crazy story. But the thing is, this guy, Alonso Fall—he was super cool.*

Felix: *How cool?* (Felix cocks an eyebrow.)

Cassidy: *Very cool! Way ahead of his time. And the curse on the family began with him and his brother. Came up in my reading.*

Felix: *Wait, what family?*

Cassidy: *The Falls. The descendants of this guy Alonso Fall. They still live in The Town.*

Felix: (He grins.) *And we believe in curses?*

Cassidy: *You might if I tell you the story. I'll tell it like my mom used to tell me stories when I was little.*

Felix: *Go on, Scheherazade. Take me away. I really could use the distraction.*

Cassidy: *Scheherazade! Love that. Okay.* (She clears her throat, smiles at her new travel companion, and begins.) *In a faraway land across the sea, in the time of forever, a boy was born magnificent . . .*

PART
THREE

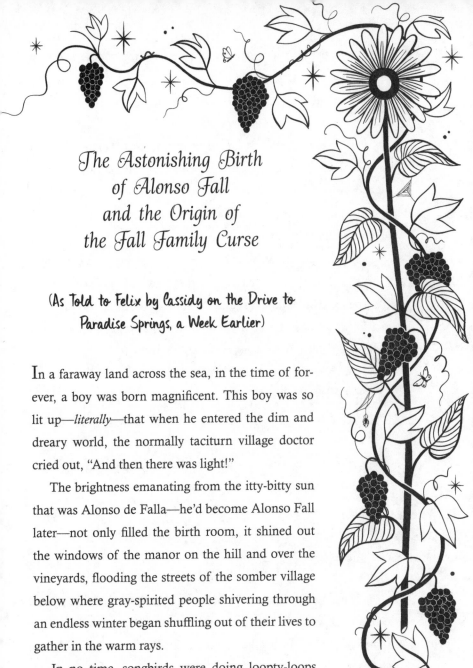

The Astonishing Birth
of Alonso Fall
and the Origin of
the Fall Family Curse

(As Told to Felix by Cassidy on the Drive to
Paradise Springs, a Week Earlier)

In a faraway land across the sea, in the time of forever, a boy was born magnificent. This boy was so lit up—*literally*—that when he entered the dim and dreary world, the normally taciturn village doctor cried out, "And then there was light!"

The brightness emanating from the itty-bitty sun that was Alonso de Falla—he'd become Alonso Fall later—not only filled the birth room, it shined out the windows of the manor on the hill and over the vineyards, flooding the streets of the somber village below where gray-spirited people shivering through an endless winter began shuffling out of their lives to gather in the warm rays.

In no time, songbirds were doing loopty-loops and barrel rolls in the air as women in fluttery dresses laid out picnics, and daffodils pushed their heads

through tired earth to bloom in the shafts of this sudden summer.

So it was, because of Alonso, everyone in this glum faraway town got new eyes, slid into love, slipped into the marvelous.

Everyone doted on the golden boy.

Tailors made him splendid little clothes, bakers baked him splendid little cakes. For Alonso, chickens laid their biggest eggs and cows released their silkiest milk. They spoke to the boy too—the animals did—and he spoke back to them unaware that he was the only one who could do so.

Soon, painters arrived, hearing tell of "a glowing boy," and to this day, all over this region, there are paintings of Alonso hanging in hotels and restaurants, in living rooms and bedrooms, paintings that still, well over a hundred years later, give off a certain light even in the deepest dark of night.

Yet, there was one who didn't get new eyes or slip into the marvelous, whose heart did not grow but shrank in the boy's presence. One who was not warmed and illuminated by his strange glow. This person made a point of wearing a long dark coat through the never-ending summer of Alonso's first years, of shielding his eyes at the boy's tiresome luminosity and scrunching paper into his ears so he didn't have to hear the boy's impossibly easy laugh.

It was instant: Alonso's father's lack of regard for his firstborn son.

Diego de Falla was light-haired and dark-tempered, a squat, unpleasant man who moved like a spider in fast bursts at odd angles. He had a black heart and no one liked him. No one. Not Alonso's mother, Sofia. Not the prostitute Luciana Magdalena, whom he paid to wash his feet before the act. Certainly not the flies that cleared a room the moment he entered it.

"Well, it's fine not to be liked if I'm respected," Diego would say, before hollering at his wife, Sofia, that his soup was too hot, the house too loud, and on top of it, she smelled dreadful, and why oh why couldn't she just smell right for one minute of one day?

This was the root of Diego's misery: the odor of his wife.

For Sofia carried another man's scent on her, even after that other man had sailed off for the Americas, even after the reports that the other man had died at sea. "How can it be?" Diego would ask his odious reflection in the mirror, in the pond, in his knife at the dinner table. How can a dead man's smell fasten itself to a living woman? To *his* living woman? And not just any man, but that ridiculous penniless poet Esteban with his ridiculous chiseled face, his ridiculous cascading brown locks, his ridiculous tree-like height. And why oh why did the ridiculous man's ridiculous scent have to be so wonderful? Diego couldn't get away from it. He'd open a drawer for a pair of socks and there it would be—*so painfully delicious*—wafting out and nearly knocking him over. At night, he would pace from room to room, trying to escape it, often ending up at a window sucking in air from outside like a drowning man reaching the surface.

But Alonso's birth was more than Diego could bear. He'd known the moment he laid eyes on the boy with his ridiculous chiseled features. Another man's son was in his house. At his table. And not just any son. This hullabaloo of a boy! This eternal jack-o'-lantern!

Sofia, for her part, found her husband, Diego, to be invisible. Even when he was right in front of her, she couldn't have said what color his eyes were. Occasionally, she heard his words, his chewing, his footsteps, but most often not. She focused on Alonso, putting a bell around his neck so she wouldn't lose him.

"A great love is inside you," she'd murmur to her son as he drifted off to sleep. Then all through the night the bell would ring and ring as he sleep-ran through the trees.

But every morning was anguish for young Alonso.

He would follow his father into the vineyard, where Diego would pick him up like he was a smelly fish and return him to the house. "Why do you hate me so?" Alonso asked his father once after being deposited back on the veranda.

Diego took Alonso by the shoulders and lifted him into the air so Alonso could smell the sour of onion, bitterness, and something far worse on his father's breath. "No matter how hard you try, Alonso," he said, "you will never be my son." Then he dropped the boy on his face. Alonso didn't get up for weeks and when he did, he had a scar from cheek to chin.

Alonso gave up trying to win his father's love after that. For the first time since his birth, he emitted no light, and lamps had to be lit and fires set in the house.

The boy went quiet.

He was not a son a father could love.

He no longer needed to wear the bell. He stayed still as a stone in his bed all night long.

In his dreams, he turned to ash.

It was in this terrible time that Alonso got a brother and his trouble compounded. Diego brought Hector home when Alonso was nine years old. Hector was a beetle of a boy, close to Alonso's age, a little human gargoyle and miniature version of Diego, with a note on his vest that said: *I am Hector, the son of Diego de Falla. My mother can't take care of me anymore.* It was signed: *Luciana Magdalena.*

Not comprehending the dark mood or giving too much

thought to the logistics of family planning, Alonso was thrilled at this unexpected development. "A brother!" he cried with joy, and threw his arms around Hector. Hector, in turn, grabbed a handful of Alonso's hair and tugged it so hard, his head jerked back. Alonso yelped and jumped away, stunned. Diego smiled and patted the head of his new son Hector. "My boy," he murmured.

Every day after, Diego escorted Hector into the vineyard, guiding him through the vines, divulging to Hector the de Falla family's wine-making secrets. But unbeknownst to either of them, always a few paces and a shadow behind them, was Alonso, picking up and storing away every sacred word.

Hector didn't care one iota about making wine. He cared about not being hungry anymore, about rodents no longer nibbling on his feet while he slept, about not having to pickpocket his way through the village. He cared about not watching his mother and her slobbering clients through a crack in the wall.

At first, he was baffled by his new life as the son of Diego de Falla. He was afraid he would boil in the copper tub filled with water for his bath, had no idea the brush next to the basin was meant for his teeth so used it on his head, and he was accustomed to wearing the same clothes until he grew out of them so didn't put on the tailor-made trousers and shirts that hung pristinely in his wardrobe. His body odor stunk up the whole house, which delighted his father, because finally, there was a stench that overpowered that of Esteban the Dead Penniless Poet's, not to mention the rot of Diego's own soul, which these days seemed to escape every time he opened his mouth.

But in time, Hector became accustomed to the smooth soft shirts, the steamy baths, the rich meals of roast rabbit and po-

tatoes fried in duck fat and began scheming of ways to hold on to these comforts forever. It began to dawn on him that he had power. Privilege. There were people here whom he could humiliate as he'd been humiliated his whole life as the son of the town prostitute. He'd send back his dinner plate three times before eating it, sometimes spitting out the food for dramatic effect. He'd urinate outside his chamber pot only to watch with delight as the maid got down on her hands and knees to clean it.

"My son," Diego said with pride to the ten-year-old tyrant each time he saw him. "My son."

But everyone else favored Alonso, and this rattled Hector.

His envy grew as sharp as his hunger once was.

Hector envied Alonso his looks, so he cut off Alonso's hair while he slept and broke every mirror in the house.

He envied Alonso his brains, so he covered Alonso's tutor's chair with fire ants.

He envied Alonso his athleticism, so he embedded nails in Alonso's shoes.

He envied Alonso his imagination, so he ripped the pages out of Alonso's favorite books and ate them.

They were eleven years old when Hector rigged the stairwell with string, and Alonso tumbled a flight and broke his arm. As he lay at the bottom of the stairs trying to keep himself from moaning, Hector said, "One day I'll kill you and everything will be mine."

"But I don't want anything, you stupid meatball," Alonso replied.

"I'll kill you anyway. You're the stupid meatball."

And with those murderous words, from this moment on, a curse became manifest in the Fall family, a Cain and Abel curse in a family that would exclusively bear males, brothers, Cains and Abels, for over a hundred years.

A curse that has led to very bad ends for the Falls, generation after generation.

Very, *very* bad ends.

MILES

Miles sailed through the hospital lobby en route to what was likely another terrible decision. His first internet hookup. He kept his head down so as not to have to talk to anyone and pretend to feel all the appropriate things he wasn't feeling about Wynton's condition and hide all the awful, inappropriate things he was. Not to mention the awful things he was feeling about himself after Dean Richards's visit this morning. He'd almost reached the exit when something—a foot?—got caught beneath his shoe.

"Oh damn, sorry," Miles heard as he catapulted forward, somehow finding his balance mid-flight and pitching backward as if he had invisible armrests, until he landed upright, saving himself from a spectacular face-plant in the hospital lobby. "Whoa, dude. That was a stellar recovery. Gold medal. Wow. Sorry about that." The offending foot (and voice) belonged to an enormous guy with a handlebar mustache in mirrored sunglasses. He was standing beside Miles in a bewildering (wallpaper-influenced?) getup under a chef's coat from The Blue Spoonful.

"No problem," Miles muttered, and resumed his beeline to the exit. He'd only taken a few steps when he heard, "Hey!"

Miles spun around. It was Hipster Hercules again. "Yeah?" Miles said, but the guy had nothing. He was just standing there, head grazing the ceiling, looking in Miles's direction with the movie-star shades on. Miles looked over his shoulder, wondering if the smile and *hey* were for someone else, but no one was behind him. "Yeah?" Miles said again to the dude who was still staring at Miles. "You all right, man?"

The guy nodded. "Oh yeah. Fine, fine. Really good. And you? How are you?"

Miles felt his brows rise at the supreme oddness that was this interaction. "Good, yeah. Got to run." Miles pointed toward the door.

"Sure, of course. Yup." The guy pointed toward the door too. "You go run."

What a total effing weirdo, Miles thought, turning back around. He should tell his mother that Finn hired a lunatic.

Then right before Miles reached the doors, once again, he heard, "Hey!"

Annoyed, Miles turned around. Again.

"I'm Felix Rivera from Denver, Colorado," said the loon.

"Ur, okay, Miles, uh, Fall, from here."

"Miles Fall? Oh! Hey! Hi! Another descendant of Alonso Fall! Heard *all* about him recently. I work at your mom's restaurant. I fed Dizzy a moment ago. Oh, that sounded weird, like she's a dog. And that sounded weirder. Chef Finn was concerned because she hasn't been eating." The guy exhaled mightily. "Changing lanes here. So sorry about your brother. Your sister's worried when he wakes, he'll think he's a race car driver or you even. I told her not to sweat that." He twirled his bonkers 'stache. "Um. Sorry. Those were probably not good words either. Must do better with the words." A smile filled up the guy's face then, corner to corner. He looked batshit. Miles wanted to laugh—an unusual feeling for him. He noted the purple paisley shirt, the gray pinstripe pants, the wing tips, the suspenders. Suspenders! Dude was living in ALL CAPS. Also, hella weird this guy was calling Miles out as a descendent of Alonso Fall. Maybe when he "fed Dizzy" she mentioned their great-grandfather, along with those coma theories that Miles had already heard?

Miles nodded a farewell, then turned around, but before he pushed open the door, curiosity made him turn around yet again. The guy had freed his hair from the confines of a hairband, and it made him look like he should have a bass guitar in his hands—total rock star vibes. His shades were resting on his head now and his light eyes, heretofore hidden, were on full display. They were cool-looking. "You kind of glow too," he said to Miles.

Um. What the fuck? Did he just say Miles *glowed*? Seriously, what was with this guy? And what about the *too*? Who else was he referring to? Or maybe Miles misheard. He must have.

"Excuse me?" Miles said.

"I said you kind of glow too."

Okay then! Miles, totally baffled, turned and pushed through the doors and out of the hospital into a finally cooler day.

MILES

Miles bent down to pet Sandro, who was waiting for him by a willow tree. The rain had stopped, and sunlight was breaking through the clouds in thick children-drawing beams. A cool breeze grazed Miles's skin. The Devil Winds had finally blown away to another town. Miles wanted to blow away too.

Just met a really tall weirdo who said I glowed, he told the dog.

You kind of do.

Really?

Sandro didn't reply, instead said, *Did you find her yet?*

Not yet. But I know her name now. He hadn't seen Sandro since they found out.

Moxie?

No.

Lucy?

No.

I know! Sugar-pie. Oh! Beauty?

No. You won't guess. It's Cassidy.

Sandro put his paws on Miles's thigh. *How are we going to find her?*

Not sure.

How could she not come back for us?

Don't know. Miles put his forehead to Sandro's. Like the dog, his *sehnsucht,* or inconsolable longing, was for Cassidy, to see her again, and he didn't know why.

Dizzy thinks Cassidy can bring Wynton out of his coma, he told Sandro.

She brought us out of ours.

215

This jolted Miles. Because it was kind of true, wasn't it? What if Dizzy was right? Hadn't Cassidy completely transformed and revitalized both him and Sandro in the course of a morning? Didn't she somehow make him feel like he made sense? Like *life* did? And she literally saved both Wynton's and Dizzy's lives. Damn. Maybe she *was* an angel or Energy Being or whatever Dizzy had been calling her—what did he know? But how to find her? He'd humored Dizzy and searched the internet with her first name and anything they could think of: Cassidy/literature, Cassidy/orange truck, Cassidy/tattoos, Cassidy/beautiful, etc. and yes, for Dizzy: Cassidy/angel, Cassidy/Energy Being, Cassidy/Divine Messenger. Of course, they'd come up blank.

I'm feeling bad again, Miles. Like I did when Beauty ran away.

Me too.

Maybe we need antidepressants, Sandro said.

Maybe, doggo.

Or to go to therapy.

Yeah.

But it means you have to tell someone about our moods.

I think they know now. The dean of my school came to the hospital today.

His mom had gotten an earful from Dean Richards, who said he felt terrible about delivering this news under the circumstances but he hadn't been able to reach her by email or calling the house—plus he must have an old cell number—and he was that worried about Miles. He told her Miles was on academic probation and his scholarship was in jeopardy. The dean also talked to her about "a worrisome pattern of social withdrawal and internal preoccupation" (someone had noticed this?). He'd given his mother the name of a psychiatrist.

So.

Good riddance Perfect Miles.

Since the dean's visit this morning, Miles kept catching his mother and

Dizzy looking at him, his mom with concern, and Dizzy with curiosity, like he was new to the family. He heard Dizzy telling Wynton that maybe Miles had just been pretending to be perfect all this time—true enough. His mother tried to talk to him about it all, of course, but he hadn't known what to say. He felt like a whopping disappointment loser even if she said the opposite, even if a tiny part of him was glad she finally knew.

Miles buried his face deep into Sandro's coat, feeling a bolt of love for the dog so strong, he thought he might cry if he were a normal person. It really did make him feel unhuman that he never cried, especially over the last few days with his mother and sister probably setting a Guinness World Record for weeping. Well, nonhuman animals didn't cry either, he thought. He always suspected he was one of them—a sad old goat maybe? A cow? A lone deer?—and someone had cast a spell on him, the frog-prince in reverse, and if the right person came along and kissed him or whatever, he'd turn back into his true goat self.

It'd explain a lot. A lot a lot.

I wish I were a dog, he told the dog.

Oh, yes! You'd be a fabulous canine, Miles. So fast!

You could be me?

No way. I don't want him as a brother.

Shhh. Don't say that while he's in a coma.

He still did what he did to you. Bastard.

I know.

So far, Miles had mostly avoided looking directly at Wynton. Only once did he really take in the tubes, the casts, the blood-seeped bandages, the bruises, the staples, the pins, the still face, the slack mouth. He'd been alone in the room and had vomited into a trash can. Sometimes he tried to read, but all the sentences blurred, so he switched to sifting through wine notes online, futilely searching for his father, while feeling like his breastbone was splitting open.

Panic was so thick in the hospital room. (Except when Dizzy did some nutso thing like zombie-walk around like a nun!) When he couldn't take it anymore, he'd escape to a nearby supply closet, where he counted the 1,394 tiles on the floor or watched porn on his phone, particularly one video where two burly bears made out ferociously while doing it, like two Jericho Blanes from *Live Forever Now*. Yeah. But it was better than thinking about suffocating his brother with a pillow (yes, this occurred to him one fleeting moment) or shaking him awake only to say: *I still hate you.*

It all made him want to throw himself at a wall.

He was so far away from his mother and Dizzy, like there could be tumbleweeds blowing through the endless desert between them in that hospital room. When, yesterday, his mother had beckoned him into her arms, all he'd wanted was to run into them, to join her and Dizzy, to fold into their embrace, but he couldn't do it. He had no idea how to travel the distance.

The cool air made Miles's skin tingle. He scanned the parking lot for orange trucks. None. If only he could go off with Cassidy and they could be nemophilists together and live happily ever after, reading novels in some forest.

"Miles!" A girl's voice interrupted his thoughts. He turned and saw Madison from the left-for-dead-in-a-Dumpster night rushing toward him. His stomach lurched. Oh no. Seriously, oh effing no. He'd hoped he'd never see her again. Had she helped Wynton throw him in the Dumpster? Probably. He wanted to take off across the parking lot, but it was too late—she was already so close he could smell the coconut lotion. Ugh, that same lotion. Her hair was no longer pink and spiky but brown and coiffed conservatively around her face. There was no dolphin nose ring, just an indentation where it had been. Oh man, why couldn't he remember what they'd done together? Had they gone all the way? Did they use a condom? What if she was pregnant? That thought hadn't occurred to him until this moment! What if he was going to be a father at seventeen?

What if he fainted on the spot? "I'm so sorry, Miles," she said, her round eyes concerned. "I kept thinking of you after I heard about Wynton." She bit her lip. "You must be so devastated. I'd do anything to have an older brother like him. I still can't believe he went to jail for you and everything. God, that night, I—"

Static filled Miles's head, blasting through his thoughts. "What?" Did he just hear what he heard? "What?"

Her expression changed, her brow creasing. "Wait, what? Really? You don't remember?"

"Remember what?" *Went to jail for him?*

"I guess you really were that far gone." She exhaled slowly. "My fault, I guess. Not okay what I did, giving you that pill, I know that now. So, I'm sober—well, since I heard about Wyn."

Miles's heart was slamming around in his chest. He could barely get out words. "What did I do?"

"You really don't remember driving into that statue?"

Miles tried to compute. "*I* drove into the statue of Alonso Fall?" He'd assumed this had happened after he'd been chucked into the Dumpster to be eaten alive by rats.

Her face brightened and her hands took to the air. "Oh my God, Miles, you totally grabbed the keys from Wynton when we were leaving the party. You got in the driver's side and started the truck and peeled out like a maniac. We had to chase after you to get in! You kept yelling *I'm not perfect! I'm not perfect!* Wynton was trying to get you to stop the car the whole time. You slammed into that statue on purpose!" She pointed to her forehead. There was a jagged line barely visible through makeup. Miles sucked in air. "You can still see the cut from when I hit the window. Wyn told us all to run when we heard sirens. But he didn't. He slipped into the driver's seat and waited. Bettina and I watched the cops handcuff him from the alley. We didn't know where you went."

He had totaled his mother's work truck? *He* had destroyed the statue of Alonso Fall? Wynton hadn't thrown him into the Dumpster with this girl's help? He'd chucked his own ass into it? Hid in it probably? And he didn't remember any of this?

"Also, I'm sorry I tried to—Okay. How to say this. I thought you were into me until Wynton said . . ." She looked down, a flush rising in her cheeks. "Until he said you were too wasted to, like, to know what you were doing or whatever. I'm sorry if I . . . I . . ." She shook her head. "First time anyone's pulled me off a guy. *Get off my little brother!*" she said, imitating a drunken Wynton. Wynton had pulled her off of Miles? *His little brother?* "So, I'm sorry . . . and like in case you don't remember or something, nothing happened between us." She raised her hand, gestured helplessly toward the hospital. "I hope he'll be okay. Sure, he's reckless, but there's such a good heart in there. But you know that better than anyone."

What. The. Actual. Fuck.

What the actual fuck? repeated Sandro, who then began barking. Miles wanted to bark.

The conversation was a demolition derby inside him, wrecking everything he'd ever thought about his brother, about himself.

What's true? he thought.

Depends on who's telling the story, Sandro replied even though Miles hadn't been talking to the dog. *Your specialty is the woe-is-me story.*

Oh man, Sandro, ouch, that's not nice.

Miles watched Madison walk away and enter the hospital, noticed the tall weirdo dude from Denver holding the door like it was his job, dramatically bowing before her. What a kook. Miles leaned against a telephone pole, feeling woozy, disoriented. The tall guy was now motioning Madison into the hospital with a dramatic hand twirl. Madison smiled flirtatiously and curtsied before him. Whatever.

Miles's thoughts spun. He'd put all their lives in danger that night?

Why couldn't he remember? What kind of drug had Madison given him? Why had he drank so much? And Wynton had protected him? Had spent the night in jail for him and had never said a word about it, not even to their mother when she kicked him out of the house? And what had Miles done? Broken the bow he'd sold his motorcycle to buy. For the gig that would change his life.

Only now he might not have a life.

Miles felt like he might be hyperventilating. He made himself inhale deeply. In, out, in, out—

His phone dinged.

Hear! the message said. Lord. The guy couldn't spell. This morning in the supply closet he'd opened the app Lookn and uploaded a photo, then swiped right on this guy Rod, who in pics looked like Hot AP English Teacher Mr. Gelman. Rod was nineteen (or said he was), on his way to Oregon, and was stopping in Paradise Springs for a bite. *Of you maybe,* he'd joked in the message to Miles. Hardy har har.

Did he still want to do this? He did. He wanted to do other things too. Like uproot trees, hurl houses, smash his fist through windows. Oh, holy hell, who was he? He'd yelled, *I'm not perfect!* and driven a truck full of people into the fifteen-foot statue of his great-grandfather Alonso Fall.

Miles broke into a run and Sandro barked joyfully as the two of them raced to the fire road.

Where are we going, Miles?

Nowhere.

I love nowhere!

Miles could see the back of the truck now, a self-loading logging truck with no logs.

This wasn't the first time Miles had opened Lookn. After being indoctrinated into the religion of kissing a boy in a hurry in a restaurant refrigerator, Miles had downloaded Lookn, an app that wasn't connected to other social media, so he could easily sign on saying he was eighteen. He'd uploaded a photo of someone else, made a skeleton profile, then spent hours, then weeks, ignoring messages and swiping through guys until his eyes were bleary, until his room was full of these phantoms: the short hot guy who liked rugby sitting in his desk chair, the skinny redhead into musicals splayed on the bed, the hefty guy who loved to eat Mexican food lying on his side on the floor, the surfer standing by the window. It was a little like reading a novel that had doors so the characters could get out and join you.

At first, he searched for the refrigerator-kiss guy Nico, then he didn't know whom or what he was searching for, just that he couldn't stop swiping, imagining, pulling guy after guy out of his phone and into his room to keep him company. The men were mostly that: men, and in many of their pics, naked or half-naked. Their bodies fascinated frightened dared aroused obsessed Miles with their smooth jacked chests, their hairy sunken ones, their lanky frames and squat ones, their freckles and moles and mouths and eyes. Their dicks and dicks and dicks and dicks and more dicks. (And measurements of said dicks!)

His school wasn't like the ones on TV and in movies with LGBTQ+ centers and Gay/Straight Alliances or whatever. There wasn't one out gay person at his small Catholic school. He did have suspicions about this guy Conner on the track team and once had clumsily tried to investigate but got nowhere. He knew statistically there had to be others like him making out with the wrong people—in his case: girls—under bleachers or in the hallways at dances. And sure, he could be the first to come out. Except Perfect Miles didn't rock the boat. He didn't even get in the boat.

But night after night, back then, he indulged, looking and looking. Some of the guys were nearby too, and a few he knew personally. The assistant track coach at Paradise Springs High. Tony Sanchez, an older guy who owned the hardware store. It was like walking by your neighbor's house and suddenly the walls turned see-through. Miles went to the hardware store the next day after he spotted Tony on the site and lurked in the electrical aisle, spying on the man with his big toothy smile, before finally buying a box of nails. At the checkout, Tony said to him, "You're looking more and more like your father every day."

Miles had heard this his whole life but even more so as he got older.

"Were you and my dad friends?" Miles asked Tony that day, handing him the money for nails he did not need.

Miles saw it then. The monster mask that was Tony's face too and the unmistakable longing beneath it. "Nah, he was older. Didn't know I existed, as they say." He smiled at Miles. "Everyone knew your dad. Your mom and uncle too. They were the cool kids. But your dad, he was a special guy, made everyone feel good, went out of his way to, you know?" He slowly made change like it was a kind of sorcery and Miles felt certain Tony'd had a crush on his father in high school. "He'll come back," Tony said after bagging the nails. "The story's not over until it's over, right?"

"Right," Miles said. He'd had this same conversation with Paradise Springs's old-timers often. Everyone thought his father would return one day. Miles wanted him to, imagined it all the time, but had given up on it actually happening long ago. Anyway, Miles had left the hardware store that day unable to fit "Are you gay, Tony?" into the conversation.

Back then, he'd been too chicken to actually message anyone on Lookn or post his real picture. But this morning in the supply closet, he'd done it. He just couldn't count the tiles or watch any more Jericho Blane porn or think so many wrong things about his possibly dying brother. Who'd saved his hide!

He'd messaged Rod.

Miles slowed to a fast walk when he saw the guy leaning—posing—against the cab of the truck. He was more manly than in his pic—was he really nineteen? He had a bandana around the top of his head, and he looked like he rode a Harley. He's probably in a motorcycle gang, Miles thought. He'd watched a TV show about motorcycle gangs because of an extremely hot actor who starred in it, so he was familiar with their automatic weapons. The way they buried people alive. Set people on fire. Miles slowed further. He could see Rod's expression now, a lot of Christmas morning in it on spotting Miles. Miles stopped. Why was he doing this? He didn't know. He just was. He started walking again. Jesus. He was a (secret) criminal now to boot, who needed a psychiatrist and probably was going to get kicked out of school. A criminal whose asshole (comatose!) brother went to jail for him and pulled a girl off of him because he couldn't consent (did Wynton suspect Miles was gay?), acting after seventeen years like he might actually care about Miles. How to deal with any of it?

Wait a second, Sandro said, halting mid-trot. *Is this a date? With some rando? It is! Oh my Dog, I do not condone this life choice, Miles. Miles! Bad human! Bad Miles!*

There's dignity in risk.

Who said that?

I did.

Oh. Well said. But there's also idiocy in it.

"Hey," Rod said as Miles approached. "Even better in person. That never happens." Miles was engulfed in aftershave. Rod's hand landed on his shoulder and squeezed it like he was testing a melon. Miles didn't know how to greet him, didn't know what to do with his hands. Should they shake? Bro tap? Oh, too late now. Miles put his hands in his pockets, caught Rod checking him out, down and up. Miles didn't know where to look. Where did people usually look? He settled on the name of the truck: *Kenworth.*

This idea had been better in his mind.

Rod whose name was ROD was indeed handsome in the rugged Hot

Mr. Gelman–like way. He could ford a river on horseback maybe when he wasn't setting people on fire for his motorcycle gang.

"You talk, man?"

Miles nodded mutely and Rod laughed. Miles wasn't sure he actually could talk, like even if someone put a gun to his head. God, he hoped no one was going to put a gun to his head! Because this was stupid, right? Incredibly stupid. He should make a run for it. What if Rod took him somewhere and a group of guys was waiting with crowbars? He'd seen that movie, that TV show, read that article, that post, that book. And, was this guy even gay? He didn't really seem it, did he? But Miles didn't seem gay either, he didn't think. Not that Miles even knew what seeming gay meant, not really. He'd taken the bus down to San Francisco once. He'd peered into the windows of bars and cafés in the Castro and felt like the hickiest hick of all hicks. Like a potato with ears and feet. He'd taken the next bus back to Paradise Springs. And it was worse when Miles watched movies and TV shows. He couldn't find himself anywhere. He certainly wasn't fun or flamboyant. He wasn't into musicals or clothes. He was a terrible dancer. He hated theater. He knew nothing about music. He hated iced coffee! Could you fail at being gay, because he might. He could relate to some of the gay guys in books, but they were made of words. Where were the gay guys who were quiet and gloomy, who liked to read all night and talk to dogs and run? That's not how gay guys were ever portrayed. That's not how *any* guys were portrayed, actually. Would he have to learn how to be gay like he'd had to learn how to be Perfect Miles? Would he ever just be able to be himself? (With anyone other than Cassidy and Sandro.) Surely other people just were who they were, weren't they?

So far all he knew about his gay self was that he was mute.

Rod reached up and opened the passenger door. "Climb on up, Jack."

Jack?

Shut up.

Jack!

Please shut up, Sandro.

Miles hopped onto the platform. He paused for a second to check out the cab, looking for . . . he didn't know what, a gun, maybe? A machete? Doll heads? An arm? It smelled like cigarettes and old food. There were Dunkin' Donuts coffee cups everywhere and crumpled fast-food bags. Was he really going to get in?

"Go on. I don't bite," Rod said. "Well, I do bite, like I said in my message, but only if you want me to." He chuckled in a goofy way. Okay. Harmless. Miles climbed into the cab and settled into the passenger seat.

Sandro, get in.

Not a chance.

C'mon, I mean it.

Reluctantly, Sandro jumped onto the platform and then into the cab. *Under protest, Miles. And only to bite this box of stupid if necessary.*

Miles closed the door, quickly put his hand over his mouth to check his breath. His heart raced. What were the rules anyway? Should he tell him before what he did and didn't want to do? He wasn't ready to try certain things. Not with someone he didn't know. Oh man. What the hell was he doing? And doing it when his brother was in a coma!

Rod and his cloud of aftershave climbed in. His arms were streaked with grease or dirt. Miles wanted to ask where they were going to go but he couldn't even manage that.

"You're really hot," Rod said.

Stop hissing at him! Miles told Sandro.

He smells funny and I don't think he has your best interests at heart.

Who does?

I do.

Miles petted Sandro and it calmed both boy and dog. Rod reached over, tried to pet Sandro. The dog growled.

"Don't seem to like me."

"It takes him a minute."

Ah, he spoke! Now that his vocal cords were working, he and Rod began discussing heading down Hidden Highway, but when he glanced out the window, he saw a sight: The thirty-foot-tall maniac from Denver with the handlebar mustache on a glittering pink kid's bike charging across the dirt lot, waving at Miles with one hand.

"What the—"

"What is it?" said Rod.

"Nothing, let's head out."

Sandro started to bark. Rod lit up the engine. And . . . there was loud banging on the bottom of Miles's door. Miles looked out the window. Colorado guy had ditched the pink bike and was standing below, windshield-wiping his arms and shouting, "Miles! Miles Fall! Miles Fall!" Sandro got up on his hind legs, put his paws on the window ledge.

We're being rescued! He started to bark loudly.

"Sorry, just a sec," Miles said to Rod, opening the door. Sandro bolted out. "What the hell? Did something happen to my bro—" Miles said to the giant guy, his cheeks burning.

"Oh, what? No. Everything's okay I think, as far as I know," he said—Felix, that was his name. Felix was now opening the door further and stepping up onto the platform. He lifted his sunglasses. Whoa. Those eyes again, now up close. The contrast of the light gray irises and dark inky lashes was startling. Felix gave Rod a death stare.

"Look. Don't wanna get between anyone," Rod said. "Don't want any trouble. This your boyfriend, I'm presuming?"

"Boyfriend? No! I don't even . . ." Miles realized he was being hoisted out of the truck by Felix, very much like Felix was his jealous and quite berserk boyfriend. Sandro had his paws up on the platform: *Get out while you can, Miles!*

Miles said to Felix, "Why are you doing this?" which wasn't the real question. The real question was why Miles was allowing it, no, actually helping Felix get him out of the truck. "Really sorry, Rod," Miles said as Felix guided more than manhandled Miles off the platform and onto the road, where Miles flung Felix off more for show than anything else. "Seriously, what the hell?" Miles said to Felix. "Who are you? Why is this any of your business? What's wrong with you?"

Felix slammed the truck door. His shades were down again. "What's wrong with me? What's up with you getting in a truck with a total stranger? He is a stranger, isn't he?"

Rod revved the engine and pulled out as Miles sputtered, too exasperated to get out the words to express the irony of this, Felix being a total stranger as well! A huge and more unpredictable stranger in the most bizarre getup Miles had ever seen. Not to mention the mustache! "I know he's a stranger," Felix scolded. "I saw that awkward greeting. Ever hear of meeting in a public place first? You could get killed. Is this something you do? Like the secret life of the high school football star? Been done. He could've been homicidal. He looked homicidal. He could've been an ax murderer. He could've been a rapist. He could've been a kidnapper. He could've been a strangler. He could've been a . . . oh damn." He looked up. His mouth bunched to one side. He twirled his bonkers 'stache. "Damn, damn it, totally tapped out early."

"A cannibal," Miles said.

"Oh wow. Good one. Thanks. A cannibal. He could've been a cannibal. Or . . . a slasher." He looked at Miles, his eyebrow raised expectantly above the mirror of his glasses.

"He could've been a serial killer," Miles offered.

"He could've been a chainsaw massacre-er."

"Vampire."

"No way. Different list," Felix said.

"Okay, an escaped convict," Miles said.

"Nice. Out of the box." Miles felt a flash of pride. "Hmm." Felix's mouth bunched to the side again as he thought. "A gunslinger."

"A gunslinger?" Miles shook his head. "I'll allow but barely . . . I'm out."

"Me too." Then Felix snorted as he said, "Um, did I hear you call him Rod? Seriously, tell me that guy's name wasn't *Rod?*" Felix started to laugh. It had a lot of giggle in it for such an enormous person and Miles had to bite his cheek so not to smile as they watched the truck chug slowly down the fire road. What had just happened? It was like the novel he'd been reading got switched mid-sentence.

Felix bent down. "And who's this?"

Sandro was doing joy-circles at Felix's feet.

"That's Sandro."

And this is the biggest human being I've ever encountered. Are you sure he's in your same species? He's ginormous, humongous, gigantastic, gigantor, a big old badonka, mongo man!

Sandro's tail wagged as Felix scratched his ears and Miles took in the glittering pink bicycle with flowered banana seat and white basket with flowers woven in it. "Nice ride," Miles said.

"Yeah," Felix replied, standing and nearly brushing a cloud with the top of his head. "I knew it would put the fear of God in Rod the Cannibal when I chose it." He twirled the mustache, his lips curling upward. Miles noted the wide planes of Felix's cheeks, one of them dimpling with the grin. Then tried to unnote it. He loved a good cheek dimple on a guy.

As they walked back to the rack from where Felix had "borrowed" the bike, Felix said, "So do you do that a lot? I think you need to develop a better sense of Stranger Danger."

"You're a stranger!" Miles blurted finally.

"Yeah," Felix said dismissively. "But I'm me."

"In the fifteen minutes since I met you, you've stalked me, stolen a bike, and you were about to start a fight with Rod the Cannibal. Plus, you're like three of me."

"Yeah, dude, but I'm me," Felix said again, smiling and dimpling. Despite himself, Miles caught the grin and unbelievably raised him some. It was a little alarming how charming this guy was.

What's going on, Sandro?

I think you're making a friend.

I don't have friends except you.

There was Cassidy.

There was.

Also, Miles, maybe he's queer like us. The real human McCoy, not an honorary like me.

Straight as they come.

Could be bi?

He's just city. A hipster or whatever.

Miles didn't want to go back to the hospital, especially after the dean's visit, and Felix didn't seem like he had anywhere to be, so Miles led them down a path to the river, the temperature luxurious, no longer trying to broil or suffocate them. Walking with Felix on the trail, he quickly discovered, was like hiking with a wildly enthusiastic (i.e., off his rocker) nature guide. He stopped repeatedly to bellow and whoop at what he was seeing. Miles kept trying not to laugh each time he exclaimed "Wooooooooooow!" at a redwood, "Hooooooooly crap!" at the mossy oaks gathered together like circles of hunched old men, "Amaaaaaaaaaazing!" at the bougainvillea bushes bursting with red and purple blooms, "Do you freaking see this?" at the sunlight reflecting off damp boulders.

"How old are you anyway?" Miles asked, catching Felix between exclamations.

"Nineteen, took a gap year last year, and to answer your next questions,

I'm six feet, seven and a half inches, and no, I don't play basketball."

Those had indeed been Miles's next questions.

"You came all the way from Colorado to work at my mom's restaurant?"

"Kind of," Felix replied, but Miles couldn't ask for elaboration because Felix got distracted by a hawk circling above them. "Are you seeing this, man?"

The three of them ambled through the trees, Felix exclaiming and Sandro chasing critters through the brush. Miles tried not to laugh out loud at Felix's outbursts while in his head he began rewriting his family history with Wynton as hero, not villain. For one reckless moment, he imagined himself as a little kid not secretly spying on his siblings from the stairwell but flopped on the red couch with them watching movies, doing puzzles, clobbering each other with pillows. And then he found himself swept into a cheesy movie: He'd go back to the hospital and put his hand on Wynton's chest, Wynton's eyes would open, his first words, "Little brother."

No. Miles cringed, shook it off. Wynton was a venomous striking snake. Who cared if he did one brotherly thing in seventeen years? He'd terrorized Miles. He'd kicked him out of his own family, out of his own life.

"You okay?" Felix asked. Miles realized he'd stopped and was staring at his feet. He looked up. Felix's sunglasses were resting on his head and Miles was once again taken aback by the guy's amazing eyes—the color of wet slate, he thought, no no, oh no, his eyes were *the color of mist* like Jericho effing Blane's! Made even more lethal because of the intensity of Felix's gaze, which was currently x-raying Miles, shifting things around in Miles's stomach, making his neck warm. Could Sandro be right? I mean, did straight guys eyeball gay guys like this? Not at his school, they didn't. He sure didn't want to look away, so did precisely that.

Also, how had he not noticed right away how good-looking Felix was—he must've gotten thrown off by the outfit, the mustache, the strangeness of their first encounter. But now, well. Hot Hercules definitely had appeal. This guy looked like he ate three other guys. There was so much of him to imagine naked, which was what Miles was doing. Was it true what they said about foot-size? Because whoa.

"All good," Miles said.

Felix smiled, then dropped the shades, and continued down the path. Miles followed, thinking about Felix stealing some kid's bike, then practically forcing himself into the truck to pull Miles out of it. Should he be mad about it? He wasn't. Ashamed? Not in the slightest. Should he be freaked because this was the first person besides Nico the sauté cook and Rod the Cannibal who knew he was gay? He wasn't. Like not at all. In fact, he felt a little lighter, relieved. It probably would've been fine with Rod, but maybe Miles wouldn't have been so fine after? Maybe it had been a bad idea. Miles caught up to Felix. "So, um, thanks for—" He was going to say "caring," but the word sounded so corny, he stopped himself.

Felix nodded like he heard it anyway, then rested a—friendly?—hand on Miles's shoulder. Miles hadn't known there were so many nerve endings in his body. Oh man. A swarm of bees took residence in his stomach. He was feeling it. *Rest in peace, Miles Fall,* he thought as Felix took his hand away and they pushed on deeper into the forest.

The Heart-Wrenching Love Story of Alonso Fall and Sebastian Ortega Begins

(As Told to Felix by Cassidy on the Drive to Paradise Springs, a Week Earlier)

Back in the time of forever, Alonso was twelve years old and strolling down a quiet wooded road, when, looking over a stone wall, he saw a boy reading under a tree in a rose garden. The boy had long, curly blond hair, a cascade of it, and his eyes were the faraway kind of people in paintings gazing at horizons. His cheeks were freckled from the sun. He was so immersed in his book that he didn't even stir when a butterfly landed on an eyelash. Alonso climbed a tree so he could watch the boy unnoticed, and only then did he realize that the boy's body was not touching the ground.

A floating boy.

The floating boy read and read and Alonso stared and stared until a man's voice rang out from the stone house. "Sebastian, put that book down! Your sisters

233

left for school over an hour ago." The boy—*Sebastian*—rose to his feet, which still didn't mean his feet touched the ground. Alonso watched an old man come into the garden. He handed Sebastian two rocks and Alonso observed, mouth agape, as Sebastian, now with a rock in each hand, gently lowered to the ground.

The older man was thin and pale with a stooped, spindly posture. He said to the boy, "Keep them in your pockets all day at school. Not letting you float up to heaven like your mama."

"Don't worry so much, Papa," the boy said, his voice lazy and loving. He smiled at his father. Alonso had never seen a smile like this boy's, so open and unselfconscious, so *lovely*. It made something in his chest come loose. It seemed to have the same effect on Sebastian's father, who patted the boy's head and said, "My sweet boy."

Alonso's body and soul contracted. To have a kind father like this.

Sebastian walked to the gate, opened it, then continued down the quiet dirt road, holding the book in front of his face with one hand, perfectly adept at reading and walking at the same time.

He had a very particular stride, more hop than walk.

Alonso stealthily followed Sebastian, who, now cloaked by the trees, took the rocks out of his pockets and tossed them to the ground, then continued to walk and read, only now, he was doing so inches above the ground.

It became Alonso's ritual. Each morning before his tutoring began, he'd sneak down the hill, slip through the village, and then turn down the dirt road and climb a tree to spy on the floating boy reading in the garden, before furtively trailing him through the forest to school.

Then, one morning, halfway down the path in a thick and

shadowy part of the woods, the floating boy turned around and said to the air, "Why do you follow me every day? I don't see you. I don't hear you. But it's brighter when you're nearby. It's easier to read my book. I know who you are. You're the boy from The Time of Light." (This was how townspeople referred to Alonso's birth and the illuminated years that followed.)

Hiding behind a tree, Alonso decided the best course of action was to squat down, close his eyes, and tuck his head in his knees and panic. When he glanced up a few moments later, to his surprise, the boy's freckled face was looking down on him with that same soft smile. Alonso hadn't heard him approach because the boy had no footsteps.

Sebastian reached out his hand to Alonso, and to Alonso's astonishment, when he held it, he too rose several inches into the air.

The boys smiled at each other.

People in the village began calling them The Inseparables.

For Alonso, having a best friend was like having a secret suitcase full of sky, of rivers, of endless summer afternoons.

Soon they had a ceremony in a meadow so they could be blood brothers. Under the shining sun, they cut their fingers and pressed them together.

"How long do we have to keep them like this to become brothers?" Sebastian asked.

"I think it has to be a long time. Like an hour," Alonso said, a flickery warmth spreading through him.

"Feel that?" Alonso asked Sebastian.

"What?"

"I don't know," Alonso said, but he did know. That was the moment he knew.

Day after day, Alonso's horrid brother, Hector, listened

through the wall to Alonso and Sebastian talking, laughing, and unbeknownst to him, floating around the room. Hector fumed about how Alonso, who in Hector's meatball mind already had everything, now had a best friend too. It was more than Hector could bear. His envy, which had been like hunger, became actual hunger. He took a bite out of the wall. Then another. It made him feel better.

That was the day Hector began eating the house.

Though The Inseparables looked a bit alike but for their hair color, they were not alike. Whereas Alonso was restless and daring, Sebastian was placid and careful. Whereas Alonso was impatient for the next moment even while in the present one, Sebastian was so calm, he made moments seem like they went on forever.

Whereas Alonso had dreams, Sebastian was dreamy.

One day, Alonso was walking home from the village through the woods with a bullfrog in each hand, having just raced them with Sebastian behind the bakery. At the creek, he placed the frogs on a rock and was shooing them back to their frog-lives when a shadow fell over him and he realized someone was behind him.

Someone enormous like he'd been eating a house.

It all happened so fast.

Alonso turned to see his brother, Hector, about seven feet tall and three feet wide now, looming above, holding a stone slab in his hands.

He dropped it murderously on the two frogs.

Without thinking, Alonso flew at Hector's legs, catching him off guard, and despite Hector's size, Alonso knocked him down. Alonso began punching him as hard as he could, enraged at his brutality toward the poor innocent frogs, not to mention at Alonso since the day they met. "How could you do that?" Alonso cried.

And: "You're a monster just like our father!"

And finally: "Your mother's a prostitute who abandoned you!" Because he'd heard the cook talking.

Alonso, however, was not prepared for his brother's retort. Through clenched teeth, Hector cried out, "At least my father's not dead!" Because he too had heard the cook talking.

"What?" Alonso asked, stilling his fists, not understanding.

Hector sat up, pushing Alonso off him with ease. "Your father died on a ship to America. To some horrible place called California." Then he added, like it was the greatest insult, "He was a *poet.*"

Just like at Alonso's birth, light began radiating off of him in every direction, like he was the sun.

Alonso watched Hector, blinded by light, scurry away, a seven-foot insect.

Was it true? Was Diego de Falla not his father? Was Hector de Falla not his brother? Alonso got brighter and brighter thinking of it.

He found his mother in the garden.

"Tell me about my real father," Alonso said.

"I've been waiting for this moment," Sofia replied, her hand shading her eyes from her son's glare. She told Alonso everything. How a poet named Esteban had ridden into town two months before her wedding to Diego (a wedding planned by her father that she'd protested body and soul). She'd taken one look at Esteban and he her, and she'd climbed onto his horse, and they'd galloped off, following the moon across the sky, talking all night, their spirits twining so that nothing, not even death, could untwine them. "Sometimes you live more in a week than you do

in a lifetime," she said to Alonso, showing him the sapphire-and-diamond ring on her hand. "From Esteban when he asked me to marry him. His one valuable possession."

Their secret plan, she told Alonso, had been to stow away on a ship to California, but Diego, her betrothed, found out and showed up at the harbor with a posse. The men had ripped her from Esteban's arms, from her destiny. She lifted the sleeves of her dress to reveal fingerprints around her arms. "This is how hard Esteban held on to me. The marks have never gone away. He's still holding on to me, Alonso." Then she told her son how they forced Esteban on the ship, how he cried her name until they gagged him, how they tied him up in the cargo hold, where he slowly starved. A vicious death. She said she would have died too, of grief, had she not found out she was pregnant with Esteban's baby, with Alonso.

Me, Alonso thought. This is who I am.

Alonso and his mother didn't notice time passing, but as she spoke of Esteban, of how proud he would be of Alonso, *his son,* Alonso's chest filled out. He grew inches taller, a faint mustache appeared over his lip, his voice deepened, and when they finally stopped talking, three years had passed, and Alonso was sixteen years old.

They walked hand in hand out of the garden. "Can you see him over there?" his mother said, and for the first time, Alonso saw his father's ghost. "Sometimes I find poems from him," his mother told him.

"What do they say?" Alonso asked, not quite used to his deeper voice.

"They're blank," she replied. "But that doesn't mean they don't speak to me."

Alonso left his mother and walked down the hill to reunite with Sebastian. The two teenagers with their strange new bodies and with their older, more complicated minds and hearts took each other in. Alonso noted his best friend's broad chest, his height, and deep voice, his same smile like the moon was shining through it. When they hugged, Alonso reached his hand into Sebastian's pocket and removed a rock, then he did the same with the other pocket, so the boys rose into the air, not a few inches, but high in the sky so they could have some privacy.

They did not come down for weeks. And when they did, everything would change for them.

"I'm going to ask Esperanza to the dance," Sebastian said as they walked home one evening from a café. These words punched Alonso squarely in the chest, but he didn't let on. He was used to the disproportionate physical reactions he had to Sebastian's words. Sometimes, like in this moment, Sebastian would say something innocuous like taking Esperanza to a dance, and Alonso would be certain he'd taken his last breath. "I've never kissed a girl, Alonso," Sebastian said. "You have."

"Never?" Alonso asked, unsure where this conversation was headed.

"I was thinking you could teach me."

Alonso's heart stopped beating. "To kiss?" he asked. Truly, Alonso wasn't sure if he was still alive in this moment.

"Oh," muttered Sebastian, confusing Alonso's expression for one of displeasure when it was one of rapture. "I don't know why I said that, Alonso, how could I have said that? I—" Then Sebastian gave up on words and took off running in the direction of his house, leaving Alonso alone in the moonlit road.

Alonso's legs were trembling so that he couldn't take a step.

He sat down in the middle of the road and tried to slow his breathing, his racing heart. He'd known happiness but never like this. He was going to kiss Sebastian! He imagined and imagined exactly how he was going to do it, and what might happen after and after and after that. Then in a giddy fit, he jumped to his feet and ran on wobbly legs as fast as he could muster to the stone house. His blood sang as he climbed up the trellis and into the open window of Sebastian's room. He sat on Sebastian's bed. His friend was already asleep, rocks on his chest to keep him bed-bound. Anticipation consumed Alonso, until he couldn't stand it, couldn't stand it, couldn't stand it.

He gently touched Sebastian's mouth with his index finger and Sebastian's eyes fluttered open.

"I want to teach you to kiss," Alonso said. Moonlight flooded the room, splashing over them. They stared at each other. Alonso could hear both their hearts beating.

Sebastian's face was serious. "Okay."

When their lips met, the world began to swing and sway.

The bright beautiful world.

Sebastian never asked Esperanza to the dance.

After that, the boys couldn't keep their hands off each other. They began sneaking into the back room at the bakery, running into the woods, pulling each other behind doors. Even though it occurred to them to hide their new romance, it never occurred to either of them that it was wrong, for nothing had ever felt so right in all their lives. It made Alonso feel holy, holier than he ever had in church. Or anywhere.

Their passion grew and grew.

One day, unable to keep it in another moment, Alonso declared his love to Sebastian by using the corresponding colors, for Alonso had a sense-blending condition where words came in colors. It was discovered by his tutor. For him, *I love you* was: *purple green blue*. That became their secret code.

If people bear the trauma of their ancestors, doesn't it follow they also bear their rhapsodies? If there is generational pain passed down, mustn't there also be generational joy? If there are family curses that drop through time, mustn't there also be family blessings that do the same?

MILES

Miles still had no interest in returning to the hospital—Felix was an off-ramp from misery and he was taking it. He made Miles feel like there was more air in the air. The two wandered through the woods, sunlight tumbling through trees and across the forest floor, while Sandro tromped beside them.

He's so . . . excited about everything, isn't he, Sandro?

He's a rapturous human being.

Yeah! Rapturous.

He's probably an ecstatic like lots of us dogs. It's our dominant religion.

Dogs have religion?

Sure.

Yes, Miles had been certain Felix was straight at first, but now, he again found himself wondering if Sandro had been correct. Because why had he looked at Miles so intensely—hungrily?—in the hospital lobby and a couple other times since? Why did he say Miles glowed? (*So* weird, no matter what Sandro said.) Why did he follow Miles? And wasn't breaking Miles out of the truck the cock-block of the century? And that hand-on-shoulder moment? What was that? Plus, his expressive (insane) personal style. Miles had attributed it to his being a city boy or to his big banging personality, but what did Miles know. Maybe this was how gay guys dressed in Denver? His gaydar was clearly unreliable (nonexistent) from living in the boonies his whole life.

And there was something else he'd begun to notice about Felix. His face would dim sometimes, as if he'd ducked into The Gloom Room or was caught in some impossible thicket in his own mind. Miles sensed secrets, stories. "So, you came all the way here from Denver to work at my mom's restaurant?" he asked again, hoping for more of an answer this time than *kind of.*

Felix was absently slapping branches with the palm of his hand as he passed them. "Only found out about your mom's restaurant on the drive down," he said. "The girl I got a ride with mentioned aphrodisiacal soufflés and a Michelin Star. That was it. I was sold." Felix turned his head and Miles could see himself distorted in the mirrors of the sunglasses. "I guess Chef Finn and your mom had been looking for a sauté cook for a while, so I lucked out."

Miles's stomach took a dive. Felix had taken Nico's spot on the line? Nico of the walk-in kiss. This had to mean something!

As the trail narrowed and Felix took the lead, Miles began to recast the walk-in kiss with Felix in the starring role. It was Felix now slipping out of the shadows, all six feet seven and a half inches of him, pressing into Miles from behind, his hand on Miles's shoulder. "Can I join you in there?" he'd whisper into Miles's ear, lighting the world on fire. Then the thud of the walk-in door closing them in. Felix pushing Miles against the cold wall, one hand against Miles's chest, the other reaching for Miles's belt, unfastening it, popping the button of Miles's jeans with ease. Miles closed his eyes.

TMI, Miles! I'm here too.

Sorry.

Sandro took off into the trees. Miles's heart was pounding. Boy did he have to slow his roll. "No college?" he asked, attempting to retrieve himself from the fever dream he was now caught in.

"Took a gap year to get experience," Felix said, unaware how furiously their mouths had just pressed together in Miles's mind, how passion had licked through their blood like flames. "Worked at this criminally hip Denver restaurant called It as a sauté. Took me months to convince my parents—both professors—that I should skip college and go to culinary school."

"How'd you convince them?"

"A twelve-course French-Mexican menu—my real grandfather was Mexican and my in-my-dreams grandfather is Auguste Escoffier, so that's my thing. Me and a buddy took ages to create the menu."

A buddy? What kind of buddy? Miles wondered. Instead, he asked, "So you're going to chef school?"

"I was supposed to start in two weeks," Felix said. "Changed my mind. Don't ask."

Miles was about to do just that when a rabbit hopped onto the trail in front of them. Felix stopped and then so did Miles. Felix looked at the bunny, then back at Miles. "You're seeing this too?"

Miles laughed.

"Dude!" Felix whispered more loudly than his normal speaking voice. "Look at its ears! I didn't know rabbits had such long dopey ears, did you?" Even with the sunglasses, it was clear Felix's face was being over-run by *rapture*. Sandro was right on, that's exactly what it was. "Didn't know rabbits were so, I don't know, so . . . rabbit-y." He flapped his arms like a kid. "I have to hold it." All at once, Felix lunged, taking a flying leap that ended in a colossal belly flop on the trail, a beached whale, his huge hands holding a pile of air as the rabbit bolted into the brush. Miles had to use all his self-control not to collapse into hysterics at the absurd sight. He held his hand over his mouth, bit his cheek, and tried to still his body that was beginning to shake. He knew he should say, "You okay?" but he didn't trust himself to speak. Then when Felix rolled onto his back, saying, "Thought I had the little fucker," and cracked up himself, Miles took his hand from his mouth, snorted, and dissolved into laughter. The image of Felix's leap, his spectacular flop, combined with the guy laughing so freely, so unreservedly, at himself, was sweeping Miles up, taking him somewhere he'd never been before, somewhere without self-consciousness or uneasiness, erasing for him a world where there were hospitals and comas and Dumpsters and monster-suits and visits from deans, until he was bent over, gasping for breath and Felix was saying "Can't believe I didn't catch *the little bunny!*" while pounding the ground with his hand, neither of them able to jump off the carousel of glee, so around and around they went.

When they finally calmed, Miles was certain all the blood in his body had been replaced with a new batch, certain if he looked in the mirror, he wouldn't see himself peering back. He'd never laughed like that before. Did people do this all the time? It had felt so much more intimate than what he'd only moments before conjured with him and Felix in the walk-in refrigerator.

A door in Miles's chest—one he hadn't realized was there—swung open.

He knew he should get back to the hospital, but he didn't want to. Ever.

Sandro loped over to them, then after assessing the situation, curled into a ball in a crevice between Felix's arm and his chest. Felix's hair was splayed on the ground like a demented halo, dotted with pine needles. He smiled warmly at Miles. "Join us?"

Um. Yes! Miles thought, but he didn't know what Felix meant. Was this something straight guys did? Laid on the ground together in the woods? How would he know? Would it turn into more? He wanted more. He wanted their bodies to melt together like hot wax. But how close should he plant himself? Stiffly, Miles sat about a foot away, dropped onto his back. Then lay there like a board. A most rigid board. He didn't dare look at Felix, at how close their hands might be, their beating hearts. He remained utterly immobile, until a few minutes later, when he noticed that the earth felt like it was holding him. He breathed in the scent of pine and river, dug his hands in the loamy soil, and soon, his muscles relaxed for the first time in . . . well, maybe ever, and the two of them remained like that, side by side, under the trees, in a companionable silence, staring through branches at blue sky and scattered meringue-like clouds. He hadn't ever done this before with anyone either. It felt secret, private, *intimate,* just like the laughing spree had. He hadn't known there were all these incidental intimacies you could have with someone.

Miles realized he'd somehow walked out of his life and into a new one, a much better one. He closed his eyes, felt like he and Felix were lying in the air together. He wanted to write in his pad: *There's a secret world within this one. A wind has blown us there.* A few moments later, he heard Felix say, "I used to think about playing beer pong and how to adjust pound cake recipes for altitude so they didn't fall, now all I think about is beauty."

Whoa. Left field. And excellent surprise ending to the sentence. A poem. Way better than Miles's lines. He wanted to write it in his pocket pad too. Or eat it. If only he could ingest certain words, certain sentences. It also felt like an admission of some kind, but Miles wasn't sure of what. He didn't know how to respond. Finally, he said, "Did something happen?"

Felix didn't answer. Miles lifted onto his elbows to steal a glance. Felix's glasses were off, his eyes were closed, his brow was furrowed, his expression troubled. Felix definitely divided his time between rapture and despair, and Miles wanted to know why.

He lay back down, keyed into the sound of the river in the distance and tried not to obsess on Felix for a second. He let his mind drift and drift it did back to Wynton, to Madison's revelation. "My brother's always been a prick," Miles said to the sky, feeling as though he were telling the whole forest, along with Felix, his thoughts. "But I did this really messed-up thing recently and just found out he took the blame. He went to jail for me."

"Jail?" Felix said. "What'd you do? Dude. Jail, for real? Whoa. The big house." He paused. "The joint."

Miles smiled. This again. "The clink," he offered.

"Prison."

"Slammer."

"Pokey."

"Penitentiary."

"Correctional facility."

Miles thought for a second. "Hoosegow," he said proudly, lifting his head to see Felix's reaction.

Felix's arms were now crossed behind his head like he was lying on a bed. His eyes were open. One side of his mouth had curled up in an ironic way, showcasing the dimple. It was unbearable how into Felix's face Miles was becoming, all its private language. He wanted to watch him sleep. He wanted to watch him breathe. "Hoosegow. Nice one, Mr. Fall," Felix said. "Take a bow and now tell me what you did that was jail-worthy. Need to know before I head any deeper into the woods with you." He'd called Miles Mr. Fall! No one had ever called him that. The only nickname he'd ever been given—Perfect—he despised.

Miles lifted up onto his elbows again. "I don't even remember doing it, but I guess I drove into this statue and totaled my mom's truck. I don't even drink or do drugs or drive for that matter—only have a permit—but I did that night. I must've been in a black-out state, I don't know. I can't believe I'm telling you all this. I usually don't talk to anyone." Miles shook his head. "Dude, you're like the only one who knows I'm gay." The confession made Miles's stomach flutter.

"Really?" Felix looked perplexed. Was he surprised that Miles wasn't out? Or that Felix was the only one who knew Miles was gay? Or that he didn't have anyone to talk to? Probably all of the above. Felix most likely hadn't gathered yet that Miles was more goat than human.

"What's weird is, there was this other person recently," Miles told him. "A girl. Her name was Cassidy. I could really talk to her too. She just showed up the other day in this cool vintage orange truck. My sister thinks she's an angel and can save Wynton's life. She looks like one."

"Need to tell you something. A few things actually," Felix said, sitting up. He frowned, like he might be trying to figure out which of the things he was going to say first. "Okay. The reason I'm here is I ran away." Whoa. He ran away? From what? Why? Miles sat up too. He was at attention. Felix continued. "Left a note for my parents and little brother, Elvis. Left my phone so they couldn't reach me. Emailed the Culinary Academy, told them I wouldn't be coming for the summer session." He sighed. "Broke up with my girlfriend by text, like a total dick." Miles tried not to let the disappointment at this girlfriend-news register on his face. Felix must've caught it anyway, because he quickly said, "No. I mean, I'm bi, I see guys too." Holy hell! Miles now tried not to pop to his feet and do a jig. Instead, he coughed, looked at Sandro, who started barking and circling them.

Told you he was queer like us!

You were right!

Say it again!

You were right!

Felix stared at his hands, bit his bottom lip. "I'm not available though. Like I'm really, *really* unavailable . . ."

Ugh. Ugh. Ugh. "Oh okay, don't worry, I'm not . . ." Miles said, again trying to hide the disappointment. He could feel blood rushing to his face.

"Oh, yeah, I know you aren't," Felix replied, "of course not. I didn't mean . . ."

"No, I know, I didn't think you did."

"Okay, all good." Felix's cheeks were as flushed as Miles's must be.

"All good."

"How about I dig a hole and we both jump in?" Felix said, and they each laughed a nervous, awkward laugh, nothing like the train of hilarity they'd boarded together earlier. Felix went on. "But what I *really* need to tell you is that when I left, I got a ride from Denver to this tiny Northern California town, about five hours away from here, spent a week at these hippie hot springs up there, then got a ride down to Paradise Springs with this girl named Cassidy in a super cool vintage orange truck."

Miles's heart blew open. He jumped to his feet. "Cassidy? No way!" The relief, the joy, caught him off guard. "You know her? Wow, dude. So that means you know where she lives?"

"I know the town she lives in," he told Miles. "I know where she works too."

"Holy shit!" Miles said. "Let's go. This is amazing! We'll bring her back. She'll wake my brother from his coma!" Miles was entirely aware he sounded like Dizzy. "Yes, I know, dude. I sound wacko," Miles said. "But we have to find her! Got a driver's license?"

Two hours later, Felix, Miles, and Sandro were heading north on Hidden Highway on a mission to find Cassidy. Miles was in a flurry of hope, half-bewitched even, like if he spoke to the trees hugging the winding road outside the window, they might speak back.

CASSIDY

Starting where I left off, Wynton. Had to slip out for some coffee to keep going. I really do feel like Scheherazade. Felix, the guy I drove down here with, was right on about that. He's a trip. I can't wait for you to meet him.

Okay. Mom and I are creeping south on Hidden Highway, headed straight for the second betrayal. And our meeting—yours and mine, Wynton—in the meadow when we were thirteen. I can't wait for you to enter this story! Hidden Highway is the kind of road we usually avoid in Sadie, but it's the only way to get to Paradise Springs (your town!) from the north. The only way to find Dave Caputo, who, if you recall, weeks before, left us in the night after asking my mother to marry him and me to be his daughter. Do you know him? So strange it was Dave who led me to you.

Anyway, Paradise Springs is in a valley we've never noticed on the map before—which we find odd. I'm in the passenger seat of Sadie, scraping a peanut butter jar clean with a spoon. We've never been this low on supplies before. We've never been so skinny either. Weeks with Mom in The Silent World and me waiting for the sound of Dave's rig returning have taken a toll. All I want is to see him again, to become a fearsome threesome like he promised, to be his sous chef, to have him carry me around again like a surfboard. I've never known a want so unwieldy, so consuming. Nor have I known a fear like the one gnawing into my every thought, making my heart beat too fast: It can't be Mom and me alone anymore.

"We'll get there in a month at this speed," I say. We're going ten miles per hour now instead of the thousand mph of earlier.

"So be it."

I unbuckle myself and go in back, sit at the table.

"Aren't you going to tell me to fasten my seat belt?" I yell up at her.

She doesn't answer, making my rebellion useless. I strap myself in, then ball my hands into fists, letting my ragged dirty nails dig into my palms until I see blood.

I think a terrible thing: Maybe Dave will take me and be my father even if he doesn't want to marry Mom anymore.

I'm holding my breath for as long as I can, in rounds. On the fifteenth go, I hear Mom say in a strange voice, "Cassidy, come up here, please."

Mom's pulled Sadie into an overlook on the side of the road, so I walk easily to the driver's seat to peer over her head out the panoramic front windows. We're on a ridge over a valley blanketed in vineyards. There are hot-air balloons in bright colors floating at different heights. It's gorgeous, but I know that's not what has swept my mother's face clean of heartbreak and disappointment, of *acedia*—her spiritual torpor. She points and says, "See there?"

In the distance, surrounded by vineyards and orchards and redwood forest is a hillside town that, from this angle, looks like it's floating in the air. There's a river wending and winding back and forth through it all the way to the valley beneath.

"The Town," I whisper, not quite believing my eyes.

"Maybe," she says, taking my hand. "I think so. Finally."

We descend a mountain road full of hairpin turns. I buckle into the passenger seat. The river begins cutting into the highway so we're crossing rickety wooden bridges and catching glimpses of waterfalls cascading down rock walls. We've rolled down the windows and Sadie is full of the sound of rushing water, the scents of eucalyptus and pine, and a sweet thick aroma we can't place until we hit the valley floor and trucks loaded with grapes begin joining us and the road turns more and more purple as we go, as clusters of grapes fall off trucks and are smashed by tires, including ours.

"I think I'm getting drunk from the air," Mom says. "Must be harvest time."

"It's the purple brick road," I say.

As we ride along with the grape trucks, I notice orchards of avocados, olives, figs. I see a brown horse and a black one side by side, their coats gleaming in the sun. Fields of cows chomping on grass. One vineyard we pass has a band of fiddlers playing while women in flowery dresses like we wear stomp grapes in a giant wooden vat.

Their laughter sounds like bells as we pass.

I pinch my arm to make sure I'm awake.

"No wonder it's called paradise," Mom says.

It occurs to me we've crossed over into one of her *In the Time of Forever* stories. I'm imagining how we're going to live happily ever after with Dave in his dream shack in The Town, this place we've been looking for almost my entire life. "Makes me wish I could paint," Mom says, awe in her voice, her eyes fixed to the window. "I told you we'd feel it in our bones, didn't I?" I nod. She was right. I feel it in every bone. "I just don't understand how we missed this whole valley," she says. "Why didn't I notice it on the map before?"

"Maybe it wasn't on the map before."

She looks at me and smiles. I know she's thinking those words could've come out of her mouth and I'm feeling it too, our sameness again, but it doesn't feel treacherous like it has lately.

"You're my best friend," I say to my mother.

I see her eyes fill up. "And you're mine." I can't believe all the bad things I've felt and thought about Mom in the last few minutes and weeks (and years!) and how they've all been erased by the feeling I have now as we approach The Town together in Sadie Mae.

We take the turn-off for Paradise Springs holding hands, full of hope.

CASSIDY

And then Sadie Mae is parked outside of Robert D. Caputo's house, the address we found at the library in Jackson. If Dave's wreck of a rig weren't in the driveway, it would be inconceivable that this is where he lives. The house is palatial, a glass castle in the middle of the forest. There's a wildflower garden on one side of the house and a spectacular succulent garden on the other. Rhododendron bushes line the path to the door and trellises with waterfalls of peach polka roses are all over. There's a grand redwood tree in the center of the yard.

Edenic, adj. *of or resembling the Garden of Eden.*

"Oh boy," Mom says. "Didn't expect this. Expected more of a hippie shack."

"He built it," I say. "With his hands."

"But he said it was a shack. I'm sure he did. Didn't he?" I nod. She goes on. "You know what I'd like to do? I'd like to ram Sadie right into that wall of windows." I look at Mom, shocked. "What? I would." A sudden storm of mirth breaks over us and we both start to laugh. "We could roll Sadie through this gorgeous flower garden on the way." This breaks us up further, giggling and chortling in the front seat, feeling like criminals. "C'mon," she says. "Let's do this. Let's find my betrothed."

"My stepfather-to-be."

We open Sadie's doors, full of bluster, full of some righteous purpose, a feeling that he's ours, that this is our dream, our town, finally. A feeling of Mama Bear, Papa Bear, and Baby Bear living happily ever after in The Town. It's like we've forgotten that he left us without a word, that he lied to us, tricked us. I have anyway. Mom takes my hand, and we walk down the pristine path to the house.

(Wynton, I need to remind you here that we haven't bathed or brushed our hair or teeth or eaten much for weeks. We smell rank and are skeleton-thin and our skin's a mosaic of dirt and residual despair. Our sundresses look like used napkins. Our hair could nest flocks of birds, or more likely, bats. Mom's bare feet are so black, they leave prints on the light gray slate path as we approach the glass mansion. We must look like creepy ragamuffin dream-creatures, out of time and out of place, but we don't realize this yet.)

We knock on the door, our spirits high and hopeful as they've ever been.

Then there he is: Dave.

Because the house is mostly glass, we see him coming toward us down the long white hallway.

Let's stop time here: Because this is a moment of tumbling joy for me. It's the marooned me seeing a plane circling over my desert island, me waving my hands, me climbing up a rope rescue ladder out of a terrible untenable predicament. Delightful Dave the Dazzling Dick Weasel, I'm thinking repeatedly in this moment. I don't care how different he looks, that he's cut his hair and shaved his face, that he's so *clean,* so scrubbed of the elements, of us and our time together. I don't care that there's this new thing about him I can't identify because it's so unfamiliar to me, but I will tell you now what it is: wealth. Dave looks rich. He has that casual, easy air of entitlement, of safety, of predictability. He's wearing loose-fitting jeans with a long-sleeved crew-neck burgundy shirt that hugs his chest. He glides gracefully through the glass house, like water.

A geyser of hope goes off in me.

"Dave!" I exclaim under my breath, jumping in place, thinking: Papa Bear! Unable not to think it.

Because we've stopped time, I can tell you for this split second, before tick turns to tock, before my heart breaks, betrayed for the second time, before my mother's and my world spirals even further into uncharted despair, I see that the first expression that crosses Dave's face on seeing us through the glass wall of the glass house is an expression of relief, of joy, of Thank God. That, for him, for this split second anyway, we are his rescuers too.

Mom grabs my hand and I squeeze hers.

But time doesn't stop when we want it to—Wynton, you know this more than anyone—when we need it to; it plows ahead like a runaway train with no conductor, and so there's a woman, also gliding gracefully down the hallway behind Dave, a woman with long brown hair in a loose ponytail, an elegant pretty woman in flowing black pants and a tank top, a woman, I imagine, with a closet full of shoes and a kitchen with marble counters who goes to Pilates class and maybe runs a company from a corner office. A woman I've only ever encountered on celluloid. She's followed by two children, a dark-haired girl who seems to be four or five years younger than me with bright eyes carrying a stuffed purple hippo and an even younger boy, a wild-haired, milk-mustached kid who looks more like the Dave I remember than the Dave before us. He's holding his sister's hand. Dave's frozen in place now; any remnant of relief or joy on his face has been replaced by terror. Except for Dave's expression, this family, *Dave's family, clearly*, looks like a stock photo trapped in a frame behind glass.

And we're about to shatter that glass.

Dave jumps into action. We watch like it's a movie as he tries to herd his wife and kids away from the door, shooing them back down the long white hallway, but it's too late because the woman's opened the door and the kids have bottlenecked at her feet. There's fury in her eyes.

Mom's making a choking noise beside me. I sneak a glance at her, see she's swaying like her knees may be buckling. She grabs my shoulder and nearly pushes me to the ground. My heart's never beat like this. I wonder if my chest's going to burst.

Dave's saying, "I got this, Joanne." Joanne. Joanne's face has gone so pale, it seems like it would be cold to the touch. I can smell her perfume. She doesn't wear jasmine oil like we do, but the kind of perfume people spray at us when we go to department stores to buy Mom's lacy underwear.

Joanne turns to Dave and says, "This is them?" Says it like we're roadkill that's been brought to her doorstep. But he's told her about us? Mom pulls me to her as if to shield me from the woman's disdain. The woman flips a dismissive hand at us, her nail polish like little fires at the end of her long fingers. "This is them?" she repeats, staring at us, something even more disdainful than disdain in her voice now: amusement.

Her nose twitches then, and that's when I realize we smell.

Mom, Dave, and I all seem to have lost the ability to speak. My stomach growls and everyone looks at me. This seems to plug Dave's faulty cable in. "Yes," he says to Joanne. "This is Marigold and Cassidy." Then to Mom, he says, "Marigold, I'm so sorry. This is my family."

"Are they homeless people?" asks the little girl.

"They stink," says the boy, breaking into a fit of giggles.

I gasp. I'm a dirty smelly girl with a dirty smelly mother.

"They need a bath," the boy says.

"Who are you?" the girl asks me.

"They're no one," says Joanne, gathering her kids up in her long arms. "A client of Daddy's."

The girl says, "But why's she crying?" It takes me a moment to realize she means me. I wish my mother would say something.

The woman squats and says to the kids, "Who's hungry for popovers? Last one to the kitchen's a rotten egg." And then she says to Dave, "Get rid of them."

Get rid of them.

I can't breathe.

They're no one.

How is everyone else breathing? Before the woman follows her children to the kitchen for popovers (my stomach's hollow with hunger) she meets my mother's eyes and says, "Leave my family alone. Leave this town and never come back."

My mother, who still hasn't spoken, nods at the woman. "I didn't know," she whispers.

Something passes between the two of them, something I don't understand, but whatever it is, it wipes the meanness off the woman's face for an instant, and underneath it there's a sadness to match our own. She nods at my mother, then turns and sweeps down the hallway without looking back.

Dave exhales, shuts the front door with them on the inside and the three of us on the outside. Dave and I are both looking at Mom. She seems to be vanishing like a blue morpho butterfly that looks as if it's appearing and disappearing when it flies away from you. I'm scared she's already in The Silent World, but a new standing-up version.

Except then, like the blue morpho, she blazes back to us. "How could you do that to me?" Her face is rigid, her eyes hard, and her voice is about as fierce as I've ever heard it. "How could you do that to Cassidy?" Her eyes are lasers shooting into him. Not a blue morpho but an assassin bug now that injects its poison right into the body of its prey. "You're a monster. A lying, hypocritical monster in Gucci jeans in a fucking literal glass house." She's spitting the words at him. "You disgust me."

He reaches for her arm, but she pulls it away from him. "Do not touch me."

"You're right. I am a monster," he says, his voice reeling with emotion. "I'm so sorry, Marigold. There's no excuse for what I did. I got so carried away. I wanted to be that guy, not this guy." He gestures toward the glass palace. That's when I notice Dave's shrinking, as if vertebrae are being pulled out of his spine one at a time. "I never left that master's program, never drove away from everything expected of me. I wanted to but didn't have the guts. I'm a coward. I've never done anything not expected of me. Until you. My father, he just—I am an architect with my dad's firm in San Francisco. This is his house. We summer here." He points to the rig. "Mushrooming's a hobby."

"Like us," Mom says. "We were this summer's hobby."

Does Mom notice that Dave's shrinking?

He closes his eyes. "No. I fell in love with you, Marigold. I didn't know what to do." His voice has matched hers with its fierceness. "I fell in love with both of you. Felt more at home in your life than I ever have in mine. I couldn't resist. You were living my dream, and I lost my mind. I was so happy up there with you two." He's like a devil's flower mantis, I think, an insect that pretends to be the flower it sits on. He pretended to be like us but he's not like us. "So many times, I wanted to tell you but . . ." He meets Mom's eyes. His voice breaks when he says, "I just didn't want to ruin it. I felt like . . . like I was inside the sun for that month. Or it was inside me. I've never had that feeling before, not even close." He runs his hands through his hair, messing it up so it's more like I remember. "I meant everything, every word I said to you. I left that morning to come here and tell Joanne I was leaving her. And I did. I told her everything. She asked me to stay for a few days. To give them that. That I owed them that. A few days turned into a few more. Then a few more. And it all started to feel like some dream. Like some make-believe—"

Mom's crying now and it's too much. Dave's words are too much. Dave's shrinking is too much. It's all too much. "I don't want to be the make-believe part!" I shout. "I hate make-believe. I've *always* hated make-believe. I hate you both!" Then I'm running away from the big glass house, from my make-believe mother in her make-believe world, from Dave, who's someone else's father, not mine. I'm running from weeks of living in the cramped sour squalor of my mother's psychic vacancy. I'm running from this feeling of existential unworthiness I never knew was in me until: *This is them?* Until: *They stink.* Until: *They're no one. Get rid of them.* Running from the cleanliness and order and predictability of these rich people who make me feel like—no—make me see what I am: a dirty smelly girl who belongs to a dirty smelly mother who is not right in the head and never will be.

CASSIDY

I run and run, faster than a tiger beetle, the fastest insect alive who goes blind with its own velocity. I run straight into the woods, not looking around to see if they're following me, not wanting to be found, not like last time I was lost in the woods. I break out onto a fire road and run down it, down, down, down, until I come to a meadow. I catapult myself into the tall grass, out of breath, heart cartwheeling in my chest. It's just me in the hissing knee-length grass, so I pound my feet on the ground and rip up handfuls of the long, scratchy grass and throw them and rip up more. Then I scream, just let it out, a shuddering, piercing primal scream, until I fall down on my back, enraged, disappointed, heartbroken.

This, Wynton, if it's not obvious, is the second betrayal.

That's when I hear something and sit up. Across the meadow, there's a skinny boy playing the violin. Except he's not actually playing it, he's attacking the strings with a bow making awful screechy sounds.

You. Finally, you, Wynton.

You have blond stringy hair, and your long face is pale as the moon. You're looking at me with equal parts alarm and curiosity. I duck down. Had you been there this whole time hidden in the grass? Did you see my fit, hear me scream? You must have. You're dressed like the kids at RV camps who scare me the most. Cool raggedy boys with metal in their faces, clunky black boots, ripped T-shirts with band names on them, boys who vape and try to get people to buy them beer. Boys, my mother calls punks, who look like they live at the end of the world, who make me so curious though I don't dare go near them for fear of the mean things they may say to me.

Peeking through reeds, I watch you, listen to the chaos you're making with the instrument. A cat being tortured to death, I think. Or worse. I half expect the trees to run off, the sky to rip open. When I can't take it anymore, I cover my ears with my hands and then you're standing above me, blocking the sun. "Go away," I say. (Remember? Sorry.)

"I will if you want me to." Your voice is surprisingly gentle. "I was trying to play what I saw, what I heard."

I lift my head. "What you saw?" And then I get it. "You mean me? Before?"

You nod.

"Oh." My neck prickles. You were trying to play *me*? Your eyes are too intense, too full of questions. "Don't look at me." (Sorry again, Wynton.)

"Okay." You turn the other way, wait for a second, then lift your violin to your shoulder and start to play again, but this time it's different. This time it makes the skin at the back of my neck start to tingle, then the skin on my arms, until I'm tingling everywhere. As you promised, you're not looking at me, but I can see you, your furrowed brow, your mouth contorted in concentration, your eyes opening and then closing. Your upper body sways like a tree in wind. I'm surprised colors aren't coming out of the violin, bright swirling paint filling the air, that's how beautiful the sound you're making is now, like you're walking through the house that is me flipping up shades, letting light in.

(Thank you, Wynton. I can't tell you how many times I've relived this moment.)

I find I can't stay sitting while I listen to you, so I lower myself onto my back and look up at the blue sky. It seems so much bluer with you playing. You note my change of position with a smile, but then it's gone. Your face is so serious when you play. A lady bug lands on my hand, then a butterfly and a yellow jacket. When I turn my head, I see there are daisies and dahlias all over this field, hidden in the long grass. How did

I miss the flowers before? More yellow jackets have come too. Now a hummingbird. And another.

I close my eyes and when I open them, I notice tears on your cheeks.

"Can I look at you now?" you say quietly.

"Yes," I say, and we lock eyes. You have a crooked smile that completely transforms your face and unsettles something in my stomach. I point to your cheeks, still wet with tears.

Your face reddens. "Can't help it," you say. "It happens when I play. Usually, I wear sunglasses, but I didn't think anyone would be here."

You point to my cheeks, also still wet.

I shake my head. There's no way I can tell you why I'm crying.

"Since you're sad, I mean, I can play sitting down if you want to sit back-to-back."

(Isn't this the weirdest offer you made, Wynton? To this day, it might be the sweetest thing a stranger has ever suggested to me. Or anyone. I thought about it all the time in years to come, but that day I'm still so socially naive that I think maybe this is something kids do.)

I shrug and you take it as a yes, which is what it indeed was, and then your boniness is against mine, your bigger back against my smaller one, a perfect backrest. I'm glad you can't see the smile overtaking my face. I cover it up with my hand. If you notice that I smell, you don't say anything, and anyway, you kind of smell yourself, sweaty and sharp, so I'm thinking we cancel each other out. Soon, you're playing again, and I can feel it, literally. I feel your spine undulate, your elbow touch and flee my rib cage, your head swiveling, and the music's replacing the darkness in me, note by colorful note, like I'm part of the song. Tears well up again, but not because I'm sad, because it's just you and me on earth now, back-to-back, hidden like two daisies in long grass.

I don't notice the moment you stop playing either, just zone back in sometime later to find that the grass is hissing, the dahlias are swaying, and the yellow jackets are buzzing. I hear birds chirping, a river rushing, and kids shouting, maybe in a playground nearby. I don't usually focus on sounds like this. It's like being a cricket and hearing through my legs and arms. "I think I'm hearing through your ears," I say.

"Yeah? Do you hear a trumpet playing in the distance?"

I listen for a trumpet. "No."

I feel his head nodding. "No one does."

"Who is it?"

He doesn't answer for so long I think he's not going to tell me but then he says, "It's my dad playing."

"Where is he?"

"I don't know. Somewhere. He left."

"You always hear it?"

"Not always." You sigh. "Sometimes I think it's in my head but other times I'm sure it isn't. I heard it today though for sure. That's why I'm here. I was following it, trying to get closer to the sound. I was lying in the grass listening to it when I heard you scream."

"You still hear it? Like right now."

There's a long silence in which I guess you're listening. "No. Not anymore."

Your hair's tickling my neck. Is mine tickling yours, I wonder. I lean back, into you, wanting my hair to tickle your neck. Then you lean back too. I smile again, then say, "My dad's dead, he drowned, and my mom is somewhere else even when she's right there." I feel you nod like you understand and I'm loving talking to someone my own age. It's like sharing magic beans, only I didn't know I had any magic beans to share. I'm surprised I don't feel shy with you. I add, "I thought I was going to have a stepdad, but he ran away from us."

This crushes me all over again. You must know I'm crying, because my whole body's shaking you with the misery of the last few weeks, with what's to come without Dave. You gently press your back into mine and when I settle back down, you say, "Your voice doesn't seem to come out of you. If I just heard it, I'd think it came out of a tree, some old oak, like that one maybe." He points to a hunched-over oak tree covered in long stringy cob-webby Spanish moss. "If I had it, I'd talk all the time nonstop all day long."

"Really?" This is the coolest thing anyone's ever said about my voice, which I know sounds like a boy's.

"Totally."

My stomach growls loud and we both laugh.

"Stomach in B flat. Mine's in C sharp usually." My stomach's in B flat! "Are you hungry?" you ask me.

"I'm so hungry."

"Want a soufflé? Saturday is chocolate. My mother makes them at her café."

I spin around. "Your mother's Bernadette?" You nod, turning too, and then we're both cross-legged, knees touching. *Knees touching.* It's different being able to see each other and have our bodies touching, and shyness overtakes me. I get a close-up look at your face then, the pale skin, the full froggy lips, the freckles like a map of lonely stars, eyes the electric blue of a dragonfly wing. You could play the alien in a sci-fi movie. (You still could, Wynton, and I mean this as the highest compliment.) I could not imagine you on a horse. I could imagine you onstage though. Or on a magic carpet. You push hair out of your eyes, and it immediately falls right back into them. I get up the nerve to say, "Do people really fall in love if they eat the soufflés?"

Your smile makes your whole face go topsy-turvy. It's the gap between your front teeth, I decide. (For years I'll think about your grin: the way it makes someone want to say yes before even hearing the question.)

"They only make you fall in love if you're already old," you say.

"I don't believe you," I say, looking at my hands to avoid your smile, your eyes, our touching knees.

"I guess if I'm wrong and I'm the first person you see after you eat one, then it'll be me you love." I raise my head, shocked by your words. "For the rest of your life."

"Shut up," I say, but can't stop smiling no matter how hard I bite my lip. I have a revelation then that you're flirting with me! No one's ever flirted with me before. Obviously. I've never even talked to a boy before. It's making me feel so much better. I didn't know that flirting was so fun. I want to thank you for flirting with me but even I know that'd be weird. I'm pretty sure my mother's going to find me, but if she doesn't, I'm thinking I'll just ask you if I can go home with you and maybe live secretly in your closet, subsisting on soufflés and violin music until I'm old enough to go to college. "Do you live in a house?" I ask.

He nods. "A big white one. Super old. My little sister Dizzy sees ghosts looking in the windows all the time." Your eyes soften when you say the name Dizzy. "Do you?"

"See ghosts?" I ask. "No."

"I meant live in a house?"

Before I can answer, you stand and reach for my hand to pull me up like we're friends. Then we're walking together in the meadow grass like we're friends and then stomping down the riverbank like we're friends and then single-filing it on a path through redwood trees like we're friends and then we're at the town square and we are friends. "I live in an RV named Sadie Mae," I say, remembering your question. On the walk, you talked about your father and how he's a musician too and how he smelled like leaves.

"An RV? All the time?" you say, confused. "So, you live nowhere?" You stop walking. "Or everywhere, right? That is so cool. Like a band."

I want to ask more about your father who smelled like leaves and the little sister who sees ghosts but now you can't stop asking questions about full-timing and boondocking and saying "That's so cool!" to all my answers.

I have no idea my life is cool.

The square in The Town has massive redwoods in the middle of it and a waterfall bombing down a slope on one side that feeds into a creek that cuts the plaza in half. The square's full of teenagers on skateboards, parents with strollers, people throwing balls and dogs catching them. There's a woman playing guitar by a large statue of a man in a cowboy hat.

The Town.

I feel it in my bones.

And permeating the air is a chocolate smell. "Is that . . ."

You nod. "Yeah. I've already had three today. Dizzy'll sneak us some out the back." You trill the violin. "That's how I get her attention."

I notice the others then, Soufflé Zombies, you call them, walking like we are, transfixed by the aroma, all of us headed to the same café where the line runs down the long block, the same café Dave told me about, where someone named Bernadette—your mother!—is inside making soufflés. You're biting your lip, looking nervous, as you say, "Maybe my dad wanted me to meet you and that's why his music made me go to that meadow today. I've never been there before."

This thrills me. "Like destiny?" I say, loving this idea, like we were predetermined to sit back-to-back in that meadow.

Or maybe it isn't destiny after all, I think, because there's Sadie Mae parked on the far corner of the square. She's dirt-spattered and faded, a pale sun-bleached yellow, not the old bright canary yellow she used to be. And the flower decals, once so bouncy and joyful, are now indistinguishable blobs peeling off to varying degrees. Our sagging sad-sack home on wheels. I spot my mother talking to two police officers. Dave's nowhere in sight. She's showing them her digital camera. I notice her bony shoulders, her frail frame on which a rag of a yellow dress hangs. She's still barefoot.

What picture is she showing them of me? Of us? Is it one of the photographs of us in the air? I feel a pain in my chest so sharp, my breath catches. A part of me wants to duck my head, to continue walking like a Soufflé Zombie with the exciting boy that is you, but even as I'm thinking that, without a word, I break away from you and run toward my mother as fast as I'd run away from her earlier, caring only about her, wanting only to be with her. Always. Because she, and she alone, is my destiny. No one else.

"Cassidy!" she cries, seeing me hurtling toward her, and then we're locked in each other's arms. "We're going to be okay," she tells me. "I promise. I really promise. We don't need him or anyone else. We have each other."

"I'm sorry I ran—"

"Don't be sorry for anything. You're perfect. This is all my fault. I never should've fallen for such a weakling. Let's go. Let's get the hell away from this godforsaken town we've spent the last seven years looking for." She says this with a smile. "Okay?"

I return the smile. "Okay."

"Remember when we studied irony?"

"Yes," I say. "The opposite outcome from the expected one."

"Exactly. This is irony. I never want to come back here. Let's cross The Town off the map."

I turn around, wanting to say goodbye to you, thinking I'll never see you again, Wynton. I scan the square but you're nowhere. I open the passenger door and get in Sadie Mae and I'm asking Mom if we can get a soufflé before we go, thinking I could at least leave a goodbye note for you with your mother, but Mom wants nothing more to do with The Town. She's talking about whether to hit the diner we saw one town over when I notice a little girl with a whole lot of frizzy hair loping toward us with a cardboard tray and what looks like a steaming cupcake on it. At her heels is a barking black dog. I unstrap my seat belt, knowing immediately who she is because her grin is a toothless, nuttier version of yours.

"Here." She's panting and out of breath from running. "My brother said to give you this." The girl pops her head in Sadie as I step onto the street. "Oh! Do you live back there? Oh my God!" she cries. "You're so lucky. Your house goes places."

Mom looks up from the map and smiles at the girl whose name I remember is Dizzy.

"Do you really see ghosts?" I ask her.

She glances down at her purple sparkly sneakers. The chocolate smell has engulfed me, making it difficult to wait for her answer, to not grab the soufflé out of her hand. She raises her eyes, studying me as if to see if she can trust me. "There's the kissing male ghosts and their lady friend with the flowers growing out of her head. They're mute. I mean, they move their mouths sometimes, but no sound comes out."

This all seems like it's lifted from one of my mother's stories. I decide then I'll write it down the moment I get back in Sadie. "Really?" I say, at a loss for words, but liking this odd girl.

She nods, her face serious as stone, and I have the thought that we should switch places, that this little girl who sees ghosts would make a better daughter for my mother, and what I would give for a white house in The Town, a brother with a violin, a mother who makes soufflés all day, a house that doesn't go places.

The dog's sniffing at my legs. I squat down to pet it. "I don't like dogs," Dizzy says.

"I love them," I say, wrapping my arms around the dog's neck. "If I were in charge, all dogs would live forever. Especially you."

I love you too! I hear, to my utter surprise. Right in my head. *I love you so much! I want to live forever! You smell so good! Like flowers!*

"Do dogs talk here? Like directly into your head?" I ask without thinking.

Her face crinkles like what I've said is preposterous, which of course it is, but it's not like she hasn't just been going on about mute ghosts. "Dogs can't talk," she says, like I'm dim-witted.

"I know that," I say. "But . . ." Okay, get a grip, I think, convincing myself it's the chocolate aroma combined with my month-long hunger, and I can't test it anyway because the dog's already out of my arms and scampering after a dark-haired boy on a skateboard who's whistling at him, the hand-in-mouth kind of whistle Dave taught me. The boy is beautiful, like a prince in a storybook. Him, I think, I could imagine on a horse. Maybe a purple one.

I stand up. "Thank you," I say to Dizzy, taking the soufflé and turning around to climb back into Sadie.

"Wait, take a bite first," she says.

"Now?"

"Yes, while I watch. Wynton said so."

"Is that your brother's name?"

She nods. "We're all named after our missing father's favorite jazz trumpeters, only they're all men and Black and we're white and I'm a girl and Wynton's the only one who plays an instrument. Dizzy Gillespie is me. He's already dead. Wynton Marsalis is Wynton. And the boy who just skated by that you couldn't stop staring at is Miles, named after Miles Davis."

"I wasn't staring at him."

"Everyone stares at him."

"Where did your other brother go? Wynton?"

She shrugs and hands me the plastic spoon. When our hands touch, we both look up and our eyes hold for a moment and before I know what I'm doing, I touch her nose—*bop*—and she laughs, surprised, then does it back.

I sink the spoon into the soufflé. Steam escapes and, with it, a chocolate scent so rich and thick, it makes me want to gulp at the air. The texture surprises me, light but spongy, an edible cloud. It melts the moment it finds my tongue, filling my whole mouth, my whole existence, with delight. I take another bite and I'm unable to keep the moan in. I feel my eyes rolling back in my head.

Violin music shatters the gustatory (adj. *concerned with tasting*) ambrosial (adj. *of or relating to food of the gods*) swoon I'm in, and I glance upward at the source of the music.

On the roof of a nearby building is you. I see the lopsided smile even from this distance and think about one of my mother's stories: *In a faraway land in the time of forever, there was a lightning bolt who became a boy.* Your bow's pointed right at my heart, and I know exactly what you're thinking as you hold my gaze because I am too. Since you're the first person I laid eyes on after biting into the soufflé: *I will love you for the rest of my life.*

"You will marry me now," you yell. "Right?"

"I will," I yell as I get back in Sadie, soufflé in hand, happiness unbreaking my broken heart for a moment. You smile and start playing again. I listen to your music as we drive away.

But I hear it for years. I still hear it. I hear it right this minute as I sit by your side in this hospital room, Wynton.

But back then, Mom and I pass the soufflé back and forth—I notice she looks in the mirror after her first bite, but I don't mention to her what that might mean—as we follow the signs for Hidden Highway, aiming to get as far away as possible from The Town.

If I'm being honest, Wynton, I couldn't get you out of my head for, well, forever, after that day. I haven't been able to forget you. Silly, I know, to think about this marriage proposal because we were just kids. But then the other night, you asked me again! Did I dream that moment with you in the moonlight? Our dance? I've never experienced anything like it in my life. Have you?

This is a secret: Every time I get close to a guy, I hear your violin so loud and clear, I turn around half expecting you to be standing behind me.

Each and every time.

WYNTON

You played an instrument that could do anything, make a rose bloom in someone's hand, a bomb detonate in their heart, a staircase reach all the way to a star.

But most important: Violin music was the map that would lead to your father.

If you got good enough. If your fingers flew faster over the strings, with more dexterity, more precision.

If he read about you in the paper or online. If he saw you on YouTube, heard you on the radio.

Every time you played, no matter how large the crowd, there was only one man in a cowboy hat sitting in the audience.

Every tonal pattern you found alone in your room was an imaginary conversation with him, an imaginary reunion with him.

But music was the map that led to you too.

You thought in music, breathed in music, dreamed in music, loved in music, fought in music, lived in music.

No, that's not right.

You heard that Miles Davis once pointed to a woman stumbling in the street and said to his band, "Play that."

You played that. All the thats and thises. And you played them hard.

Music was never a noun for you, it was always a verb. The only verb. You music-ed through the days and nights of your life.

But you will never again, and it is excruciating.

You thought you needed a body to feel pain. You don't.

You're free of it only when Cassidy's beside you smelling like a garden, telling her story in that magnificent cave of a voice.

It's like she's introducing you to every last bit of her.

Are stories prayers? Invitations? Mirrors? Storms?

Or maybe they're homes.

Listening to her, sitting with her back-to-back in the meadow, swaying with her in your arms in the moonlight, are the only times you've ever felt like yourself without a violin and bow in your hands.

MILES

They were headed north on Hidden Highway on the way to the hot springs where Cassidy worked when Sandro started in. The dog was rolled up contentedly on the floor between Felix, who was driving, and Miles, who was trying not to fall in love with the driver. Sandro's snout rested on his paw, his eyes focused upward on Miles.

I, for one, love a big dog, if you know what I mean, Miles.

Stop. He says he's unavailable. But, fuck yeah, definitely know what you mean.

Sascrotch, human dude, Sascrotch.

Don't be bigdickulous, doggo.

Oh no, it's the cockapocalypse.

Cockasaurus-rex.

The baloney pony that broke the dick-ter-scale.

Miles tried not to laugh, gently pressing his foot on Sandro's paw in commiseration, grateful there was a creature on earth with whom he could be this goofy. Miles had been pretty surprised when Felix said he was bi, then hella thrilled—everything in his mind had started gleaming—until the *unavailable* comment. But still, the ease and comfort with which he'd told Miles had made an impression, even if Felix didn't like Miles that way, which was fine, totally fine.

Ugh, *so* not fine.

But Felix seemed to want to be friends with Miles and Miles *really* wanted to be friends with Felix. He'd just have to avoid eye contact, and eye-mouth contact, eye-abs contact, eye-ass contact. Except then it occurred to Miles that maybe Felix had a crush on Cassidy and that was why he so readily agreed to the road trip, saying only that he needed to be back for his shift at the restaurant in a few days, assuming it reopened. Was that why he was unavailable?

Who knew?

Still, Miles was stoked that he was going to be in this cab barely a foot away from Felix for five straight hours. He'd just have to get used to Felix releasing the wheel to rapturously exclaim and point at clouds, redwoods, the dilapidated bridges poised high above the river, as the three of them traversed switchback after switchback up the first of many mountains on this drive to Whispering River, the northern town where Cassidy lived.

So, when you're bi, you're equally into girls as you are boys? Or are some people more like 80/20? I don't get it.

No clue. We dogs aren't label-fluent, human dude. Why don't you ask him?

You ask him.

It had taken them a while to get on the road. First Miles had needed to go to the Bell Ranch next door to see if Rory Bell, who for as long as Miles could remember referred to Miles as Sandro's co-parent, would let him kidnap the dog for a day or two. He knew he'd never hear the end of it from Sandro if he didn't take him on the pilgrimage to find Cassidy. He told Rory Bell this, and it made the solitary, windswept ranch woman, a decade or two older than his mother, laugh before she agreed to part with the pooch.

After that, he and Felix had trekked to Miles's place through the pinot noir vineyard to pick up the camper truck. They'd popped grapes into their mouths as they walked along in the golden light, letting the warm tart juice sluice down their throats, an experience Miles had regularly, but sent Felix into paroxysms of joy, which ended in him borrowing Miles's pocket pad to write a recipe for a stilton and sour grape galette. A dish, Miles was pretty sure, his mom had already invented, but he kept that to himself as Felix said ten thousand times, "It's going to be *epic,* man!"

At Miles's house, Felix had walked around like he was in a museum, peering into photos, immediately discerning the faint blue, green, and purple stripes that were visible under the faded white paint of Miles's bedroom walls. (No matter how many times they painted his room, those three colors still broke through—it was bizarre.) For Miles, being home made him feel ill. When glancing into Wynton's room, eyeing the piles of sheet music, the stand, the amps, his knees buckled, and he staggered into the bathroom to wait out a tsunami of nausea and dread.

Did he really believe Cassidy would be able to wake Wynton from the coma?

As irrational as it might be, he kind of did.

Next, they'd gone to the youth hostel where Felix was staying until he found a roommate situation, maybe with other staff from The Blue Spoonful. Felix hadn't yet had to share the room at the hostel, which was good because it was barely big enough for the bunk bed and desk that filled it. One small cob-webbed window looked out onto the creek. Miles noted that Felix had traveled the thousand miles from Colorado with a *Larousse,* the French cooking encyclopedia, as well as *Tu Casa Mi Casa* by Enrique Olvera, plus a memoir by Auguste Escoffier (Felix's dream-grandfather, he'd said), all books that sat on Miles's mother's kitchen bookshelf as well. No wonder Felix had been hired.

Miles leaned against the desk, eyed the bunk bed, and oh hello perfect scenario: *Sorry, you two are going to have to share a room, only one left.* "Tell me about the trip down with Cassidy," Miles said to distract himself from the X-rated moment beginning to live-stream in his head. The porn marathon in the hospital supply closet had surely warped him. Though now he wanted those other things with Felix too: laughing fits, looking at the sky in silence, all the talking. He watched as Felix threw some wildly inappropriate things for a road trip into a backpack: a purple-and-yellow-striped shirt, another pair of striped pants, a checkered vest, more suspenders (!), a fedora (!!), other wingtip shoes (!!!).

"We had fun. Super cool girl," Felix said.

"And?"

Felix lowered his sunglasses. Damn those eyes. "And she's writing about you guys."

"Wait, what? Who guys?"

"Your family." He twirled his mustache with his thumb and index finger, a habit that was growing on Miles. Way too much about Felix was growing on Miles. "For college, a paper or whatever. On California history, the wine families of Paradise Springs or something, and she's focusing on yours but from way back, starting with the European settlers. The de Fallas. She said she might even write a novella."

"Wait, de Fallas? That's us? Really? A novella? About Alonso and Maria? Why didn't she tell me? Why didn't you tell me? And we weren't always Falls?" Is this why Felix had said in the hospital lobby he'd just heard *all* about Alonso Fall? From Cassidy? Must be.

"I *am* telling you. Not just Alonso and Maria. There was Alonso's evil brother Hector and his even more evil father, um, what was his name, oh yeah Diego and his mother who was in love with some penniless poet whose amazing scent attached itself to her after he died. And there's a family curse. Oh and Sebastian, of course. And everyone who came after them. Like you, dude. She told the stories in this weird way, kind of like fairy tales. Though I nodded off after a while, so I think I missed a bunch."

Miles was baffled. "I don't know what you're talking about. Seriously, I don't know who any of those people are. Who are they?" Miles sat down on the bottom bunk, which was covered in an itchy green army blanket. "So that's why she was parked on the property that day? She was doing research?" He remembered there'd been several books on California history on the seat. He'd read some of one at the swimming hole. When he raised his head to say so, he saw that Felix was unbuttoning his shirt. Oh no, no, no, because: *Oh yes.* Hot AF Hercules is right. Felix was half-turned toward the window so Miles could watch uninhibitedly as Felix undid the last button and slipped the shirt off one shoulder, then the other. He was broad, lean, and tan, and, oh man, with his dark loose tousled hair hanging past his shoulders, not to mention the misty eyes, he really and truly was Jericho Blane. A giant bisexual Jericho Blane! A Jericho Blane who liked guys. He'd won the effing lottery.

Except he was unavailable.

Deep breath.

Just leave the sunglasses on, Miles psychically begged, and as if in response, Felix turned, lifted them, and smiled at Miles. "Whatever should I wear?" he said, throwing up his arms. Ack—and that was adorable. How would he survive a road trip?

He'd been attracted to unavailable, i.e., straight, guys at school, of course, like every one of them, or most of them anyway, his body reacting to, reveling in the smallest most carefree gestures: Conner Foley reaching up to grab his hat in his locker before practice, Hot AP English Teacher Mr. Gelman tilting his head exposing his neck while he read aloud to the class, Rhett Clemens kicking his legs up on his desk like he owned the air. He collected these moments, then relived them safely, constantly, privately when he ran, when he read, when he showered, when he breathed.

Felix pulled a plain black T-shirt out of his duffel, and thank the Lord, his sunglasses fell back down over his eyes like a curtain. "These are prescription by the way," he said to Miles, pointing to the shades. "Have eye issues. Don't want you to think I'm pretentious."

Miles nodded. He didn't think Felix was pretentious. He thought he was amazing and unlike anyone he'd ever met—funny, smart, weird, warm, mysterious and open at the same time, hot. Miles sighed, studied his hands in detail trying to unthink the Hot AF Hercules part. He was unavailable. Maybe he broke up with the girlfriend because he now had a boyfriend? Or another girlfriend? Maybe Cassidy? Or maybe he wanted to be single? Or wasn't attracted to Miles? Maybe it had turned him off that

Miles had gotten in the truck with Rod? Maybe he thought Miles was, well, a slut. He wanted to blurt out that he'd never done anything like that before. He also wanted to ask him a thousand questions about why he ran away and what it was like to be bisexual and if he laughed like that and laid on forest floors with everyone. Maybe he made everyone feel the same fizzy way he was making Miles feel?

"Hey, you okay?" Felix's hand landed in the crevice between Miles's shoulder and neck. His *neck*. Miles lifted his head. "You must be really worried about your brother," Felix said to him, having misinterpreted Miles's expression.

Felix's shades were up again and his absolutely gorgeous eyes—let's just be honest—were gazing down at Miles sympathetically, causing the blood in Miles's body to switch directions. Was it normal for an unavailable guy to touch an available guy like this? This felt even less platonic than the shoulder tap in the woods. Further, Felix hadn't yet put on the T-shirt, and the tan swath of his stomach was so close, Miles could place the flat of his palm on it, so close he could run his finger under the waistband of Felix's pants, so close he could see the Calvin Klein logo on the briefs. Miles breathed in, smelled sweat. The light in the room was shadowy, the music of the river loud and secluding. They were alone. So alone. This was so much better than being in a restaurant walk-in refrigerator. Miles closed his eyes.

Fuck it. He let himself imagine it all: How he'd stand and place his palms on Felix's stomach, his chest, his arms, feeling the heat of Felix's skin under his hands. He imagined Felix's arms closing around him, the two of them falling back onto the lower bunk, their bodies entwining. Their hands traveling. His heart began to race.

This wasn't good.

Miles flicked Felix's fingers off his shoulder more brusquely than he'd intended, saw Felix's expression become confused, then embarrassed. "I need some air," Miles said, pivoting as he stood so Felix couldn't see his erection.

Miles got himself marginally sorted through a talk with Sandro, who was waiting outside (no pets in the hostel), and when he returned to the room, Felix was dressed and sitting on the bed, his bag packed. He looked upset.

"Sorry, I . . ." Miles didn't know how to finish the sentence. *Sorry I was in a porn video before while you were just being a nice guy.*

Felix shook his head. "No way. Don't apologize. I can't imagine what you're going through with your brother. Even if—"

"That's the thing," Miles said, relieved the misunderstanding was still in play. "It's just hard to suddenly stop hating someone, you know? I mean, how do you do that?"

"You try to understand them," Felix said matter-of-factly.

"Why are you like so, I don't know, mature or something?"

"Therapy."

This shut Miles up.

They'd gone to the hospital then. His mother had seemed happy that Miles and Felix, her new sauté cook, had somehow become friends, but hadn't understood the point of their driving a third of the state in search of Cassidy. Ultimately, she gave in, telling Miles that it was probably healthy for him to take a break from the hospital. She said she'd text if there was news. Then she'd held Miles's face in her hands and said quietly so only he could hear, "I always seem to forget I need to worry about you too. I'm so sorry, honey."

And now here they were at dusk, Miles, Felix, and Sandro cruising up Hidden Highway, heading deep into the forest, past Jeremiah Falls, where he and Cassidy had floated in the pool on their backs like two water lilies. The sun was setting over the mountain, filling the road with ghostly shapes as the river raced by them, like time.

Miles,

The sun walks beside you, always has, like it did your father.

When you were little, people would line up behind me wherever we were to catch a glimpse of you in the stroller. "Can stop the heart, beauty like his," they'd say.

Beauty inside and out.

But now I know there is a lost boy hiding inside my boy, and it is him I need to find.

Mom

MILES

Only the sky remained lit by the unseen sun as Miles and Felix continued north, Felix yakking about Whispering River, the town where Cassidy lived. Each had a hand out his window as if trying to capture the dusk in his palm.

"It's a picture-perfect western town in the redwoods," Felix said. "Couldn't believe it when I got there—I'd never been to California before. Looked like there could be a shootout any minute with actual cowboys. We're talking saloon doors that swing, except in the saloon you can get your aura read. No shit. There's a sign outside. And the hot springs where Cassidy works! It's this total New Age-y spot called The Community and everyone there talks about astrology"—he cocks an eyebrow—"with absolutely no irony whatsoever and says things like 'Turn your face to the sun, and all the shadows will fall behind you.' And 'We're all just walking each other home, man.'"

Miles was laughing.

"Yeah, mental," Felix went on. "But it was cool too. Like visiting another planet where the inhabitants are all just really . . . open. Oh, and I need to warn you. No one wears any clothes at The Community, like at all, except in the restaurant."

"Dude!"

Miles pet Sandro, who was in a happy ball on the seat between them.

We're going to see him naked, Sandro! All of him!

It's cockapalooza!

"Yeah, I had some mind-expanding experiences at The Community, let's leave it at that. What goes on at the hot springs stays at the hot springs."

"No, let's not leave it at that." Miles said, leaning over to see the gas gauge from the passenger seat. He'd been so distracted by Felix and Felix and Felix, he'd forgotten to check. "Oh no."

Felix followed Miles's gaze. "Do not tell me we're out of gas, Mr. Fall."

"Okay."

"No, nope, no way," Felix said. "This is not happening. You've got to be kidding. Haven't you ever seen a horror movie? They all begin like this. Two guys in a truck on an empty highway in the middle of nowhere USA."

"Other kinds of movies too," Miles did not say. "We're good," he did say, pointing to the gauge. "One bar left. Just take it out of gear when we're going downhill. We'll make it to the next town." Miles tried to ignore the stranded-with-Felix porn event now rolling in his head.

Sandro looked up at him. *You planned this, didn't you, Miles? Seems convenient. Actually, didn't it happen in that romance novel you read all time? Live Forever Now?*

Shut up. I don't read romance novels.

"The next town?" Felix said. "This isn't the kind of highway that has towns . . . Uh-oh. *Oh no.*"

"What?"

"It just occurred to me that *you're* the ax murderer! Of course you are!"

Miles laughed again. "Except you could take me in a heartbeat, ax or no ax."

Take you? He could take you?

Seriously, shut up, Sandro. And it was a yacht that ran out of gas at sea and Jericho Blane and Samantha Brooksweather floated around and drank champagne and had sex for a week.

Um. The state rests its case, Your Honor.

Miles said, "We'll find a farm or ranch that'll give us some fuel, and that'll get us to a gas station."

Felix took off his shades and put them on the dash. "That's a goddamn legit plan. This is how you local yokels roll!" He twirled his mustache with his fingers. "Okay listen, Miles, if we get ambushed by a gang of thieves or something and we need to communicate, we'll speak backwards, okay?"

"Yako."

"Doog."

Felix reached in his back pocket and pulled out a case with another pair of glasses in it, which he put on. Black nerd ones, kind of like Dizzy's. "Better for night," he said. Miles noted that he looked extremely intellectual in the new specs. It made him, ugh, even cuter.

You need a cold shower.

Thank you, Captain Obvious.

I like when you call me Captain.

They rode on through the shadowy twilight, the smell of river brine in the air. Miles wanted to ask Felix about the stories Cassidy had told him, but more than that, he quite suddenly wanted to tell Felix every single thing that had ever happened to him, like from birth onward. In great detail.

"Can I tell you something?" Miles said.

"I think I can fit you in between appointments."

Miles took a breath. To keep some semblance of cool, he'd stick to his immediate predicament and avoid the trials and tribulations, of let's say, preschool. "So, I quit everything recently. Track. Math club. Academic Decathlon. Volunteering. I stopped going to school. Stopped everything."

"Why?"

"Don't know. I mean, that thing happened with my brother—the black-out night I told you about—but it wasn't just that. It's like everything in me powered down or something." Miles couldn't stop himself from spilling, like when he was with Cassidy.

"My friend Eddie deals with depression," Felix said.

"I mean, is anyone actually happy?" Miles shifted in his seat, put a knee on the dash.

"Yeah, they are," Felix said. "I am. Like right now, this instant, hangin' with you, running out of gas on this spooky-ass road, I'm happy AF."

Miles looked out the passenger-side window. He didn't want Felix to see the smile stampeding across his face.

"Maybe quitting everything is your version of leaving home in the middle of the night," Felix said after a bit. "Maybe we were meant to meet because we're both on the verge . . ."

"On the verge of what?"

"No clue, dude," Felix said, and they laughed.

Miles was well aware his brother was in a coma and they were on an urgent mission to find Cassidy, but a very big part of him never wanted to get out of this truck. He had a weird feeling, like he was becoming more himself with every moment that passed.

"Your friend Eddie. How does he say it is, being depressed?"

"He says it's like being trapped in cement that's slowly drying."

"Whoa."

"Meds helped him. It's weird. We're tight, like *really* tight, and I never even knew he was depressed until it got bad this one time and he couldn't get out of bed. He kept it from everyone." Felix's face filled with emotion. "He's *the* funniest guy on the planet."

Miles wanted to stick his head straight into the ground.

You're jealous, Miles.

No, I'm not. Shut up.

You shut up. Stop telling me to shut up.

"Hey, what's the most amazing thing you've ever seen?" Felix said, changing the subject. Miles was grateful to not have to hear more rave reviews of Eddie, who was probably the buddy who helped Felix make the twelve-course meal for his parents. Miles was not loving how Felix's face softened when he said the guy's name.

"Like a concert?" Miles asked.

"No, like anything." Felix looked expectantly at Miles and Miles had the urge to say, "Those eyes of yours, dude."

Beauty's face is the most amazing thing these canine eyes have seen.

Sheesh, cornball.

Takes one to know one.

Miles gave Felix's question some thought. "You know the waterfall on the town square?" he said. "When the sun hits it sometimes, it looks like light's tumbling down, not water. I can't handle it. It's so cool. What about you?"

"Faces," Felix said without hesitation.

"Like all of them?"

"Pretty much," Felix replied. Miles loved this answer. Then Felix turned to him. "You have such a cool face. Noticed in the hospital lobby. Probably why I followed you." Miles's stomach dropped to his feet, then plowed further down all the way to the middle of the earth. And now, one side of Felix's mouth was curving into the deadly half-smile. He added, "Definitely why I followed you, actually."

Um, did he just say that, or did I imagine it?

Sorry, I wasn't paying attention.

Sandro!

He said it, Romeo.

This was possibly the happiest moment of Miles's life. He didn't trust himself to say anything—he might hoot or whoop—so he just secretly grinned, once again, like an idiot, out the window. Miles thought about the moment Felix touched his neck at the hostel. Was it possible it hadn't been just a friendly gesture? Could it be that Felix had also wanted something to happen? Had it been a pass? Felix had been half-undressed after all. Oh man. And what about when he said "Join us?" in the woods. Maybe nothing had happened then because Miles had been busy impersonating a board! The nervous buzzing resumed its residence in Miles's stomach. Ditto a whole new level of effervescence in his chest.

Miles snuck a glance at Felix. His gaze was on the road, his expression neutral, like nothing had changed. Okay. Miles had to chill. Maybe the guy often followed people whose faces he thought were cool. And barged into and pulled them out of their internet hookups.

A few months later, after Miles settled down, he asked, "So why'd you run away, then?"

"Next question," Felix said.

This was most definitely a No Trespassing Zone and Miles suspected the reason Felix wandered into despair sometimes.

Why do you think he ran away, Sandro?

Maybe he didn't like the kibble.

"What's your favorite thing to cook?" Miles asked.

"A tie between Julia Child's beef bourguignon and pozole rojo—my grandfather's recipe. I'm old-school."

"I'm a vegetarian."

He grinned. "I have an epic veggie version of pozole rojo. Epic. Like you won't be able to handle how good it is."

He's going to cook for you!

I know!

"Were you close with your grandfather?"

Felix shook his head. "Never met him, but he had a recipe box full of killer Mexican recipes that I'm now in possession of. My parents are useless in a kitchen. It was Eddie who got me into cooking. He's an incredible cook. His parents own this soul food restaurant and I used to hang out in that kitchen after school. Felt like home." The smile now on Felix's face from talking about Eddie was impossible for Miles to endure. "Eddie's way into pizza. There's this white pizza he makes with grilled calamari, fontina, and garlic aioli. A-mazing. He's on the US Pizza Team."

Um, WTF is the US Pizza Team?

Eddie, Eddie, Eddie, said Sandro.

Right? Is this why he's unavailable? Must be.

Miles wanted to change the subject from the champion pizza-maker so was glad when Felix said, "Your dad's a winemaker, right?"

Miles nodded, then after a pause, said, "My dad disappeared twelve years ago. Just drove off one night."

"And never came back?" Felix asked.

"Nope. Just split. My mother hired a detective and everything. She makes him a plate of food every night at the restaurant. You'll see it under the heat lamp late night. Leaves a glass of wine out too. The closing bartender always eats it. It's a thing. Really weird and sad. She's never even dated anyone else. She says my dad's her beshert."

Felix's face turned into a question mark.

"Yiddish for *soul mate*," Miles explained. "*Beshert* means both destiny and your destiny in a person." Miles really couldn't seem to shut his trap. "Sometimes I wonder if he left because he was depressed . . ." He was about to add *like me* when he realized at this moment, he was anything but. Maybe he'd just been lonely his whole life. He hadn't known other people could remix your DNA until Cassidy and Felix. He hadn't known all this time he was a door waiting to be opened.

Felix glanced at Miles, his expression intense, like he wanted to tell him something. Or possibly *do* something? Did he have this feeling in his chest too? Did he want to say *Is something going on here*? Did he too want to reach across the seat and grab a swath of Miles's T-shirt in his hand and pull Miles to him, so they could kiss, in one furious go, for two straight weeks, the average lifetime kissing allotment Dizzy had told Miles a person usually uses?

I want him to tell me why he's unavailable.

Ask him, human dude.

I can't.

Why?

I don't know.

They drove on in silence until Miles couldn't take it anymore and said, "So what's it like? Do you like girls more than guys or guys more? I don't get it."

Felix kept his eyes on the road. "I went out with girls until my junior year. But that summer, there was this guy on the line at the restaurant where I did prep—older, gay, out, almost tall as me—and he'd look at me and smile way over everyone else's heads and I'd lose my shit. I nearly chopped off all my fingers watching him pull the rib-eyes out of the wood oven."

Does he only like fellow giants? Miles wondered. "Don't tell me. You hooked up in the walk-in?"

Felix laughed. "Right. Like the hot springs, what goes on in the walk-in stays in the walk-in. But I kind of knew before that even, kept wondering if I was gay or straight, kept going back and forth, totally confused, neither felt right, then I realized there's that B. In LGBTQ, you know? And I started reading about it and was like *this is me*. Went to my senior prom with a guy."

"Bold. The walk-in guy?"

"No. Avi Patel. Not really bold. At my high school, everyone wanted to be queer. Kind of annoying really." His expression changed. "The thing I wasn't expecting was how some gay guys don't take me seriously, but whatever. You'd think the more queer people the better, right?"

Did gay people not take bisexual people seriously? "I totally take you seriously, Felix," Miles said. Felix's smile was big as the outdoors and sincere. Miles went on. "But so can't imagine a school like yours. No one's out at mine. Not one person. It's tiny. And Catholic." He wanted to shriek: *Why did you run away? Why are you unavailable?!* And while he was at it: *I'm so into you!*

"How about you?" Felix asked. "How'd you figure it all out?"

"First crush. Second-grade teacher, Mr. Quittner."

"You don't want to come out?" Felix asked with curiosity, not judgment. "Suppose it's different out here in the sticks."

"Maybe," Miles said. "I'm not ashamed or anything. It's not that. At least I don't think it is." He looked out the window. "It's like I don't want the world ruining it."

"I get that."

"And not a fan of being in a club. Kind of feel like I just want everyone off my island." Was this even true? He certainly wanted Felix on his island. And to be in a club with him. Oh, he didn't know anything about anything. He was such a rough draft, had no idea what parts of himself would make it, what crap parts would be cut. He was aware too that deep down he feared people would kick *him* off the island if they really knew him, like his siblings had. So much safer being in a monster suit all these years, being Perfect Miles. Except here he was being himself and he wasn't being booted at all. And it had been like this with Cassidy too.

"I'm the opposite," Felix said. "I want to be part of *everything*. Like when I read a book or see a movie, I move in." It was taking everything in Miles to not fall in love on the spot at this. Felix's gaze fell to the gas gauge. "We're not passing any farms, are we?"

"Nope." Running out of gas was not good, *obviously,* but hanging with Felix under the stars until someone drove by—jackpot. "So, want to tell me about—what'd you say we were? The de Fallas?"

Felix smiled at Miles. "Totally. You *so* need to hear more about your great-grandfather." His eyes were dancing behind the specs. "Because, dude, according to Cassidy, Sebastian—the guy I mentioned before—was Alonso Fall's *boyfriend*."

"His boyfriend?" Wait, what? Miles's mind began to tip. Alonso Fall, the statue on the square that he drove into and beheaded, was gay? "But what about Maria? They were married." That he did know.

"It was an arrangement thing. Though they did do it once, hence your existence. Want me to tell—"

"Hell yeah. Start at the beginning."

Felix was at the beginning of Alonso Fall's story, in what Cassidy had apparently called *"the time of forever,"* where Alonso was born into the world like a sun bolt, when the truck started to sputter. Felix pulled to the side of the road, killed the engine.

They sat for a moment, not talking. Through the open windows, Miles could hear mockingbirds, the whoosh of a nearby creek. The sky above them was already drunk with stars. "Is it a long story, Felix? Because we got time," Miles said as a knocking sound filled the cab. Felix and Miles whipped around as Sandro leaped to all fours and barked at the back glass.

"Are we there?" a muffled voice said. Behind the window to the flatbed was Dizzy's sleepy face. "Can't believe I crashed out like that."

Alonso Fall's Terrible Choice Between His Heart or His Destiny

(As Told to Felix by Cassidy on the Drive to Paradise Springs, a Week Earlier)

In the time of forever, Alonso and Sebastian's joy wouldn't last.

It was the year they turned eighteen. Alonso's tutoring was long finished. The house was more than two-thirds eaten by his "brother" Hector. Moreover, the rot in his "father" Diego's soul wafted from his mouth with an ever-insistent pungency that shriveled grapes, ruining vintage after vintage of wine.

The de Fallas were in a dire financial way, and looming poverty made Diego and Hector even more cruel to Alonso than ever. For amusement, Hector— so large now, his head kept busting through the ceiling—would sit on Alonso, threatening to pluck off his limbs, while Diego laughed, breathing his noxious fumes into Alonso's face until he passed out. Once, Hector ambushed Alonso in town, stuffed him into a suitcase, and threw it (Alonso!) onto the back

of a carriage headed far into the mountains. It had taken Alonso a week to find his way home.

Alonso's spirit was in constant jeopardy, not to mention his person.

He dreamed only of running away with Sebastian.

Then one evening, Sofia and Diego sat him down at the half-eaten dining room table. "I have an announcement," Diego said, his breath curdling the air. Alonso and his mother held their noses to survive the next sentence. "Maria Guerrero's father has a way to restore our fortune, but he won't help us unless you and Maria marry at the next Harvest Feast."

Now Alonso was being choked by Diego's words too. "I won't," he said. "I cannot marry a girl I do not love."

"Why not?" said Diego.

Maria Guerrero was Sebastian and Alonso's dearest friend. She had fire-red hair, liked to run through the de Falla vineyards, and was the daughter of the village's most renowned gambler, schemer, and bon vivant. She wore trousers under her dresses and straddled her horse like a boy, before galloping into the hills or to the sea, all on her own. She had a rough rowdy laugh and was constantly losing her shoes, so walked scandalously barefoot through the streets.

"But I thought you loved her, Alonso," Sofia said. "I was certain of it, the way you walk into things and can't get your buttons right or eat a bite of food. All signs of love. I've seen the way you, Sebastian, and Maria run through the vineyard. The way you, Sebastian, and Maria stay at the café so late into the night. The way you, Sebastian . . ." Something seemed to dawn on his mother. A flush rose in her cheeks. She swallowed.

"No," Alonso said to his mother. "I do not love Maria." They shared a look, and he thought maybe she understood.

"Well, you will marry her," Diego said resolutely, oblivious of the silent words that had been exchanged between mother and son. "That is that."

But that wasn't that. Alonso went to Maria and told her they couldn't marry because he loved someone else. Her red hair was loose and unbrushed. She was in trousers with no dress over it. "I don't want to marry at all," she told Alonso. "I've never wanted to marry. I want to—well, I don't know what I want to do, but I don't want to marry." Her expression was serious. "My father wants your father's land and your father needs my father's vines."

"What vines?"

"My father spent our entire savings on twelve of them. He says wine from these grapes will make the angels sing. But his plan depends on your father's land."

When Alonso returned home, all had changed. His mother, realizing her mistake, convinced Diego to arrange the marriage between Maria and Hector instead. By then, Hector was twenty feet tall and four feet wide from his diet of house, and more recently, vineyard, so when he heard of his betrothal to Maria, his celebratory dance caused most of the village to crumble.

Maria, on hearing the news, burst through the door of the still-standing bakery where Alonso was working behind the counter with Sebastian. She threw herself at his feet, begged him to marry her so she didn't have to marry Hector, who had already eaten the front door off her house so he could enter at will. She divulged that she knew about Alonso and Sebastian and didn't care. She said they could work it out.

Alonso was distraught. He couldn't condemn Maria to a life with his brother. He realized how naive he'd been. It had never occurred to him he'd have to marry. The future hadn't existed. The clock had had no hands, but now it did. Everywhere he went he heard time. The cuckoo in his room. The church bells. Sebastian's pocket watch.

The world had turned into one giant tick-tock.

Going to fight in a war together occurred to them (Maria would dress as a man, they mused), but there was no war at the moment. They had no choice. They could not let Maria marry Hector, who would most certainly try to eat her one day. Alonso told his mother and Diego that he'd changed his mind, and he would indeed marry Maria.

But Diego wouldn't hear of it. He said he'd never take away this newfound happiness from Hector.

Life had trapped Alonso, Sebastian, and Maria.

Their future shrank as did their hearts.

Maria refused to speak.

Her red hair turned ghost-white.

Then one day, their fortunes changed as fortunes do. A boarder who was renting a room in the uneaten part of the de Falla house began talking to Alonso about an outlaw city in California on the west coast of America. It was called San Francisco, or sometimes Sodom by the Sea, the boarder said, chuckling. A place where there were no laws, no rules, where men danced with men and women with women, where men dressed like women and women men, where people did what they pleased, lived any way they wanted.

The whole sky flew into Alonso's chest.

The boarder also told Alonso that north of this city were trees that touched the sky and rivers full of gold. He said you could dip your hand in and pull out enough nuggets to live (to buy a house, a bakery, a vineyard!). Said the sun-drenched hills north of the city were perfect for growing grapes.

Alonso formed a plan.

He, Sebastian, and Maria would take the special grapevines and finish the voyage Alonso's mother and real father, Esteban the Penniless Poet, had started. They would go to California. They would plant a winery in the hills north of San Francisco.

But Sebastian resisted.

He reminded Alonso how he'd promised his father on his death bed that he'd always take care of his sisters. He couldn't see past that promise. He assured Alonso that even if they each married and had families, they could still see each together.

But what Sebastian described felt like a diminished life. Alonso wanted to pull gold out of a river and buy a house with it where he and Sebastian could live, floating around together from room to room. He wanted to be somewhere lawless where men danced with men. He wanted to be far, far away from Diego and Hector and their cruelty.

He wanted to follow his father Esteban's path to freedom.

Destiny roiled inside him.

But Alonso couldn't convince Sebastian, and since Alonso wasn't going anywhere without Sebastian, he didn't share the plan of escape with Maria.

It was in this heart-crushing period that for the first time in Alonso's life, instead of emitting light, he began emitting darkness—so much so that people in the village needed to use lanterns all day long. Flowers slunk back into the ground. Trees lay down in roads. All over the village, people fell asleep on

their feet. Sebastian couldn't find Alonso anywhere. No one could. The night around him was impenetrable. His soul had switched off. Sometimes Alonso heard Sebastian calling his name, but the darkness around him was too thick for Sebastian to ever locate him.

After weeks of this desperate gloom, Sebastian made a roaring bonfire outside the half-eaten manor. Alonso found his way to the front door, and with the blaze, he could almost make out Sebastian's silhouette.

"When we had that ceremony in the meadow when we were twelve," Alonso pronounced into the dark, "that's when I knew."

Sebastian's voice was full of emotion. "I knew before that. I knew when you were following me to school, lighting my path through the forest. I've always known, Alonso."

"Purple, green, blue," Alonso said, their code for *I love you.*

"I'll go with you to San Francisco," Sebastian replied, and just like that, the darkness began to recede.

That same day, in the dawning world, they knocked softly at Maria's bedroom window. They shared their plan. How the three of them would stow away in the cargo hold of the next ship leaving for San Francisco. She wouldn't have to marry Hector. They told her about sky-high trees, about women who dressed like men. They told her how they'd build a house, buy a bakery for Sebastian. How they'd plant a vineyard in the sunny hills north of the city. How they'd buy her a horse she could ride all the way to the ocean and back before lunch.

She stared at them as though they'd lost their minds.

Then they told her why else they'd come.

"If we had those vines, Maria, we'd have a wine like no other on the new continent."

She refused outright. She said she'd never betray her father like that. She'd resigned herself to marrying Hector.

In the days that followed, Sebastian tried to keep it from Alonso that he was losing conviction. But he couldn't. His feet hadn't risen off the ground since he'd committed to going. There were other stories about that city, San Francisco, he'd say, different from the ones Alonso told. Stories about people shooting each other for no reason, about rivers emptied of gold for decades and decades, about the city's wild revelry being long over. About men full of greed who had sex with prostitutes, smoked opium, and beat each other senseless in the streets. What if they ended up vagrants? he'd say. They didn't even speak the language. They didn't know the customs. They didn't know the first thing about the other side of the world.

Except then, Sebastian would pivot and tell Alonso that he was only half a man without him, and he didn't want to half live a half life as a half man.

On the day of their departure, Sebastian was to meet Alonso at the port at three p.m.

At two p.m., Alonso arrived, the adventure ahead of them churning in his mind, in his soul. When he'd told his mother the secret plan, she'd given him the sapphire-and-diamond engagement ring from Esteban and a gold bracelet, pieces she'd kept when she sold all else. "I don't want you to stow away," she'd said to him. "I don't want you to hide, Alonso, not ever. Sell the bracelet and buy a ticket for you and Sebastian. I want you to sail to your new life with pride. Write me only care of the bakery so Hector and Diego will never know where you are."

Alonso had sold the bracelet. Two tickets were in his pocket.

He kept his eyes on the road, but each time he thought he saw

Sebastian in the distance, he was mistaken. Then at almost three p.m., he glimpsed Sebastian and his heart soared.

Until Alonso saw his expression. And that he had no suitcase.

"I can't" was all Sebastian said, looking down at his feet, which were planted on the ground. Alonso could smell the bakery on him.

"You can," Alonso said. Sebastian lifted his head and their eyes met. So much love flooded Alonso, he wasn't sure he could remain standing.

"I'm so sorry, Alonso. I'm not brave like you." The way Sebastian said this, Alonso knew he couldn't change Sebastian's mind. His heart felt as if it were dying in his chest. Sebastian whispered in his ear, "I'll always love you, Alonso." Then he added, "It was losing your dream that took away your light. You must go." Sebastian pressed an envelope into Alonso's coat pocket and then broke from Alonso and ran. He did not look back.

Alonso gazed down at his arms. Even though he was mortally sad, he was still aglow.

He wanted to follow Sebastian back to their life, which certainly wasn't perfect, but it was a life that had both of them in it. He was certain if he stayed, there'd be breaks in the darkness where he'd be able to see Sebastian happy and floating around. That could be enough? He watched Sebastian get smaller, then he looked out to sea, then further, to the land he'd conjured in his mind, this paradisical place pulsing with color, life, freedom. He knew his destiny was on that boat. California had become his religion. But his heart was here with Sebastian and always would be.

Do you follow your destiny or your heart when they aren't one and the same?

Which pull is stronger?

Alonso didn't know. Even as he made his way slowly up the gangplank, he didn't know. What if he single-handedly brought permanent darkness to America? Or got the ship lost at sea? He was still contemplating going back to Sebastian when he heard someone calling his name. He spun around, and there was Maria with a large cloth bag draped over both of her arms.

He walked back down the gangplank to his friend. "I took six of the vines," she told him. "I heard my father talking to yours. From one good vine you can make many. Take them." She smiled. "You will make the most monumental wine in California."

Alonso threw his arms around her, and she flinched. "What?"

She opened her coat; her neck and chest had enormous handprints on them. "I defended you," she said. "Hector said terrible things."

"Don't marry him," Alonso said. "Stay if you must but marry anyone else. Marry Sebastian. He's not coming." Alonso could barely say the words.

"Oh no," Maria said. "I assumed he was already on the ship."

Alonso squeezed his eyes tight. When he could speak again, he said, "Hector's an ogre—"

"Marrying Hector is the only way for my father—"

"Your father can find another way." And then the idea bloomed inside Alonso—no, not bloomed; it appeared as if it had always been there. "Use Sebastian's ticket. I think it's destiny. Our destiny. Yours and mine, Maria. And six magic vines."

And it was.

299

That was how Maria and Alonso arrived together, people assumed as husband and wife, one month later at the harbor of San Francisco Bay, with arms full of vines that were to make the angels sing.

MILES

"You've been back here this whole time?" Miles said to Dizzy, shining the flashlight from his phone into the sleeper bed. The truck was tucked onto the highway's shoulder. All around them were trees and stars and not a hint of civilization. But now, reality—along with Dizzy—was crashing into the dream state Miles had been lost in all afternoon and evening with Felix. He felt like a siren was going off in his head. His phone had no signal and his sister being here meant their mother was all alone. What if she needed them? What if something happened to Wynton? Miles couldn't remember the last time he saw another car either. Anxiety pulsed through him—they'd be out of cell phone range all night if no one drove by.

"I knew we had to get past the point where you'd drive me back," Dizzy said, interrupting his doom spiral. "And then I fell asleep. Where are we anyway? Why are we nowhere?"

"Good question," said Felix, who was now leaning into the flatbed, phone flashlight in hand. Sandro scurried in next, rushing and sniffing Dizzy, who stiffened at the dog's affection.

"I had to come," she said. "I know you don't think Cassidy's an angel but—"

"Does Mom even know where you are?" Miles interrupted, hearing the irritation in his voice. Well, he was irritated. No way their mom agreed to this, and he certainly wasn't thrilled about his little sister parachuting into his time with Felix.

"Yes, she knows. We texted," Dizzy said, then looked at Felix. "So, what did Cassidy tell you in the orange truck? In the chapel you said she was really chatty on the drive down with you, remember?"

"Oh . . . she told stories," Felix said, smiling at her. "Which I'll tell you soon."

Dizzy beamed at him. Miles glanced his way too—was his great-grandfather really gay? It had never even occurred to him to research his ancestors. He returned his attention to Dizzy, putting his hand out. "Let me see your phone, Diz." He needed confirmation that his mother wasn't at this very moment reporting her missing to the cops.

"I texted her before we got out of range. She's totally fine with it."

Miles wiggled his fingers impatiently. Dizzy made an exasperated face, then placed her phone in his hand. There was indeed a text exchange between Dizzy and their mom, who was decidedly not fine with it, but at least she knew where Dizzy was.

"You two met in the hospital, right?" Miles said.

Felix nodded. "Best face in town by a mile. And I'm a face expert."

"No way," Dizzy said. "Miles's face is perfect if you haven't noticed."

"I've noticed," Felix said, and Miles briefly lost consciousness.

Here we go again with your face, said Sandro.

"Got any food?" Felix asked Dizzy. "Miles here only thought to bring food for Sandro."

"Do I ever! I raided Chef Finn's hospital refrigerator. Are we sleeping here? Like outside?"

"Afraid so, if no one comes along. We're out of gas," said Miles. "In the morning we'll have to hoof it to a farm or ranch or something."

"It's like we're in a horror movie!" Dizzy said gleefully.

"You and me are of one mind," said Felix, and Dizzy's face became joy itself, but then the reality, the potential calamity, of the situation seemed to filter in.

"But what if we don't find Cassidy in time now?" she asked.

Felix said, "Cassidy wouldn't be at the hot springs—the place where she works—at night anyway." This seemed to pacify Dizzy, and it did Miles too. He hadn't thought of that. Miles told himself if no one drove by tonight, he'd wake at dawn, climb a tree, and hopefully he'd spot some-place nearby where they could get some fuel. His mother would be fine for a night. So would Wynton. Everything would be okay.

Miles popped off the camper top, the anxiety seeping out of him. It didn't feel anything like a horror movie to him with Felix now exclaiming about the beauty of the stars, and Dizzy telling them how Energy Beings, of which angels and possibly even giants like Felix are a subcategory, have healed countless people throughout human history. "It's a well-known fact," she said. "I've been reading up on it for days. Energy Beings are . . ." And she was off again. Miles would have to hear about his great-grandfather later. His sister's voice and soon Felix's intermingled with the sound of rustling leaves and the babble of a creek, the noisy quiet of nowhere. It lulled Miles, making him feel a little floaty again, like he was drifting into yet another dream.

By lantern light, they sat on the flatbed as Dizzy unloaded a backpack, pulling out a large container of gumbo, an aluminum blob that she un-wrapped to reveal a loaf of cornbread, a ramekin of lavender butter, and three forks.

"I love you," Felix said.

"I love you too!" Dizzy replied enthusiastically, sincerely, her cheeks flushing. Miles sucked back a laugh. What a trip his sister was. What would it be like to be so unselfconscious?

Miles broke off some cornbread and handed it to Felix, who was seated beside him. Their knees were touching—no big deal, Miles thought. No. Big. Deal. Dizzy opened the container of gumbo and the chili aroma spun into the air. She handed it to Felix with a fork. "At the hot springs," he said, taking the container from her, "I had a meal with some of the residents of"—he made finger-quotes—" 'The Community.' It's going to sound really weird, but everyone ate from one bowl like we're doing, except we all fed each other. It was part of their spiritual practice."

"Oh," Dizzy said. "Let's do that. I'm very spiritual."

Felix and Miles exchanged a glance, Miles fighting again to keep from laughing.

"At first I thought it was silly and embarrassing," Felix went on. "But I got into it." He stuck a piece of sausage with the fork, then added some rice and peppers to the bite with his fingers. "I made this andouille sausage this morning. I have a way with sausage, if I do say so myself."

A way with sausage! Omg, lol, roflmao, as you young humans say.

Miles laughed out loud this time.

"What?" said Dizzy.

"Don't pay attention to Miles," Felix said, guiding a forkful of food into her mouth. "His mind's in the gutter."

Sandro, remember how I told you he touched my neck?

Yeah.

He touched my neck!

You told me.

After an elaborate sequence of moans, Dizzy said, "It tastes so much more delicious than when I had it at lunch."

"That's the point," Felix said. "They say food tastes exponentially better if someone else feeds it to you." He speared another piece of sausage. "Now you," he said to Miles. Was Miles imagining it or did he say *Now you* in a provocative way? A sexual way? Felix drew one of the camping lanterns closer, then worked for some time designing the perfect bite. "Bon appétit, Miles," Felix said, and Miles parted his lips, feeling ridiculous, vulnerable, and turned on all at once. Their eyes met, held. Felix lowered the fork, resting it on Miles's bottom lip for a second before tipping the forkful onto Miles's tongue. Miles closed his eyes as Felix slipped the fork out of his mouth, as flavor burst on the roof of his mouth, filling his whole head.

"Holy God," Miles said.

"Really makes you taste each and every spice, doesn't it?" Felix said. His eyes were still on Miles's mouth and that was making Miles feel breathless. He licked his bottom lip. Felix swallowed. Was he imagining this? He wanted to holler, "ARE YOU SUDDENLY AVAILABLE?"

"Wait!" Dizzy cried. "Miles, you're a vegetarian!"

Miles hadn't remembered. He was gone.

I'm losing it, Sandro.

"Ah! Sorry, forgot," Felix said to Miles. Miles shrugged it off—he wasn't strict, cheated sometimes, and anyway, he was too preoccupied to worry about it. Because it wasn't just their knees that were touching now but half their thighs too. When had that happened? Had he moved closer to Felix without realizing it? Or had Felix moved closer to him? When he *fed* Miles maybe? Miles's hands were getting sweaty and there was the matter of his heartbeat. They were flirting—*right?*—except he wasn't sure. But whatever it was they were doing, it was much easier to do since they weren't alone. He was now *so* glad Dizzy crashed the party.

Why's it this easy to be with him? he asked Sandro.

Maybe you knew him in a past life.

You don't believe in past lives.

Oh yes, I do. When I met Beauty, I was certain we'd been together in turn-of-the-century France.

I thought you didn't believe in New Age stuff.

It isn't New Age. The concept of reincarnation has been in various human religions for over three thousand years.

Really?

I used to be your wife in one of our lives together. We've had three.

I had a wife? And it was YOU?

Sandro started barking in delight. Miles tried not to laugh out loud.

"Wait, we have to feed Felix," Dizzy said to Miles. "I'll do it."

There was nothing Miles wanted more in that moment than to feed Felix. He watched mournfully as Felix passed the plastic container to Dizzy, catching Miles's eye as he did. Did he want Miles to feed him too? Miles was already reliving—in slowest motion—the moment Felix placed that bite of food on his tongue—the way Felix had held his gaze, then stared at his mouth, then swallowed like that.

"Why are you being so normal?" Dizzy asked him, interrupting his reverie as she prepared Felix's bite with great care. "He's never like this," she said to Felix. "I told him the most amazing thing the morning before Wynton's accident, and he didn't even look up from his book."

"What'd you tell him?" Felix asked.

Miles watched the fork rise to Felix's mouth, to Felix's mouth, to Felix's mouth. "About this woman who has orgasms from brushing her teeth."

Good, Miles thought, let's all talk about orgasms. Perfect.

Felix almost spit out the bite Dizzy fed him. "That's not true."

"It is. It's a well-known fact."

"No way it is," Miles said, joining in. "Dizzy needs a checkup from the neck up."

Did I say you could use my material?

Both Felix and Dizzy peered at him, their eyebrows raised. "What?" Miles said. "It's slang."

"From when?" asked Felix. "The 1940s?"

Felix and Dizzy were laughing, saying back and forth: *You need a checkup from the neck up,* and the teasing was making Miles feel warm, included. This is what it was like, he thought, to not feel like a hole in the air. What it was like being with Dizzy when Wynton wasn't around. Then a loathsome crocodile of a thought rose from the deep dark swamp of his mind: *He hoped he'd never be around again.* So what if one time in seventeen years he acted like a brother, even if it was a biggie like going to effing jail for Miles. What about all the times he acted like an ogre? Humiliating Miles, making him feel like a mite—

No. Jesus. Miles tried to unthink it. He didn't want Wynton to die, of course not, he wanted to save him, didn't he? Hence this whole trip. Miles wished he'd stop being a human roller coaster, careening from one extreme to the next, whenever he thought about his brother.

When they were finished eating, the three of them lay on their backs in the flatbed looking up at the sky, like Felix and Miles had in the forest earlier in the day, except now Dizzy was a shield between them.

The night pulsed with stars.

"Why don't you like Wynton?" Dizzy asked, turning her head to Miles.

"I guess because he's never liked me."

"Why don't you like me, then?"

Miles heard himself gasp; his heart sank. He rolled onto his side, so he was facing his sister. "I do. You're the coolest. I wish I were more like you. I was thinking that tonight. Truth."

"Really?" Her voice was frail. He remembered her at the dance a few weeks ago, all alone like a scared bird, remembered her convulsing in sobs by Wynton's side this morning. He touched her shoulder and she leaned into the touch. "Lizard doesn't like me anymore," she said. "And Wyn—" Her voice broke. "He's my only other friend."

"I'm your friend too. Okay?" Miles squeezed her shoulder. "Starting now."

"And me too," Felix said, which made Dizzy clap her hands together. She turned her head to him. "I decided you're too normal to be sent from above."

"Ouch," Felix replied.

"It's okay. Me too. Human through and through. Miles also, now that he's not perfect anymore."

Something was dawning on Miles. Was it actually his fault he and Dizzy weren't close? Could that be right? Had he kicked her off the island? No, Wynton had always hated him, treated him like crap, and made Dizzy hate him too. It was like they were allergic to him his whole life. But Dizzy didn't seem to hate him now. And why did Wynton go to jail for him? He thought of the moment in the hospital room yesterday when he couldn't bring himself to let his mother and sister comfort him—even though he'd so badly wanted to.

He pulled Dizzy into his arms.

"I've never been this close to you," she exclaimed. "I didn't know you smell the color of a California poppy!" It was like hugging a bundle of sticks. Was what she just said true? Had he never hugged his sister before? Ugh. What was wrong with him?

"I've been a bad big brother to you, haven't I?" he whispered. Dizzy didn't answer, which was the answer. "Wynton's going to be okay and we're going to find Cassidy," he said, his chin resting on her head. It fit perfectly. He was so glad Dizzy stowed away, but now, to feel this. This tenderness toward her. This sunrise inside. "Now tell me what happened with Lizard."

After a long time, she said, "I thought love was always two ways."

"Oh, me too, Diz," said Miles.

"Me three, Diz," said Felix.

Me four, Diz. I love bonding! We're all bonding! I'm so happy! Everything smells so good!

When Dizzy was breathing steadily and deeply, Miles picked her up and carried her into the cab and covered her with his sleeping bag. Then, instead of going straight back to the flatbed, he walked down the road into darkness.

He leaned against a tree, thinking about how close he'd felt to Dizzy tonight. He only had one memory of feeling similarly about Wynton, a moment that washed over him sometimes and raised the hair on his skin when it did, like the memory was part of his body. Miles had been really young. Their father was pushing him and Wynton on swings. This was one of Miles's only clear memories of him too. He and Wyn were both pumping their legs trying to get higher. All he could see was Wynton and all he could hear were his own happy hoots. Then Wynton jumped, so Miles did too, and as they scrambled on the ground, Wynton reached for Miles's hand, laughter tumbling out of them. Two brothers hand in hand with a father running after them. Evidence that he and Wynton had been tight once. But sometime after this, Wynton had stopped talking to him, even looking at him, no matter what Miles did. He thought about what Felix said today. How you stop hating someone by trying to understand them. Had he ever tried to understand his brother?

When Miles returned to the flatbed, Felix and Sandro were crashed. Because he'd given Dizzy his sleeping bag, he scooted gingerly onto the bed of the truck and rolled himself up in a tarp on the other side from Felix so he didn't, accidentally, in the night, ravish him, and then marry him on a beach in Hawaii. He turned off the lantern.

"Hey, want to . . ." he heard Felix say. Miles stilled. "Want to, um . . . ?"

Miles tried to make his voice even as lightning shot through him. "Totally, yeah. Totally." His voice did not come out even.

Felix took a breath and exhaled slowly, said quietly, "Not like that."

Panic assailed Miles. Uh-oh. He tried to cover. "No. I didn't think—" But he did think, he *so* did, and they both knew it. He buried his burning face in his hands, grateful for the darkness. He'd been so off. Felix was just being caring in the hostel. And friendly in the woods. Nothing more. People didn't say they were unavailable unless they were unavailable.

"It's going to sound weird," Felix said. "But I want to close my eyes and for you to tell me what I'd see if they were open."

"What?" This was odd. "You mean like describe the stars?"

"Describe everything."

Was this some kind of good-night ritual Felix's mother did when he was a kid or something? Seemed like it might be. It was such a personal and strange request that it made Miles less self-conscious about what he'd just thought and said. And hoped.

"You don't have to," Felix said. Was he embarrassed?

"Your eyes closed?" Miles asked.

"Yeah." Miles could hear the smile in Felix's voice.

Miles breathed deeply, looking around. "So the sky's like this charcoal-black dome all around us, no"—he sat up—"that's not quite it. There's a sheen to it. Like velvet. No, this is better: It's like a glimmering dome of black water. Know what I mean?"

"Yeah. Awesome."

Miles felt the smile on his own face now. He lay back down. "Okay, and around the periphery toward the horizon, there's a kind of lazy spattering of stars but rushing into the center of the dome there's this full-on flood of them. Like a river overflowing the banks, like so many freaking stars, dude, a tidal wave of them, which is the Milky Way. It's dimensional, and the thing is: you can almost see it all vibrating tonight."

Miles rolled onto his side, could discern the outline of Felix's body, could see his hand was over his eyes. He wanted to lift Felix's hand and replace it with his own. Whatever this was they were doing felt wholly private and it was bringing Miles right to the edge of the cliff that was his heart. Yes, he thought constantly about having sex with guys, but even with his secret compulsive rereads of *Live Forever Now,* he didn't realize how little he thought about loving them. Until now.

Miles said, "Did you know that the atoms in human bodies are billions of years old, some as old as The Big Bang, and so we're literally stardust, which means you, me, and everyone who's ever lived is made of this . . . I don't know, this elemental brightness. Like we are the stars. We are made of their light. We *are* light."

Miles could not believe what was coming out of his mouth and got self-conscious, but Felix said, "So cool," and joy radiated through Miles. He felt again like he was somehow talking a new person into existence, and that new person was himself, the real deep-down him. He continued. "There's blackened-out mountains in the distance, silhouettes of trees on top of them, of redwoods shooting into the sky all around us."

"You're good at this, Miles."

Miles talked and talked, and after a while Felix's breathing got steadier, but even after Miles was sure Felix was asleep, he kept talking, telling him all that he saw in the dark.

When Miles woke later, it was to Felix's muffled sobs. Sandro was up too.

Do something, he told the dog.

What?

I don't know. Lick him.

You lick him.

I can't lick him! C'mon, be a dog. Make him feel better. That's why you were put on earth.

That is so human-centric, Miles. As if we were put on earth for your—

Don't get all righteous—sorry, that was insensitive of me. Just help him!

Sandro licked Felix's face. "Good boy, thanks boy," Felix murmured.

"You okay, Felix?" Miles said softly.

"Oh yeah, totally," he said. "Really fine, good. Go back to sleep."

"You sure?"

"It's just really . . . it's just . . . so beautiful here."

Miles flopped onto his back. "Oh my God. You scared me." He noticed Sandro was still bombing Felix with affection.

You can stop licking him, he's okay.

He tastes good.

He does?

"Felix?"

"Hmm."

"What was the mind-expanding experience that happened at the hot springs?"

"I had a threesome in the mineral pool one night. It lasted approximately thirty seconds."

This turned Miles into a human spark plug. He had to know the gender ratio of this threesome immediately, but he couldn't bring himself to ask. He was bi, so it could be any combination. It was probably with two girls. Two friends who thought he was hot. Naked friends. Didn't he say no one wore clothes at this place? Oh, he had to find out if it was two girls or a guy and a girl or two guys (!), how he wanted it to be two guys, but he waited too long, because Felix said, "Night dude."

It took him an eternity of Felix threesome events to fall back asleep.

Perv.

Yeah, I know. Someone should club me.

The next time Miles opened his eyes, it was still dark, but the moon was beaming down on them. He could see Felix in silhouette, could hear his regular breathing. Miles gazed at the moon, the fading stars, thinking how he'd describe it all to Felix. How strange had that been? And then the guy had cried because the night was so beautiful. Even stranger. A thought fell straight into Miles's head. Because hadn't Felix also asked Miles to share the best thing he'd ever seen? And the dude practically jumped for joy at the sight of birds, rabbits, rickety old bridges, whatever. And he'd mentioned he had eye issues. Was something going on? With his vision? Was he trying to tell Miles in his way?

Oh God, or maybe—was he *dying*? Hence the rapture, the despair!

No. That was ridiculous.

He was only thinking like this because of his brother and all that Wynton might lose if he didn't come out of the coma.

And if he did.

Miles woke for a third time at dawn, this time in a panic, no idea where he was, and when he recalled where indeed he was, the panic gripped him harder. The siren was blaring again. What in the world were they doing in the middle of freaking nowhere with no way for their mother to contact them? What if something had happened in the night? They had to get gas, find Cassidy, and hurry back to the hospital.

He threw off the tarp and sat up. The dawn air was cool, the world still dim and muted. The creek was roaring at him, like it too didn't know what they were doing there. While the others slept, he climbed a massive alder tree, feeling jittery the whole way up. Sweat beaded down his neck and back as he maneuvered into a makeshift seat on a high branch. The sun was breaking over the mountain, and in the distance, he could see an orchard of some sort, probably oranges or lemons, and beyond that were hills covered in grapevines.

He found himself reeling with the beauty of it all, like he was Felix, and then remembered what had occurred to him in the night. Was he right? Was there something wrong with Felix? He gripped the branch above him, digging his fingers into the bark. And Wynton—would he play violin again? Would he make it, period? Oh man. His thoughts whirled. Why was he in a tree? And why in the world had he thought finding Cassidy was so crucial? What could she do to save Wynton that a staff of doctors couldn't? Dizzy had brainwashed him. It was all magical thinking, all an excuse because Miles had so badly wanted to see Cassidy again—

Oh! He spotted a barn. A moving tractor! There'd be someone who'd give them enough gas to get to a station. It'd be a walk though.

Less than a half hour later, they began the trek to the farm down the leafy, sun-dappled one-lane highway. Miles walked with the empty gas can, setting a fast pace, consumed as he was with a deluxe guilt-dread combo. His mind was too loud. He couldn't shake the thought that something terrible might've happened in Paradise Springs, while he was up here, quite possibly having the best time of his life.

"Feel like telling us Cassidy's stories, Felix?" Miles asked, needing to stop pinwheeling, hoping to lose himself in the refuge that was Felix's voice, wanting to hear about a gay great-grandfather, whether true or not.

"Yes!" Dizzy cried. "I want to know everything Cassidy told you!"

Felix nodded. "For sure. Time you kids learned about your ancestors." Then he slid his sunglasses down his nose and winked at Miles in a ridiculously *available* way. "You in particular, Mr. Fall," he said, and just like that, Miles forgot all his concerns as his inner Samantha Brooksweather swooned onto a fainting couch.

However, as they walked, and Felix began telling them about Alonso Fall's younger years, Miles grew agitated. He was not in the mood to hear some fable about brothers who hated each other—he'd had enough of that in his own life—but when the story became about a glowing boy and a floating boy in love, and he realized this was why Felix had said to Miles in the hospital lobby *You kind of glow too,* he began to get lost in the tale.

The End of One Dream, the Beginning of Another

(As Told to Felix by Cassidy on the Drive to Paradise Springs, a Week Earlier)

In the time of forever, Alonso stood at the stern of the ship to San Francisco, alone, wind in his face, the spiraling wake beneath him. He was eighteen years old, and his heart was in ruins. This was not the crossing he had imagined. It would not be the life he imagined. He watched the distance between him and Sebastian growing, the familiar port receding, the green hills, the stone houses blending into silhouette, then shadow, then disappearing into horizon.

He'd made a terrible mistake. What mad spell had allowed him to walk onto this ship? He began climbing up and over the railing, thinking he'd jump into the sea, swim back to the port, and run, sea-drenched, to town, to Sebastian's, where he'd hop the stone fence, climb up the trellis of the stone house, like he had so many times, like he had the very first time, bliss in his blood, when he'd taught Sebastian

to kiss. He'd take the rocks off Sebastian's sleeping chest and then lie next to him, holding hands, both of them a few feet above the bed until they became old men.

Instead, he climbed back down to the deck and returned to the cabin. He curled up beside the six vines that Maria had spread out on moist sheets on the bed, as she, before his eyes, transformed into a new person. While he wept in their cabin, she went around the ship introducing herself, learning about San Francisco, practicing English with those who spoke the strange language, talking about Alonso, how they planned to start a winery. She found the English speakers had trouble with de Falla so began using Falla, then Fall.

Each time she came back to the cabin with food for Alonso that he couldn't eat, more of her white hair had returned to its former color of fire. It was as if the girl who'd always been wild and bold had been a mere caterpillar and the moment she stepped aboard this ship, she began transforming into a startlingly beautiful creature that might at any moment sprout wings.

And then she did sprout wings, two nubs on her shoulder blades.

She was giddy about that, about everything. She reeled with relief, with liberation, with the uncertain future. "I can't believe my life can be anything," she'd say to Alonso, examining the wing nubs in the small mirror. "It never occurred to me that I could actually do what I wanted, when I wanted, how I wanted. Thank you, Alonso."

Toward the end of the sea voyage, Alonso came out of his despair long enough to remember that Sebastian had put something in his coat pocket. He reached in and found an envelope. There was some money in it, a note, and the leather bracelet

Sebastian had worn since he was a boy. Alonso wrapped the leather band around his own wrist and made an oath that he would never take it off, that he would never love another. Then he unfolded the note.

It said: *Maybe one day I will have the courage to come find you.*

Hope filled Alonso. He saw it again then: He and Sebastian on the porch of a big white house, Sebastian reading inches above his rocking chair, Alonso looking out over their vineyard. The two of them under one roof, free to float around all night long, all life long. A bakery for Sebastian on a town square. It would happen. Alonso would build this dream for them. He would build it for his father, Esteban, who'd died, maybe on this very ship, and for his mother, who'd been ripped out of his father's arms at the same port where Sebastian turned his back on Alonso. He would follow his parents' unwalked path. He would never give up hope. Like Sebastian had said, Alonso was a dreamer, and dreamers dream.

Alonso and Maria settled in a lush, flower-filled valley hundreds of miles north of San Francisco that was perfect for growing grapes. The pair became as close as the dearest brother and sister. They teased, laughed, fought, and most importantly, lived and let live. Maria said nothing when Alonso took off for the city, coming home reeking of alcohol, tobacco, men, reeking of disappointment and desperation for Sebastian. Alonso said nothing when Maria rode in before dawn and snuck into the house wearing the same clothes as the day before, said nothing when he saw her sneaking into or out of the barn with a certain female ranch hand named Rebecca or a male one named Sal.

It was the Wild West after all. Rivers rushed. Rain came

317

in deluges. There were few rules, little accounting, and hardly any witnesses. They did as they pleased. The land awakened something dormant in both Alonso and Maria, freeing their spirits.

One day, crocuses bloomed in Maria's hair, then larkspurs, then poppies, each season bringing new flowers. People assumed she wove them into her hair daily, but she didn't. She burned her shoes, her corsets, anything that restrained her, and would spend the rest of her life in trousers, untethered, and most important to her, autonomous, soul-single, a wondrous one-ly woman. Soon, the nubs on her back did grow into wings that she kept discreetly tucked into her shirts. Once, Alonso asked her if she could fly, as he'd never seen her take to the air. She smiled coyly. Alas, every-one has their secrets.

It felt close enough to Paradise, so that's what they called their town.

In time, after much work and struggle—the rivers had been empty of gold for decades when they arrived—the white house was built, the hills harvested, and then, the first batch of wine from the special grapevines was ready. Alonso and Maria stood by the barrel, glasses in hand. When Alonso uncorked the keg, the color of wine that splashed into their glasses shocked them. It was not the dark rich color they'd expected, but ruby-colored light. "I want to jump into the glass!" Alonso cried, and when they sipped, they found it hard to remain standing. It tasted like berry-crushed delight, like the giddiest happiness, like new love. In practical terms, the notes were: lilacs, chocolate, cherry, and sun-baked stone. But there were unsung notes too, personal ones: Alonso tasted the brine from the ocean that they crossed, the yeast from Sebastian's bakery, the perfume his mother wore, his persistent heartbreak and unending hope for Sebastian's arrival. Maria tasted the pine scent of riding through trees, the leather of her saddle, the marvelous fragrances of the flowers that now grew out of her head, and the freedom in her soul.

The wine rocked the valley. Word spread about the vintners from abroad and their magic vines, and soon Alonso and Maria were sending home letters full of money. Maria to her father, who'd forgiven her both for stealing the vines and for running away, and Alonso to his mother, Sofia, care of the bakery, begging her to cross the ocean and live with them in the white house, but she refused to leave Esteban's ghost. Through Sofia's letters, Alonso kept up. He learned Diego had died. He did not shed a tear. Learned Hector had married a woman his mother called Unlucky Fernanda and they'd had a child, a brutish boy named Victor. His mother warned him of the hatred in Hector's heart in every letter, how he believed Alonso not only stole his wife, but his future prosperity. *Always have eyes in the back of your head, my son.*

Occasionally, she'd mention Sebastian, and this was why he'd rip open her letters like his own beating heart was inside the envelope. He didn't understand why Sebastian never wrote him back, but he gleaned from his mother's letters that he still hadn't married, though his sisters had. And most upsetting for Alonso, that he no longer seemed to rise into the air (his mother had seen Sebastian's proclivity when he used to read in her library). Whenever Alonso thought about Sebastian permanently grounded, he had to take to his bed.

As the years passed, Alonso stopped writing letters to Sebastian. Instead, every week he'd put a blank piece of paper in an envelope and send it to him, knowing with confidence that Se-

bastian would open the envelope and understand everything that was in Alonso's broken heart, and in this way, Alonso finally comprehended the wordless poems his ghost father wrote to his lovelorn mother.

One cool evening, after a long day of work, when Alonso and Maria were sitting on the porch sipping wine and eating olives, Maria said, "I want a baby and I want you to be the father."

"Me?"

"Who else? The other men I see are . . . I don't know. One becomes the next. Same with the women. I'm not built for long-term romance. But you are my long-term unromance, my dearest friend, my family."

"I don't know if . . . I've never . . ."

"I do know. Look out at the oak tree. I'm always imagining a boy on a swing."

"A boy?"

She nodded. "We will call him Sebastian Junior."

Alonso smiled. He liked thinking of a son called Sebastian Jr. The idea steeped in his mind those next days, altering its very color like tea in hot water. A child for whom he could be as different a father from Diego as possible.

Alonso and Maria were twenty-six years old, when, for the first time since they crossed the ocean, they shared the same bed for several nights in a row and, less than a year later, Sebastian Jr. was born with a full head of bright red locks, like his mother.

They called him Bazzy for short, and how he reminded Alonso of his namesake too, the way he walked and stared at books even though he couldn't read, the way he smiled at nothing, the way Alonso loved him.

Every morning, Alonso would put Bazzy on his shoulders, and together they'd hike the vineyard, Alonso throwing grapes upward, and Bazzy trying to catch them in his mouth.

He called his son el bicho del amor, *love bug,* and the two were rarely apart.

Then one spring day, it happened.

Alonso and Maria were on the porch with seven-year-old Bazzy, who was telling them the scent of the air was magenta that afternoon—he'd inherited Alonso's sense-blending condition but had a different variation—when they saw someone striding down the driveway.

Someone, who, Alonso realized as he got closer, had a hopping kind of walk.

Could it be?

Alonso rose so quickly, he knocked over his chair. He did not think a thought, but began to run, and with each step Alonso's light shone brighter. He'd thought he'd been alive all these years without Sebastian only to realize in this moment he'd been a dead man for over fifteen years.

Sebastian saw this sun in clothes running toward him, and because his feet had stayed firmly planted on the ground since Alonso left, he'd long ago stopped weighting his boots or placing rocks in his pockets. He began to rise into the air.

"Hurry!" Sebastian cried. Alonso made it to him in time to catch his foot and rise with him into the sky.

"You look like a wild man," Sebastian said to Alonso on their way up.

"It's a wild land," Alonso said. "You look like you, Sebastian. Maybe sadder."

"Not anymore."

"Not anymore."

They kissed for a fortnight tucked away in a corner of the sky before Sebastian was able to calm down enough to lower them to the ground.

Bazzy watched their descent and walked over to greet them on their landing.

"This is the man I've told you so much about, love bug," Alonso told his son. "The man I love so much, I gave his name to you." Alonso choked up saying these words as he had in the sky when he told Sebastian about Bazzy. It was too much seeing these two together on this land he and Maria owned, in front of the house they built and vineyards they sowed.

"Will you teach me to float?" Bazzy asked Sebastian.

Sebastian smiled at the redheaded boy. "Yes," he said, after Alonso translated. "I'd love to."

"Soon he'll teach you, love bug. Now he needs to rest after his voyage. Come Sebastian," Alonso said. "I will show you our room."

Many years before, Alonso had painted the walls of his bedroom purple, green, and blue stripes specifically for this day he hoped would one day come.

Alonso and Sebastian did not come out of their room for a month. Maria left food outside the door for them. Even a spate of earthquakes didn't bring them out. When they were told of them later, they smiled at each other like fools, for they'd assumed the two of them were responsible for the shaking earth.

And maybe they were.

So that's how it was. The four of them lived together, joys compounding, until the three parents wizened, their waists growing thicker, voices deeper. They bought a storefront on the town square where Sebastian became Paradise Springs's beloved baker, his shop called Sebastian's Spanish Bakery.

Alonso's dream had come true.

If only time stopped here. If only.

If only we could have joys without sorrows, blessings without curses.

MILES

Felix had told Miles that when he read a novel or watched a movie, *he moved in*. Well, Miles had moved into Alonso and Sebastian's story, as told by Felix, and now he was standing in the middle of this strange, fantastical place with all of his moving boxes and furniture, wondering if any part of it was true. He knew he shouldn't be thinking of fairy-tale men—his IQ was surely tanking—knew they needed to find Cassidy and hightail it back to the hospital, but all he wanted was to grab Felix's hand and float up into the sky and be done with it, leave the real world behind.

Beyond the window, in the roadside deli, his travel companions waited in line for takeout. They were a sight—Gulliver with a Lilliputian in tow. Luckily, Felix was of the gentle variety of giant unlike that monster Hector, whom Miles had just met in the time of forever.

Could the love story of Alonso and Sebastian really belong to his family? To him?

There'd been moments on the walk to get gas and then the drive to the roadside sandwich shop where they now were, when Miles was certain Felix was adding his own flourishes to the stories. Like, when, with half-grin, gorgeous effing misty-colored Jericho Blane eyes, and mustache twirl, he'd said, "They stayed in bed for a month—no, for one year, Miles. *One whole year*. And the earthquakes that occurred from their reunion sex could be felt all the way in my home state of Colorado. Further even."

However, now, Miles, who'd been hopping from one delirium to the next since meeting Felix, needed to snap out of it. He had to call his mother, who'd been sitting by the side of her comatose son all alone because they'd abandoned her. He still didn't have a signal on his phone, but the cashier at the sandwich shop said he could use their Wi-Fi to call the hospital. Sandro was outside with him, lapping water from a bowl Miles had just filled. Because they'd woken up so early, it was still morning.

His stomach tightened as he punched in the number, birds cawing joyfully, obliviously, in the tree above him. What was going on down there? He was flooded with shame that they'd run off on this fool's errand. And they were still a couple hours away from Whispering River, where Cassidy lived, and from the hot springs where she worked. But would she even want to come back with them to the hospital? *Why* would she? What the hell had they been thinking? What a deranged idea this was!

The phone rang and rang and when his mother finally answered, her voice was weak, almost unrecognizable.

"How is he?" Miles asked instead of hello.

His mother cleared her throat. "Well, when I was talking to him yesterday afternoon, I swear his head turned toward my voice. Just slightly. I don't know if I imagined it, because Doc Larry said it was something to look for. But if it indeed happened, it's good news."

Okay, okay. Miles relaxed a little. He gave Dizzy and Felix, who were now staring at him from inside the shop with nervous expressions, a thumbs-up sign, and the two did some high five into a goofy hand-dance. Dorks. "Sorry we left you alone, Mom."

"Miles, sorry I left *you* alone. I've been thinking about it all night." Miles sat down on the stoop, and Sandro, done drinking, curled up on his shoes so he wouldn't move. He loved when the dog did this. "I can't honestly say I didn't know something was up with you, Miles. I did. I just—"

"I should've said something." Though he had no idea what he would have said. *Morning Mom, I feel like a crime scene, like mold on a wall, like I'm trapped in drying cement today, you?*

"No, it's my job to pay attention. Things will be different from now on, okay?"

"Okay." Felix had Dizzy on his shoulders now. They were placing the order and the woman behind the counter was laughing at something they'd said. "Mom? Do you know about a curse on Fall brothers?"

"Miles!" She was laughing. "One car ride and your sister has you believing in curses!"

"Apparently this curse, it started ages ago with Alonso and Hector."

"Alonso the now headless statue? Where'd you hear this?" Miles felt a rush of blood to his cheeks—headless because of *him*. "And who's Hector?"

"Hector's Alonso's evil brother." Oh, what the hell. "He was a giant—like he ate half the house back in the old country so got really big."

"Miles, are you okay? You don't sound like yourself."

He laughed. "I'm good. Really good actually. What about Alonso and Sebastian? Do you know about them?"

I do.

C'mon, Sandro. Shhhh.

I won't shush. Also, I wish there'd been one dog in the stories. Talk about a lack of representation. If you ever become a writer, Miles, I hope you give me a voice.

Promise, Miles told Sandro, reaching his hand down to shake his paw.

"Who's Sebastian?" his mother asked. "And why are you thinking about this right now? Seriously, Miles, are you okay?" She paused. "All I know is that Alonso and Maria came from Spain and started the vineyard with six magic vines. Ha! I sound nuts too. But I do remember your grandfather Victor telling us about the magic vines the day I met your father. I was just writing about that. Anyway, Alonso founded the town in—can't remember—early 1900s maybe? But who is Sebastian?"

"He was Alonso's *boyfriend*," Miles said.

"Miles, where are you getting this information? Alonso was married to Maria." She paused, then exclaimed, "Wait! Sebastian's Spanish Bakery was the name of the café we leased when my parents and I arrived in Paradise Springs. The place that became our soufflé shop. It wasn't owned by the Falls then though, some out-of-towner. I remember it had been empty for decades. My father thought it was beshert, like it had been waiting for us." This jarred Miles. Could there be some truth to the stories, then? Was it the same Sebastian? How he wanted it to be.

"Apparently Cassidy's researching Alonso Fall for some college course on California history because he founded the town. She told Felix all these stories about him when they drove down together, weird ones full of giants and floating people and curses. Obviously, she took artistic license."

"That's odd."

"I guess she came down to do more research or something."

"Well, if it's true, couldn't have been easy being gay back then."

Miles thought about this. How over a century ago, his great-grandfather seemed to live his life more on his own terms than Miles did. He had an impulse to tell his mother then and there that he too was gay. Instead, he said, "We'll be back soon. Promise."

"Please. I need you both. I think Wyn does too."

"Mom?"

"Yeah?"

Miles spotted a hawk soaring above the treetops, followed it with his eyes. "I have this memory of Wynton and me on swings and Dad was there, and we were close, like really really close. I don't know what happened . . ." He hadn't known he was going to share this.

His mother was silent for a moment and then said, "I think it was very hard on your brother when your dad left. He changed after that and—"

"But he and Dizzy are so tight . . . so . . . why not . . . me?" He hardly ever talked like this with his mom. But something had shifted in him. He didn't know if it was Wynton's accident or finding out Wynton went to jail for him or Dean Richards telling his mother the truth about him. Or maybe it was hanging out with Dizzy and Felix last night and Cassidy before that. Or who knows? Perhaps it was Cassidy's stories now rolling around in his head. But he definitely felt different, like all the rooms inside him were being redecorated.

"Oh Miles. Maybe this is the wake-up call. When Wynton's better, hopefully you two will finally be able to have a real relationship."

"Maybe," he said. But that seemed impossible to imagine. It was easier to believe that they were cursed. Their relationship *felt* cursed to Miles.

He said goodbye and slipped his phone into his back pocket. He looked upward half expecting to see Alonso and Sebastian waving to him from above, but there were only a few puffy clouds idling over the treetops. Miles had been hearing about and dismissing the existence of Dizzy's floating ghosts for a very long time—she'd freaked when Alonso and Sebastian rose into the air for the first time in Felix's story. "It's the kissing ghosts, Miles! I knew one of them was Alonso Fall! I just knew it!" Sure, he wanted floating spectral ancestors who were queer. I mean, seriously, who wouldn't?

Too bad he didn't believe in ghosts.

Wish we could float too, he told the dog.

Oh, me too! Sandro the levitating Lab!

Miles laughed. *And Miles the hovering homo!*

Miles rubbed noses with Sandro, then stood as Dizzy and Felix spilled out of the shop, grub in hand. Miles shared that Wynton might've made some progress, then Dizzy started in about the kissing ghosts again.

"I'm so happy the kissing ghosts are Alonso and Sebastian!" she said for the hundredth time that morning. She handed Miles a wrapped sandwich. "I so want to be like Maria Guerrero, don't you? She just does whatever she pleases."

"She's the giver of zero fucks," Felix said.

"I want to be like Alonso Fall," Miles said as he began unwrapping his sandwich, curious what the chef got him.

"You *are* Alonso Fall, Miles!" Dizzy and Felix both blurted, their voices overlapping.

"Except Miles isn't gay," Dizzy said matter-of-factly to Felix.

"I am actually," Miles said, the words falling from his lips easy as rain.

There was surprise in Dizzy's expression, and excitement. "Really?"

"Really."

"Oh my God! You are *so* Alonso Fall. I had no idea you were cool this whole time!"

Miles realized he was shaking. Because he'd just done that. He'd actually done it! "I think I'm having a spiritual awakening," he said, hoping he sounded at least a little ironic.

"I am too," Felix replied with no irony.

"Oh good," said Dizzy. "Maybe you're both mystics like me."

"Mystics in the middle of freaking nowhere," Felix said, and they laughed. Then Felix's hand landed on Miles's shoulder. "Good work, Mr. Fall," he said. Miles's throat tightened and eyes burned at the gesture, the words, the acknowledgment of what had just happened. Telling Dizzy was the equivalent of yelling from the rooftops. He'd come out. For the briefest, boldest moment, Miles rested his trembling hand on Felix's, which still was on his shoulder, and when their eyes locked, he was certain all the doors in all the world blew open.

He felt as winged as Maria, exultant, like his heart was expanding in his chest in fast motion. There was some fear too, at the edges, for how everyone else was going to respond, but for now they ate their sandwiches (Felix had gotten him egg salad with avocado on pumpernickel). Between bites, they all smiled at each other like they were legit brainless.

"Keep going, Felix," Miles said as they climbed back into the truck. "What happens next?"

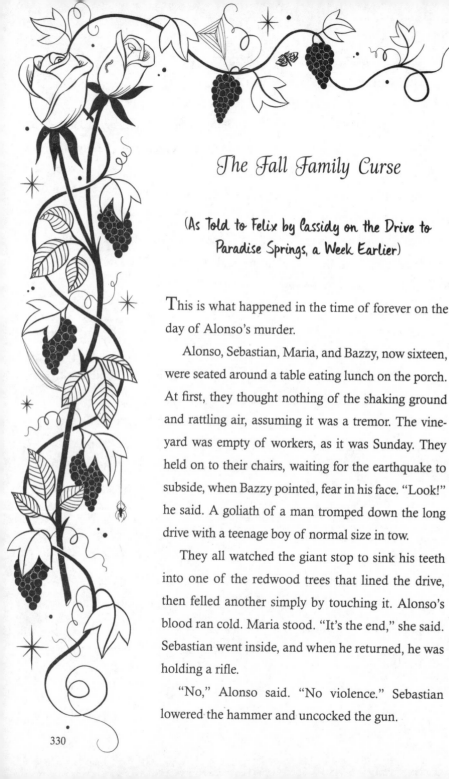

The Fall Family Curse

(As Told to Felix by Cassidy on the Drive to Paradise Springs, a Week Earlier)

This is what happened in the time of forever on the day of Alonso's murder.

Alonso, Sebastian, Maria, and Bazzy, now sixteen, were seated around a table eating lunch on the porch. At first, they thought nothing of the shaking ground and rattling air, assuming it was a tremor. The vineyard was empty of workers, as it was Sunday. They held on to their chairs, waiting for the earthquake to subside, when Bazzy pointed, fear in his face. "Look!" he said. A goliath of a man tromped down the long drive with a teenage boy of normal size in tow.

They all watched the giant stop to sink his teeth into one of the redwood trees that lined the drive, then felled another simply by touching it. Alonso's blood ran cold. Maria stood. "It's the end," she said. Sebastian went inside, and when he returned, he was holding a rifle.

"No," Alonso said. "No violence." Sebastian lowered the hammer and uncocked the gun.

"But who is it? *What* is it?" asked Bazzy, nervous.

"That giant man is my brother. But not a good kind of brother. Not one in blood or spirit," Alonso said. He took a breath, met Sebastian's eyes, said, "Purple green blue."

"Purple green blue, Alonso."

Some families have their sorrows doled out over a lifetime, a little tragedy here, a little there, still others seem to live joyfully for decades only to have the suffering come all at once, one tragedy piling up on the next. This family was the latter. For years, there was barely a raised voice, barely a tear shed in the big white house. There were birthday parties, harvest feasts, hikes to waterfalls, endless dinners in the vineyard with friends from town. There was the delight of raising Bazzy, who spent his afternoons after school crashed in the vineyard reading books—the black dog from down the way always by his side—and his nights kissing neighborhood girls on rocks in the moon-filled river. But to Alonso, Bazzy, with his wildfire hair that now nearly grazed his shoulders, remained his love bug, no matter the boy's age.

The world darkened as the shadow of Hector fell across the porch, across the life Alonso and Maria had built from nothing. Alonso walked down the driveway toward his colossus of a brother and, he assumed, his son, Victor, trying to control his gait so as not to reveal his quaking terror. He told himself that surely all Hector wanted was money, and Alonso could and would be generous with him. Bygones be bygones.

But Hector had something else in mind. He lifted his massive hand out of his massive pocket and at the end of it was a gun.

In a flash, Sebastian re-cocked the rifle, pointed it at Hector's heart, and pulled the trigger, but he wasn't quick enough. Sebastian's bullet didn't save Alonso's life as it took Hector's.

Both Fall men fell dead in the same moment. Then, right there on his feet, Sebastian released a soul-shattering cry and died of grief, which made it easier for his spirit to hop-walk out of his body, down the porch steps, just in time to reach for the hand of Alonso's spirit the moment it struggled free of Alonso's body. Alonso and Sebastian, in spirit form now, entwined, then retired to the sky to get reacquainted in their new incarnation. (Who knows what happened to Hector's spirit? Perhaps he didn't have one.)

Three men dead, and for what?

Bazzy and Maria laid Alonso's and Sebastian's bodies side by side on their bed in the purple green blue room. The wailing of mother and son could be heard as far as the city, as could the vengeful words of Hector's son, Victor, directed at Bazzy: "I will take your life for my father's."

By morning, Alonso's and Sebastian's dead bodies were holding hands. No one could explain this. A real love story is not falling in love once, but again and again through all sorts of incarnations. Theirs was a real love story.

A statue of Alonso was erected on the town square.

Bazzy, grief-stricken over the loss of his father and Sebastian, cut off his fire-red locks and enlisted in the air force when he turned eighteen. While overseas, he fell in love with a British nurse named Ingrid who died in childbirth. He returned home to Paradise Springs with his three-month-old baby in his arms: Theo Fall.

Maria called her grandson, Theo, love bug.

Despite her sorrows, Maria lived on for son Bazzy and grandson Theo, her hair never graying, instead growing redder, and perpetually tumbling with flowers. It filled her entire bedroom while she slept, and when she walked to town, she was her own floral procession. She spent her days writing in a journal, recording everything that had happened.

But there was Hector's son, of course. Victor was equally as cruel as his father, but far cleverer. He never returned to the half-eaten manor across the sea. Instead he moved into the white house and learned to keep his nefarious intentions to himself, play-acting as a brother to Bazzy, and eventually marrying a woman named Eva, with whom he had a son, Clive.

Then at the age of twenty-four, Bazzy was killed in a tractor "accident"—Victor, the only witness. Well, the only sentient witness. Alonso and Sebastian saw the murder of their son by his "brother," Victor, who wanted the Fall vineyards for himself.

You see? Another generation, different Fall boys, different circumstances, same tragic outcome.

After Bazzy's death, Victor's wife Eva, who was kind, insisted on raising Bazzy's two-year-old son Theo alongside their own son Clive, much to Victor's displeasure. The boys were brought up as brothers.

The grief of losing Bazzy, after the deaths of Alonso and Sebastian, was too much for Maria to bear. She became ill, and one day, after she hid her journal in a safe place, she climbed onto the roof of the house and took off her blouse. Her wings burst forth into a glorious span. They flapped a few times, lifting Maria off her feet. She then glided around the property surveying all she, Alonso, Sebastian, and Bazzy had created together, her hair streaming across the sky. This was how Maria—the freest spirit of all of them—left the living world and crossed into the next, dying mid-flight.

It was a sight. Alonso and Sebastian watched it all from their perch above the vineyard.

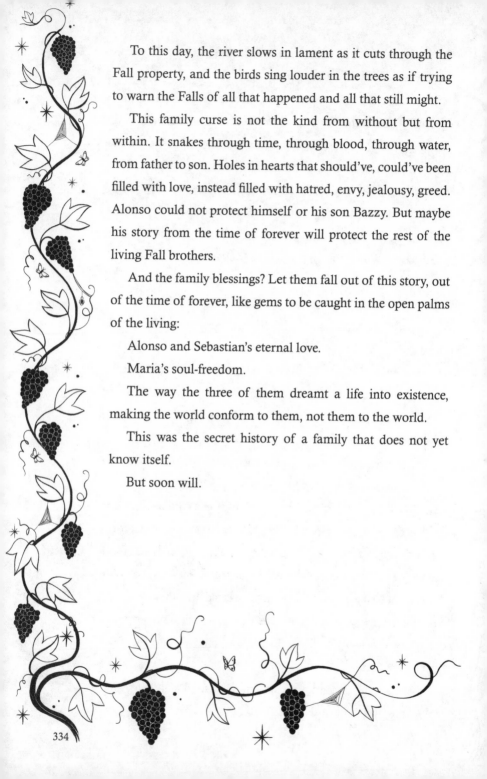

To this day, the river slows in lament as it cuts through the Fall property, and the birds sing louder in the trees as if trying to warn the Falls of all that happened and all that still might.

This family curse is not the kind from without but from within. It snakes through time, through blood, through water, from father to son. Holes in hearts that should've, could've been filled with love, instead filled with hatred, envy, jealousy, greed. Alonso could not protect himself or his son Bazzy. But maybe his story from the time of forever will protect the rest of the living Fall brothers.

And the family blessings? Let them fall out of this story, out of the time of forever, like gems to be caught in the open palms of the living:

Alonso and Sebastian's eternal love.

Maria's soul-freedom.

The way the three of them dreamt a life into existence, making the world conform to them, not them to the world.

This was the secret history of a family that does not yet know itself.

But soon will.

334

WYNTON

Cassidy says she needs a break before telling you the third betrayal, the most crushing of all. She says she's going to tell you the stories of your ancestors instead.

The stories are weird and they upset you. You have way too much in common with the villain Hector.

You want her to stop talking about envies and jealousies and curses between brothers. You want her to stop holding up this magnifying glass to your rotten soul. You beg her to shut up, but the story goes on and leads exactly where you think it will.

After she leaves, you turn the stories around and around in your mind. You realize something.

This is why your heart stops.

MILES

Miles's phone blew up the moment they crossed into cell service range, right as Felix was describing Maria's winged ascent to her death.

"Uh-oh," Dizzy said, gripping Miles's arm.

Miles called their mother, who told him that Wynton had gone into cardiac arrest and had been resuscitated by the nursing staff with chest compressions and medication. Miles wanted different words, not these lit matches, wanted his mother not to sound frantic and somehow hollowed out at the same time. And now, a high-pitched humming noise was coming out of Dizzy, who'd surely heard, because her head was glued to the other side of his phone. Miles tried to keep his own voice steady so as not to scare Dizzy further, then ended the call.

Behind smudged glasses, Dizzy's eyes were blurred with tears and fear. Miles realized he was rocking in his seat, made himself stop, put an arm around his sister, which quieted the terrible humming sound. "He's going to make it," Miles said with confidence despite the fear pounding through him. Since they were only a couple miles outside of Whispering River, they decided they'd head home if they couldn't find Cassidy right away.

They drove in silence, in dread, the thick tree cover allowing in little light. Miles stared at the ancient redwoods, so full of time—thousands of years—unlike them, who had so little. How had he not understood this before? How had the severity of Wynton's situation not penetrated until this moment? A wave of compassion swept over him. Poor Wynton. He was the guy full of voltage and fury, who blew the lids off jars, who walked into a room and electrocuted all present. How could this have happened to him? And why hadn't Miles tried to talk to him in the hospital? He'd been so caught up in his own stingy miseries, his preoccupations, his victimhood. God, why had he *never* tried to talk to his brother when he wasn't in a coma? Not once. Maybe he was also to blame for their shitty relationship. Really, why did Miles never take the reins in his own life at all? He was the anti–Alonso Fall. He was the object of a preposition, never the subject of the sentence that was his life. It was like he'd been in the closet about *everything,* not only being gay.

But how to change this? How to change anything? How to be a brother? How to be a *person*? He wanted to be . . . more, to do better.

Miles squeezed Dizzy to him, then he took a breath, and said, "Love you, Diz." It was the first time he'd ever told her, and in response, she plastered herself to his side, clamping both arms around his waist like he'd seen koalas do to tree trunks. It melted him.

Storytime was over, and what about those stories anyway? Could there be truth to them? Did Hector really murder Alonso? And Victor, Bazzy? Didn't seem possible, did it? Felix said he'd gotten confused by all the names at this point, started spacing, and then fell asleep, but if it happened, even some of it, what was wrong with his family? What kind of family outside the Bible had all these murders? Maybe they really were cursed. And he and Wyn as much as the rest of them.

"This is the sign for the hot springs," Felix said, pointing at a big yellow arrow on a wood board. "For those in the know. Cassidy works in the reception kiosk." Dizzy disentwined from Miles and sat up straight. Miles wiped clammy palms on his jeans. This was it. Would Cassidy be there? Would she think they'd lost their marbles? Of course she would. Because they had. He'd only ever spent a few hours with the girl! Still, he felt a little breathless at the thought of seeing her again. Possibly in mere minutes.

Felix turned onto a dirt road that traversed a mountain face at a steep pitch. "Forgot to mention this road's gnarly," he said. On both sides, homemade signs were nailed to trees either with arrows or warnings:

"Slow down" and "That means you!" They barreled downward until bottoming out in a gully where a sign said: "Welcome! You've Arrived!"

There was a thatched hut with three flags on its roof: a peace sign, a rainbow, and a yin-yang. Beyond it was a path through old oak trees where Miles supposed the hot springs were. "Cassidy works here as a greeter," Felix said, driving up to the kiosk. Would she be inside? God, Miles hoped so. And maybe she'd wake Wyn after all? How could he believe something and unequivocally not believe it at the same time?

Felix rolled down the window and reggae music filled the cab. Two girls with sunburned cheeks, neither of whom was Cassidy, were inside in flowery skirts and tank tops. Miles's heart sank. Even more so when he saw that one of the girls who wasn't Cassidy broke into a blinding grin at the sight of Felix. "Couldn't stay away from me?" she said. Felix lifted his shades and returned the grin, adding dimple to the mix. Miles wanted to ream him with his elbow, suddenly certain that this was the threesome: Felix and these two girls. UGH.

"You guys want a day or camping pass?" she asked.

"We're looking for Cassidy," Felix said. "It's pretty important. You know where she is?"

"Haven't seen her since she came in for her last paycheck, over a week ago. But you can check her house, just a few miles away. Sixty-eight Dandelion Road." She took out a map for guests, drew a dot on it, and handed it to Felix.

Dandelion Road was a quiet tree-lined street with ranches on either side, surrounded by golden hills blanketed with vineyards. Sixty-eight, where Cassidy lived, was a yellow house, with a vegetable garden on one side, orchards on the other, and flowers everywhere else. There was a barn, horses in a corral, pigs in a pen. Miles could see the same stainless-steel wine casks and other wine-making machinery that were rusting on their property at home. Parked in the driveway was a purple RV.

"This looks exactly like where an angel would live on earth, doesn't it?" said Dizzy. There was a bounce again to her voice.

"It really does," said Felix.

"Some Energy Beings double as people for periods of time, like I told you guys," Dizzy said nervously.

"Okay," Miles said, just to say something. All his excitement at seeing Cassidy had morphed into apprehension. What were they going to say to her? We need you to come back with us and wake our comatose brother because Dizzy thinks you're an angel? They were basically stalkers. No, worse, they were kidnappers! He *really* hadn't thought this through.

The four of them shuffled down the path to the yellow house. "Kind of feels like *The Wizard of Oz,* doesn't it?" Miles said. "The scene where—"

"Totally, dude," Felix said.

"Totally, dude," Dizzy repeated, in perfect Felix.

"Totally, dudes," Miles added in exaggerated surfer, teasing them both. He swatted Dizzy, and she him, then both of them started swatting Felix as they hopped up the steps onto the porch, so when Felix rang the bell and the front door opened, they were laughing and behaving like an unruly litter of puppies.

"Pardon us, sir. We're looking for Cassidy," Felix said, the first of them to regain composure.

The man who answered the door was tall with a black cowboy hat cocked low and when he lifted his head to say "Cassidy's away for a few days," and Miles saw his face, Miles began choking on the word rising to his lips. He grabbed Dizzy's hand.

"Dad?" Miles said.

"Dad?" Dizzy repeated.

Sandro barked so loud, the roof blew off the world.

Dear Repeating Dream,

Stop taking my teeth.

Sometimes, they're in my cupped hand, and I am shaking them like dice. Sometimes, I'll be having a conversation with someone, and tooth by tooth, they fall out of my mouth. Other times, someone else has my teeth and won't give them back to me. It's usually Theo. He opens his hand and in his palm are my incisors, canines, molars, then he shoves them all into his own mouth.

But worst are the nights like last night when my whole mouth is gone and there is only skin from nose to chin.

No way to eat or talk.

No way to tell my secrets.

DIZZY

Bells were ringing and clanging in Dizzy's head as she stared in disbelief at the tall man in a cowboy hat who was her father. This man, who could've strolled out of the photograph she kept framed on her dresser.

How could this be happening? Was it happening? Or had they somehow driven out of the real world?

No.

This was God hollering at the top of His lungs.

Finally.

Oh, but she had to calm down, to stop shaking, to wrap her mind around the immensity. Okay, okay, they'd driven hours and were directed to a yellow house and a door opened and behind it was their missing father whom she'd never met. After twelve years, her whole lifetime, they'd found him without even looking for him at the moment they needed him most.

Well-known fact: Things like this didn't happen.

Unless a great mystical gale had blown them all together through all improbability.

Thank you, she thought. Thank you, world.

"This is a full-on miracle!" Dizzy said, but the ringing was still so loud in her ears, she couldn't hear her own voice. Or maybe she hadn't said it out loud, because no one responded. She realized Miles was squeezing her hand hard enough to break her fingers.

When they each had said *Dad,* the man who was their father had lost his footing and staggered back. Dizzy wondered if he was going to fall, but he steadied himself on the doorframe. She felt the same—she needed a doorframe. She untwisted her fingers from Miles's and walked on unsteady legs to the man. She pressed her index finger into his thigh. "You're real," she whispered. She heard herself this time. "I worried you were one of the mute ghosts."

"Not mute. Just speechless." His voice was deep, gravelly. She'd only ever heard it when she was in the womb. Is that why it sounded familiar? Is that why it sounded as she'd always imagined it would? Like heavy rain. The man who was her father seemed to be having trouble making his face look like a face. Dizzy inhaled deeply. He smelled a rich rust color. This was what a father smelled like, she thought. *Her* father. The man's gaze traveled from her to Miles and back. Sandro, at Miles's feet, was howling like he was dying maybe, and then all of a sudden, the dog bolted to the man and jumped into his arms.

"Hey boy, hey Sandro," the man said, petting the dog as Sandro licked his face, his neck, his hands, because, Dizzy realized with surprise, the man and the dog already knew each other. Sandro knew her father better than she did. She turned to see how her cohorts were reacting to this miracle. Maybe not so well, she thought. Felix was hunched over so he almost looked normal size, and his hand was clasped over his mouth. Miles's eyes were huge, and he kept blinking and swallowing. He couldn't make his face into a regular face either.

Behind them, one of the horses neighed and reared, then both horses began loping around the corral, like they knew what was going on. She turned back around, feeling suddenly like she could jump into the sky. Because this was the best end of a treasure hunt in the history of treasure hunts. "I saw you once before, right?" Dizzy asked him. "On the ridge above our house, in that same hat?"

He nodded, putting Sandro down. "I think so." Her father looked as though he might be having trouble breathing. And standing. And being.

"Everyone said I was imagining things," Dizzy told him. "Everyone always says that about me." There were so many questions queuing up inside her, but there was one way out in front of the pack. She cleared her throat. "Why'd you leave us?"

This question seemed to shoot her father in the gut.

"Dizzy," Miles said, his voice strained. "Come here, okay? You too, Sandro."

Dizzy turned to her brother, shook her head. Sandro had again made his way into the man's arms, and was now nuzzling into his chest. Now pawing at his shirt, as if trying to get inside it. This did not seem like normal dog behavior to Dizzy. And now Sandro was succeeding—his whole head was engulfed. Their father extricated the dog, and once again, gently rested him on the ground, but instead of heeding Miles, Sandro planted himself by the man's feet, then *on* the man's feet, gazing up at him like he was God of dogs.

She could relate.

She reached for her father's hand, and he took it. It was large and rough as the burlap sack she used at the farmer's market. She held on to it, and it didn't feel wrong. Au contraire. *She was a girl holding her father's hand on a porch in the sunshine.* She'd never been a girl who could do that before. Oh, there was a buzzy feeling in her chest now. In her soul too. By far, this was the buzziest she'd ever felt in her whole life. Her blood had been replaced with electricity. It had to be God's work, didn't it? And she somehow already felt like she knew her father. She already felt like she might love him. She squeezed his hand and he squeezed hers back, and then, he looked at Dizzy in the same way her mother did after she kissed Dizzy's forehead, her favorite way to be looked at.

A peace had fallen over her. She knew why they were there now. She understood what had happened. Everything was clear. She'd been wrong about only one thing.

"Do you know what beshert is?" she asked her father.

"Destiny," he said.

"Exactly," Dizzy said. "This is beshert." She turned around and faced Miles and told him what she now understood. "Cassidy sent us here through Felix because our father is going to wake Wynton. Not Cassidy." She looked at the man. "Do you still play trumpet?" Wynton spent his whole life following their father's ghost-music around Paradise Springs— Wynton had told her this so many times. Now he would follow the real trumpet music played by their real live father back to them from wherever he was. Relief fountained inside her. Wynton would be okay. She knew it now. They'd been granted a miracle without her even having to step foot in a convent. She didn't have to become a nun! Further, this was absolutely a sign she'd been forgiven for leaving the keys out for Wynton the day of the accident. Grace had crashed into all of them.

"Wake Wynton?" their father said, not understanding. "And you know Cassidy?" His voice broke on the name. Dizzy had thought it was her hand that was trembling, but realized it was her father's.

"Yes, we know her. First, she drove down with Felix and told him stories, then she saved my life," Dizzy said. "The next day, she drove around and went swimming with Miles and Sandro, then she saved Wynton's life by doing CPR and taking him to the hospital after he was hit by a car. Now she sent us here so you can wake Wynton from a coma with your trumpet. She's our Energy Being."

Their father was nodding slowly, trying to process what Dizzy was saying. His eyes traveled to Miles, looking at him too in that post-forehead-kissing way. "Miles." The name scraped their father's throat on its way out. "Tell me more about what's happened to Wynton."

Dizzy had no idea Miles was a dormant volcano until he erupted.

His hands flew into the air as he cried out, "I'm seventeen fucking years old!" Miles's jaw was set, and his face was tomato red now. "Are you kidding me?" He was more furious than the day he broke Wyn's bow. His eyes bore holes into the man. "Seriously, are you kidding me?" Sandro started barking. Felix stepped toward Miles like he wanted to hug him or shield him or hold him back. "You've just been here this whole time"—Miles looked around, sputtered—"feeding pigs and riding horses and making wine?" Dizzy could see her brother's heart breaking in his face. "Why?" It was a bellow, a one-word war cry that seemed to come from the very center of Miles's being.

Only to be interrupted by a lanky guy who appeared in the doorway, wearing a windbreaker that said *Dexter Brown Wines*. "Sorry, I got it," the man said to their father, taking them all in. "No tastings, no tours," he said. "You're all a little young anyway."

"They're not here for a tour, Nigel."

"What for then, Dexter?" Nigel asked.

"Who's Dexter?" Dizzy said. "This is our missing father, Theo Fall. We were looking for Cassidy but found him instead."

PART
FOUR

CASSIDY

Wynton, this is the most difficult part of the story. I've been loath to relive it by telling it, but you need to know what happens next. And next and next and next.

Yes, *need* to.

Despite Mom's promise, after we leave Paradise Springs (You! The Town! Our time in the meadow!), we aren't okay, and a year later, by the time of the third betrayal, we are unrecognizable. At fourteen, I look so much like my mother did at eighteen, at the beginning of The Great Adventure, that I get confused sometimes when going through photos whether it's me or her. It doesn't help that I'm usually wearing her old clothes, having shot up and out of my own wardrobe. And at thirty-two, the last age I'll see my mother, she's so changed, it steals the breath. To look at all our photos chronologically, it's as if she's under a witch's spell and the life force is slowly being drained out of her.

Sadie Mae dies on our way out of Paradise Springs. No joke. She stops running for no reason, like she wants to stay in The Town or wants us to—that's what I think now anyway, that we were supposed to stay there, despite Lying Dave Caputo, not because of him, and Sadie knew it. (Kind of like your father's ghost-music, Wynton, bringing you to the meadow that day to meet me. Don't you think there's so much at play in the universe that we barely perceive?) Now I believe Dave's gift was luring us to The Town, to a spot on the map that didn't seem to exist before he did. I believe that Sadie Mae was always bringing us to The Town and the town was The Town because you, your brother, and your sister were in it.

I think it's possible to *live* our lives without believing in destiny, with-

349

out feeling it at work in the choices we make, or the choices that are made for us. But it feels impossible to *tell* the story of our lives without it. Stories give our lives structure, and that structure is destiny.

Okay, onward to the third betrayal, the most devastating of all.

The mechanic couldn't figure out what was wrong with Sadie Mae, so we ended up selling her to him for parts. Sadie for parts. It was crushing, like, here sir, have my heart, my kidney, my soul. And you can see in this photo of Mom and me in Purple Rain how wrong this new RV is for us. How our rag rug clashes with the industrial carpet. How our colorful dresses look absurd hanging in the open metallic closets. How our sheer lavender curtains don't fit the windows nor our pink polka-dotted quilts the beds. And us. Don't we look as out of place? God, look at our expressions. Especially mine. I look like I've been taken hostage, which is how I'll feel for many months to come.

So many of the photographs I have from this time could've gotten Mom arrested for child endangerment. Here's one of me, age thirteen, sitting on the lap of some drugged-out Jesus Impersonator in Purple Rain as he holds my face over a bong, Mom beside us laughing because it's just so funny.

And another of me wandering through a house party of wastrels in some skimpy negligee, age thirteen, with an open beer in my hand that someone gave me, my eyes done up like Cleopatra, the rest of my face coated in makeup, because some women thought it would be fun to doll me up and put lingerie on me.

Here's one where I'm jumping with a group of tripping adults on a trampoline. As you can see, I'm about fifteen feet in the air and Mom's nowhere in sight.

Like I said, I've been dreading telling you this part of the story, Wynton. And please know that like everything with my mother, I don't know if I'm remembering it right. When I think about The Great Adventure now, it's more like dreaming than remembering, and if so, now is when the nightmare begins.

In the months following our visit to Paradise Springs, my mother starts partying (self-medicating, I think now). Gone are the days of boondocking perched on cliffs and mountaintops. Gone are nature walks, meditation, aura fluffing, astrocartography, hugging trees, beet juice, and fevered talks about modern pioneers and enlightenment and how *we are California*. Gone are *In the Time of Forever* stories. (She threw all her notebooks into a Dumpster when we moved from Sadie to Purple Rain. All I have of her writings are the scraps of paper I stole over the years and kept under my mattress, her bag of words.)

It doesn't happen all at once, our demise. At first, we try to get back to our old rhythm of hooking up at an RV park for a few days, getting supplies, doing banking, going to doctors, movies, diners, bookstores, whatever, then heading for the hills and boondocking as far away from civilization as possible for anywhere from a month to three months. But gradually our hookup times get longer and our boondocking times shorter as Mom becomes more and more social, venturing out to the fire pit or to a nearby bar to party, then returning to Purple Rain with crews of ragtag revelers: "Everyone! Sleeping Beauty over there is my daughter, Cassidy. Cassidy, this is absolutely everyone under forty at this godforsaken RV park! Where's that bottle opener? Rolling papers are in the drawer, guys."

I sleep under Purple Rain in my sleeping bag too many nights to count.

And soon, we're rolling from RV park to RV park, the kind Mom used to call cement hellscapes. We buy our food in gas station mini-marts. The only fruits we eat are mealy apples, desiccated oranges, and underripe bananas. We go to the ATM all the time, but I never see what Mom's buying with the money. She no longer reads or writes or studies California history or religion or whatever. She eats hot dogs, not tofu pups, and drags me to parties: house parties, beach parties, roof parties, every kind of party, festival, or fair, where she does drugs, drinks vats of alcohol, and looks for Dave. (One time at a wine festival, from afar, I really thought it was Dave she was talking to so animatedly, but when I got up close, I realized it was just some older guy selling jelly and stuff.)

Her new credo is Transcendent Living, which came to her in a vision. Remember how when I was younger, I thought of my mother in pieces? I do again in this period. She's a freaking kaleidoscope, Wynton. It's like having a hundred RV-mates. More. I never know who I'm going to get either. There's the mother who sways on top of Purple Rain talking to the planet Jupiter, the one who tells me she loves me a hundred times in an hour, the one who sobs so loud in the bathroom, I have to reassure the people in neighboring RVs that everything's okay. Then there's the mother who keeps touching my face saying that I'm glittering, the one who breaks all the dishes because Dave abandoned us, and her mother and father abandoned us, and everyone on earth abandoned us. There's the one who says she can reverse time and see the dead, the one who sits in a daze staring out a window all night long, the one who hosts a steady stream of Dave look-alikes (*The only men who interest me now are the ones who are setting fire to the status quo.*) who stay with us for days at a time and call me kiddo.

And most reliably, there's the mother who retreats to The Silent World for weeks at a time.

So very many moms.

I have a sense that she no longer writes her *In the Time of Forever* stories because she's living inside one of them now. Maybe all of them at once, I don't know. "Drugs have always been used by indigenous cultures to open the brain's pathways, Cassidy. You can meditate or you can take E or peyote or acid or have sex or so many things. You can't let society dictate where you take your consciousness or how you get there. There are so many paths to transcendence."

"Yes, Marigold," I say all day long. She's decided I should call her by her name instead of Mom because the parent/child dynamic is oppressive and limiting to both of us.

"Why bridle our relationship is all I'm saying. Let's explore all the possibilities. Let's bust through boundaries. Let's be authentic and make our own rules. Let's—"

"Yes, Marigold."

So much of the time, I don't feel like I'm there.

I learn you can be sitting next to someone and be in different time zones.

I learn you can unknow someone.

And you can unknow yourself too.

I do school by myself. I read novels, no, not read, I tear them open and crawl inside them and hide in between the words. I read the dictionary still, methodically, devotionally, like a Bible.

I start to run and I'm fast because I need to get away from Marigold, then even faster because I need to get back to her. "Oh, there you are, Cass. Greg's going to be staying with us, just for tonight. He's a shaman and thinks I'm a reincarnation of a goddess. Maybe you could make that pasta dish, the one with all that cheese. Don't be put off by this, but he always keeps his eyes closed, I mean always, so we're going to have to help him eat and get around and stuff."

"Yes, Marigold."

"Honey, this is Dylan."

"Yes, Marigold."

Honey, this is Michael. Honey, this is Doug. Honey, these are the twins Calvin and Lester.

"Yes, Marigold."

I go quiet, so quiet that she starts again with "I can't hear you!" and "Oh there you are!" and "Stop sneaking up on me, Cassidy!" But I have nothing to say to her. I feel like a ghost, like a candle that's been snuffed out, a kid that's been thrown off a carousel.

Like I've been sold for parts.

This is when I start finding the really good words like Desiderium, n. *an ardent desire for something lost.*

From Marigold's Bag of Words Under Cassidy's Mattress:

In the time of forever, a woman couldn't get out of a burning house. She got used to a bed that was on fire. She learned to sleep with her back to the flames.

Fuck the time of forever.

I forgot where I put my life. (Retrace all the places you've been since you last had it, Marigold.) I wish I were Keith Richards. Or Joan Didion. Or anyone anywhere. I can't get out of this. I gnash my teeth. I teeth my gnash. Watch me climb out of a window into a different sky. Sky out of a climb into a different window.

The despair walks on two legs.

The despair has its own set of keys.

CASSIDY

Some RV parks have computers for public use and when they do, I spend hours futilely searching pictures of "mothers," picking out ones I'd rather have, and "thirteen-year-old girls" so I can pick all the girls I'd rather be. I also search "What's going to happen to me?" and "Please help me!" and "How do thirteen-year-olds act?" (I still avoid the other kids at RV parks, mostly now because: How to explain Marigold?) The rest of my computer time is spent watching videos of animals being rescued: goats from under a bridge, a dog from an uninhabited island, a cow stuck in a fence, a baby elephant trapped in a well. I watch for hours and hours weeping in the final moments where the cow/elephant/dog/goat is freed and able to live happily ever after.

Other times, I get practical and search for help for Marigold: treatments for alcoholism and drug abuse, treatments for depression, grief, trauma, but nothing ever goes anywhere because she says she won't take medication or go to AA or NA or talk to a therapist. "I'm fine, Cass! Why are you so bleak? Why are you such a worrywart? Why are you so, well, I hate to say it, but I will: boring, yes, you've gotten dull. You used to be so much more fun before you became this sad sack, this judge of me, this moral arbiter. I just need some life in my existence! So do you! We're in the civilization stage of The Great Adventure, that's all. Life is about change. Life is about experimentation. Life is about finding magic by any means necessary, Cassidy."

When she says things like this, I get confused and think that maybe she's right and this is all normal and it's me who's changed, that I am a boring dull sad sack now. I try to be upbeat then, try to jump on her

Transcendent Living train, but the train always ends up derailing with her too high to talk or too drunk to walk, or worse. I get confused too because sometimes everything feels okay and it's us again and we do our old things like go to used bookstores or thrift stores or the doctor, and I think I imagined there was a problem because what does it matter if she parties a little and why am I such a stick in the mud?

All I know is I never feel okay anymore except when I imagine I'm in the meadow with you, Wynton, which I do all the time.

All the time.

The most right I ever felt was with you and I don't know why.

I hear your violin too. Maybe like you hear your father's trumpet. Calling on me to come find it. Find *you*.

Sometimes I think about college even though it's years away and then feel guilty because what will Mom do without me? It's me who makes sure she eats. It's me who's there when she comes out of The Silent World. It's me who waits up for her, who empties Purple Rain of derelicts in the morning, who listens to her constant proselytizing, who is the emergency driver (yes at thirteen!) when she's too wasted. It's me who worries, who loves her, who's afraid to leave her side, because if I do, I know something really bad will happen to her.

The problem is no one's worried about something bad happening to me.

And then it does.

Usually, I'm the only kid at the parties we go to and I develop a routine. It consists of this: Watch over Mom so she doesn't die until she inevitably goes off with some Dave look-alike, and then I find the room where the coats are all piled on a bed and wait under the mound of them until Marigold's ready to leave.

I like the weight of all of the coats on me at once. It feels safe.

It isn't.

A month before my fourteenth birthday, we go to a party at a farmhouse in the foothills of the Sierras. The people that live there are part of an intentional community called Soul on Fire (these are kind of like modern communes). Mom met some of the members at a music festival the weekend before where she jumped onstage with her Hula-Hoop. Two security guards escorted her to safety in a trailer with medics. Matt and Emily were in the medical trailer with us (they took bad peyote) and they bonded with Mom while I read *Crime and Punishment*.

That's when they invited us to this party.

Per usual, I find the room with the coats and lie down and pile the coats over me and sigh with relief to be hidden, disappeared. (Why I thought this was a better idea than hiding in a closet I have no idea.) I fall asleep because I'm exhausted from sleeping (or not sleeping) under *Purple Rain* for so many nights while Mom entertained.

When I wake up, there is someone on the bed, pressing into me from behind.

Two arms are wrapped around me, and hands are pushing up my shirt, then are inside my shirt, touching my bare stomach, then squeezing my breasts. I gasp, twisting and turning to get away from the rank breath, the insistent grip, trying to find purchase with the coats, the bedclothes, but can't. *I can't get away.* When I yell out, a hand finds my mouth and clamps over it. I try to bite it, to scream, but the door's closed and the music's loud and he's shushing me and pushing rhythmically into my back, slurring that it's okay because I have my clothes on, and he isn't going to go inside me and because all people have one communal soul. I go limp then, drowning in his body stench and fish breath, drowning in the pounding into my back with his groin, his hand on my mouth, the weight of him burying me in the bed, clenching the coats in my hands as his moaning, shaking, gasping goes on and on and on.

After, I watch him stumble away, barely able to walk, one hand in his greasy stringy hair, the other ahead of him as if he's bushwhacking, a wet stain on his khaki pants. He thanks me on his way out, which is just so disgusting. I throw up once, again, then panic about the vomit on the coats and frantically flip the whole pile so the soiled ones are hidden on the bottom, all the while thinking how he'd said it was all okay because he kept his pants on and didn't enter me, like I was a house. I still have doodles in one of my school notebooks that I drew after this happened. They're of me with doors in different places on my body. All barricaded.

I don't tell my mother. The shame makes it hard for me to speak at all. She doesn't notice. She doesn't notice how many times a day I bathe or how raw and red my skin is from scrubbing. She doesn't notice the weeping at night.

Like always, well, since we left The Town, the only thing that makes me feel better, Wynton, is thinking how you let me cry that day in the meadow and didn't ask why, just softly pressed your back into mine, letting me know you were there.

A month after this happens, the night before my fourteenth birthday, I'm coming back at dusk from a computer session where I watched little ducklings getting rescued from a sewage pipe when I see my mother behind the mini-mart with a Grizzly Man in a jean jacket. He's pressing her against a wall, and at first, I think she's being pinned against her will, like what happened to me. I start sprinting toward them, except as I get closer, I realize, unlike me, she's an enthusiastic participant. I see way too much.

When she stumbles into Purple Rain hours later, I watch her in the ghostly glow of the night-light staggering around wasted, getting a glass of water, missing her mouth with it, then practically falling up the ladder to my bed. I retreat to the far corner of the bunk, not sure if she wants to sleep with me or if she went up the wrong ladder. She smells exactly like The Man in the Coats, the same sour stench and fish breath. "I don't want you in my bed," I say.

"Okay," she whispers weakly, and climbs down the ladder. "I don't blame you."

"Well, I blame you!" I scream.

She doesn't reply.

When dusk rolls around on my birthday and she's still not awake, I do something out of character. I leave to find some kids.

The lights at the RV park have just turned on and I follow the path I've seen young people traipse down day and night for the three weeks we've been here until I spot the group of teenagers, as I knew I would, in the dunes. They're sitting around a bonfire drinking beers and smoking weed, the scent wafting in my direction. I watch them from a safe distance, my heart racing.

Do I dare?

All their heads turn as I shuffle up to them. My sweaty hands are fisted in my hoodie pocket. I realize I'm biting the inside of my mouth. "Hey," one of the boys says. He's cute, with white-blond surfer hair. "How long you guys here for?"

"Don't know," I say, the words sounding scratchy and rough. I'd been talking so little. "A week, more maybe."

"Whoa, deep voice," the surfer boy says. I start to flush, and he must notice my embarrassment, because he quickly says, "Us too. You full-timers?"

I nod and one of the girls says, "Your mom homeschools you?" I nod again, astonished how easy this is. "Us too," she says. "I'm Lucy and this is my brother Mark and sister Cali, we're triplets. We're outa here tomorrow. Going to Colorado. These other idiots are Max and Sam, they're brothers. And dimples there who greeted you is Surfer Ollie. He's been talking about you nonstop for days"—she rolls her eyes—"but was way too shy to knock on your door."

I don't know who's blushing more, me or Surfer Ollie. He throws a handful of sand at Lucy. "Don't listen to her. She's high." He takes a hit off a vape pen and passes it to me. Despite all the parties I've been to and access to drugs I've had, I've never smoked or vaped weed or drank any alcohol except for a sip or two of beer. I bring the pen to my lips and inhale, sucking the vapor deep into my lungs like I've seen others do. It burns my throat and I start coughing and choking—it's awful!—and everyone laughs but not in a mean way. I hand the pen to Cali, who motions for me to sit between her and Surfer Ollie. Cali tells me she's in love with our rig. "It's purple! So cool!" I tell her its name is Purple Rain and then everyone jumps in saying the names of their rigs: Waldo, Blue Moon, Sweet Potato.

Ollie reaches into a cooler and offers me a beer. I look over at Purple Rain, still dark with Mom passed out inside and think: Just following in your footsteps, Marigold, and take the beer. It's so cold, I have to pull my sleeve over my fingers to hold it, the first beer of my life.

I'd been avoiding so many groups of kids at the RV parks, worried I'd have to explain why my mother was howling at the moon or having sex with someone's dad, but this conversation is all about where we've been and where we're going next. I find it easy to chime in, having been so many places. I open a second beer, start laughing at jokes, even make a couple, remembering what it was like with Dave, who'd said I have the gift of gab. Not like it is with Marigold, who lectures me, makes declarations, never asking me anything, because she's not interested in me, the sad sack, the moral arbiter. Is that why I've gotten so quiet?

Soon my head's woozy, my body's relaxed, and out of nowhere a feeling of delight comes over me, a field-of-daisies kind of delight, like everything's going to be okay, and I'm thinking why *am* I so worried all the time? I look around the circle at all the friendly faces. It's my birthday and I have friends! No wonder my mother drinks and smokes weed, I think, my head swimming, the girl next to me telling me how annoying her mother is. "Not nearly as annoying as mine, I bet," I say, rolling my eyes like she did, and feeling some combination of wicked and ecstatic at this betrayal, loving this freedom, this camaraderie, this hour free of worry. I realize I'm having fun! You see, Marigold, I *am* fun, I think. I'm only a sad sack *because of you.*

And because of . . .

I try not to let The Man in the Coats break into my mind. Though he's banging on the barricaded door. Rattling the doorknob. I place my hand on Ollie's leg defiantly because I somehow think it will help keep The Man in the Coats out, and I watch as the surprise on Surfer Ollie's face turns into a joy so raw, it both scares and thrills me. I can't believe I made his face do that by touching him.

"Let's go down to the water," I say to Ollie, getting up. The others say things like: "Uh-huh. There they go." Ollie casually rises, following my command, then is loping after me like a happy mutt. It's like I'm all-powerful, I think. The opposite of the way it felt in the coats. As we stumble down the path together, he takes my hand in his. It's warm and a little sticky. I've never held a boy's hand before. "You're really pretty," Ollie says.

Groan, I think, remembering then all the cool things you had to say, Wynton, about your father's music and about my voice coming out of a tree and my stomach being in B flat and how you asked me to marry you. I don't know then that it will always be this way, that you'll always be somewhere in my mind when I'm with other guys.

"It's my birthday," I tell him.

"Whoa. How old?"

"Sixteen," I lie.

"I'm seventeen," he says, believing me. How easy it is to lie, I think, to pretend to be someone different, someone new. Like Dave did with us.

We sit on the shore and look out at the waves. The sand's cold but the air's still sultry and the sky's a glory of post-sunset violet and orange puffs.

"Happy birthday," he says, then leans toward me like he's going to kiss me. "Can I?"

Suddenly I don't want to. "No," I say, pushing him back.

His eyes widen. "Oh, okay. I thought—okay. Sorry."

"Let's just—"

"Yeah. Fine." And I can tell it *is* fine with him. I nod, filling with relief. I take a breath and we watch the waves some more. "I like your name," he says after a while.

"Yours too," I say.

"After *Oliver Twist*," he says. "My mom's favorite book. She used to be an English teacher. What's your favorite book?" Maybe he's not such a dope after all.

"I can only pick one?"

"Okay, pick three or—"

I notice a shadow coming at us, one I realize is turning into my mother. Oh no. And then a moment later, she's pulling me up by my hoodie and saying to Ollie, "She's thirteen. You hear me? Thirteen. What's wrong with you?"

He looks at me questioningly, both shock and hurt in his face. He doesn't tell her that I lied about my age. He just says, "I'm sorry, ma'am. Nothing happened. I promise."

"That better be the case!" my mother says, then her hand is like a claw at my neck as she escorts me down the beach in the waning daylight. I see Ollie fast-walking away from us back down the path. "Are you serious, Cassidy? He's probably eighteen years old! You can't just go off with strange boys, strange *men*. And have you been drinking? You're not allowed to drink."

I'm flabbergasted. Truly flabbergasted. *Who is this person?* I wonder. For a minute I'm too stunned at the hypocrisy to speak, but then the words start to flow. "You do!" I cry out. "That's all you do is run off with men!" I break free of her hold and spin around. "And like you care. Why are you pretending you care?" I say it angrily, practically growl at her, but on the inside something else is happening—it's like a fountain going off and fireworks bursting and confetti dropping all at once. Because she's acting like a parent, one that actually cares about her child. What a revelation it is that she can so easily become a mother. Is this all I have to do? Run off with some older boy?

"Pretending? Cassidy, of course I care. You're all I care about. I know I've been—"

I can barely speak through the fury. "I'm all you care about? Right. First of all, I'm fourteen today. Happy birthday to me. Thanks for remembering." I try to get my breathing under control. "And—God—Like—I'm just—" I put my hands on my waist, make myself say the words slowly. "I'm just doing what you do, *Marigold*." I fill her name with as much ugliness as I can. "Except I didn't take acid or E or peyote or cocaine or whatever else you do to expand your stupid selfish consciousness." Words and words and words coming now. "At least I don't go behind the mini-mart and rut with some gorilla. I saw you! You're disgusting! You're useless! And you're—Do you know I google 'crazy mothers,' do you know that? Because I don't know what to do anymore. Ever. And seriously, Mom—I mean, *Marigold*—if you really cared about me, you wouldn't take me to parties where men . . ."

Her expression changes. "Where men what? Cassidy?"

I'm crying now.

"Cassidy?"

"What! Nothing, nothing happened!" I'm shrieking the words. "Nothing happened! Nothing happened! Nothing happened." I can't stop screaming this at her.

"Cassidy," she says, taking my shoulder. "Tell me what happened."

"Some man, he—It was outside my clothes, so don't worry. It's not like—"

"Oh my God. He what? What was outside your clothes? Did someone hurt you? Or make you—Cassidy, tell me. Oh honey. Oh God. No. How come you didn't tell me?"

I stare at her, dumbfounded. "How come I didn't tell you? When should I have told you? When you're in The Silent World? When you're having sex behind the mini-mart? When you're partying all night with Greg, who won't open his eyes or whoever? You're not there! You're never there! You're not even there when you are there! You're always high or drunk. You're like your father now: A sad drunk giant. And like your crazy mother too. Lucky me, I get both." I know I should shut up, but I just can't make myself. "You're the worst mother! The worst mother in any movie I've ever seen, and remember, we've seen *Mommie Dearest*! Any book I've read, and I've read *East of Eden*! You're probably the worst mother in the world! I hate you. I hate this life." These are the words I'll replay again and again for years to come. "You keep me trapped in Purple Rain with you. I have no friends. I have no one. And I don't even have you anymore! I don't have a mother! Marigold, I am *your mother*! I'm afraid to leave you for a moment because you might die or something. I don't have a mother. I don't have anyone."

She takes me in her arms and holds me so tight, I have to struggle to breathe. "Tell me what happened to you."

I tell her about The Man in the Coats.

Later, when we're back in Purple Rain, she climbs up the ladder to my bunk, puts her hand gently on my hair. "I'm going to fix this, I promise you. You're the best thing that's ever happened to me. The very best thing. Do you know that? But I've done it all wrong. Everything. You deserve better. Nothing can ever happen to you." Her face is calm. "I'm going to fix this," she says again.

I think this is the moment she decides. It must be.

We head into the mountains to celebrate my birthday and for a week it's like the old days in Sadie Mae. We do school together and hike for hours through pine trees and eucalyptus groves. We hold hands and lie on our backs and watch clouds. We hike to peaks and dive into waterholes. We read for hours in our chairs. I'm certain she's been miraculously cured or fixed or whatever. It feels like the beginning of something, a new us. Every night we sit outside by a fire and drink hot apple cider and look at the stars, talking about all the books I've been reading and how much I like running and we talk about college. It's so strange to have the focus on me, it makes me feel like I'm blooming in fast motion from seed to flower.

One of those nights, she tells me she thinks I should go to college at Berkeley, where she would've gone if—

And that's the last thing I remember before waking up in my bunk, groggy, mouth dry, head throbbing, thoughts reeling, sick. I must be sick, I think. I'm so attuned to Mom, her energy, her breathing, perhaps her heartbeat that I know even with my eyes still closed, even with this flu, that she's already up and out of Purple Rain. I imagine she's reading outside in her chair or has gone for a swim in the nearby creek. I gingerly climb down from my bunk to find her, to tell her that I'm sick or dying even, that's how bad I feel.

But when I push open the curtains, I see that we're no longer at the state park where we've been boondocking but in a driveway on a rural street with ranch-like houses on either side. On the other end of the drive-way is a pretty house. It's canary yellow, the color Sadie Mae was when she was new. There's a vineyard on one side and a vegetable garden on the other. Flowering bushes are everywhere—jasmine, wisteria, rhododen-dron, and another I don't know the name of. There are lemon trees, two fig trees, an avocado tree, and on the other side of the vegetable garden is a small round stable with a brown horse and a calf.

I blink, confused. What the—

I see the note on the counter then.

And I know.

I know before reading one line.

I read one line: *You are not safe with me . . .*

I push the note away, there's no breath in my lungs.

I spot a hammer on the counter and pick it up and smash it into the mirror with everything I have, this mirror my mother and I have spent so much time inside together.

Welcome to the third betrayal.

Is your seat belt on, Wynton? Here we go.

I stare at my shattered reflection, the swollen eyes and cracked lips, thinking I'm really ill, I must be, because why is Purple Rain spinning like this, why am I so nauseated. I sit at the table, put my head in my hands, then when the spinning subsides, I slide the note toward me. Maybe she went for a walk? I think. Maybe she went to get me medicine? I've half convinced myself of this and then I read more.

> *You are not safe with me, not physically, not mentally, not spiritually. I thought I could outrun it. I really thought we could be like the pioneers settling the state in the 19th century. Marigold and Cassidy on The Great Adventure. I thought that I could escape the past and find "gold" like all the desperadoes before us. I thought we could build a new beautiful civilization of you and me. Our own utopia. And we did for a time, didn't we? But I am not well, as you know. After all my efforts, it was you who finally woke me up. I can't take care of you when I can't take care of me. You haven't been safe, not to mention happy, for a while, and I'm so ashamed. I'm so ashamed about what happened to you that night and how it never should've*

happened and how it could've been so much worse. I need
help and I'm going to get it so I can be a mother to you, the
mother you deserve. I said once I wanted you to be like me.
It's the other way around, Cassidy. I want to be like you.
You are the light in my body. I will get better, and I will
find you and you will tell me amazing stories. It's you who
are the writer, but you don't know it yet. Know it. You are
empathy and compassion, my darling dictionary-reader.
I am sorry to leave like this, sudden and in the night, but
I don't have the strength to do it any other way. You're
the strong one, not me. You will be safe here and happy,
I think. You'll find out I haven't been honest with you. I
wish now I had been—

I rip up the note.

She just left me all alone on some road in some rural town? It's so hard to think with my head pounding like it is, with the world spinning . . . Except. Wait. How come I don't remember driving here? How come I don't remember going to bed? Did she drug me? Because why do I feel this way? The last thing I remember we were talking outside under the stars about college, drinking hot cider. Did she drug the cider? And then I'm certain that's exactly what she did.

There's a knock on the door of Purple Rain.

Mom! Relief courses through me. It doesn't occur to me that she wouldn't knock. I run to the door and fling it open, ready to fall into her arms, to promise her anything so long as it can be the two of us again: Cassidy and Marigold on The Great Adventure.

But it's not my mother. It's a man in a black cowboy hat.

I close the door in his face.

A plan's forming in my mind, and he, whoever he is, is not in it. I have to find my mother. I scramble to the front of Purple Rain, stumbling across the floor, which seems to be moving now, and fall twice. Did she leave me the keys? I pull open the glove compartment and there they are! I ignore the exhaustion in my limbs, the jackhammer in my head, and get in the driver's seat. I try to insert the key into the ignition, but my hand's shaking so intensely, I miss again and again, then drop the keys. Bending over the seat, reaching for the keys, I feel so dizzy, I forget what I'm doing and what species I am. Then I remember I'm going after her, and sit up, keys victoriously in hand, when there's another knock. I lock the doors.

"Can we talk for a moment, Cassidy?" the cowboy says through the door.

How does he know my name? Who is he? And man, am I woozy.

She definitely drugged me.

And then left me all alone on a street in the world.

I'm inside out as I finally get the key in and start the rig. Also, did she just walk off? I should've checked her closet. Did she take her toothbrush? WHERE IS SHE? The engine thrums alive and the knocking on the door gets more insistent.

"I don't think you're old enough to drive! Please open up!"

Yeah, right buddy, I think as I peel Purple Rain onto the quiet rural street, burning rubber, which is extremely hard to do with this RV, and then I'm barreling down the road with no plan, no destination, no mother, only a head full of fuzziness and misery, wondering how she could do this to me, and worse, how it's my fault for telling her what a terrible mother she is.

And who the hell is this man who's now following me in an old orange truck. Help!

I step on the gas and Purple Rain lurches forward. How could she have just discarded me like this? Thrown me away like a cruddy old shoe!

Especially when things were finally good again, except then, I realize that she'd been saying goodbye in the mountains. That's what the last week had been—not a fourteenth birthday celebration, but one long farewell.

I'm driving down a narrow road going about eighty miles an hour. I pass a casino, some ranches, vineyards, but the only living person I see is behind me, hatless now with his hand firmly planted on the blaring horn. He looks angry, I can tell that from here. His face is sun-leathered, craggy. What am I doing? I've only driven in emergencies when Mom was too blotto to get behind the wheel. I look at the speedometer and press my foot on the gas until it settles in at around 95 mph. Wow. I didn't even know Purple Rain had it in him to go this fast. I pat the dash, feeling the first blast of affection for the vehicle.

"Help me," I say to the rig. "Let's lose this guy. Then you're going to help me find her. I know you are."

The adrenaline of the escape has cleared my head a little, which unfortunately, means the words in the note from my mother come back to me: *You will be safe here.* Where is here? Who leaves their child by themselves after drugging them? Oh my God. How can this be happening to me? Why did I tell her I hated her? All the love I have for her is filling me up up up. I love her more than anyone, anything. She's everything. She's everyone. She's me, I think.

My only person.

The only person.

My throat starts to constrict until I'm gulping air, certain I'm choking. I'm an orphan now, I think, and orphans go into the system, I know this from movies. Foster care. The RV's swaying like it's going to capsize as the world outside the window grows more and more blurry. I don't bother wiping the tears away, just grip the steering wheel tight and floor it. Because I'm in the basket floating down the river like Moses. I feel a hot stream running down my leg. Oh no. I look down at the expanding wet splotch on my pajama bottoms and remember the last time this happened when I was lost in the woods and how that panic and desperation was nothing compared to this. She's not going to blow a whistle so I know where she is this time. She's not going to find a police officer like she did in The Town.

I fly through a stoplight only realizing it's red when I'm through it. The craggy-faced man blows through it too, his hand still on the horn. *I have to lose him.* I steer Purple Rain down a road, then another, and another, then recognize the casino again, the ranches, the winery, think I may have made a circle. I try to calm down, manage to get a few deep breaths in my lungs, mop the tears with the bottom of my shirt, concentrate on the blurry road, trying not to think of anything except driving, of never stopping this vehicle. How could I have peed my pants? And then I'm crying hard, sobs tearing out of me as I drive on.

The man lets up on the horn.

I'm winding Purple Rain up a mountain now, taking the hairpin turns like a pro if I do say so myself. I feel a little calmer. Dizzy still, but calmer. I've settled into my sticky seat. The smell of eucalyptus is filling Purple Rain, replacing the acrid smell of urine and fear. The redwoods are getting taller and the light softer. I look in my rearview mirror. The man waves at me. I can see the irritation in his face, but also maybe amusement? I don't know why, but I wave back, then turn Purple Rain down a road because I see a yellow sign with a giant arrow on it, just an arrow and no words. Then there are signs telling me to slow down. Well, too late, I'm hurtling down a steep incline a little too fast—no, a lot too fast. This road's definitely not meant for RVs, and the man behind me is honking again as I blow past signs that say "Slow Down" and "That Means You" and finally a huge one near the bottom of the slope saying "Welcome! You've Arrived," and I think I've arrived where? as I fly by some kind of thatched hut with flags on top of it. I'm riding the screeching brakes, but Purple Rain has other ideas. I close my eyes the moment I see the gully and then: impact.

"Open the door," the man says to me a moment later, because I'm still alive even though I wasn't wearing my seat belt and I'm turned around so my head's against the window and my legs are over the gear shift. I shake my head. He goes away. That was easy, I think.

I straighten up and turn the key and the engine starts. "I love you!" I say to Purple Rain. "I'm sorry I haven't been nicer to you." But when I put the car in reverse and gas it, the wheels spin. "I take that back," I say. The man's returned with a slim jim and in maybe two and a half seconds the driver's door is open and he's not just a man in a mirror but a man so close, I can smell some kind of shampoo or soap.

"You okay?"

I nod.

"You bang your head?"

I shake my unbanged head, self-conscious that he might see the wet spot on my pajama bottoms, but he doesn't look down and if he smells anything, his face doesn't show it.

"You think you can make it out of this rig on your own?"

"I'm not getting out."

"Okay. Fine. Just glad you're all right." His shoulders relax. He looks like he's going to say something else but doesn't. He's studying me, and I watch as tenderness breaks into the ruggedness of his face. He closes the door gently, taps it once before walking away. I look in my rearview mirror, see that he's talking to two naked people, a man and a woman. Naked people who are naked. Naked people in the middle of the road, absolutely positively irrefutably naked.

I blink a few times, thinking I've for sure been drugged and am now hallucinating, but when I look again there's more naked people, a whole tribe of nakeds, some pointing at Purple Rain's tires, all of them facing my way. Naked! What's going on here? "Oh please," I whisper. "Be dreaming, Cassidy."

I head back into the living space to change into shorts and clean myself up. I see the shattered mirror, shreds of the note all over the floor. Why did I do that? Maybe she said where she was going? I wasn't thinking. I'm still not, can't. I'm sick to my stomach and so tired. I sit on the bench, decide I'll put the note back together later. I open the curtain a crack to see that the naked tribe has members of all different shapes, sizes, and ages. I can't not look. So many penises. I've never seen a penis before, except in an anatomy book. I had no idea it looked like that. And that. And that. And *that*. So much variation.

Craggy Face is back at Purple Rain's driver's-side window, knocking on it. I walk up front, press the button so the window lowers. "We're going to try to get your RV out of this gully. The only damage I see is to the right bumper. Kind of amazing really. It'd be easier if you got out and let me have a go at the wheel. Not that you're not impressive behind the wheel." I think he's being sarcastic, considering the predicament Purple Rain is in, but then he says, "That was some damn good driving."

"Thank you," I say, a sudden surprising surge of pride filling my chest and making my cheeks hot.

"Well?" he says.

"Well, what?"

"Can I take that wheel for a minute while Bob here puts that plank of wood under your wheels? It's not their first rodeo with this."

"Is Bob naked?"

"Afraid so."

"Why?"

I wouldn't say it was a laugh that comes out of Craggy's mouth, more a mirthful guffaw. "Hell if I know, to tell you the truth. Now, get on out of there before more of them descend on us from the hot springs like ants on a picnic."

I get out of Purple Rain, realize I'm still in my pajama top, which would probably render me underdressed anywhere else on earth. Several of the nakeds smile and wave at me. This is certainly a friendly part of the Milky Way I've found myself in. I try not to look at breasts and penises and balls hanging like wind chimes on one old guy. Whoa, didn't know about that either.

I hear laughter coming from a grove of oaks to my right and see a small boy and an older boy watching the show from a tree branch, like two birds. Not naked, I note with relief. The not naked young boy's waving. He's a skinny stick with a tangle of brown curls on top. I wave back at him. The older boy must not realize the little boy had been waving at me so thinks I'm waving at him. His face breaks into a smile and then he's waving at me too. He has dark straight hair and a baseball cap. Okay, potential allies, I think. We, the clothed, shall stick together. (Who knew I would lose my virginity and go to the prom with this person years later? It ended a few weeks after we graduated.)

Naked Bob is a very large man, which is great because it means I can't see his PENIS (!) under his enormous hairy belly when he comes up to me and says, "Hello! You look younger than an acorn. Can't believe they gave you a license. Well, don't worry, we'll get your rig out of here in no time. Any friend of Dexter's is a friend of mine."

Dexter. Craggy's name is Dexter. Does not ring a bell. "Thank you," I say, noticing a police car gliding up the road toward us. He pulls in behind Dexter's truck. I have a very clear vision of myself in jail.

"What happened here?" says a mustached man getting out of the patrol car. He looks around at me, the nakeds, Dexter. His eyes even track to the boys in the tree. "Who was driving this here RV?"

"I was," says Dexter.

"Oh yeah? Then who was driving your truck, Dexter?"

"I was," says Naked Bob.

The police officer looks at Bob. "Like that?"

"You got a problem with my God-given attributes, Bruce?"

"And who are you?" he says to me. "Because I heard a little girl was driving a purple RV at the speed of light down Highway 43."

Dexter walks over. "Well, you heard wrong. This here's my niece Cassidy. She was riding in the back when the rig spun out of my control. She and my sister are visiting from Oregon, and I wanted to show her the sights and take her for a morning dip in the hot pools. I was just giving the leg a stretch on 43."

"Stop hassling us and give us a hand now, will you, Bruce?" Naked Bob says impatiently.

And just like that, I've been sprung from jail, no more questions asked, just all of them, some dressed, some not, yelling at each other, quite loud at times, on how best to get Purple Rain out of the ditch.

I watch them, still unable to think straight, waves of dizziness and nausea coming and going, my legs feeling weak beneath me, thoughts spinning around and around. Why did Craggy Dexter say I was his niece? *Am I* his niece? Did Mom have a brother? How does he know my name? And why did he cover for me? Where did my mother go? What am I going to do? Why is everyone naked? Around and around until eventually only one thought is left and it's just me and it. What I've been terrified of my entire life has happened:

My mother's abandoned me.

I give in to the lightheadedness, the exhaustion, feel my legs give out and . . .

CASSIDY

When I wake, I'm in my bunk in Purple Rain. I bolt upright, thinking for a gorgeous fleeting minute that I dreamt it all . . . I stick my head out of the bunk and look down, see the mirror shards have been cleaned up and the remains of Mom's note are in a neat pile on the table. Next to it is a plate of pastries, a bowl of blueberries, a jar of jelly.

I part the curtain, see that Dexter's outside in a beach chair, a guitar in his arms. My warden. Did Mom have a brother she never told me about? Is that why I'm here? He does kind of look like us. Behind him is the yellow house where Mom abandoned me.

I climb down the ladder, take a deep breath, and open the closet. Mom's side is as it always is, like a clothes explosion, unlike mine, which is tidy and organized. "You're so anal, Cassidy!" she'd said once, taking handfuls of my carefully folded shirts and throwing them into the air. I sigh. Her side is still her side, everything balled up and shoved in, ten dresses to one hanger and the rest of the hangers empty. It doesn't look like she took anything. I pick up a yellow sundress and bring it to my face and breathe in. "Where are you?" I say quietly. Then: "How could you do this to me?" I pull out her light blue dress from the corner it's jammed in. Her favorite. The one she wore the night Dave proposed. I lift a few strands of stray blond hair from it and carefully tie them around my finger. I put on the blue dress, then go into the bathroom. Her toiletry bag is still there, her toothbrush, soap, shampoo. Her jasmine oil.

I dab some on my neck and wrists. (Though I don't understand it, Wynton, long after I finish this bottle, to this very day in fact, I swear I continue to smell like this perfume, this scent that I associate with my mother and our time together.) Then I go to the table and pick up pieces of the note she left, wishing I hadn't done such a good job of shredding it. I can't remember much of it now that whatever she gave me has worn off. There's no doubt in my mind that she drugged me. I get the Scotch tape and sit on the bench and start putting the note back together. Maybe in the part I didn't read, it said when she'd be back. Maybe it said who Dexter was.

Not sure how much time goes by.

I continue with the note, sticking my finger in the jar of jelly periodically because it's incredible. Like manna. I look at the label: Dexter Brown's Grape Jelly. He makes this jelly? I study the label because it's familiar. Then I stand and open the cupboard behind me because as I suspected, there's another jar just like it, and next to it a bottle of Dexter Brown's Red Vinegar and a bottle of Dexter Brown's Pinot Noir.

A day comes back to me. Mom and I were at a wine festival up north and she was talking to a man selling jars of something or other. He looked like Dave from behind, same messy hair and lanky frame, same easy gait as he stood and slowly walked over to her. Nothing new. She was always talking to men who looked like Dave. But this time my heart had started fluttering because they were hugging like they knew each other. As I walked toward them, I got more and more certain it was really Dave. Maybe he'd left Joanne and had been scouring the state looking for us? Dave turned around and all that hope retreated inside me. It was some older man, more weathered and just not Dave. I went back to Purple Rain. When Mom joined me, she had the jelly, the vinegar, and the wine. I try to remember what she said to me about the man who must've been Dexter but can't. I pick up the bottle of jelly. There on the back is an address and an email.

I go to the window and look at the man strumming his guitar under his cowboy hat. There's a harmonica around his neck. He really does look so much like us. Could it be her brother? Why would she tell me she was an only child then? My mind whirs and whirs and then I'm thinking how easy it would be to imagine him on a horse. Is he an old boyfriend? Why would she leave me with some rando ex-boyfriend?

Unless . . .

I look at the shattered girl in the remains of the mirror.

Unless . . . he doesn't look like *us,* he looks like *me.*

Because . . .

But what about Jimmy the Dead Drowned Dad?

I haven't been honest with you—

No, not possible, right, Wynton?

I run back to the note, continue working on it. Soon, I make my way through her barely legible words:

> *I haven't always been honest with you. I met your father at a bluegrass festival in San Diego, spent one beautiful afternoon together, and that was it. I never knew his name or where he lived and figured it'd be easier for you if you thought he was dead rather than out there somewhere with no way to find him. Like all my decisions, it wasn't very thought through. We ran into each other recently and he was as wonderful as I remembered. I think you'll find you have a lot in common. After communicating with him by email, I know he will keep you safe in ways I can't . . .*

The note continues but she doesn't tell me where she's gone or when she'll be back for me. The final part of the note is about money. She says there are two bank accounts in my name, a college fund and a savings account that I can use for living expenses and that there's a bank card in the drawer with a sticky note attached that has the PIN.

I open the drawer. There's a bank card in it that has two names on it:

Cassidy Snow and Mary Snow. Her name isn't even Marigold; it's fucking Mary. Mary Snow. A stranger's name.

I go to the window and peek out the curtain.

He's still out there, waiting. For me. There's something about his face, a stony patience, that tells me he'd wait forever. I walk across Purple Rain, grab the door handle, and open it. I say to the man sitting in the chair, "You're not my uncle."

"No."

"I know who you are."

"Makes one of us," he says, and I catch a smile in his eyes that reaches nowhere else in his face. "You hungry?"

I nod, step down from Purple Rain. His bones crack as he rises from the chair.

As we walk to the yellow house, the sun's warm and welcoming on my skin, and its rays dapple the path, so it looks like my father and I are walking on water.

"You don't seem surprised," I say quietly.

"Are you kidding? This is me surprised out of my goddamn mind."

This makes me laugh and it feels so good. "Really?"

"You have no idea." The smile in his eyes this time is so fleeting, I barely catch it.

"So, if you win the lottery or get struck by lightning, this is you," I say, thinking we're already shooting the shit, like I did with Dave.

"Oh, I've been struck by lightning—it was nothing compared to this."

It's probably premature to like him. It's probably premature to feel like I'm jumping on a trampoline inside myself because I have a father. A father who makes dry jokes, who waits for me, who smiles only in his eyes. Then he stops mid-step and when he speaks next, his voice is full of emotion. "I need to tell you that I didn't know about you until a few weeks ago when your mom emailed me."

"Did she get your email from the jelly jar?" I ask, still trying to put all this together.

He nods. "Not sure if you were at the festival that day. The moment I saw her, I knew who she was. Hard to forget your mom, she's like a meteor." Eye-smile. "She didn't recognize me at first. Had to remind her how she lured me away from my favorite bluegrass band eons ago, telling me she had to know everything about me that very minute, said it was destiny we met. Something about how she could imagine me on a horse and then she went on about Jupiter being conjunct to something or other. Never done anything like that before or since, don't have an explanation either, felt like I was under some kind of spell. But it turns out she was right, it was destiny." The smile this time finds his mouth. "You are that destiny." He shakes his head. "I must've read that email from your mom fifty times." He laughs and it makes me feel warm inside. "Asked Nigel— my vineyard manager—to print it out, and to be a hundred percent honest and I will admit this to you only, I slept with it under my pillow that night so I could look at it first thing when I woke up. Couldn't believe I had a daughter. I felt—" He swallows, his face brimming with emotion. "I don't know how to describe it. It felt like some kind of redemption. Some kind of grace."

I'm confused by this story, by all the feeling in his words, on his face. My voice comes out slight, tinselly. "You mean you were happy?"

I've always been a burden, a leech.

"*Happy* doesn't come close. I felt, well, don't know how to describe it. Like someone switched on the lights. I emailed back, inviting you and your mom to visit. Painted the house even—" The canary yellow? "Then didn't hear back, just about gave up, tried the email again but it bounced back. Then woke up yesterday to a purple rig in my driveway. Next thing I knew I was involved in the first car chase of my life." He eyeballs me, lifting an index finger. "Never again, by the way. No more driving until you get a license." I laugh to mask that I'm welling up, realizing I finally have an honest-to-God parent.

The summer days pass.

Then the years do, and Wynton, for the first time in my life, they're safe and happy ones.

There's this Louise Glück poem I love now. I've tattooed my favorite line from it on my shin: *Of two sisters one is always the watcher, one the dancer.* That was Mom and me. I was always the watcher, but with my father's eyes on me, in these years, I become the dancer.

WYNTON

You know Cassidy's there because you smell flowers, but she's not saying anything. For hours, lifetimes, it seems. Is she reading? Just sitting and staring at you?

You hope she's touching your arm. You remember how she brushed your face with her fingers in the moonlit road, like you were something precious.

You remember how when you played violin you tried to find the ache between notes with your bow.

Now you are that ache.

Finally, you hear, "I'm not sure what you know about your family and what you don't, Wynton, but I need to tell you that we're okay, you and me—we're okay."

Then the scent of flowers is gone.

DIZZY

Standing on the porch in the yellowy sunlight holding *her father's* hand, Dizzy no longer felt like the walking-talking paint splatter of a person she usually did, instead like a calm fearless one who was no longer afraid her big brother was going to die. A girl who wasn't even afraid of being face-farted again or being ugly forever or even being without her one best friend. She felt taller. Maybe she *was* taller? She remembered the moment in the Alonso Fall story when Alonso found out the truth about his real father and started giving off light, and how maybe she was undergoing such a transformation herself. Because didn't Alonso *actually* get taller in that moment? Maybe the same magic from Cassidy's stories was in Dizzy's family in the here and now, but it was more subtle, so you had to look harder for it. She wanted to ask the others if she was indeed growing in fast motion, but read the room and kept it in.

Miles was still seething, his face like thunder, his eyes pinned to the man in the cowboy hat, their *dad*. "What kind of father leaves his whole family and never comes back?" Miles cried out, clearly not yet realizing they were in a miracle. Dizzy had read once that there were at least two hundred reported cases of spontaneous human combustion in the last century, and watching Miles in this moment she wondered if she was about to witness another. "I just don't get it," he raged on. "Do you know how much I needed you?" He gestured toward Dizzy. "All of us! You've never even met Dizzy—the most incredible kid—and she's twelve years old!" Dizzy's mouth fell open. Miles thought she was an incredible kid? It made her feel like an incredible kid! She bit her cheek so as not to smile. Who would've thought she'd be having these kinds of epic moments right in the middle of the absolute worst week of her life?

Her father was taking Miles's outbursts as if they were physical blows, and she felt the man retract each time another one hit. She held on tighter to his hand trying to tell him through her touch that everything would be okay now that they'd found each other. She scanned the others. The guy in the doorway, whoever he was, looked like he was watching two cars colliding at top speed and there was nothing he could do to stop it. Sandro was barking desperately at Miles from their father's feet. Felix looked like he wanted to bark too. Dizzy noticed the pigs in the sty had pushed their snouts through the fencing of their pen. A row of sunflowers that Dizzy could've sworn had been facing the road were now looking their way.

The whole world was at attention.

"I understand how angry you are, Miles," their father said. "You have every right to be." His voice was tight, like the words might be choking him. "There's no excuse for what I—"

"No, there isn't!" Miles stamped his foot, then pointed at the house. "Please explain to us how it's okay that all this time you've just been up here being someone else's father?"

Wait, Dizzy thought. *Whose* father? She regarded the young man in the doorway whom, she remembered now, their father had called Nigel. He caught Dizzy's gaze and at the same time she said, "Are you his son?" Nigel said, "Not me," and Miles said, "No, Dizzy. *Cassidy!* This is her house, remember?"

A brand-new chord in Dizzy began vibrating. In all the shock and excitement and hallelujah, not to mention her potential personal physical transformation, she had not remembered. She felt like she might fall off her own legs. That meant . . . "Cassidy is my sister?" She whispered the words, dropping her father's hand, bringing both of hers to her chest. She had a sister? A big sister? And it was *Cassidy*. Her *sister* had pushed her out of the way of that truck and saved her life. And Wynton's too. Oh, oh, oh. This was an even bigger miracle than she'd thought. A mega-miracle was happening. Her body felt like a live wire. Holy cow cow cow. This was better than any miraculous event she'd ever researched. She'd rather have a father and sister drop out of the sky than shoot fire from her fingers like Buddha or fly through the air like Saint Joseph of Cupertino. Even if this news meant Cassidy wasn't an angel or Energy Being. Because how could she be if this man was Cassidy's father, just like he was Dizzy's? But Dizzy didn't care about that anymore.

She'd much rather have a big sister than an angel.

But the most irrefutable part of the mega-miracle was that her sister had led them to their father so he could wake Wynton with his trumpet. This was such a good, solid, feasible plan, unlike prayer-walking and lying prostrate on dirty floors and becoming a nun. The extra bonus obviously being Dizzy's fiery furnace would never have to go cold and dark in a convent.

"We need to get to the hospital now," she said. She looked at her father. "Please go get the trumpet so you can wake Wynton."

"I can't, Dizzy," he said to the porch floor.

"You can't get the trumpet, or you can't go to the hospital?" Dizzy said.

Her father began massaging his forehead under the rim of his hat like he had a headache. "I can't go. I'm sorry."

Dizzy couldn't believe what she was hearing.

"No," Miles said. "No way. Dizzy's right. Your *son* is in a coma and maybe you can save him. Please go get the trumpet."

Dizzy and Miles smiled at each other on the inside without doing so on the outside. Miles believed in the plan. She wanted to jump on his shoulders. She wanted to tell him he too was a white truffle with lightning inside him. She had two favorite brothers now.

And a favorite sister!

Their father went into the house and Dizzy relaxed, believing Miles had convinced him and he was getting the trumpet. Nigel went inside too. Dizzy wanted to follow them. She wished she could see every corner of that house and especially her sister's bedroom. She wanted to open all the drawers, read every secret thing, put on all her sister's clothes, but there wasn't time for that.

A minute later, their father was back on the porch, trumpet in hand. But something was wrong. His cowboy hat was missing, and it seemed his life-force was as well. Had someone inside the house unplugged him? Or broken him?

"I can't go to Paradise Springs." He said it definitively, and the buzzing in Dizzy silenced. She heard music coming from the house; had it been playing the whole time? Jazz maybe? "I'm so sorry," he continued. "To see you both has meant . . ." His face crumpled. "I can't tell you." He grabbed the doorframe for support. "But I can't do it." He held out the trumpet to Dizzy. "Clive can play it."

"What do you mean?" Dizzy said. "Wynton's been missing you his whole life. You're the one who can bring him back to us."

"I'm sorry," he said again.

"But all you need to do is get in the truck with us," she said. She could hear the shrillness, the desperation in her own voice.

Their father looked at her, then at Miles, as if to record their faces in his mind, then rested the shiny trumpet on the arm of a rocking chair and went back inside, shutting the door behind him.

Dizzy went to the door and tried to turn the knob, but it was locked. She knocked. "Please," she said, standing on tip-toes, trying to see the wrong way through the peephole. "You have to come with us." Hysteria was rising in her. She could feel it like a storm. She turned to Miles.

He looked like she felt—wrecked. He held out his hand, but she couldn't move. "We have to get back," Miles said. "We don't need him, Dizzy. Never have." She nodded, but she felt the opposite. She picked up the trumpet and dragged her dead-limbed body to Miles. Felix joined them. She realized the dog was gone. Was he inside? Had he gone back to the truck? Everything she'd felt moments before had flipped. She was still the shortest twelve-year-old on earth. She was the same scared, ugly, friendless paint splatter of a girl with hair you could see from outer space whose brother might die. There was nothing miraculous happening here. Nothing normal either. Because even if their father didn't believe in the plan, which she understood might not sound entirely logical to certain people, Dizzy couldn't fathom why he didn't want to be by his son's side at least, to talk to him and tell him stories, to place his ear to his heart like she and her mother had. It made her chest ache for Wynton, for all of them. She knew how much Wynton loved this man, and how she'd begun to in just a few moments.

Once again, she was faced with the fact that love didn't always go two ways.

Their father didn't love them back. That's why he left. That's why he wouldn't come to the hospital.

Life was a terrible place to live.

She was halfway down the path to the truck, feeling like every last thing had been swept off the shelf inside her, when she heard Miles say, "Does Mom know you're here?"

She turned to see that their father had opened the door and was now silhouetted in the narrow opening watching them leave. A shadow, not a man. He shook his head, said, "When I left, I told her to never try to find me."

Miles swallowed. Dizzy could see the light seeping out of her brother's face. "I always thought if we met, I'd look up to you," he said to their father. "I thought I'd want to be just like you. I can't imagine what happened to make you like this."

Dear Wynton, Miles, and Dizzy,

This is what happened.

So many things I haven't told you.

So many things I thought I'd never tell you.

But everything feels different now as I sit in this hospital room by Wynton's side with only a pen and terror as companions.

I'll try to be as honest as I can.

The day I met your father, my family had only been in Paradise Springs for a couple weeks. Your grandfather Victor Fall called my parents and told them he wanted to do a private wine tasting in the hope that we might serve Fall wines exclusively at Christophe's Soufflé Shop when it opened. They freaked. To my parents, your grandfather was a celebrity. For years, my mother had seen him splashed over the society pages of the *San Francisco Chronicle*. "He looks like a blond Clark Gable, no?" she'd say, staring at the debonair, imposing (evil) man, always with his elegant wife Eva on his arm. (I'll just say I'm glad none of you met Victor, and that alcohol took him before he could ruin any more lives.)

All that morning, my mother kept repeating, "Who are we for Victor Fall to visit us? Nobodies! C'est incroyable!" as she snuck peeks in the mirror and brushed powdered sugar from her nose, while we scrubbed and polished, trying to turn Sebastian's Spanish Bakery into Christophe's Soufflé Shop before his arrival.

My parents dressed for the occasion, which meant they took off their aprons, a rarity. My father put on his black beret instead of the burgundy, and my mother expertly twirled her best scarf into a meringue around her neck. I was being forced to "look nice" too so I put on my less beat up black boots, less ripped jeans. I added Christophe's red flannel plaid shirt, then his black leather jacket, which I rarely took off. "You look like you live under a bridge!" my mother told me often back then, which made me very proud. With spiky hair and heart, I was committed to sarcasm and outrage, keeping private the ocean of emotion that roiled inside me.

Until your father.

Anyway, Victor charged into our world that day, one hand in the air presenting himself, the other on the bony shoulder of Clive, a scrawnier and punkier version of his father. "Victor Fall here," he announced to the room like he was beginning a prepared speech, which he was. "I understand you're French, Monsieur and Madame Fournier, and as such you may think you prefer your old-world burgundies to our California pinots, but that is simply because you've not tried mine. My relatives from the old country, Alonso and Maria Fall"—he pointed to something out the window and we all followed the gesture to the grand stone statue of a man—"they absconded from Spain with six rare, remarkable—some say magical—vines to start a new life in America. This is why my vintages have that old-world magic." His booming voice reverberated around the café finding a captive audience in my parents who were gazing at him with a mixture of intimidation and awe as he began pulling wineglasses out of a bag. "And what is that heavenly smell?" he asked, lifting his nose into the air. The nose-lift was what everyone did when they entered one of my parents' cafés. No one baked like them, though I predict you, Dizzy, will give them a run for their money one day.

"That is some old-world magic too," my father said proudly. "My chocolate raspberry soufflé will make you fall in love."

I watched Victor shake my father's hand too vigorously, then hold my mother's fingers a moment too long, making both of them blush. Next to him, my parents seemed even more diminutive, grief-stricken, and old-fashioned, like they'd popped out of a sepia photograph, washing up on the shore of a new century where this man was the king.

"This is my son Clive," Victor said then, pulling the boy to him. My dad stared at the father and son with so much longing, I had to look away.

"And this is our beautiful daughter Bernadette," my father said after a pause in which I heard the proud introduction he'd never make again: *Voilà my son Christophe.* I sighed, knowing I'd never be enough.

"Beautiful indeed," Victor said, drawing out the words as he gazed at me. My, what big teeth you have, I thought.

Clive bulged his eyes at me in a *get me out of here* expression and covertly mimed slashing his own throat. I laughed and he returned a quick cockeyed grin.

"Unfortunately, Clive didn't get his mother's genes," Victor said. "He got stuck with mine, poor kid. My wife's the beauty." How mean, I thought, watching Clive flinch. Clive had a mangy look, yes, but we all had the same "living under a bridge" fashion sense back then. I was impressed that Clive's hair had green streaks in it and liked how it hung straight and mostly in his face, like a curtain. He had on a worn-out leather jacket like mine, rose-colored sunglasses perched on his head, and black brick-like boots, also like mine.

But despite the mosh pit attire, Clive's face had none of Victor's scowl. His eyes were almond-shaped and kind. Freckles lined his pale cheeks. He was cool-looking and I suspected a world of trouble (how right I was), which intrigued me. "If only this one got my brains though," Victor said, continuing the public takedown of his son. His hand was gripped like a vise on Clive's neck. "This one thinks school's a joke," he went on. A cloud of embarrassment passed over Clive's face as his gaze fell to the floor. I looked at my parents and knew they too were wondering how a parent could be so cruel, could so take a child for granted. Clive squirmed out of his father's grasp and began pulling bottles of red and white wine out of the other bags that he and Victor had carried in, lining them up on the table and uncorking several. "This one, he is going into the tenth grade and he never—"

"Soufflés are ready, Papa," I interrupted so Victor couldn't insult Clive again.

Clive glanced up at me, his expression grateful. My father's forehead creased. He had an oven timer in his head and knew there was no way the soufflés were ready. "A few more minutes, mon ange." I nodded and scrubbed the already-clean spout on the espresso machine, surreptitiously studying Clive, asking myself, like I did about everyone then, friend or foe?

After Christophe died, I'd stopped hanging around with my friends in San Francisco. I felt like they could no longer understand me, nor me them. Nor did I understand myself anymore. The person I was had died with my brother. I felt empty and blank, like a nothing-girl. But one who wanted to take apart the world with her bare hands.

After the bottles were set up, the tasting began. Your grandfather Victor splashed wine into glasses with flair, pouring from a ridiculous height, as he introduced the different vintages to my parents. Clive shuffled over to the counter where I was cleaning the sparkling-clean espresso machine for the tenth time since they'd arrived.

"You like cows?" Clive said to me, hopping onto a stool.

I thought I'd misheard. Was he asking me to get high? Is that what they called it up here in the boondocks? Or maybe Cows were a band? "Cows?" I asked. "Like moo?" Clive nodded, his face serious while he waited for my response. "I guess so," I said, not having thought too much about cows.

He smiled. "Yeah, me too, they're the best. Like so chill. They spend twelve hours a day lying down. Only sleep for four. They have favorites too and when they're not with them they get super stressed and sad. I'm kind of like that when my brother's not around."

My heart skipped. *I'm kind of like that when my brother's not around.* That was me too. I was a cow that had lost my favorite.

Clive unzipped his backpack and took out a stack of Polaroids. "Meet the locals." He spread the photographs before me, each a close-up of a cow's face. "I'm doing a project." He was gazing lovingly at his bovine models. From the beginning, kids, there was something disconcerting about your uncle, like the pieces of him didn't quite fit together:

the swagger, the *I've arrived, you're welcome* attitude, with the shrinking in front of his father, and now this extremely weird cow thing. I didn't know what to make of him.

"A bovine portrait project?" I asked.

"Sure," he said like the bovine portrait project had been my idea and he was agreeing to do it. What an oddball this boy is, I thought. He retrieved an old-fashioned Polaroid camera from his bag, lifted it to his face. "Can I?" he asked. I nodded. "You have cow eyes actually," he said. "I noticed when I walked in." He snapped a picture of me.

"You can't tell a girl she looks like a cow!" I cried.

He placed the picture of me next to the others to develop. "I didn't. I said you have cow eyes. It's the highest compliment." He pointed to a brown cow's face. "You see? Those are the saddest eyes in the world. Like you can see the whole tragedy of mortal existence in them."

Friend, I decided then and there. Friend, friend, friend. Then Clive handed me the picture he'd just taken. My image was slowly emerging out of darkness. He'd caught me laughing. Had I laughed when he told me I looked like a cow? Apparently so. He lifted the camera again. I gave him the finger with both hands. "Bernadette!" my mother exclaimed from across the room. "Be polite."

"Don't dare be polite, Bernadette," whispered Clive, and his raised eyebrow and devious grin made me laugh. Again.

"I like your hair," I said.

He nodded as in *of course you do*. This guy. "How old?" he asked me.

"Fifteen."

"I'm already sixteen," he said with superiority, but then added to my surprise, "My mother's really sick. She has cancer." He took another picture of me.

"My big brother died," I said, surprising myself. I didn't talk about Christophe's death to anyone but my parents.

Emotion stormed his face. "Oh no. No. That's awful. Oh man. I couldn't survive that. If anything happened to my brother—"

"That's how I feel," I said. He nodded, and somehow, I knew he got it. We both looked down at the images of me getting clearer. "I want pink streaks."

"Easy peasy," he said. "I can help. Just so you know, I dress like this, but I don't especially like punk or grunge music."

"Oh. I like all kinds of music," I said.

"I only like David Bowie," he said. "I can play every single one of his songs on the piano and I know all the words. On other instruments too—"

Just then I heard music, a trumpet maybe. "That's Theo," Clive said with pride, and the bells on the door sounded. And there was your father. Seventeen years old, tall, with long brown ringleted hair and an angel face. I actually gasped at the sight of him but pretended it was a cough. He walked over to us, horn in one hand, a book in the other, and a battered old cowboy hat on his head. His eyes were dark green, like seaweed, and heavily lashed. Clive and I looked like the kids who smoked cigarettes under the bleachers. Theo looked like he rode flying horses across the night sky. Unicorns even. He put his book on the counter and gave Clive's Polaroid camera, now pointed at him, the finger. Like minds, I thought happily.

The novel he was reading was *One Hundred Years of Solitude*, one of Christophe's favorites. "Meet Prince Theo," Clive said. "Don't be fooled like everyone else. He sucks." I could hear Clive's admiration for his big brother breaking through the insulting introduction. It was unmistakable in the way he was looking at Theo too. The way I used to look at Christophe. I really understood Clive in that moment. We were two adoring younger siblings who could never measure up.

"Hello Prince Theo," I said, my heart rate on an uptick.

"Milady," he replied.

I tried to imagine what it would be like walking through life with so much beauty. It's funny because in all our years of marriage, I don't think I ever saw Theo in front of a mirror. He had no idea how stunning he was.

Theo slid onto a stool next to Clive and said, "Did you know this very minute there is a hurricane on Jupiter that is twice the size of earth? And it's been raging for three hundred years!" (Dizzy, you have this same fascination for outlandish information!)

"He's not stoned," Clive said, his camera on his brother. "This is just him."

"Look who's talking," Theo said, pointing to the cows lined up on the counter. "Did my brother tell you about his spiritual experience?" Clive tried to cover Theo's mouth with his hand, but Theo wasn't having it and had Clive's hand behind his back in a flash. The brotherly tussling, so second nature, made my chest ache. Theo continued, "Clive was walking home from school through a field, and it struck him that God was inside this one cow—"

"He is!" Clive said. "You have to see this cow, Bernadette! There's something about her. Will you come see her?"

"Sure," I said quickly. Who wouldn't want to see God in a cow? And that was when I said *Thank you* in my mind to Christophe, who surely sent these two wonderful wackos to me. I gazed down at the Polaroids Clive took of me, three now. In them was a version of myself that got happier from picture to picture. I remember you, I thought.

Feeling eyes on me, I looked up and met my mother's gaze. She was smiling. Perhaps she'd heard me laugh, a rare occurrence those days. My father was sipping wine, eyes closed, delight on his face, oblivious to anything but his palate. My gaze then traveled to Victor, and my breath hitched. He was leering at us—no, not at all of us, at Theo. There was way too much wolf in the look.

It was in that moment I knew something was gravely wrong in the Fall family. I had an overwhelming impulse to throw myself in front of Theo to protect him from his father. Instead, I pulled the soufflés from the oven. "One for them, one for us," I said to Theo and Clive. "Oh. And one thing you should know. They're said to be aphrodisiacal."

Both of the Fall boys smiled.

And so it began.

So, it all began.

—B

Kids—

I can't stop writing. I want to be there again. I don't think I've ever been happier than I was that first summer in Paradise Springs. I'd been so lonely and lost, so angry in my bones, just seething with the unfairness of the world and always having to keep it in, and then, there were your dad and Clive, the Fall boys.

I spent the day after I met them staring out the window, willing them both to come back. Which they did that afternoon. They returned for a soufflé to bring to their mother in the hospital, and soon after that: It was Bernadette and the Fall boys. The Fall boys and Bernadette. Sitting three in a row at the movies, on a boulder high up on the ridge, in a field staring at God in the form of a brown cow. Me always in the middle, Clive on one side, Theo on the other.

"Do you think your brother Christophe is still here, like his spirit?" Theo asked me one day. The three of us were lying on our backs in a high grass meadow, full of yellow jackets and daisies, watching the pink streamers left over by the sunset ripple across the sky. Their mother Eva was out of the hospital and doing better, but the inevitability of her death was always with them. I'm certain that was what made the three of us such fast friends. You can tell when death is near people. You can see it on a face, hear it in a voice. It's like grief is an exclusive club and members recognize each other as easily as if they were wearing name tags. We three were VIP members that summer.

"My father says Christophe visits him in the kitchen," I

said. "But I don't think he visits me." I ran my hands over the scratchy grass. "It's weird. I guess I think he has powers or something though, like he's the conductor of our lives now. I think he made us leave the city and move here, made Sebastian's Spanish Bakery be vacant and for sale, made you guys come in. I think he wants the three of us to be friends—" At that, to my surprise, at the same moment, from opposite sides, both Theo and Clive touched my hand.

"We're only friends with you for the soufflés," Theo said, turning his head toward me and smiling. He rolled onto his side. "And because we needed a sister." These words. These words of Theo's, to this day. I felt something long forgotten opening up inside me: joy. I had an impulse then to touch Theo's face. What if I had? Would things have turned out differently? I think maybe so. But I left my hand by my side. "You know what's strange?" Theo said. "I'm pretty sure I saw Mom's ghost the other night. I sleepwalked and woke up in the hammock and she was standing in the field. I went to her, but she disappeared. I wasn't dreaming either. I know it doesn't make sense because she's not dead." The word *yet* hovered in the air. I wanted to reach for Theo's hand. Again, I didn't.

It was getting dark, the meadow filling with shadows.

Clive stood. "Let's go swimming," he said, his voice breaking. "Let's fucking jump in the river."

"Ever swim at night?" Theo asked me. "We have the best spot. Jeremiah Falls. It's off Hidden Highway. We'll have to hitchhike there. My truck's dead."

I, of course, had never swum at night. Or hitchhiked. Or had two friends like Theo and Clive.

For the first time in a long while, I felt lucky. That night we swam in the river until there wasn't a trace of death left on any of us. I think of that night often, all of us young and alive in the moonlight.

It was weeks later I learned more about Victor.

We were crashed in the Fall vineyard in our sleeping bags under a full moon. I thought we were outside for fun but would soon understand that Theo and Clive had started to sleep in the vineyard to avoid their father.

I remember that night so clearly, the intimacy of it. The way all our voices intermingled in the dark, like our spirits were braiding together. By then, I felt like I could trust them with anything. And they must've felt the same about me, because after a lull in conversation, Theo said to Clive, "Can I tell her?"

"Tell me what?" I asked.

"I won't if you don't want me to," Theo said.

"It's okay." Clive said. "She's our sister now."

Again, these words.

Theo sat up so he was half in, half out of his sleeping bag. "Our dad taught us to fight," Theo said as coyotes howled in the distance. "Both wrestling and boxing. We've been fighting each other since I was seven and Clive was six." Clive rolled onto his side in his bag. The moon was bright enough to see the despair in his face. "It used to be fine," Theo went on. "Like fun. I mean, Dad's always made us compete with each other, for everything. Like when we were little, he'd tell us he only had one hug and whoever told him a better joke would get it."

Clive said, "Theo would tell the worst joke, something that didn't even make sense, so I'd get the hug."

"Or Dad would drop us off at Pan's Ridge," Theo said.

"And he'd tell us whoever got home first would get to go with him to town for an ice cream." There was a bitterness in Theo's voice I'd never heard before. I thought then of the way Victor had glowered at Theo in the café so many weeks ago. "Our mom hates it," Theo said. "Hates all of it so much."

"I always fell for it," Clive said. "I always wanted the ice cream or the hug, wanted to win, which I always did, not realizing until I got older that Theo was letting me. But we'd have these epic battles."

"Yeah, Clive's scrappy," Theo said warmly. "But I did always let him win."

"Not always!"

"Always, Clive," Theo said. I remember looking at Theo in this moment and thinking how he looked aglow in the moonlight. So many times since, I thought this same thing. "But since Mom's been in the hospital, Dad's been . . . I don't know what's going on. The other night he got us out of bed to fight and when we got in the ring—our ring is the living room, we move the red couch—he started saying these totally awful things to get us riled up, so we'd take it out on each other. It was sick."

"What kind of things?" I asked.

"It's me who got so riled, Theo. Not you." Clive sat up, flailed his arms helplessly. "I was trying so hard not to let Dad get to me, but he was saying how everyone likes Theo more. How Theo's better than me at everything. He said I was pathetic, useless. He said—"

"He didn't mean it," Theo said, cutting Clive off. "He only said that shit so you'd—"

"What? So, I'd whale on you?" Clive exhaled loudly,

miserably. "It worked. Theo wouldn't fight back. He faked it, kept it together no matter what Dad said, but I lost it—"

"It's okay," Theo said to Clive. "You didn't hurt me." I sat up too then, a queasy feeling in my stomach. "He wants us to hate each other, and the closer we are, the more it pisses Dad off."

"Why?" I asked. "Why would any father want his kids to hate each other?" I was horrified. "He can't *make* you fight each other. Can't you just say no?"

"We tried that," Clive said. "The next night, it happened again. Theo said he didn't want to fight me anymore. Dad went crazy." Clive turned on his flashlight and pointed it at Theo's chest. "Show her."

Theo lifted his shirt to reveal a blue galaxy streaming across his side. "Dad shoved Theo into the banister when he was trying to get away." Clive looked at his brother and said, "It won't happen again though. Dad's just upset because of Mom."

"It's going to happen again, Clive." The way Theo said this sent a chill through me.

"Has your dad hurt you before, Theo?" I asked.

Clive's body clenched. Theo studied Clive, then shook his head.

But Theo was lying.

That night, I stayed awake long after they both fell asleep, watching how they turned toward each other in their slumber, how Theo's arm settled protectively on Clive. I had the sense then that Theo would do anything for Clive. Anything.

And then the wildest thing happened.

Theo rose out of his bag and began sleepwalking deep

into the vineyard, holding his trumpet in his hand. I couldn't believe it. I hadn't even known he had the trumpet with him.

I woke Clive.

I'd never seen a sleepwalker before, couldn't believe how gracefully he was moving down the row of grapevines. Clive and I scrambled after him like two uncoordinated crabs. At first, we couldn't stop giggling, tripping, bumping into each other, while Theo sailed effortlessly through the night, negotiating roots and rocks as if he were wearing night-vision goggles.

Half boy, half wind, I thought, watching Theo, and when he got to the edge of the vineyard, he brought the trumpet to his lips and started playing. In his sleep! My spine tingled. Clive and I followed Theo up and down the rows, the music— jazz maybe? Classical maybe?—floating in the air, until the first sprays of morning light filled the sky.

Once a year on the Jewish high holy days, back then, my family road-tripped to the one temple in the area, which was over eighty miles away. At the Yom Kippur service, I'd spend my time scoping out the other kids who were as bored as I was with all the standing and sitting, the incomprehensible Hebrew, not to mention that we were all starving from the fast. I never felt God there or in Clive's cow or anywhere. I figured if he existed, he would've shown himself when Christophe died. Before he died. He would've saved my brother.

But there in that vineyard with Theo sleep-playing this dream-music and Clive by my side, for the first time in my life, I felt a presence of something I only had the word *God* to describe. It felt like a divine hand had landed on my shoulder. Clive smiled at me, and I knew he was feeling it too. Something more.

More world, I remember thinking. More and more and then some more world. (Be on the lookout for these moments, my children.)

"Look," I whispered to Clive, pointing to the end of the row. A black dog, several squirrels, and two deer were poised there like they'd been called by the music. "I wish we had this on video," I said to Clive. "He's not going to believe this."

"I don't believe this." Clive's voice was filled with awe.

Theo stopped playing then, concert over, and lowered to the ground, curling up, the waning moonlight finding him so that he glimmered there in the dirt. Clive and I huddled together, watching as the animals slowly approached Theo and then sat down around him.

"What's happening?" Clive whispered.

"He's magic," I said.

"I think there's something wrong with me," Clive whispered. "Don't make fun of me, Bernie, but I feel like I love him too much. Like it makes my chest kill."

I wanted to say, *Me too*, but held it in.

This night might have been the night I fell in love with your father. It is one of my favorite memories.

Clive pointed to the menagerie with Theo curled up in the middle of it. "That black Lab Sandro is the Bells' dog, but he sneaks into Theo's room at night. And sometimes birds fly to his window and perch there on the sill while he sleeps," Clive said.

"Really?"

"Girls too. They camp out in the tree outside his window."

"Why?" Ugh. I did not like this idea.

Clive shrugged. "One girl, Lucinda Paul, wouldn't leave until he said he'd take her to some dance."

"Did he?"

"Yeah. But just to stop Dad from calling her parents about the tree thing." He gestured toward Theo. "Dad says mean things to me, but it's Theo he hates. He won't let Theo play the trumpet in the house, says it hurts his ears, but always sings along when I play the piano or guitar or whatever. He never goes to Theo's track meets or comments on his perfect report cards, but if I get a C, he makes sundaes." Clive turned to face me. "We played hide-and-seek this one time when we were little, and my dad found me and took me to town for an ice cream. We just left Theo in his hiding spot. For hours. I went along with it, thought it was so funny until we got back. I found Theo still hiding in the laundry basket. He was crying, and Theo never cries. He wouldn't talk to me for days." Clive's gaze dropped to his feet. "Those days were the worst of my entire life. Not lying."

"I get it," I said. Looking at Theo sleeping on the ground surrounded by animals, I understood how someone's world would go dark without Theo.

And I was right. It has.

—Mom

MILES

Miles spent his whole life hiding his emotions only to have them all tornado out of him at once on meeting his father. He didn't know what to do with himself as he walked back to the truck, could barely keep his skin on. Dizzy and Felix were already inside the cab. Miles called for Sandro and climbed in the truck to see Dizzy hugging the trumpet tightly to her chest, devastated.

"We don't need him, Diz," he said.

"We actually do. Didn't you feel it?"

He had felt it. *It,* for him, being everything. "But we have the trumpet," he said, trying to make her feel better. "That'll work, right?"

She looked at him like he was boneheaded. "We need him with us because he's our father, Miles."

He studied his little sister. She was wearing this heartbreak differently than the heartbreak of previous days. The perpetual bubble of optimism that made Dizzy Dizzy had burst and hopelessness had invaded her tiny body. It was in the slumped shoulders, pained eyes, downward tilt of her neck. He couldn't bear it. What kind of dipshit father did this to a little girl? *His* little girl? Closes a door on her? How dare he? His fists were two grenades at his sides.

He leaned out the truck, unclenched his jaw, and called for Sandro again. Then he called the dog from inside his head. They had to get out of there already. Where was Sandro? He never took off like this.

"Why doesn't he want to be our father?" Dizzy said softly.

"Only an idiot wouldn't want to be your father," Felix replied. Miles smiled at him, so grateful he was there. He had an urge to give him something, like the Golden Gate Bridge or Mount Everest. But what must he be thinking of all this? Of Miles's epic meltdown?

"Be right back," Miles said. "Going to get Sandro."

"Can we talk about something else for a second?" Miles heard Felix say to Dizzy as he hopped out of the truck. "Like how awesome it is that Cassidy's your half sister."

Tenderness crushed Miles at these words. Felix was probably the most badass big brother. Miles slowed to hear Dizzy's response. "It's the best thing that's ever happened to me," she said solemnly, then added, "I guess that's how she knows our family stories, because they're her family stories too."

Now Miles was being clobbered with affection for Dizzy, but as he continued down the path, that affection began morphing into anger, and then several steps later, into a wild flailing rage with teeth and claws. The closer he got to the yellow house, more and more blood-red words filled his head—he was going to rip his father apart with them. Because what kind of monster was the man? How could he do this to Dizzy? How could he not want to see his son whose heart had just stopped? And what was wrong with Miles that he felt sick with need for this man and at the same time like he might possibly kill him? Also, who would believe that coming out to his sister would be the least consequential thing to happen to him in the past couple hours?

As he approached the door, Miles heard jazz. Had it been on this whole time? He hadn't noticed it before. He didn't knock or ring the bell. The door was ajar, probably from when the man watched them leave, thinking he was done with them.

Well, sorry, Charlie, not so fast.

Miles pushed the door open and walked into a massive room with a vaulted wood-beamed ceiling. His father wasn't there. Neither was Sandro. He shouldn't be there either, he knew that. He felt like a burglar in the airy space that was brimming with the rich luxurious sound of trumpet, bass, piano. So inappropriate, Miles thought, as was the sunlight pouring joyfully through the large windows. At the far end of the room was a wall of shelved books that had an attached ladder to reach the highest volumes. So many books. And to his left was a similarly shelved wall with a ladder, but the shelves were filled with vinyl.

Miles's hungry eyes took in the room, vacuuming up the man's life, inch by inch. On the other side of the living room area was a large dining table with a computer open on it, and behind that, a wine refrigerator with hundreds of bottles inside. To his right was a fireplace large enough for Miles to crouch in. He scanned the photos on the mantel. His father and Cassidy on horses. His father and Cassidy in the vineyard. His father and Cassidy around this very coffee table in front of the couch, on it a lopsided birthday cake crowded with candles. His father smiling from east to west about to blow them out. He hadn't seen the man's smile yet and it pierced Miles's heart. As did the evidence of his love for another child. How come he could be a father to her and not to them? There were no photos of Cassidy when she was little and none with a mother, a wife, or girlfriend. He didn't know how old Cassidy was either. Had his father had an affair? Or was Cassidy from before he married their mom? Or could she also be their mother's child? No, that didn't seem possible.

The pain in his chest was knife-sharp now.

He had an impulse to piss all over the room, to lay claim to every last bit of it.

He ran his hand across the armrest of an oversized yellow leather couch. In front of it was the large low wooden coffee table with stacks of more books and albums as well as half-played games of backgammon and Scrabble. There was a deck of cards, with a scorecard beside it: *Cassidy* and *Dad* followed by two long columns of numbers, written in what must be Cassidy's handwriting—or he supposed it could be his father's, referring to himself as *Dad*. *Her* dad. He didn't even know his own father's handwriting. His father and Cassidy had probably been playing this card game for weeks. Next to that was a vintage record player that was spinning. He had the overwhelming and unsettling sensation being in this room that this was where he'd belonged all these years, where he would've felt at home. But he hadn't been wanted here. It was worse than being rejected by Wynton and Dizzy because he'd always felt alien from them. His father and Cassidy seemed to be made of the same stuff he was, people who read like others breathed. Cassidy had had these books, these games, this music, this sunlight, this man, and he hadn't. His stomach heaved and he had to breathe through it so he didn't vomit all over the table, all over their beautiful father-daughter life.

He was a speck of dust, that's how little he mattered here.

He walked over to a wall where there was a framed photograph of Cassidy. She was sitting on a boulder in a river, her hair blond then and tumbling down her back. She seemed pensive and Miles wondered what she was thinking about. He wanted to traipse around in her mind for days, for years. How could he not have noticed how alike they looked? Except for the hair, his dark like their dad's, hers maybe light like her mother's? Who was her mother? And how long had Cassidy known about them, her half siblings in Paradise Springs? Because clearly, she knew. Had she just found out? Did she still think her father's name was Dexter? Where was her mother now? Had Cassidy come down to Paradise Springs to meet them all, but then chickened out? Had she wanted to tell Miles in the orange truck that day who she was? Miles sensed now that she had. Repeatedly. God, it was so obvious in hindsight. Of course she was his sister. She'd felt like the other half of his soul.

And Dizzy was right. The Fall family stories were Cassidy's stories too. That's how she even knew about the purple, green, and blue stripes of his bedroom walls. Her father probably relayed them to her around this very table with a fire roaring, and she'd transformed them into the magic-infused tales she told Felix. He remembered her saying, *Sometimes I don't even read in order, just read some from one book, some from another, whatever, all night long. Like all—and I mean all of everything—is just one really long story.*

He *was* glad he was in the really long story with her now. Even if her fuckface father refused to be a father to him, to them. He realized he was grinding his teeth and stopped just as he heard heavy steps clomping down the stairs, and then there was his father at the bottom of the stairwell holding Sandro in his arms.

"Sandro was hiding under my bed," the man said. "I was bringing him out to you."

Miles examined the unfamiliar man's familiar face from across the room—it took his breath as it had outside. Miles was a slighter, younger replica of this man: same model, different year. It was eerie, like he was looking at himself in the future. He wondered if his father also frequented The Gloom Room. He thought yes. (And Alonso Fall too, for that matter, because what was up with the period when he became a fountain of darkness?)

Sorrow seemed to be all over his father, in his posture, in his stare that in this moment was devouring Miles, making him feel woozy, unsteady on his feet, unsteady in soul. Yes, Miles had futilely searched wine notes and written emails to an imaginary dad over the years, but he wondered now how much of the yearning at the core of his being, the feeling of emotional exile, all the lonely hope-bitten hours, were because this man had left him. What if the deep-seated fear that there was something wrong or askew at his core *began* with this man's rejection and was only *reinforced* by his siblings? This revelation jarred him. Because what if he'd had it wrong all these years and it was his father, not Wynton, who was the Big Bang of Miles's damaged psychic universe? And probably Wynton's too.

No, not probably, definitely. His whole life, Wynton had carried the hurt and rampaging anger that Miles was only experiencing today for the first time. Because not until being in this upside-down ship of a room full of books and music and love, until being in the man's presence, did Miles understand what Wynton always knew—just how much they'd missed out.

There was a tight ball of pain in Miles's throat and a yearning the size of a continent in his heart.

Miles's gaze drifted to Sandro, so at home in his father's arms.

Traitor.

Sandro didn't respond.

What the hell, Sandro?

Nothing.

You're going to pretend you can't hear me now?

Still nothing.

Why are you ignoring me?

Sandro turned his snout to Miles but didn't make eye contact. *Because I'm staying, Miles, and I don't know how to tell you. I'm staying with Beauty.*

Beauty? What? He's *Beauty!? You've got to be kidding me, Sandro. Beauty's my father? I thought Beauty was another dog!*

Your father used to sleepwalk all around our property, then crash in the vineyard under the moon. My human-mom Rory called him Sleeping Beauty.

How come you never told me?

You never asked!

Can he hear us?

I don't think so. Beauty and I never communicated this way.

Miles couldn't stop himself. *You love him more than me?*

Don't ask me that.

I don't need to now. You just told me.

Blood sped through Miles's veins as he absorbed this, as he looked at his father standing there with Miles's very own face plastered on his skull as he held in his arms Miles's very own surrogate dog and best friend on this earth. Sandro's snout was tucked under the man's chin. He looked more content than Miles had ever seen him because this man with Miles's own private face was the love of the dog's life.

This dog who didn't love Miles enough to stay with him just as this man hadn't.

Everything Miles had prepared to say evacuated the premises. His temperature began spiking, his thoughts were in a blender. He felt like he could break rocks with his hands. He glanced over at the photograph of the man blowing out birthday candles with his pretty teenage daughter and a proud smile on his fatherly face and a dam burst. Geysers and geysers of betrayal and anger and lifelong hurt erupted in Miles, putting his previous furies to shame. He could barely see, barely breathe, thought his head might fly off his neck. Because how dare this man—this Big Bang of damaged psychic universes—have Miles's face! How dare he have all these books! How dare he raise another child! How dare he play cards with her for weeks on end! How dare he not try to save Wynton's life!

How dare he steal Miles's dog!

It was too much!

Everything was too much!

"Fuck. Off. Both. Of. You. Shitheads," Miles said, not only for himself, but for Wynton and Dizzy too, savoring each word in his mouth, making each last. "Have a happy life together."

And he was gone.

CASSIDY

When you have a yellow house, a mountain bike, a mailbox with a bird feeder on it, a smartphone, a father in a cowboy hat, an address on Dandelion Road in a town called Whispering River, a kitchen you make meals in with a funny gangly vineyard manager named Nigel, neighbors named Mrs. McGerald on one side and The Heredias on the other, two horses (Chet and Billie), two pigs (Mingus and Parker), three chickens (Coltrane, Monk, Rollins), a front stoop you sit on with your dad at sunset where he tells you why pinot noir is the heartbreak grape and how the great wines are love stories in bottles.

When you have a bedroom with a window seat and purple curtains, a real bed, a town square with a main street with Becky who works at the bakery and Ami at the hardware store. When you go to high school and dance classes and cross-country practice and the mall. When you have sleepovers, slouch in rowdy classrooms, hang by the school fountain, party with people your own age by a river. When you've logged onto and streamed so many useless things. When you've baked pies and ordered pizzas and popped popcorn and blown out birthday candles. When you have a last name.

You start to forget what it was like before.

I start to forget, Wynton, how it was to hop out of Sadie Mae after hundreds of miles of sun-blind driving onto rubbery car-legs, my neck cracking as I lift my sundress over my head and let it fall behind me as I tear across burning sand, hand in hand with my rosy maple moth of a mother, both of us yelping and whooping our way to the swimming hole we've been talking about for ten straight hours, imagining how it will feel to plunge into the cool water and then we're there, on the ledge of a rock cliff counting: three, two, and we're both too excited to wait to one, so we jump into the air, and when our desert-heated bodies sink into cool blue water, it's religion. Because like my mother promised, there were times, that, without a doubt, The Divine Force ate us up like tacos.

I forget when I'm trudging through the vineyard with my father popping grapes into my mouth, when he teaches me how to ride a horse, how to play guitar, how to drive a car (legally), how to know the difference between hard bop and West Coast jazz.

I forget when I ride horses with my dad up to the ridge where I feed Billie apples out of my hand, Billie, who's become my horse; and as my father and I sit quietly in the sun, I realize I feel more like myself when I'm with him than when I'm alone, which is strange because with Marigold I never felt like myself, never felt like I had a self apart from her.

I forget as his mystery takes the place of hers, when I find the wedding band in his pocket with its inscription: *You are my forever, my always, my only,* even though he'd told me he never married, had no one in the world but me.

I forget when I watch him staring at a wall like it's a horizon, when I hear glass shattering in his office in the converted barn and I spy through a slot in the wood my father breaking wine bottle after bottle, hurling them at the floor, while Nigel, at my side, tells me it happens sometimes. I find myself forgetting when he closes himself off in his bedroom for whole weekends and I wonder if he's in The Silent World, if I'm ruining his life now like I did Marigold's.

I forget when he asks me my favorite color and I tell him—the same as the word *love*: purple—and he exclaims that I'm a synesthete like him because he sees music as colors and it feels like the coolest club ever to belong to and I wonder if Marigold ever paid attention to anything I did or said because how could she have missed this?

I forget as I plod down the halls at school with best friends Olan and Summer, when we three get our belly buttons pierced, get tattoos of blue birds on our thighs, when we dye each other's hair red, then blue, then pink, then go all-out rainbow, when we three stay up baking brownies, when we sneak bottles of my father's wine out of the house to drink by the river, where I tell them how my mother abandoned me, walked off into the night, didn't even take her toothbrush, when I tell them what happened with The Man in the Coats, and they put their arms around me and comfort me and then tell me their own impossible stories and my arms wrap around them.

I find myself forgetting at parties, where I'm kissing first Denver Cho, then Scott Swan, then Riley somebody, though nothing comes of those kisses because I'm pining away for Peter the pizza deliverer who was the boy who watched me from the tree when I crashed Purple Rain into the gully in the Land of the Nakeds, the boy who ignores me no matter how many Denvers or Rileys I kiss, no matter how many pizzas I order, until he finally stops ignoring me, and then I forget some more and we're on our way to our senior prom.

But the thing is, Wynton: Even with all the forgetting, my mother has become my shadow, my witness, my rage, my enemy, my ally, my yearning, my joy, *my language*. I get tattooed on my arm the quote everyone thinks is by Walt Whitman but is just a paraphrase of a quote by him: *We were together, I forget the rest.* I love these words, they are my faith. And I need faith because those years with Marigold broke something inside me and it is a permanent kind of broken.

In a faraway land in the time of forever, there was a mother and a daughter, I write before I go to bed each night and the words flow. I show my mother/daughter stories to no one because this is where I sneak up on her ("Oh there you are!") and despise her and love her, where she and

I are same-souled again, and when I get the postcards, one from India, one from Bali, one from the Camino de Santiago in Spain, I toss them into her old bag of words and retreat to my closet where there is that Marigold-spot on the wall and I punch it and punch it and punch it until my knuckles bleed.

MILES

Miles swung open the passenger door of the truck and hopped in. "Let's hit it," he said.

"Where's Sandro?" asked Felix.

"He's staying," Miles said.

Felix lifted his shades, made eye contact with Miles. "Um. Dude. You sure?" The very obvious unspoken words hanging between them: *He's not your dog to give away.*

"Couldn't be more sure."

Felix's concerned gaze—like should he drive straight to a psychiatrist's office?—lingered on Miles for a few moments, then he lowered his sunglasses, lit up the engine, and pulled onto the road, somehow knowing not to ask how it went inside the house. Miles thought again about Felix saying that when he reads or watches a movie, he moves in. That's what he'd done with Miles's life in the last twenty-four hours—he'd moved in, and Miles didn't want him to move out. He dismissed the morbid thoughts from last night. Of course Felix wasn't dying. Jesus. What the eff had he been thinking? About anything.

Dizzy's face was puffy from crying and her glasses were smudged and crookedly resting on her nose. Her hair looked as if she'd put her finger in a socket. How could a father not love this child? The image of her on tiptoes peering the wrong way through the peephole of the shut door assaulted him and made ice-hot heat flush through him. He *hated* the man for that, for so many things. God. Dizzy motioned for Miles to bend down, then cupped a hand around her mouth and whispered into his ear, "Did Sandro tell you he wanted to stay?" Miles couldn't have been more shocked if his sister had suddenly spoken to him in Sanskrit. How could Dizzy possibly know this wholly secret thing about him? He nodded and then she nodded back at him, sympathy on her face. She leaned in again, whispered, "That's so sad and you were already so sad."

Oh man. He put an arm around her and pulled her in tight and the three of them drove in an unwieldy silence out of Whispering River toward the hospital where Wynton quite possibly lay dying. They were too destroyed to even rejoice about their new half sister. The shiny brass trumpet lay quiet and songless on the dashboard.

"What a jerk," Miles said, but it came out flat, false.

"He didn't seem like a jerk to me," Dizzy said. "Not on the inside."

Miles sighed. The rage was receding now, and without it, all that was left was confusion, turmoil, his mind suddenly the messiest drawer imaginable, one that doesn't shut. In the photographs with Cassidy, their father looked like such a proud everyday dad. A good dad. But he'd shut the door in their faces! What piece of the story was Miles missing? He stared out the window at the streets that must be so familiar to his father, wanting back in that upside-down ship of a room, despite everything. It was pathetic. He felt magnetized to the man, helpless. He despised his father, could taste it in his mouth, and at the same time, Miles never wanted to let him out of his sight again. He wanted to sit on him or tie him up and make him play cards on the yellow leather couch. He wanted to jump into the photographs on the walls and never come out of them. He wanted to hide under the man's bed like Sandro had.

He wanted his dog back!

There was a splintering pain in his chest now. He could barely tolerate it. He felt like birds were pecking at his mind.

And now he was having trouble with his whole body, being in it, making it sit in the truck. Dizzy released herself from his embrace as he shifted this way and that. Why did his limbs feel so excessively long suddenly? So ungainly? How did anyone deal with having these ridiculous appendages? And this head? Just bobbling around on his neck like this? It was unbearable. He felt like he had twenty elbows, fifty knees, four heads as he readjusted and readjusted and readjusted, until they were about to enter the ramp for the highway home, and Miles said, "So sorry, Felix, but we need to go back."

MILES

When Miles walked through the door of his father's house for the second time, he had no words prepared, no idea what was going to happen. He remembered learning in physics that the strongest magnet ever built had 100,000 times the magnetic field of Earth itself.

That giant magnet was his father, and Miles was a tiny metal shaving.

The man was sitting on the yellow couch with Sandro as if waiting for Miles, as if he'd decreed his return, and maybe he had. The same jazz music filled the room. The expression on the man's face was softer, less walled up than it had been earlier. His eyes were red-rimmed. Had he been crying? Miles hoped so. He motioned for Miles to sit but Miles shook his head even though his legs felt weak and wobbly.

He thought of the epic tantrum he'd thrown earlier—two of them now!—not to mention that he'd told the man to fuck off and called him a shithead. Embarrassment eked its way through him, but indignation too. Hell if he was going to apologize. Still, he'd never acted that way in his life—like a petulant child. Maybe the little boy he used to be had blown back through time at the sight of the man who'd left him. The man, who, Miles somehow knew, had loved Miles for the first years of his life because the memory of it was in his bones though he never knew it until now.

Miles spent a great deal of time studying boys and men. His father was the kind of man who commanded a room simply by entering it. Tall, rugged, stoic, a freaking wine-making cowboy, for Pete's sake, face full of time and topography. Miles turned his gaze away. Looking at his father made the floor drop under his feet.

Then he turned back because here was his father.

Miles took a deep breath, then exhaled slowly. He'd keep it together this time. "Dizzy's just a little kid," he said. "You've crushed her. And her heart was already crushed because of Wynton." As the words came out, Miles understood he was also talking about himself.

"I know," the man said, sighing. Miles studied his father's hair, the dark curly tendrils, just like his own, except streaked with gray. The man reached across the table and lifted the needle on the record player. Miles fixated on the man's hands, the long fingers, again, so much like Miles's, except the older man's had vineyard scars and nicks, earth under the nails. The room, emptied now of musical paint, was less welcoming, less homey, which was a relief. His father took the album off the player, careful to hold it by its edges. "I want to come with you," he said, sliding the album into its sleeve: *Kind of Blue* by Miles Davis. His namesake. "That's the truth."

"Then why don't you?"

The man lifted his head and looked at Miles dead-on. He's a mirror, Miles thought. "I don't belong there," his father said.

"I don't understand that," said Miles. "Of course you do. What do you mean?" All he had were questions upon questions upon questions. "Why do you think that? What happened? How come you never came back? Not once. Can you at least try to explain it to me?"

His father's mouth twisted to one side. Miles could tell he was contemplating what to tell Miles, what not to. *Tell me everything,* Miles willed. "What does your mother say about it?"

"She doesn't," Miles replied. His father nodded slowly. "I mean, she says she doesn't know why you left. She just makes you dinner. Like every single night. Leaves a plate under the heat lamp in the restaurant when she takes off for the night. With pairings of wine." This was not what Miles had expected to be talking about, but he suddenly felt compelled to let his father know this. "So that's twelve years times three hundred sixty-five days, um, yeah, excluding holidays, so probably over four thousand meals she's made you." Was that a light in his father's eyes? Was he surprised? It encouraged Miles. "The bartenders love it. They get to eat the meal after closing. I think maybe she got the idea from how we leave the wine out for Elijah's ghost on Passover. I don't know. No one gets it." His father swallowed.

"And I write you, you know? Emails. I have a folder." He was on a roll now. "I call it *Help Me!* And I also search wine websites studying the wine notes, looking for ones that are as weird as the ones your wines used to get. For a while, I was sure I'd be able to find you that way." Miles recited from memory, " 'With his new Pinot Noir, Theo Fall has done the impossible—he has concocted true love out of grapes. With hints of black cherry, forest floor, and pure zingy bliss, you can pair this juicy wine with game birds, fatty fish, and the one who got away, because this wine is sure to bring them back. It's a dance you didn't know you knew until the music came on.' " The surprise on the man's face had morphed into shock.

"I imagine you all the time," Miles continued, unable to stop now. "Sitting in the bleachers at my track meets, standing in the doorway of my bedroom saying good night, eating alone at some restaurant. You'd be sitting in the back at a table with a whiskey in front of you, swirling the ice with your finger, like in the movies. I imagine and imagine you, you know? And Wynton, he's spent more hours staring at pictures of you than playing the violin and all the guy does is play violin. I think he plays it for you. I think he believes if he gets good enough, you'll hear about him and come back. And he cries when he plays. Always. I'm pretty sure it's because of how much he misses you." Miles didn't know he thought any of this but was suddenly certain of it all, as if a decade's worth of dust was blowing off the past. He was also suddenly certain he didn't hate his brother. His mother had said Wynton changed after their father left. Had Wynton been taking out his anger about their dad leaving on Miles all these years? For some reason? Miles didn't know, but maybe this was him starting to understand his brother a little, or trying to, anyway.

"When we were young," he went on, "Wynton would spend whole days looking out the window, down the driveway. I knew he was waiting for you to come home. We all knew it. But you never came back." Miles felt a tugging in his chest—he'd loved that kid who'd stared out the window all day long. What if he still did? "Wynton still sleeps with that trumpet you left him." Miles would go into Wynton's room when he went out, the only time he could enter without getting a shoe hurled at his head, and he'd see the lump under the covers.

"We've spent the last twelve years living inside your . . . your goneness. All of us. It's like we breathe it, speak it, sleep alongside it." Miles had no clue where this speech was coming from. Maybe he'd subconsciously been preparing it his whole life. "I've spent so much time wishing you were there to save me from so many things, things you know nothing about because you weren't there. I've spent so much time wondering what it would be like to have you as a father, how you'd tell me everything was going to be okay, because everything has not been okay for me." Miles's throat was getting tight. "I know it sounds inconceivable, but how do you know that your trumpet, your music, your voice, just being there in the hospital room, your smell even—Wynton once told me you smelled like leaves—how do you know that your actual presence in that hospital room after all these years of Wynton longing for it won't bring him back? I don't know it and I'm the most rational person in this family. I'd think if there was even the smallest chance that you could do that for Wynton, for us, you would."

Bravo.

Fuck you, I'm not speaking to you, Judas.

Miles could tell his words were affecting this man who'd missed everything in their lives, absolutely everything. "I just assumed," his father said. "I've always thought. I don't know . . ." He seemed genuinely perplexed.

"That we'd all forgotten about you?"

"Well, yeah." He swallowed.

"How could you think that?"

The man leaned over his knees, lifted his head. "Look, Miles, not that this will make the slightest difference, but I've watched pretty much every one of your track meets—they're all on your school's video channel, up to the last relay where you inexplicably took off with the baton mid-race. And I read the school's online paper, *The Oracle*, every day."

Now it was Miles's turn to be shocked. He didn't even know his school newspaper had an online edition or that his school had a video channel, for that matter.

His father continued. "I followed the whole academic decathlon you competed in last year and was furious that you guys lost regionals on that stupid technicality in the music category." He smiles in his eyes, Miles thought. "I read and reread the three poems you published in your school's literary journal, *The Phoenix*—I especially loved the wonderful recent one called 'Finding Religion in a Walk-in Refrigerator,' where the narrator's in the walk-in, smelling bleach and blood from the marinating steaks and meditating on life, but I sensed—though it's never stated outright—that there was another presence, a paramour even, in the walk-in with the narrator, but you, the writer, wanted that to be a secret." All the hairs on Miles's body stood on end. "I've been wanting to ask you about that for weeks. It's an incredible poem. You're really good, Miles. It reminded me of John Berryman's *The Dream Songs*." He was scanning a stack of books on the table, then reached out and grabbed a chunky one and slid it across the table. "Here. Have you read him?"

Miles shook his head. Yes, the poem was about the kiss with the sauté cook Nico in the walk-in, but Miles hadn't wanted anyone to know that. And no one had. Not even Hot AP English Teacher Mr. Gelman, who'd talked to Miles extensively about his take on it. But his father, sitting on this couch probably with a computer on his lap, had, unbeknownst to Miles, read the poem close enough to get it. "How many times did you read it?" Miles asked.

His father shrugged, then for the first time since they'd arrived, a smile flashed across his entire face, there, and then as quickly, it was gone. "Not too many. Fifty max."

Miles was always hearing people talk about feeling seen by someone else, but he never truly knew what they meant until this moment. No one had ever paid him this kind of selfless undivided passionate attention, as ironic as that might be. "There was someone else in the walk-in," Miles told his father. "And it was a secret. That is exactly what the poem is about." He felt see-through, way more so than when he'd told Dizzy he was gay hours earlier.

His father had found him, the real hiding him, deep inside a pile of his words. He'd crawled into Miles's poem and pulled Miles out of it.

"I think of you, your sister, and your brother every waking minute of every day and that is not hyperbole. It's fact."

"I think you should change your mind," Miles said. "I think you should get up off the couch and try to save your son's life. Please."

They took each other in, all the empty years coursing between them, years of words never said, of promises not made, of walks not taken, of meals not eaten, of a love never explored, a love Miles could feel standing before the man in his belly, his bones, his blood.

His father rose from the couch. Miles heard the man's bones creak and crack. Sandro scrambled to his father's feet. Then, before Miles had an inkling what was happening, his father had jumped the table, moving with the same kind of agility with which Miles was gifted, and then he was standing next to Miles.

His father's hand fell hard and determined on Miles's back, like the man was about to pull Miles into an embrace, into his life. Miles's body went rigid. He was quite suddenly made of stone. No, he thought, no, no, no way. The hot ball of pain was back in his throat, and his eyes were burning. "I can't . . ." Miles said. They were so close, he could feel the heat radiating off his father's skin. He was engulfed in the man's scent. Wynton had been right. Leaves, yes, but also earth, sun, sweat, hope. Miles's breathing was getting fast, too fast. His father's hand was still on his back, and he was peering into Miles's face, but Miles wouldn't allow it. No. He couldn't. He looked anywhere but at this man, then covered his face with his hands. Everything felt different now with his father so close so real so father-y rather than safely across a room talking about a dumb poem. Who cared if he read Miles's poem? How could it matter after what he'd done? How could he let this man breathe the same air as him? "I can't forgive . . ."

But before Miles could say *you,* his father said, "I can't either," and pulled Miles into his arms with gravitational force. Miles let him. Miles let his body melt into the embrace, feeling like a boy, like a tiny little boy being hugged by his mountain of a father. He heard a sound, a wail, and realized it had come from him. And then he was falling through years of pain and sadness, through nights spent alone and humiliated in his room while laughter rang out from downstairs, through so many days of not belonging, of hiding. He let himself fall and fall, because, as unlikely as it might be, considering what this man had done, Miles intuitively felt that here was someone who knew how to catch him, here was someone who knew he needed catching.

Miles heard his own words again: *I think you should get up off the couch and try to save your son's life.* And that was what his father was doing, only in this moment, Miles realized he was the son who was being saved.

"I'll come," his father whispered, and for the first time in as long as he could remember, Miles burst into tears.

From Bernadette's Notebook of Unsent Letters:

Dear No One,

I changed my mind. I'll never share what happened next. And next. And next. I'm going to rip these pages out of this notebook, but for now, sitting in this hospital room, with the past crashing around inside me, I need to get it out.

All of it.

The night everything changed, I was seventeen, Clive was eighteen, Theo was nineteen and out of school. The three of us were sitting together by Eva's deathbed, then by her grave. Theo and Clive told me Victor had started waking them up again (he'd stopped when their mom's cancer went into remission), cajoling them drunkenly into impromptu wrestling matches. When they resisted, Victor said, "You'll fight each other, or you'll fight me."

They chose each other. Theo held back, as always, trying to playact his way through it, not wanting to hurt Clive. But then, one day, Clive confided to me that Victor had gotten to him and he'd unleashed his fists on Theo, crushing them into Theo's gut, jaw, reveling in the thuds, realizing in the animal moment, egged on by his father's drunk sneering words, how pissed he was at Theo for his perfect grades perfect girlfriends perfect looks, his ability to tilt the world so everything always slid in his direction.

Clive's face had gone pale as he told me how it had infuriated him that Theo wouldn't lose control and so he'd gone after him even harder. This confession scared me. It

426

stayed with me, repulsed me. I hadn't known what to say to Clive. I couldn't believe Victor was turning this sweet boy who liked cows and David Bowie mean, bitter, violent.

Maybe Theo sensed that Victor was getting to Clive too, because, when, soon after that, Victor again said, "You'll fight each other, or you'll fight me," Theo apparently said, "I'll fight you."

I saw only the aftereffects. Theo sitting on my bed, head in his hands, while I placed icepacks on his cracked ribs. Clive was there too that night, pacing, his face flushed, eyes frightened. "I should've stopped him."

"Did you just watch this happen?" I asked Clive, disgusted.

"Leave him alone," Theo said to me. "It's better this way."

Clive was at my bedroom window, looking out over the square. "I'm scared."

"I know you are," Theo said gently to his brother.

"Of Dad."

"I know, Clive."

"Aren't you?"

"No," Theo said.

They came into a new kind of focus after this. I realized then that Theo, for all his head-in-the-clouds rhapsodies, was tough as a boot and would protect Clive at all costs, would always sacrifice himself for his brother, and that Clive, for all his bravado and recklessness, was fragile.

Was that what upset our equilibrium? Maybe. Maybe what had kept the three of us so perfectly in balance for years was that my affection for each brother was equal.

No more.

That night when I was placing the icepack on Theo's torso, he looked up at me and when our eyes met, something wordless passed between us. I'm certain he felt it too, because after that, his sleepwalking began taking him to me. Every week or so, my father would find him curled up on the bench outside the café at dawn, usually with several dogs and pigeons around him. I loved that his subconscious mind was guiding him to me. He joked it was the scent of my father's croissants in the oven, but it wasn't.

It was then I knew Theo was my beshert, my destiny in a person.

I'd wait at the window, sometimes all night, for the magical boy that was Theo to walk out of the darkness. No, he was a man by then. Nineteen and taking classes in enology and literature at the community college and working on his first batch of pinot noir. He'd gotten admitted to Davis, but didn't go, confiding to me that he was afraid to leave Clive alone with Victor.

Then one day at dawn, I was at my window lookout, and there Theo came, wide-awake this time, walking across the square toward our café, looking like a sun that had fallen out of the sky. He stopped when he saw me in the window and our eyes locked. My heart felt like it was going to burst as I climbed out onto the fire escape, flew down the ladder, and ran to him, throwing my arms around his neck.

"Oh God, finally," he said, lifting me off my feet like we were in a movie. Then he pressed me against a tree and kissed me until the tree disappeared, then the square, then the town. Until it was only the two of us left in the bright beautiful world.

I fell so in love with him.

I'm still so in love with him.

Stopping here because I have to stay in this moment.

I need this moment.

I don't know who I'd be without the regret for what I did next.

It has defined me, ruined me.

CASSIDY

My story is catching up to the present, Wynton, but we're not there yet.

Okay, a month ago, I'm working at the hot springs, dating assorted ding-dongs—which I'd been doing since the breakup with Peter the pizza deliverer post-prom—having deferred my admission to Stanford because I don't want to leave the yellow house, my purple bedroom, my horse Billie, not to mention my father, who's become my favorite human being. I also don't want to leave Nigel, the ranch manager, his wife, Lupé, and their toddler, Valentina, who has corkscrew curls and runs after me like a wobbly little drunk. They live in a house on the property and are family. Then there's my tabby Mazie, whom I rescued from the animal shelter where I volunteer on the weekends. All to say, the residents at Dandelion Road in Whispering River are doing just fine, thank you. Particularly this resident.

But some part of me knows the last years have only been a reprieve and that my life on Dandelion Road will one day be ripped from me just like my life with Marigold was.

This is that moment.

I wake to banging on the front door and thick choking smoke in the air. From the top of the stairs, I see two firefighters talking to my father and I do the least brave thing imaginable. I run back to my room, throw myself under the covers, and pretend it's not happening.

Then my father's there, shaking the covers off me. "We need to evacuate, honey. There's a wildfire. We have a few hours max. Get together what you want to take and meet me downstairs. I'm going to round up the animals and take them to a farm outside the fire zone. I want us to take Purple Rain if that's okay."

"Sure," I say.

"You all right? You understand what's happening?"

"Yup."

"I'm coming right back for you."

"Okay."

"Cassidy, everything's going to be fine."

"I know." My voice is barely audible. I'm not sure what's happening inside me, but it's not good. Have you ever seen a fast-motion video of a fern unfurling? Imagine that in reverse.

"I'm coming back for you. Do you hear me? Say it to me."

I couldn't say it, Wynton, because I didn't believe it. The people I love don't come back for me. This is why I'm so afraid you too won't come back.

"Please say it, Cassidy," my father insists. "I need you to believe it."

"You're coming back for me."

"Okay." He smiles with his whole face. A rarity. "A suitcase for a few nights. And whatever else you can't live without."

I do not pack a suitcase. I don't go out to help Nigel and Lupé. I go to my desk, open my notebook, and escape into the time of forever with my mother until it's time to go, then I grab three things.

It's telling what people take when there's a wall of fire bearing down on them.

An hour later, driving away with my dad in Purple Rain, I have Mom's digital camera with all our pictures safe inside it. I have my notebooks of *In the Time of Forever* stories about my mother and me. And I have Marigold's bag of words, which now also contains the postcards. That's it. I didn't empty out the drawer where I keep all the little gifts and mementos guys have given me. I didn't bring the framed photo of my friends Olan and Summer and me the night of our junior prom when we jumped into the river in our dresses and arrived drenched to the dance.

I leave with only my mother, her words, my stories, and my father.

My father, who I still think in this moment is my safe harbor and worthy of my trust. How can we be so wrong about people?

When he returned from the temporary animal sanctuary, he took a ladder out of the hallway closet, placed it right outside my room. In the ceiling was a hatch I'd never noticed before and my father disappeared into this secret part of the house and emerged with what he could not live without: two cardboard boxes. I had no idea we even had an attic.

"What's in them?" I ask as we crawl down Highway 43 in our face masks, with the air purifier humming at its highest speed. There's a line of vehicles stretching in front of us as far as I can see. The air is full of smoke because of the winds, but we're apparently not in fire danger yet. I think my father's pretending he didn't hear me. Not happening. "What's in the boxes, Dad?"

"Just some papers."

"What kind?"

"You know. The kind you need to take in a fire." I normally do not push my father. I tread lightly, not wanting to upset him, always sensing I could with too many questions. I have a lot of training in not wanting to rock the mental boats of parents. He's not unstable like my mother; he's the opposite, a fortress.

"Like deeds and leases? Stuff like that?" I ask.

"More or less."

"Less, I think. Those are in the file cabinets in your office." I know I'm challenging him, threatening our equilibrium, penetrating the fortress. Maybe it's the actual masks we're wearing that's giving me the courage to do this. "Tell me what's in them."

We drive in silence for a while and I've reconciled myself to not getting an answer when he says, "There are things I can't talk about, Cassidy."

"Why can't you talk about them?" I ask, which isn't fair. There's so much about my life with my mother I can't talk about, probably will never talk about. Things I've left out of the story I'm telling you, Wynton, shameful things I saw and did, things you might feel in between my words, maybe. Like the white spaces on a page. I think we have those same white spaces in our lives, where the untold parts are. There's so much about life on the road with Marigold that I still don't have words for, no matter how many dictionaries I conquer. So much that must stay in the time of forever. But I can't seem to give my dad a break this day with a raging wildfire on our tail. "You keep a wedding ring in your pocket."

"One day. Not today."

"It's inscribed: *You are my forever, my always, my only.*"

"Cassidy, please."

I can't let it rest. "What are you hiding from me? *Who* are you hiding from me?"

He swallows, then removes his mask and looks at me. There's fear in his eyes. "I can't," he says.

I unclick my seat belt and rise, about to dive into the back to open the boxes, but my father slams on the brakes. I lose my footing and fall to my knees. "I said no," he yells, and I mean *yells.*

A window in my heart that's taken four years to pry open slams shut in this instant.

I don't know who this man is, I think as I get up off my knees, chastened and afraid, and return to the passenger seat.

From Bernadette's Notebook of Unsent Letters:

Dear Shame,

This is the confessional then.

I quickly realized being in love with Theo was no different from having a marvelous crippling flu. It had been a few days since the kiss on the square, and my stomach felt like a hot coiling snake. Not to mention that I couldn't stop sweating, writing his name on any available surface, and hallucinating that he was wrapping his arms around me, kissing my neck until I had to run from my post behind the cash register at the café to collapse in a helpless heap of passion on the sacks of flour in the back room.

All very un-me-like behavior.

Theo and I hadn't been alone since the kiss and our plan was to meet up this morning before anyone else woke, particularly before Clive woke. I tossed off the covers at five a.m. and crept as quietly as possible to the bathroom to brush my teeth and splash water on my face. I had two hours before I had to be back under these same covers, where my mother would wake me for school with a "Morning chouchou," like she did every day. I was vibrating at the prospect of being alone with Theo as I slipped on my sneakers, and a moment later, I was out the window and on the front fire escape.

All I wanted was to bolt down the ladder, but I could hear my father humming inside the café as he set up the tables like he did every morning.

Finally, the humming faded out, which meant my father had retreated into the kitchen. I quickly descended and then was on the quiet, empty town square. In the distance, the sun was climbing over the mountain, lighting up the golden hills, but the waterfall that abutted the square still looked gray at this hour, as stony as the statue of Alonso Fall in front of it.

I began to run and soon I was out of the square, peeling through vineyards, until I was on the long road to the big white house where the Fall boys lived, my two best friends, the best friends I'd ever had, until days ago when Theo had become so much more to me.

As I barreled desperately toward him, it occurred to me I was now just like that stupid girl who slept in a tree outside his window. And not just her. I knew about all his other lovesick ex-girlfriends too, and in detail. I'd known when he lost his virginity with Sierra McMeel at the river and they both got poison oak and came to school scratching *everywhere*. I'd known when he brought Aiko Yamamoto to the abandoned cabin, our hangout, leaving all the candles melted into flat color-blobs. These girls were slim and delicate-looking, unlike me, who was voluminous and could bench-press a redwood probably from all my work with dough. I'd always figured Theo liked skinny girls. But apparently not, because after our kiss he'd said, "You're gorgeous, Bernadette. Inside and out." Said it like those skinny bird girls didn't matter.

I stopped then, bulldozed by thoughts of that kiss, the taste of him, the passion that had overtaken us. My legs went weak. I was sure I was having palpitations. I wanted his hands on me again.

But suddenly I couldn't move.

Now it was guilt leveling me. Because what were we doing? This wasn't good or right. What would it do to Clive, who was so vulnerable, so volatile, who loved us both so fiercely? Who knew how he'd react? He was so unpredictable, so readily turned into human dynamite. He was always getting into fights at school at this time, not to mention shoplifting, drinking to obliteration. I secretly liked it because of the part of me then that wanted to fight too, to be obliterated, to break rules, to break the world that broke me by taking my brother from me. And there was Clive inviting me to ditch school, to steal wine bottles out of the Fall cellar and drink them up on the ridge, to graffiti walls, to smoke cigarettes in the parking lot, to key the cars of those who wronged us.

He was my devil, Theo, my angel. With Clive I was the plain old screwed-up person I was. With Theo I became the person I wanted to be.

No. Theo was way more than that to me then. It was like my very soul was lured out of hiding by Theo. His kindness made me hopeful. His dreaminess made me freer. His strength made me feel like I could do anything. Until him, I didn't know just standing next to someone could feel like flying. I didn't know a conversation could feel like wishing a whole new world into existence, a really, *really* beautiful world.

And then there was that life-changing kiss.

Oh, I couldn't wait another moment. I had to see him. I began sprinting through the trees, kicking up leaves, kicking up our lives, and then finally, finally, I was throwing pebbles at Theo's window, making sure not to hit Clive's, which was only three feet to the left.

A shadow moved in front of the curtain, and then there he was, climbing out. Theo stood on the roof shirtless, hair moppy from sleep, his grin from the Pacific to the Atlantic,

and I was dying, literally dying, because surely that was
what was happening to me with the pounding in my chest,
the tightness in my throat, the hot winding river in my belly,
and my mind like someone had taken an eggbeater to all my
thoughts.

I couldn't believe this much *feeling,* this much *love* had been
trapped inside me.

"Hurry!" I whispered, somehow keeping myself from
saying, "Before I die!"

He jumped, landing on his feet, because he was that
awesome, and then he took my hand, which sent enough
electricity through me to power a city. We ran together through
the cabernet sauvignon vineyard, up up up the hill through
the sauvignon blanc vines, our breathing growing more and
more ragged as we stole glimpses of each other the whole way.
"You're this new person now," he said to me. "And the old one
at the same time." I felt the same way about him.

Who knew one kiss could turn someone into a brand-new
person?

Then we were at our spot on the ridge—well, technically it
was one of our spots with Clive, but I couldn't think about that
now. We wrapped our arms around each other in the golden
light, in the soft dawn breeze, and even as I kissed Theo, I
had a desperate feeling that I *wished* I were kissing him, that
I would never be satisfied, that I could never get enough of
him, his mouth, his breath on my neck, his hands in my hair,
his sighs and moans as my hands found new parts of him to
touch.

We whispered crazy senseless things to each other. *I would
do anything for you, Bernadette, take a bullet, run down a train, go to*

war, anything, he said as his hand pushed up my shirt, as mine trailed across his thigh. And me to him: *You make me feel alive, happy, beautiful, Theo, you're making me feel again, you're making me feel too much,* as he unclasped my bra and I trembled and he trembled, both of us knocking the other out of our senses.

Except there was one problem. One planet-sized problem.

"You have to tell him, Theo."

"I know."

"Soon, okay?"

"I promise." He took my face in his hands, brushed his thumb tenderly against my cheek. "I've always loved you, Bernadette. Everything about you. You make me laugh. You make me so damn happy. I want to be around you all the time. I only want to eat what you make. I didn't know if you felt the same—"

"I do. God, I do."

We were entwined on the ground, my shirt and bra strewn to the side, his whole body pressing into mine, chest to chest, stomach to stomach, both of us barely able to go on without exploding from the sheer joy of it when we heard someone clear their throat—

Theo jumped off me. I flew into a sitting position, covering myself with my arms.

There was Clive staring with no reserve or shyness at my chest even though my breasts were now hidden behind my hands. The hunger in his eyes, the possessiveness in his gaze startled me, unnerved me, and then, as much as I hate to admit it, began to intrigue me, even seduce me.

Because in that moment, he was having the same Clive-effect on me he always did, making me want to be bad, to dare the world, coaxing me to do what I wasn't supposed to do but what I secretly wanted to, like take my hands off my breasts, which I then did, ostensibly to grab my shirt, but in my heart of hearts, I did it because I wanted Clive to see me too.

It was a split-second decision I made. The worst of my life.

Because in that moment, wordlessly, somewhat innocently, somewhat not, I revealed that there might be room in my heart in this new way for both of them.

Theo's face collapsed. Clive smiled.

I'll never forget the look that passed between them. It made me go cold.

It still does.

As if each was saying to the other: *This time is different. This time we fight to the end.*

CASSIDY

Wynton, I spend weeks after the fire—Whispering River was spared—taking apart the house when my father's sleeping, looking for those two boxes. I have absolutely no luck until I borrow Dad's truck to drive to work at the hot springs one day and see the lockbox in the rearview mirror and somehow know that's where they are. I pull the truck onto the shoulder of the highway unable to wait another minute to see if I've found them, but, of course, it's locked.

The next morning, I set my alarm for four forty-five a.m. Dad wakes every day at five a.m. and takes a shower first thing. While he's bathing, I rummage through his jeans for the keys, which are in the same pocket with the wedding band. I take it in my fingers, read the inscription again—*You are my forever, my always, my only.* Who is his only? His forever? I feel instinctively I'm closer to finding out. I run to the truck, open the lockbox, and as I suspect, the two cardboard boxes are there. I carry them one at a time up to my room and store them under my bed, then relock the lockbox and return the keys to his pocket with the wedding band.

Yes, I feel guilty and terrified, but I can't stop myself. I wait for Dad to head into the vineyard, and then for the first time since moving into 68 Dandelion Road, I lock my door. I open the first box and it's like a scrapbook has exploded. At the top of the pile is a concert poster with an illustration in silhouette of a violinist at a venue called The Paradise Lounge. I start laughing, relief flooding me. Of course! My father's such a jazz fanatic, he takes old concert posters in a fire. Then I catch the address of the venue: *Paradise Springs,* and all the hairs on my neck stand on end.

The Town?

How can that be?

Only when I'm putting the flyer back in the box do I notice the name of the violinist: *Wynton Fall.* Wynton is not a very common name, and Wyntons who are gifted musicians and aren't Wynton Marsalis? I study the illustration on the poster more closely and my heart begins to pound because in those swirls and swishes, I think I can find the face of the boy from the meadow, now all grown up.

It's you, Wynton.

You.

My head begins to spin. I forget about my father for a moment as I practically seize with a desire to see you again. This is strange enough, right? I'm blown away by the fact that my father has a flyer of the boy who's haunted me for years, who played my dark scary inner music in that meadow all those years ago, who offered to sit with me back-to-back while I cried, who made me hear with new ears, who asked me to marry him.

Yes, totally weird enough.

But then.

I pick up another poster, a band called The Hatchets, and then, a review of this band cut out of the *Paradise Springs Gazette.* Wynton Fall's band. Beneath that is another review of a Wynton Fall concert printed from a music blog with the words *The kid is astonishing!* underlined.

Why is my father obsessed with the boy from the meadow? Is it because the kid is an astonishing violinist?

I reach further into the box and find articles printed out from a high school newspaper, *The Oracle,* a school called Western Catholic Preparatory, about a runner who got second in the two-mile at state last year and another about this same kid in an academic decathlon: Miles Fall. Next, there's a picture from the *Paradise Springs Gazette* of a little girl dressed up as an elf: Dizzy Fall. The same Dizzy I met? Wynton's sister, who told me she speaks to ghosts, *mute kissing* ghosts, I remember. I'd written that down, liking the idea. The same little girl who gave me a soufflé all those years before.

Wynton, Miles, and Dizzy Fall.

We're all named after our missing father's favorite jazz trumpeters, I also recall Dizzy telling me.

Dizzy Gillespie, Miles Davis, and Wynton Marsalis. My dad's favorites too. Probably a lot of people's favorite trumpet players, I think.

Deeper in the box, there are recipes from food magazines. Restaurant reviews of a place called The Blue Spoonful and older ones of a place called Christophe's Soufflé Shop. There's a cookbook by Bernadette Fall, Dave's soufflé-maker, the mother of the Fall children. At this point, it still isn't computing—I'm just wondering why my father, Dexter Brown, has a box that is the equivalent of a Fall family scrapbook.

I keep digging and then I see it. A photograph and article from the *Paradise Springs Gazette*: "The Resurrection of Winemaker Theo Fall," and my heart stills in my chest. In the photo is my father: Dexter Brown. Then I see an article a week later, "The Disappearance of Winemaker Theo Fall," with a picture of Bernadette, Miles, and Wynton.

It cannot be. It cannot. I think how my mother and I looked for The Town for years. How we found it. How I met Wynton and Dizzy and saw Miles fly by on his skateboard. How Sadie Mae broke down with nothing wrong with her like she wanted us to stay there.

I remember you telling me your father left but you still hear his trumpet.

Are these people, these strangers, my family? Do I have a family? Two half brothers and a half sister. A little sister who sees ghosts! Another brother who is so beautiful! And you, who understood me without trying—okay, so this is when I flip the fuck *out* and scream into my pillow!

The ick of your marriage proposal!

The ick of how you find your way into my mind at the most inappropriate moments!

Gross and revolting, right? Yes!

But.

I guess I'll tell you now straight out what I intimated earlier, so you don't have to freak like I did—I'm practically a hundred percent certain we're not related, Wynton. I'd bet the farm on it. We'll get to why soon. Perhaps you already know?

But in this moment, I *don't* know, so back to screaming into my pillow, back to every yuck ick romantic thought I had for you becoming immediately ferociously nauseating. And platonic. So so *so* platonic. One thousand percent platonic.

And soon, I'm crying at the photos at the bottom of the box: Miles and you from behind, hand in hand, running from a swing. Miles and you each in one of Bernadette's arms. Then one of Bernadette and my father in a vineyard. This picture stuns me because they're so young, probably my age, and so clearly in love. My father's face is like I've never seen it, blown open. There is no fortress.

I look again at the family photo in the *Paradise Springs Gazette* for the article about Theo Fall's disappearance. There's you, Wynton, looking crushed, and Miles looking at you with sympathy, his hand mid-gesture as if the next moment he'd touch your face to comfort you. But where's Dizzy? I look more closely and see Bernadette's hands resting protectively on her belly and think: She's pregnant.

He left her when she was pregnant.

He left all of you, Wynton.

But why? Why would he do that? How could he have done that?

My spine turns into an icicle then. This man, whom I trust more than anyone, abandoned his family. Just like Marigold abandoned me. Like Dave. The tears that had been from joy are now choking me. He's worse than my mother. At least my mother is honest about who she is.

The other box is full of notebooks my father must've taken when he left you all. The first is so old, the pages are yellow and the handwriting is rubbed off here and there by time, but very clearly on the first page it says: *Maria Guerrero*. The notebook starts off in Spanish and by the end is in English. The Spanish parts have been translated, the English words above their Spanish counterparts in my father's handwriting. Who is Maria Guerrero? I have no idea, of course. There's also Bernadette's journal—her name and address written on the inside cover—which seems to be exclusively letters to someone named Christophe. Not cool of my dad to have taken this—I assume it wasn't given to him—but I'm guessing he had his reasons. Last, there's a weathered leather notebook in Spanish, also translated in my dad's handwriting that appears to be a wine-making manual by someone named Alonso de Falla with some *very* passionate scribbling in the margins to someone called S.

I stay up all that night, reading every word. The journal of Maria Guerrero (my great-grandmother?) documents her childhood in Spain, her journey with Alonso Fall (my great-grandfather?) across the sea, the life they created in a big white house in Paradise Springs, their trials and jubilations with the vineyards, giving birth to a son they call Bazzy, Alonso's love affair with Sebastian, Maria's many dalliances, her greatest love affair being with her own freedom, *her wondrous oneliness,* as she calls it.

The last half of the journal is overrun with the grief of Alonso's and Sebastian's deaths (Alonso, murdered by his "brother" Hector from Spain!), then Bazzy's death many years later—she implies at the hands of his "brother" Victor so he'd solely inherit the vineyard. I learn that Bazzy came home with a baby he had overseas while in the air force, whose mother, a woman named Ingrid, had died in childbirth and that this baby is my father Theo Fall/Dexter Brown. He was then raised by Eva and the abominable Victor as Clive's brother even though they weren't related by blood.

I learn from Bernadette's diary that my father didn't know Victor and Eva weren't his biological parents nor Clive his biological brother until he was a teenager when he found Maria's journal under his mattress—where she'd hid it for him before she died so he'd one day know his true heritage. My father apparently told no one—for fear it would destroy Clive—until he confided in Bernadette after they married.

And from Maria's journal, I learn how hard she tried to stay alive despite the cancer, so as to protect her grandson Theo from Victor, and one day, potentially Clive, and from what she called a Cain and Abel curse on the family—even though the Fall brothers, the Cains and Abels discussed in her journal, didn't share a drop of blood—a curse she says that, like all curses, can only be reversed when it's brought into light and then becomes a blessing. Am I crazy to think you and I, Wynton, could be that blessing, a bridge finally between two lineages that have battled brothers for generations? Oh, why am I thinking like this? It must be lack of sleep—I don't believe in curses!

Except maybe I do. In the time of forever, there are plenty: girls whose wings fall off, mothers and daughters who freeze over like glaciers, dead women who sing you into silent worlds. Then it occurs to me that perhaps it's not you and me, but Dizzy and me, who might reverse the curse, because we are the first girls in the Fall family bloodlines in over a hundred years. The one thing all those cursed Fall brothers never had: Fall sisters.

Until now.

I'll just say this, Wynton. I think I know what broke my father's heart. I think I know why he left.

This is finally the fourth betrayal. Yours.

From Bernadette's Notebook of Unsent Letters:

Dear Sleeping Dogs,

There is Right and Wrong and then in the house next door there is what's True.

This is what's True.

Dear Grief,

I am fourteen years old and Christophe and I are playing jacks in our lime-green-tiled kitchen in San Francisco. Christophe's indulging me, as I'm too old for games like this. Tears run down my face as I bounce the ball and swipe the jacks into my hand again and again, hoping the game will never end. I don't want him to leave for college across the bay. He's promising me that he'll come back for Shabbat dinner in three weeks, but I can't imagine how I'm going to survive twenty-one whole days and nights without him. He's the sun around which I revolve.

This is the last moment I'll see my brother alive.

I was a child who had to face the lack of inevitability in life, the stranglehold of mortality, the revelation that life goes on, but the people you love the most don't. What does that do to the forming psyche if your first experience of all-consuming boundaryless love is one of such profound loss? If you feel such a love again, do you trust it? Do you sabotage it? Are you ever again emotionally and psychologically capable of letting go of anything? Anyone?

Dear Hunger,

There is never enough chocolate, oysters, peaches, figs, filets cooked a perfect medium rare, picnics by rivers, sky, flowers, wine, kisses, love, time. There is never enough life in life. Open the cupboards. Rip open the bags. Reach your hand in for another. Walk into the forest at midnight, splash around in moonlight. Find the people who plant the sun in your chest. Seek platters of words, jugs of bright paint, whole days made of music. Kiss for weeks at a time, kiss everyone you know. I see you and you and you and you—life-thieves like me—trying to stuff more in your pockets, your mouths, your hearts during these measly lives that will be forgotten.

Dear Heart with Two Doors,

I hate you.

I wish I never had to know you.

The years after Theo and I got together were so wonderful. I caught his brightness, his kindness, his joy. Love poured into me like sun through a window. I was Hope itself in bright dresses and high heels.

And yet.

The years were also terrible.

Because of this needling deep inside me that somehow in some impossible way I might be in love with Clive too. This was a tiny bonfire that started that day on the ridge but had become, two years later, a raging wildfire I couldn't stamp out. Because why did I catch myself thinking about him when I was salting cod? When I was pounding chicken with a hammer? When I was kneading dough, which I'd punch down so hard, again and again, I'd bruise my knuckles?

I tried to stay away from him.

And did.

Even though he pursued me relentlessly behind Theo's back.

Relentlessly.

I rebuffed him each and every time, no matter how confused I was secretly becoming.

Until.

Dear Day It Happened,

It was a week before Theo went to some bluegrass festival in San Diego. I was waiting for him in his bedroom, snooping around, when I found a black jewelry box in a dresser drawer. Inside was an antique sapphire ring with two diamonds on either side. Was Theo going to ask me to marry him with this ring? My heart swelled so much I felt like I needed a bigger rib cage. I slipped the beautiful ring onto my finger and was admiring how it glinted as I turned my hand this way and that, when I heard steps coming down the hall. Theo? I pulled at the ring, but it was stuck. I had to get it off and back in the box and the box back in the drawer and the drawer closed before he saw it on me, and the surprise was ruined.

But I didn't and it wasn't Theo.

If only it had been.

Clive sailed into the room. He must've seen me enter the house while he was working in the vineyard. I covered the ring with my other hand, which drew his eyes to it, then they rose to my face. He stared at me much like he had on the ridge that day eons ago, like he did so very often those days.

Unfortunately, always to the same effect.

He was in work clothes and boots, was covered in vineyard, his blond hair windswept, his hands streaked with dirt. I swallowed but did not look away and the air between us grew electric. Then he was walking toward me, then right behind me, and we were closer than we'd been in years. He lifted my hand off the ring, whispered in my ear. "So that's it. You're going to marry my brother even though it's me you want." I could smell cigarettes, alcohol, sweat, danger.

"I don't want you," I said, but my voice broke on the *you*.

"No?" His hand found my bare waist. My body leaned into his touch of its own accord. My mind felt radioactive. So did my blood. "Are you sure?" he said. "You don't sound sure."

"I'm sure." The words were raspy, frayed.

"Move my hand away then," he said. "Show me you don't want me." I tried to, I did. "Do it," he said. "Show me you don't want me."

I had to move his hand away. Had to. But I couldn't.

Instead, I put my hand on his. I knew I had to stop, but I wanted to feel his hand on me for a second. Just one. Then another. Then his other hand was running up my stomach toward my breasts.

"Tell me to stop. Tell me you don't want me, Bernadette," he said. I leaned into him. "Tell me."

"I can't." It was a moan.

"I know," he said in my ear, lighting my whole body on fire, all our lives on fire.

I felt his lips, warmer and rougher than Theo's, on my neck, his hands on me, allowing myself this.

For. One. More. Moment.

"I've always loved you. It's you and me who belong together," he murmured, his breath hot on my ear, his hands hungry on my hungry skin. "You and me, Bernie. We're so much more alike."

This unhinged something in me—we *were* so much more alike—and I spun around.

We stared at each other then, and as we did, his face lost the bravado, the bluster, and became naked, vulnerable, like I suddenly felt. Here again was the sweet boy who loved cows as well as the dangerous man he was becoming and all the fragile, wounded people in between. Here again was the wild young man who lived in my heart. But there was something else. In this moment, I saw in Clive something frightening and so familiar—there was a need in both of us the size of God.

And before I realized it, we were kissing. Before I realized it, we were two furious storms spinning into one, one built for mass destruction.

He left a note at the soufflé shop the next day with a wheelbarrow of handpicked wildflowers. A wheelbarrow. The note said: *I'm only me when I'm with you.* I felt the same.

But the heartbreak, the impossibility, the truth, is that I think there must've been two of me back then, because the other me felt this exact way with Theo too. Only more so.

I decided it was a one-time thing with Clive. A must-be-forgotten thing.

I tried not to think about it. It was all I thought about.

The betrayal I was committing was so great I could barely speak, couldn't add words to it.

I hated myself.

I hated myself and I couldn't stop myself.

A month later, I was pregnant, and engaged to Theo, his grandmother Maria's sapphire ring on my finger.

I moved into the white house with Theo.

Clive moved into the brown house on the hill.

For years, I tried not to be alone with Clive.

For years, I failed.

WYNTON

You're sure you've died this time. It's that quiet. But then you hear your mother's breathing, sighing, crying. A flat, B minor, C sharp, respectively. People are music, you think.

You wonder where Dizzy and Miles are. You wish you could hear their voices, their breathing, their music.

Only Cassidy and your mother speak to you now. Your mother's telling you that you're her favorite child even though she's not supposed to have favorites, and that she will, of course, deny ever having said it if you bring it up when you wake.

She tells you that you and she are kindred spirits. And then, after all these years of not-telling, of not-saying-a-goddamn-thing-about-it, she's spilling it all, and it's a symphony of *I'm sorry*.

She says she knows how much you love Theo and that's why she never told you the truth. She says she didn't want you to lose him as your father in your heart too, that the idea of Theo always seemed to be what kept you together, what kept you hopeful, what kept you making music.

She tells you Clive doesn't know because she lied to him when she got the DNA results. No one knows.

Her weeping now is in D minor. The saddest of all keys.

You want to tell her you've always known, and you don't blame her, that you've never blamed her, that you understand her, always have, because you understand making mistakes.

Boy do you ever. You understand that life—yours anyway—is—was—just a collection of mistakes.

You're pretty sure that for her, like for you, living life is like playing an out of tune instrument.

You want to tell her that you've known since that day.

That day, you're on the swings with Miles. Your dad's pushing you and your brother into the sky, one, then the other, and you're pumping your legs and so is Miles and then you jump and Miles jumps too because he does everything you do, and how you *love* that. He follows you around like you follow your father around because he thinks you're a duck and not a duckling like him. Only you can make Miles stop crying. Only you can make Miles fall asleep. Only you can make him laugh like a crazy kid.

Only you, his big brother.

That day, you're running home together, you and Miles, the music of Dad's trumpet trailing you, and you take Miles's hand because he's your monkey, your banana, your little guy.

You call him these things when you two are alone and you're not even embarrassed about it because it makes his face turn into light. You don't know how his face does this. You smile in the mirror sometimes to see if your face will do it, but you just look like a boy smiling, not a sun shining.

That day, you both burst through the front door of the white house. You race upstairs to get Mom while he goes to the kitchen.

That day, you hear the noises first and then you stand in the doorway long enough to see.

Your mother and your uncle naked-wrestling in the bed. They don't see you.

You realize they aren't wrestling when they kiss. And kiss. Like they're eating each other's faces.

That day, later on, you go to your uncle Clive's house and tell him to stay away from your mother because someone has to tell him this.

That day, he's drunk and throws you against a wall and tells you to keep your stupid mouth shut.

You keep your stupid mouth shut.

You tell your mother you got the bruise when you fell off your skateboard.

You don't know what to do.

For the longest *longest* time, you don't know what to do.

Then The Devil Winds are here, and your mom is pregnant again and your dad has a viral pneumonia and slips into a coma. He's in the hospital dying and finally you know what to do. The nurse told you people in comas can hear.

So, when you're alone with your father in the hospital room, you climb up on the bed. You whisper into his ear what you saw and heard that day.

You tell your father everything so that he'll wake up and do something about it.

Instead, he dies! You hear the machines hooked up to his heart stop beeping and turn into one long note: C sharp. The nurses rush in. No one seems to realize you're there as they try to revive him. You know he will not revive. You know you've killed your father—whom you love more than *anybody*—with your words.

No one ever finds out you were there when your dad died, a tiny ball of fear in the corner of the hospital room, watching until you can't watch anymore and sneak out and run home.

You want to tell someone that it's your fault he died, but you don't.

You want to tell the ghost of your father when he visits you and leaves you a trumpet, but you're too scared to speak.

The next day, you hear your mother tell your uncle Clive (while she bandages his face and arm) that when Theo left, he took her journal. You distinctly hear her say, "He knows everything, Clive."

Then your father's been gone for a whole year.

You look at his photo all the time because you understand a little about sex and babies by then. You keep his photo in the trumpet case, the one he gave you before he disappeared. You always stow it under the covers with you at night. You look at that picture and then you look in the mirror because you know if you could find a resemblance, any at all, a line of jaw, a shadow at the brow, a look in the eye, it would change everything.

You decide you'll grow into looking like him.

Still, at night with that picture in your hand, you watch Miles while he sleeps so you can closely study him. You see how every inch of his face resembles the picture, the curves and creases, the soft glowing skin, the shape of eyes, the brown shiny ringleted hair, the dimpled cheeks everyone wants to squeeze, even his body, so athletic, so agile, so tall, taller than you already.

It's not just the way he looks either—he has the same lie-on-your-back-in-the-sun feeling about him that your father did. You don't have that feeling about you. And then there's how words have colors for him like music did for your dad. For you and your uncle Clive, words are words, music is music, colors are colors. These things don't overlap because you and he are not magical like them.

The knowledge curdles in your gut and fills you with white-hot hate.

You try to sell Miles but that doesn't work.

You taste hate in your mouth and smell it in your sweat and you see it in the mirror. (Like Hector did and probably Victor too, you know now.)

It consumes you. The father you love so much, it crushes you to be without him, the father you wait for by the window because he is yours, the father who bought you a violin, who tossed grapes into your mouth, who made you feel like you were always lying on your back in the sun.

That man is not your father, but he is Miles's father.

When Dizzy's born funny-looking like you, you rejoice. She's yours. You ignore it when she starts saying this smells blue and that smells orange because she's your spitting image. You do research and find out yes synesthesia runs in families mostly, but not always. It's not impossible for it to spontaneously occur. You convince yourself of this. You claim her.

And now you know from Cassidy's stories that your father and Clive are not even blood brothers. Of course, this stopped your heart because the man who was once your father is not even your uncle.

Theo Fall, the king of your private universe, is nothing to you. You have no hold on him. No right to him. You share no blood. Not one drop.

This is what's making all the music fade out of you. Clive's hex was right after all.

You try to speak or squeeze your mother's hand to tell her goodbye, but you are not in your body, not in the hospital, barely in time anymore.

Soon you stop hearing voices altogether.

You're in the meadow with the daisies and yellow jackets sitting in the same spot you sat in all those years ago, back-to-back with the only girl you've ever loved who is not your sister—you did catch that.

One good—no, exceptional—outcome of the fourth betrayal.

You're prepared to stay in this meadow until the end of time waiting for her to join you.

The Note Theo left for Bernadette:

Bernadette, I understand now for you it was always both of us, and I can't live with that. Do not try to find me, ever. I beg you, give me that, you owe me that, it would destroy me. I hope you will be happy together. I mean it. There is enough money in the joint account for all of you. The house, vineyard are yours.

Email from Dexter Brown Vineyards to Wine Magazine:

To Whom It May Concern at Wine Magazine,

As we've made very clear in the past, Dexter Brown does not do interviews. Furthermore, we do not want our wine reviewed in your magazine or included in any roundups. We do not sell to restaurants or wine shops but exclusively in our tasting room and at farmer's markets and wine festivals. We prefer to keep our batches and business small, and we do not welcome media attention of any kind.

Thank You.

Nigel Garcia

On behalf of Dexter Brown

Dear World,

I know you will never forgive me. Nor will I. I was a shattered girl who loved two boys at the same time. One for his frailty, one for his strength. One for his darkness, one for his light. There were secrets. Lies. The betrayal was momentous.

There are no excuses.

In time, my relationship with Clive stopped feeling like love, more like madness or illness. When I ended it, he tried to drink the vineyard. He never forgave me. I don't blame him.

I loved Theo then more wholly than I've ever loved anyone, anything.

It was Theo leaving—long after the end of the affair—that destroyed Clive. He never recovered. Neither have I.

It's impossible to relate to the young woman who did what I did, but our yesterdays follow us around forever. I respected Theo's wishes and never tried to find him. My shame too has kept me stock-still.

Sorry is the shamble of a house I live in. I know every desperate inch.

However illogical (and self-serving) it may sound: Theo was—is—the love of both our lives. From the beginning, Clive's and my soul-bond was that we each somehow loved Theo too much and each felt like we didn't deserve him.

We were correct.

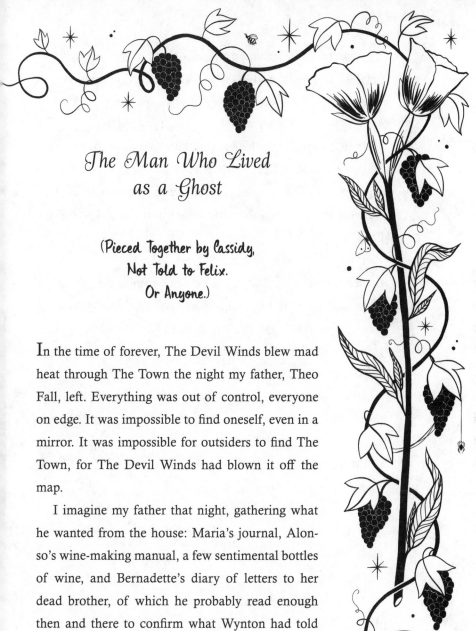

The Man Who Lived as a Ghost

(Pieced Together by Cassidy, Not Told to Felix. Or Anyone.)

In the time of forever, The Devil Winds blew mad heat through The Town the night my father, Theo Fall, left. Everything was out of control, everyone on edge. It was impossible to find oneself, even in a mirror. It was impossible for outsiders to find The Town, for The Devil Winds had blown it off the map.

I imagine my father that night, gathering what he wanted from the house: Maria's journal, Alonso's wine-making manual, a few sentimental bottles of wine, and Bernadette's diary of letters to her dead brother, of which he probably read enough then and there to confirm what Wynton had told him in his coma. And then some. He left a note for Bernadette, gave Wynton his trumpet, and it was after this, Wynton began crying when he made music. Then Theo kissed Miles's forehead and said

461

goodbye to the sleeping boy. Similarly, Miles began crying in his sleep this night, and his somnolent weeping continued.

After that, I see Theo paying Clive a visit, the same kind of cursed visit that Hector paid Alonso with gun in hand.

Perhaps at this meeting, Theo finally told Clive they weren't related by blood. The words that would hurt Clive most. I imagine it quickly came to blows between the brothers who were not brothers, and for the first time in his life, Theo did not hold back.

It was not an even match.

Bernadette dressed Clive's substantial wounds the next day.

I imagine my father, betrayed to his core, thought the right thing, the only thing to do, was to leave The Town for good, to get out of the way of Bernadette and Clive's love, to get out of the way of *their* family.

Was it hurt or love or spite that made him do this? Was it all three? Did he make a mistake? Should he have stayed? I don't know. The way the Fall family curse manifested between these two is the most painful because these men were boys who loved each other wholeheartedly.

This I do know: Since he fled, my father has gone back to The Town several times a year where he'd sit on the ridge and observe his life going on without him, very much like he was one of Dizzy's mute ghosts.

Each and every one of these times, he watched Clive enter the big white house at night. What else could he think but that Clive and Bernadette were still together? How would he know that Clive curled up and slept on the couch every night (unbeknownst to anyone but Dizzy) because he was so damn lonely?

What else could Theo Fall think except that Clive and his wife were still in love all these years later? What else could he think but that his children were Clive's, most likely in blood, definitely in spirit?

DIZZY

Dizzy was in an RV called Purple Rain, with her very own father at the wheel, speeding down a winding highway on the way back to the hospital where he was going to wake her brother from his coma by playing his trumpet.

She'd already called Chef Mom to tell her the miraculous turn of events, thinking even her skeptic of a mother would have to admit they all were knee-deep in a miracle. They'd found their father! And discovered they had a half sister! She'd told her mom the new plan regarding their father, the trumpet, and Wynton's impending revival. Her mother remained silent the whole time Dizzy recounted what had happened and what was about to happen—until Dizzy finished speaking and her mother said in a shaky voice, "Dizzy, are we awake?"

She and her father had tried calling Cassidy, but she didn't pick up. Her father then called Cassidy's friend Summer who lived in Davis, where Cassidy had said she was, but Summer told her father that Cassidy hadn't been there, and further, that she hadn't talked to Cassidy in weeks, which made her father's face worry. He believed Cassidy was still in Paradise Springs and Dizzy hoped this was the case. The whole family needed to be there for Wynton's revival. And after he woke and was home, they'd all make a family people-pile on the red couch together. Following that, Dizzy would show Cassidy her bedroom. They'd close the door, and it would be two sisters on a bed like in movies. She could barely breathe when she thought about it all.

Dizzy had been worried that she and her dad might sit there like two mute ghosts the whole drive, but boy was she wrong. To her astonishment, her father had so much pertinent information regarding existence!

For instance, in one fell swoop, he told Dizzy about a Turkish village in which people communicate by whistling—a high-pitched bird-like language that he said was as intricate as regular human language—and that they used it to send complicated messages over great distances. Then he talked about how bullfrogs don't ever sleep but certain snails can sleep for three years straight, and then about a saint named Polycarp in the second century who was fireproof. Dizzy quickly realized talking to him was way better than surfing the internet.

After she'd wrapped up a swoop of her own about how snakes can predict earthquakes (one of Lizard's), a cat called Stubbs who became the mayor of a town in Alaska, and how much Dizzy wanted to be immortal like certain jellyfish, he said, "I have a question for you."

"I'm all ears," she said, and he looked at her and smiled in his eyes and then pulled her earlobe, like fathers do to daughters, she imagined. She almost died of happiness.

"Why did your mother call her restaurant The Blue Spoonful?"

Oh! One of her favorite questions too. "Because of me—I have synesthesia. I see smells as colors. Miles has it too, but he sees words in color. Mom says when I was little, I used to sit on the counter at the old soufflé shop, Christophe's, and she would pull soufflés out of the oven and I'd breathe in and say: *blue*. I told her the most delicious desserts all smell blue." Dizzy knew she wasn't supposed to love talking about herself, but did she ever, and so had gotten caught up and hadn't noticed that her father had started looking strange. "Both you and Miles have synesthesia?" he asked even though she'd just finished saying they did, but he said it like he was asking, *You both have cancer?*

"Yeah," she said.

He turned the RV onto the shoulder and braked until it stopped. "Be back in a sec." He opened the door and jumped down the step onto the road. Did he suddenly have to go to the bathroom? Couldn't he use the one in Purple Rain? Dizzy looked in the side mirror and saw her father pacing outside the RV like a nut. Then he put his head against a tree like he was trying to mind-meld with the trunk. This was what Chef Mom called *unpredictable behavior,* usually ascribed to Wynton.

Dizzy wondered if she should've gone with Miles and Felix.

After a few minutes, her father climbed back in the driver's seat—giving no explanation—and they were back on the road. "I see sound as color," he said. "Cassidy has the same kind Miles does, words in color." He seemed to be back to normal except that he was tapping his right hand on the wheel now in a way that made Dizzy nervous.

"We must've all gotten it from you then," Dizzy said. "It's genetic. I've read all about it. It's correlated with creativity and high IQ. I think it's the coolest thing about me."

"I don't know. You seem like you have a multitude of cool things about you."

"Thank you." She felt her face get hot. She so wanted him to like her. No, she wanted him to love her like crazy like her mother and Wynton did and Miles was starting to on this trip.

"And Wynton?" he asked, his hand tapping away at the wheel. "Is he a synesthete?"

Ah, cool word alert. "Nope. It bothers him too. He wishes he was." Dizzy didn't understand why this information would cause her father to turn into a statue for a good ten minutes, but it did. She made a mental note to never talk to him again about synesthesia.

"Has my brother been good to you kids?" he asked after a while.

"Uncle Clive? Sorry to report that Mom doesn't like him to come around."

"Oh," he said, frowning. "Why?"

Dizzy shrugged. She didn't want to insult his brother by saying what

Mom said about him, that he was bad news when he drank, which was always. She looked out the window at the eucalyptus branches, hanging down like elephant trunks. "I think he's sad and lonely and that's why he drinks so much and sneaks into our house every night to sleep on the red couch. I'm the only one who knows he does that. I visit him in the brown house sometimes and so does Miles, but Wynton doesn't because he thinks Uncle Clive has bad mojo and it's catching."

This time her father didn't turn into a statue, but the opposite. Despite the air-con, he began sweating through his shirt. Dizzy noticed his neck and forehead were drenched, and his face had turned red and splotchy. His smell had grown stringent too—the color of an old rusty pipe.

She decided she better change the subject again, adding Uncle Clive to the no conversation list. She wanted to ask so many things: Why did he leave? Did he still love Mom? Did he love them? What was his favorite movie? What was the best dessert he ever had? Which music did he see as blue? Did he believe in God? Was he as afraid to die as she was? Did he like pillow fights? What did he and Cassidy do for fun? But she figured they had time for all that and she didn't want to risk him turning into a statue or pulling over the RV again. She decided to tell him what happened with Lizard and ask him what to do about it. Fathers were supposed to be great advice-givers, weren't they? After starting the story at the beginning when she and Lizard were four and ending at how he didn't come to the hospital even after all her voicemails, he asked, "Have you tried being honest with him?"

She thought about it. "Maybe not totally."

"Okay, start there. Tell him how you feel in here." He touched his chest.

Dizzy stared at the man. Did she have a real live father now for her to tell how she felt in her heart? Was he going to keep giving her advice? Was he going to kiss her forehead good night? Would she say *my father this* and *my dad that* like kids at school?

"The thing is, Father," she said, trying out the word but realizing too late it sounded wacko, like she was in a creepy old movie. She continued anyway. "We found you, you didn't find us." The man's face fell. "So, I can't be sure that you're not going to leave us again. Are you?"

He stared at her with sad eyes, marooned eyes, then reached for her hand across the aisle, which she took. But he didn't answer her for a long time. After an eternity, he said, "I'll try not to, okay?"

She'd wanted a firm no. "Okay," she said, feeling tears pool in her eyes.

They drove for miles after that, her small hand in his big one, saying nothing at all.

When they were at the station to fill up Purple Rain, she decided to take her father's advice and call Lizard and be one hundred percent honest. Listening through the recording where he called himself Tristan, it occurred to her for the first time that he might actually want to be called that. Maybe he really didn't like Lizard as a name? When it beeped, she said, "Tristan, I miss you. I wish you'd tell me why you don't like me anymore. I still like you. So much. I was so hurt you didn't come to the hospital, but I forgive you now. And guess what? I'm with *my father* in a purple RV and he knows lots of cool stuff, like us." Dizzy glanced up at the sky filled with cloud puffs. "You're not going to believe this, but I have a half sister now too. She's that angel I told you about in another voicemail, only not an angel actually. We're on our way to the hospital to wake Wynton with my dad's trumpet. My father told me to be honest with you so I am. I always thought love was two ways. Because of you I know it isn't, but I'll continue to love you even if it's just one way. This is my last message."

"Good going," her father said as he got back in and settled into his seat, because, she guessed, he had superhuman hearing so had heard her from outside.

To her astonishment, fifteen minutes later a text came in from Lizard:
never stopped liking you

Then: Should've come to hospital before

here now

came yesterday too

Followed by: Sorry

Then: There's a reason

Finally: Hurry so I can tell you

Omg, your dad!

She read the texts again and again, fireworks going off in her head.

She showed them to her father. He smiled. "As I said, good going, champ." He called her champ!

"Hurry," she whispered.

He smiled, then mussed her hair with his hand. "Pedal's to the metal."

MILES

Miles was absolutely, absurdly, certain he was Homer or Keats ever since his father said he liked his poem. He wanted to write the entire world down in his pocket pad. This new world, where he had a father and a half sister and the half sister just happened to be his favorite person he'd ever met—well, tied with Felix, who this moment had his shades down, his arm out the truck window and was in a customary rhapsody about the world around him. "You're right, man, light on water is bomb—that's some serious sorcery for sure." The Canine Traitor was sleeping at their feet as the three of them raced back to Paradise Springs.

Right before they'd left Whispering River, *his father* had put his hand on Miles's shoulder and looked at him with so much affection, it had made Miles dizzy. "You're almost a man," he'd said, his voice breaking. And Miles the human had cried again. Who knew if he could ever trust or forgive or understand the man, but somehow, he did feel like he could love him. It was possible he'd never stopped.

Miles had called his mother when they were still in Whispering River. His heart had pulsed in his ears as the phone rang. How would she take this monumental news? But Dizzy had gotten to her first. "I can't believe any of it," his mother had said to him, her voice sounding strange and far away, not at all how he'd expected. *What does your mother say about it?* his father had asked Miles earlier, which obviously meant there was a whole lot to say about him leaving that he was unwilling to say, a whole lot that his mother hadn't shared. For years. What were they hiding? Why did his father *really* run away and stay away and change his freaking name?

"We'll be back soon, Mom," he'd told her. "If anything can bring

Wynton back, it's him." He'd basically turned into Dizzy. A true believer.

"I agree," she said in the same strange voice that seemed detached from her person. "Drive safely." Was she in shock? Was she terrified to see her husband after all this time? He'd never heard her sound this way. Was it because of the infidelity that must've led to Cassidy? She'd ended the call without saying anything more, not even goodbye.

And in a few hours, they were all going to be in the hospital room together.

He noticed the purple RV was behind them again, even though they'd pulled over earlier for some reason. In the side-view mirror, he glanced at his father and Dizzy yakking away. What he never imagined in all his many imaginings of his father and his whereabouts was that the man was living five hours away in a yellow house with a daughter. So mundane. Why hadn't the detective his mother hired been able to find him? How hard could it have been? A winemaker in Northern California using an alias. Unless the detective did find him? Or maybe there was never any detective? Did his mother make that up? She must have. But why?

What was it going to be like when they were all together? This was intense.

He turned to Felix. "Did Cassidy tell you any stories about my parents? Or about the"—he made quotes—"'Fall brother curse' and how it might have manifested between my father and his brother Clive?" Miles was aware he sounded loopy and didn't care.

Felix shook his head. "I fell asleep or started spacing by then. Sorry, man. It was a lot of Fall family stories." He smiled the lethal half-smile. "I didn't know you guys then. It was about all these randos floating and glowing and killing each other."

Miles laughed. "I'm sorry, Felix. That must've been really weird back there. Sorry you got roped into such drama." Felix had had a front row seat to the most emotional moments of Miles's life. He'd seen Miles come utterly unglued. And Miles still felt comfortable around the guy. It was bizarre. More than comfortable. He made Miles feel more like himself than he ever had. He'd somehow helped Miles move into his own life.

"Are you kidding?" Felix said. "Major drama fan when it doesn't involve me. And when it does." He grinned.

He's a drama queen! Like me!

You! I'm so mad at you, Sandro! How could you choose my father over me?

I'm sorry.

How could you not have told me Beauty was my dad?

I'm sorry.

I thought Beauty was another dog! He couldn't get over it.

What does it matter? Love is love.

I know that, jeez. But I thought it was a romantic love, not our kind of love.

Sometimes platonic loves are the most profound. I thought it would upset you.

Well, you were right. It has.

Meanwhile, Felix was now half smiling at Miles, and it was making Miles's neck hot and his thoughts hotter. Per usual. He wanted to blurt out, "I fucking love you," but instead said, "What?"

"Just can't believe Cassidy's your half sister."

I can't believe it either, Sandro said.

"And I can't believe we found your dad."

I can't believe that either.

Stop repeating what Felix says. It's annoying. How old are you anyway? I thought you said you were eighty-seven in dog years, which makes you sixteen in human but if you knew my dad when he was a teenager—

That is a rude question and one I choose not to answer.

How can you be so old? Actually, how do you know all that old-time slang?

I take the Fifth!

Sandro, the immortal dog.

Has a certain ring to it.

"Now that I know it," Felix said, "I can't deal how much you and Cassidy look alike and seem alike and just wow."

Me neither. Just wow, Sandro said, jumping up on the seat between them, putting his snout right in Miles's face. *Forgive me. I love you and Beauty equally. I chose your truck, didn't I?*

Maybe you only loved me all this time because I remind you of him.

At first . . . yes.

"Really, you and Cassidy could be twins," Felix said.

You definitely could be twins.

"Oh my God, Sandro, stop repeating everything Felix says!"

Felix lifted his shades, looked at Miles with raised eyebrows.

"What? Yeah, Sandro talks, okay? Same as you. Except right into my head. I'm not crazy, well, maybe I am, but this is not a new crazy. Don't worry."

Now you've done it, Miles.

Felix was processing this, biting his lip, observing the two of them. "Will he talk to me in my head? Will you, boy? Or do I have to be a Fall?" Sandro turned on the seat, licked Felix's face. "I want to hear you too."

"And, like, what's going on here?" The words were out before Miles could stop them. He gestured in the space between him and Felix. "I mean, is there anything going on here, because it feels like there is. I'll just say it, for me, there absolutely is. I'm into you. *Really* into you, Felix. Are you for sure unavailable?"

Do you realize you said that out loud, Miles?

I don't care anymore! I feel like I'm exploding. I need to know.

Felix looked at Miles. "Not sure . . ." he said. "I really don't know . . . There's like a lot we haven't talked about."

Miles nodded. He wasn't merely rocking the boat; he'd just capsized it.

Um, Miles? Felix didn't say no about there being something going on between you.

Oh my God, you're right. He didn't say no!

He didn't say yes either.

Right. Right. But he didn't say no. He said we had to talk about things.

Miles caught himself smiling like a fool in the side mirror and next to him Felix was grinning also like a fool, and Cassidy was his sister, and his long-disappeared father had hugged him in a way that made him cry like an actual human being, and this father was going to wake his brother, whom he no longer hated despite some family curse, by playing a trumpet. So, who knew anything?

Miles looked at Felix. He wanted to move into Felix's life too. He wanted to know what was really going on with him. Miles said, "So, can we talk about all the things we haven't talked about yet?" He wanted to add, but of course didn't: *so we can make out already.*

CASSIDY

We're getting closer to the night of the accident, closer to this afternoon when I met your mother, Wynton. Yes, I just met Bernadette. I told her everything and asked her what I needed to—one of the scariest moments of my life, if not the scariest.

I honestly don't know if I just ruined all our lives or made them better.

We don't have much time left, just the two of us. Later this afternoon something thrilling and terrifying is going to happen in this room. I'm not spilling beans, but I hope you like surprises. I'm nervous as can be. And more hopeful than I ever remember being.

But before I tell you about the meeting with your mother, I need to share how it was coming back to The Town again after all these years.

Meeting you all.

So, the same night I find and go through the boxes, I throw some things into a suitcase, fill a backpack of books for company, some novels, some books on California history (I inherited my mother's interest), and leave a note that I've gone to see my friend Summer at Davis, so my dad doesn't worry. On the online ride board for the hot springs, I type in: *Heading south to Paradise Springs. Want to share fuel, driving, stories, adventure?* I'm exhausted and shaky from staying up all night reading the journals and notebook. I don't trust myself to drive alone.

I pack the truck, then wait by the greeting hut at the hot springs, hoping for a response to my post. I'm in the same spot where I bottomed out in Purple Rain all those years ago after the car chase with my father, the moment my life got bifurcated into before and after.

Like it is again now.

The dawn light's swimming through the trees, making the leaves gleam. A *glisk,* I think, tattooed on my wrist, maybe my favorite word of all. Because, ultimately and ideally, isn't that what life is: *a fleeting glance at a glittering sight.*

Soon, a response to my post comes in:

Let's go to Paradise! Not a serial killer, hoping for same in driving companion. Reached my limit on enlightenment. Get me out of here please, Felix Rivera from Colorado. PS not my phone, so respond quickly if you can. I laugh and we text back and forth, making a plan to meet by the greeting kiosk in an hour.

A giant in sunglasses shows up wearing a tie-dye shirt and plaid shorts. His hair's wrapped around some kind of something that looks like a bone. He has pine needles in his hair and a nutso mustache. "I don't normally dress like this, but I'm trying to pass," he says with a loopy smile that immediately takes away any concern he's a creep.

"Tarzan chic. Well done. Way to commit," I say.

He smiles and his cheek dimples. He's good-looking and seems sweet—a gentle giant, I think as he rifles through his backpack, saying, "You will not believe the caliber of snacks. We're talking Pringles, Fritos, Cheese Puffs, salt and vinegar potato chips."

"Where did you find the contraband?" I ask. "Salt and vinegar are the all-time fave."

He tosses me a bag. "Walked two miles to a gas station mini-mart. My personal rebellion against seven straight days of meals featuring soy strips, which in the Colorado culinary community we call leather."

"Are you part of the Colorado culinary community?" I ask, pushing aside the boxes and the backpack of books so he'll fit. I was expecting a reasonable-sized human when I packed the cab of the truck.

"I was on my way to culinary school when my plans changed," he says, but before I can inquire further, he adds, "What's all that?"

He's eyeing curiously the boxes of Fall family memorabilia and journals. What to say? "Research," I tell him, which is kind of true. "For an essay about this old wine country family that settled in Paradise Springs in the early twentieth century from a small town in Spain. Particularly this dude named Alonso Fall. But it might turn into a novella too. I don't know." An essay? A novella? Whatever. And it happens to be *my* long-lost family whom I'm going to foist myself upon and blow up my father's life and all their lives, not to mention my own! I try to hide the panic, the excitement, the uncertainty, and keep my voice even. "That's why I'm going down." I remind myself that Dizzy and Miles might not be my half sister and half brother. I'm about ninety-nine percent certain Clive is your father, Wynton, because of what's said in Bernadette's diary, but it ends years before she became pregnant with Dizzy and there are only a few entries about Miles, none revealing. I feel like I need them to be my siblings as much as I need you not to be. At this point, I've convinced myself the moment I meet them, I'll somehow know if we're related. Or not.

"You're a writer?" Felix asks.

"One day maybe."

"For school?"

"Yeah." I lie some more. "Stanford." Well, I deferred, so kind of true?

He nods, doesn't question further because he's gotten distracted. I follow his gaze to a Western bluebird sitting on a nearby branch, a male, I note, spotting the orange throat. It's amazing how much information I've retained from all the science walks with Marigold. Felix's hands are now pressed to his chest as if he's overwhelmed or possibly dying. "Holy shit, is that bird blue or what?"

I laugh, relieved to look at this little thrush for a moment with him. "He really is very blue."

I put the boxes in the lockbox on the flatbed so there's room enough for Felix in the cab, then we're on the road and Tarzan is practically giving every tree and glimpse of river a standing ovation. I've never seen anyone so overjoyed by nature, genuinely so, not performatively so, like my mother. The more I ride with him, the more I feel like *I've* never been in a forest before or on a country road or alive even, and soon the two of us are exclaiming together from one glisk to the next. It's very fun. At some point in between our outbursts, he turns to me, looking like a six-year-old and says, "So, guess what? I had my first three-way last night in the hot pool."

"Congratulations!" I say, mirroring his enthusiasm on this as well. This is not an uncommon experience at the hot springs at night, but I don't have the heart to tell him.

"It lasted less than a minute."

"Um, that blows." I tilt my head. "Or doesn't blow actually."

He cracks up. "Right? Worst threesome ever."

I'm laughing too and it's like we're already friends.

"It was with this mermaid girl and her merman boyfriend." He grins. "They surrounded me. Didn't have a chance . . . but yeah, so . . . the dude looked like my best friend Eddie. Like they could be doppelgangers." His tone changes with this reveal—there's longing in it.

I look at him. "In love with the bestie?"

"A total cliché, I know, why I left Denver." He sighs, doesn't say anything for a bit, then adds, "It wasn't just that. Why I left."

But he doesn't say more, and I don't want to pry, so I say, "Sorry you've been having a hard time."

"Yeah, it's been rough." It's clear he says this not to open a door but to close one, so I let it rest. A moment later, he turns to look at me and says, "Wait, so why are you writing about this guy again?"

I fill him in some more and he seems interested, so I begin the tale, our family story, Wynton. I weave bits and pieces from Alonso Fall's wine-making manual, from Maria's journal, from Bernadette's diary, from my old California history lessons, from my mother's *In the Time of Forever* stories, from mine, from the wind and rivers and warblers outside the window.

As we whiz down the very same highway my mother and I had on our way to The Town so many years earlier, I tell Felix about the people that populate our saga—a story of two lineages that have led us to this moment in time, that has led me to you, Wynton. Occasionally, I speculate for dramatic effect, i.e., Bazzy's witness-less death of which Maria suspected Victor in her journal. Who knows what really happened? And I admit Felix's size may have had something to do with Hector getting larger and larger in the story. I leave out a brutal beating of young Alonso and Sebastian by Hector and Diego when they were caught in Alonso's bed—which from notes in Alonso's wine-making manual seems likely the true reason he fell into a depression that led to him fleeing Spain. I couldn't bear to do that to them (again)—and to Felix—with my own words.

I leave out and mishmash other things too. It's true Alonso, Sebastian, and Maria created a perfect idyll for themselves within the walls of their house, but most of the outside community believed Alonso and Maria were husband and wife and Sebastian a dear old friend from Spain. It was still the Wild West that Marigold had described in my California history lessons, yes, but it wasn't nearly as wild, lawless, freewheeling—and gay—as it had been decades earlier when the rivers still teemed with gold and the Northern California cities and towns with men.

And I skipped over prohibition, a period that sunk a lot of wineries, but not theirs because in those years they made a sacramental wine that became very popular.

Anyway, guess what happens? Felix falls asleep! But I don't care, I blab on, realizing how much I need to tell the story, for me, to have these people as my own, to see myself apart from Marigold, to find myself in a great-grandmother like Maria, who could be a good mother and still fly, to imagine a love for myself unlike the ones Marigold modeled, but like

Alonso and Sebastian's that transcended time, distance, even death.

I also realize from the retelling that history might be one long, chaotic, fluky game of telephone.

Before long, we pull up in front of The Blue Spoonful, where Felix wants to apply for a job as a line cook after I told him about Bernadette's aphrodisiacal soufflés and her Michelin Star. He swings his bag over his shoulder. "I'm now entering your saga of the Falls, I guess," he says, gesturing toward the restaurant.

"Me too," I say, my stomach roiling.

After I say goodbye, I pull into the spot where I sat in Sadie Mae for one of the last times, my mother and me passing the chocolate soufflé back and forth, swearing to each other that after spending years and years looking for The Town, we will never, ever come back.

I look out over the square, at the waterfall catching the sun so it looks like light, not water, is tumbling down, and something clicks into place inside me like it did the first time we visited. I can't explain it any other way: It's The Town.

It's home.

I look at the café that used to be Sebastian's Spanish Bakery, then became Christophe's Soufflé Shop, and now is a dog grooming store. I imagine Bernadette on the fire escape waiting for my father to walk across the square playing his trumpet in his sleep. I imagine Alonso and Sebastian floating around inside Sebastian's bakery, Maria galloping by on a horse, her red hair whipping in the wind. I think she's my favorite one of us, a role model for me—so when I told Felix the story, I gave her wings on her back.

After much trial and error and some research on my phone, I find my way to Dave Caputo's father's glass house, but it's been sold. The name on the driveway says *The Aglins*. I sit outside the glass house for a long time missing my mother, hating my mother, loving my mother. The usual.

Then I'm ready for some serious stalking and sleuthing. I'm still thinking I'll intuitively be able to tell if Miles and Dizzy are my siblings. Won't I have a feeling of sameness in their presences? (I didn't have that sense with you all those years ago, Wynton. You felt entirely other. Thank the lordesses.)

I remember passing the middle school on the way into town. So, Dizzy first.

I park by the athletic field where kids are playing dodgeball. I watch two gym classes before a waif of a girl I recognize, with a riot of hair on her head, walks onto the field, looking lonely as a leaf. She's heartbroken, I think, and it stirs something new in me. "My sister," I say under my breath just to try out the words. But is she? The possibility makes my throat tighten. Even though it's hotter than Mars, I lower the window, hoping I'll hear her voice. I can't believe this is the same commotion of a girl I met years before. Why is she so unhappy now? And then I'm observing with horror as some bully reams a ball into her stomach and then puts his ass right in her face. Um, excuse me? I have to grip the wheel to restrain myself from getting out of the truck, jumping the fence, and taking that ball and crushing it into his face.

Then Dizzy's running away, bounding over the fence, so she misses what happens next.

A boy with gelled strawberry-blond hair rushes the dick-weasel bully and punches him in the face, telling him he better apologize to Dizzy. The bully, blindsided, is knocked off his feet. Even while the gym teacher is blowing a whistle, our ginger-haired hero sprints to the fence after Dizzy. Is it her boyfriend? If not, maybe he should be. There's a gallantry about this hero kid I like. Sadly, he doesn't get over the fence. He's halfway up when the gym teacher pulls him back down and escorts him across the field and inside, I assume, to the principal's office, while another teacher takes the bully, I assume, to the nurse.

I light up the truck and go after Dizzy. I can't help myself. And thank God, I get to her in time.

With all my might, and maybe some extra force from who knows where, I push her out of the way of a speeding truck. In that moment, I feel like one of those mothers who lifts a car to save her child, like I could've stopped time itself to save this girl. My little sister? Even though Dizzy and I only have a split second together with that truck barreling straight for us, it feels eternal.

Even so, I can't say I know for sure if she's my sister or not during our brief encounter.

After I shove her out of the way, I dive under the eighteen-wheeler as the trucker screeches to a halt over me. The sun in his eyes must've prevented him from seeing me because he has no clue why Dizzy flies into the air. As you know by now, Wynton, I have a lot of experience hiding under large vehicles, but it's broiling out and the asphalt is so hot, I have to keep rolling over so as not to blister my skin. While I rotate like a roasting chicken under the truck, I listen to Dizzy charm the pants off the driver and realize how much my father (*our* father?) is going to adore her if she is indeed his, much more than he adores me because she's so much more adorable. She's not damaged, like I am.

I'm not proud of what I feel in this moment: I don't want my dad to have another daughter. Not one bit. My father is all I have, and I decide then that I can't share him with you all, that I won't. Despite how much I want to see you again, Wynton, when Dizzy and the trucker part ways, I slip out from beneath the truck, dead set on driving back to Whispering River and locking all this away forever. I know I'm being a coward, but I also know that you guys have a mother, and I don't.

On my way out of town, I spot a big white house in the distance. Even before I see the winery sign, from both Maria's and Bernadette's descriptions, I know immediately it's the Fall house, and around it, the

Fall vineyards. Curiosity gets the better of me and I take the turnoff and park on a utility road and look up at the house, imagining Alonso, Sebastian, Maria, and Bazzy sitting on the porch. Imagining Theo and Clive as teenagers. Imagining my poor father heartbroken, fleeing in his truck, and imagining you, Wynton, Miles, and Dizzy growing up there without him. Soon fatigue begins to overtake me; I didn't sleep at all the night before because I was reading everything. I decide to nap for a minute before hitting the road again. I empty out my backpack of books, looking for something to read (even when I'm exhausted, I can't fall asleep without reading, even a sentence or two). I choose a reread of *East of Eden,* in honor of all the cursed Fall brothers. I begin to read as dusk settles over the valley, and before I know it, it's the next day and I wake to Miles and Sandro outside the window.

That morning with Miles is one of the best times of my life. (I know there must be some explanation for the Dumpster incident he told me about. I can't imagine you'd do that to him. Could you, Wynton? Have I so misjudged you?) Anyway, there's a Dutch word: *Dauwtrappen.* It means to walk barefoot in the dew-covered grass; that's how I feel talking to Miles that morning, sitting beside him, reading beside him at the waterfall, floating together on our backs like sea otters. The whole time I kept thinking: No way we're not related. No way. He rights me, like I was a painting hung crooked my whole life. And he makes me feel expansive, like a never-ending girl.

I've since done some research into siblings who meet not knowing that they're related—it's often described as a mystical experience. Meeting Miles, I feel this, feel an immediate, profound, and almost otherworldly sense of recognition, belonging, peace. Like I'm suddenly walking around in a prayer. I become convinced that morning he's my half brother and I have to stop myself from telling him the whole time we're together. But maybe it's wishful thinking. And I'm really uncertain about Dizzy.

Still, after I say goodbye to him and Sandro (whom I hear talking in my head!), I'm committed to leaving The Town, only when I'm about to cross the town line, by that bar, Better Luck Next Time, my tire goes flat. Yes. Again. Just like with Sadie Mae. I know The Town wants me to stay, and as I'm putting on the spare, I decide The Town is right this time. The need to know for sure if I have siblings in this world, and to meet you again, Wynton, is more powerful than the fear of sharing or even losing my father.

Metanoia, n. a transformative change of heart. Tattooed now on my left shoulder. I get the tattoo that afternoon at a parlor on the square. The whole time the needle drums into my skin, I look out at the statue of Alonso Fall, wondering what the hell happened to *my great-grandfather's* head. I can't believe I have a heritage now, a history to belong to, one that started long before The Great Adventure with Marigold. Like I've always wanted. And I might have siblings too! A real family! And who knows what you'll be to me!

That night is your show, Wynton, and I arrive early. Luckily I have a fake ID in my wallet that my friend Summer got me when we spent a weekend in San Francisco. When you walk on stage with your shades on, your ripped black jeans, your tattoo of a blue horse coming out of your sleeve, I know for sure you're the boy in the time of forever who was once a lightning bolt. You don't say a word, just smile at the crowd. (That smile when I was thirteen confused me, how it sent my stomach on a roller-coaster ride. At nineteen, it doesn't confuse me at all.) Yes, it's a heat wave, but it's like I've become the heat wave. I tell myself again and again: *We are not related!* Your father is Clive, your mother is Bernadette. My father is Theo, my mother is Marigold, and Clive and Theo are not related by blood. This becomes a mantra the whole mind-blowingly awesome show as my feelings for you gallop around inside me: *We are not related! We are not related!*

Remember when my mother met Dave? Remember how I asked if you believed in love at first sight? You are why I do. I think I have loved you since the day we met in the meadow all those years ago.

Once, I found under my dad's bed, a dog-eared copy of this romance novel called *Live Forever Now*. I was shocked. Nothing could've been more of a departure from my dad's literary proclivities. I read it in the bathtub that night. It's so trashy but also great. There's a couple in it who meet at thirteen and make a promise to marry (like us!). Then they don't see each other for years until they run into each other on a yacht in the Greek Isles where he is the captain and she a rich socialite. (I know, groan.) He recognizes her and falls head-over-heels at first sight (again), ensures the yacht runs out of gas so he can make her fall in love with him (again) while they're stranded at sea. There's all sorts of problematic class and gender issues with the book—but it's still ridiculously romantic and sexy. In this moment in the club, I am Jericho Blane seeing Samantha Brooksweather again after all those years.

Standing next to me is a burly guy in a hat who seems to be having similar reactions to your playing and person as I am (well, not *exactly* similar). I think his words when you start to play are, "Holy hellfire!" This makes me laugh. I catch a glimpse of his face and I recognize him as Sylvester Dennis from the band Hell Hyena and the Furniture. I know all their music because Dad is a fan. He smiles at me and says, "Who plays a goddamn sonata in a club and makes it sound like rock 'n' roll? Only this guy. This fucking guy. He's joining my band."

"Lucky you," I say.

"You're telling me."

(Wynton, it devastates me to think you might lose this opportunity. I can't imagine how you'll take it when you wake. Know that I'll be here for you.)

Sylvester Dennis and I get separated after that because I hear my mother's name being called and turn around to see a sun-leathered man rushing toward me. I gasp. It's an older, life-weary version of Dave Caputo of The Second Betrayal and he's saying, "Am I dreaming, Marigold? You don't look a day older. Not one day." Only when he's a few feet away does he realize his mistake. "Cassidy?"

He puts a hand over his mouth and looks at me for a very long time and I learn in this moment that love doesn't go away when people do. It never goes away, does it? Tears are falling down my cheeks and I'm remembering him swooping me up in his arms in the forest when I got lost. I'm remembering being his sous chef and shouting "Yes!" when he asked my mother to marry him. Then I'm waking to a horizon-less world because his rig is gone. I'm that girl again. I think in this moment how maybe I'm always all the girls I've ever been, how the now-me is just all the old-mes thrown together. And maybe you can't hang on to people, I've learned that from Marigold and from this man, but my, how we hang on to our love for them, or it hangs on to us.

Because my heart is shaking with hope at seeing Dave again, the same hope he filled me with when I was twelve, the same unwieldy love. He says, "I left my wife, left my job. I opened a custom furniture shop up here, built a dream shack. Because of you and your mom. I tried to look for you, been back to Sister Falls every year since, stay the whole month. I was hoping you guys would go back there. I never even knew your last name. Had no way to find you."

We hug then and I smell his same Dave smell. "How is she?" he asks.

"I don't know."

"What do you mean?"

"She left me . . ." I'm about to tell him what happened, about my dad being Theo Fall from this town, *The* Town, and about you all. I want to, but how can I? How can he be the first I tell? How can I trust this person after what he did to us? I can't.

But do we ever reminisce outside the club, where it's quieter. It feels so good to talk about Marigold with someone who yearns for her like I do, and he clearly does, someone who understands the spell she casts as well as the very dark shadow.

"It was real," he tells me. "That month, man. I lived more with you two than I have in all the time before and since."

When I go back inside, Wynton, you're gone. I set out to find you in my truck. Do you remember our meeting in the road? Do you remember you asked me to marry you again? Do you remember swaying together in the moonlight? It might have been the best moment of my life. Its only competition, our afternoon in the meadow.

Beshert, a word tattooed on my ankle. Dad taught it to me. I was surprised at the time he'd know a Yiddish word, but now since I've read your mother's journal and her cookbook, I know where he picked it up.

Are you my *beshert,* Wynton? Or am I making all this up?

I've been staying in Dave's guest room in his dream shack, which really is dreamy and a shack this time. No glass walls, no ostentation, except for the top-notch kitchen. Dave's "restaurant" is still awesome. Marigold would love it there. He told me he built it with her in mind and that he calls the attic room on the top floor Marigold's Nest. "To write her strange stories in." Maybe one day she'll return to The Town and find us both in it.

Each night since I arrived, I've snuck into your hospital room so I wouldn't run into your family, which might be mine too; not ready to tell them who I am. (I bribe the night staff at the hospital with Dave's incredible Everything Cookies to let me secretly sit with you—they call us Romeo and Juliet.)

At this point, I'm still so terrified to blow up my father's life, Wynton. A man who's gone to such ends to start a new one. I know Dexter Brown has no intention of ever running into Theo Fall again. What if he never forgives me for this? I don't think I could survive losing him after losing Marigold.

But I want to be part of the Falls' long and winding story. I want to claim Maria Guerrero. I want to sprout wings on my back. I want Dizzy and Miles as my sister and brother. And I want you, Wynton.

I realize my father made his choices and now I need to make mine.

So, just hours ago, after talking to the police and telling them everything I remember about the night of the accident—they still haven't found the driver—for the first time, I open the door to your hospital room during visiting hours.

Bernadette's by your side, leaning over the bed, talking to you just like I do. "Oh! You!" she says to me, rising from her chair. "She of the rainbow hair!" She's wearing a bright floral shirt and jeans. Her hair's stormy like Dizzy's. "Cassidy, right?" she says.

Wynton, I've seen your mother in photographs, but it didn't prepare me for the real thing. Her *aliveness*. How her spirit seems too big for her body. How gorgeous she is.

"My son and daughter, they're looking for you up north as we speak," she tells me. Miles and Dizzy are searching for me? How do they know where to look? Are they randomly driving around Northern California? I could imagine that actually, like Marigold and me searching for The Town. I'm about to ask your mother about it when she says, "Thank you for doing CPR and going with Wynton in the ambulance. They say you saved his life. And Dizzy says you saved hers too. Come here. How can I thank you? Can I hug you?" she says, coming toward me, arms wide open.

I know how badly she hurt my father, but it's impossible not to be swept into her warmth. No wonder he's so lost without her.

And boy, it's been a long time since I've been hugged by a mother, any mother, and your mother is kind of the quintessential one, isn't she? I try to tamp down the hunger in me for this exact type of maternal affection but can't. I also feel guilty, traitorous, deceitful because I'm pretty sure she's not going to want to hug me like this when she hears what I have to say. Not a chance. Still, I dissolve into her embrace, breathe in her musky scent, aching for my own mother who could never comfort me like this. With Marigold, the threat of her leaving was coded into her every affection. It was her unique awful sleight of hand.

But not your mom. I want to stay in her arms forever.

After a moment, she detaches from me and sweeps her lips against my forehead, a benediction, then drops her head down so that for a split second we're in Forehead-Noses. I gasp, it's like Marigold has flown into her body. Her expression is so grateful. How can I tell this woman, who's already so devastated about you, who I am? Does she even know where her husband has been all these years? Does she know he was unfaithful to her with Marigold? In this moment, I think, I can still make something up about who I am and then get in my truck and leave and not disrupt any lives, not hurt this woman, and most importantly, not risk my father's love.

"Have you told the police what you know about the driver?" she asks. "I know they've been looking for you." I nod and she says, "I better call my son and daughter and tell them to come home. Dizzy thinks you're an angel— a literal one—and that you alone can wake my boy." She regards me. "So how do you know Wynton? Are you friends from high school?" She's tilting her head, studying me. Is she noticing how much I look like Theo?

I take a breath, exhale slowly. "Wynton and I met years ago by chance . . ." I tell her. She smiles politely, waiting for more. "In a meadow, here in town. It doesn't matter, but the thing is . . ." I can't get it out. I'm a time bomb about to blow her world to pieces, my father's, everyone's.

Do I, or don't I?

What would my great-grandparents Maria Guerrero and Alonso Fall want me to do?

"The thing is what, dear?"

"The thing is . . ."

"Yes?"

"It's that you know my father."

"I do? Does he come to the restaurant?"

I blurt, "He's Theo Fall. My father was your husband."

Her hand flies to her mouth. "No." She looks around for something to grab with her other hand, but there's nothing except me, so she clasps my arm. "How old are you?"

"I'm nineteen, same as Wynton."

"Same as Wyn? I need to sit down. I need air," she says. "Let's go outside."

There's a disheveled-looking man, who I think might be Clive, sitting outside the door. When he sees your mother, he stands. "What happened, Bernie?" I smell alcohol on him.

"It's okay. Wynton's okay. Be back in a . . ." I follow your mother down the hall and through the lobby, her heels click-click-clicking like a metronome, then we're out the doors of the hospital. My pulse is flying. I don't think I've ever been this terrified—don't feel like I'm in my body.

Your mother sits down on a bench, puts a hand on either side of her. She breathes roughly, deliberately. I'm wishing I never told her, wishing I'd never come back to The Town. My mind's spiraling. What if she decides she doesn't believe me? Or worse, does and hates me for it? *I'd* hate me if I were her. Or worse, what if she tries to keep you all from me? What if she turns my father against me? How I despise Marigold in this moment for getting me into this, for putting this stick of dynamite in my hands. Further, how can I even think of asking her who the father of her kids is? Who am I to do that? And when her son is in a coma!

I want to bolt across the parking lot *and* I also desperately want her to hug me again. "Just give me a minute," she says. Blood's filling her cheeks and her eyes can't seem to focus. "Let me think, let me think. I'm spinning. This was certainly not on the bingo card for today." Her breathing's so rapid, I wonder if she needs a paper bag. I'm glad we're steps away from medical aid. "Okay, I'm okay," she says under her breath, looking at her hands. "Please tell me where he is. Where has he been living?" Before I can answer, she says, "Who's your mother? Does she live in town?"

"No, she's kind of a nomad," I say, sitting on the other side of the bench, placing my shaking hands under my thighs, reassured at least that she believes me and hasn't strangled me. Yet. "They met at a bluegrass festival. It was a one-time thing."

I can tell she's rewinding time in her mind. "In San Diego?" I figured out from her diary that this festival took place before they got married.

"Yes," I say.

Under her breath, she says, "That same week." I think I see disbelief in her face but also relief maybe? Is it because he too was unfaithful? It seems so unlike my father. Did he think of it as a last moment of recklessness before he married the love of his life and settled down? Who knows.

"You grew up with Theo?" she asks. Her eyes are following people as they enter the hospital. She nods absently to one after the next who greet her. I don't think she wants to look at me.

"Since I was fourteen," I say. "Before that I thought my father was dead. My mother abandoned me. She left me at my father—at Theo's house one night while I was sleeping."

She turns to me then, her brow creased. "Oh gosh. How awful. I'm sorry. Where was this?"

"Whispering River? Five hours north."

"So close this whole time." Her upper lip quivers. Is she going to cry? Punch me? Why did I do this? Her face is a riot of emotion as she asks, "How is he?" I see then how desperately she still loves him. It's tumbling out of her, Wynton. Same as he feels about her, I'm certain. I think of that photo of them in a vineyard, so young, happy, in love, irrepressible love.

"He's okay," I say.

She closes her eyes for a moment, then says, "A car ride away, all this time. Can't believe it. And can too. Mostly, I feel like he's still here." She laughs a sad laugh, points to the seat next to her on the bench. "I mean, like right here. This ghost in the next seat. This ghost I share my life with . . . cook for."

I want to take her hand. I want her to know she's not alone in this love that's so palpable in both their presences. "He keeps his wedding ring in his pocket."

Surprise crosses her face, then something else. Relief again? Or maybe, it's hope. She puts her hand in the pocket of her jeans, digs around, and then pulls out an identical band, places it in my palm. It has the same inscription as my father's: *You are my forever, my always, my only.* What a tragedy, I think. I don't know what really happened between Bernadette and Clive way back when, between Theo and Marigold, but these two are still somehow devoted to each other, even after all that's happened, even after so much time has passed. I find I can't even be angry at her on behalf of my father. They're both shipwrecks at the bottom of the same sea. I asked Nigel, and I don't think my dad has been on a date in all these years.

And then, something occurs to me and it's like lightning striking my soul, Wynton. We wouldn't exist but for their mistakes. Me and you. We *are* their mistakes, their trespasses. Does that change this equation? It sure does for me.

She's searching my face. "Look at you," she says. "I mean, Jesus. In walks sunshine. I can't even be . . . And you saved my kids' lives." She lifts her hand like she's going to touch my face but then lets it fall into her lap. "Does he know you've come here?"

I shake my head. "I found a box of memorabilia," I tell her. "Wynton's band posters, Miles's school stuff, pictures of you all, newspaper articles, journals of relatives, your diary—"

"You read it." Not a question. There's an edge to her voice. Shame fills me.

"Skimmed." I attempt to explain. "I needed to know why he left you all. I needed to know there was a legitimate reason. I needed to know he wasn't like my mother. He's the only person I've ever truly trusted. I needed to know—"

"If he's worthy of your trust?" She holds my eyes. "He is. It was my fault he left us."

I'm amazed at how wholly she shoulders the blame. She doesn't seem to hold my father accountable for leaving her alone to raise three kids. Is her guilt that great? Or does she love him that much? What in the world happened, Wynton?

"But you already know it was my fault, don't you?"

"I don't think . . ." Am I going to say it aloud? I am because I need to hear it from her. I need to be a thousand percent certain. "I don't think Wynton is my father's son." I don't know about Miles and Dizzy either, obviously, but this feels most important. I need confirmation. She looks down at her hands, which are fisted on her lap. "It's none of my business, I know that," I add, the shame strangling me now, but I persist because I need to know we're okay Wynton, you and me—that is, if you feel like I do. I steel myself and add, "But all the same, if that's not the case, for some reason, can you tell me, because . . . because . . ."

"Because why?" She studies my face intently. I try to keep breathing. "Because you're in love with my son," she says, again not a question.

"He's asked me to marry him twice now. Once when we were thirteen, then again, the other night."

She rubs her eyes. "This is something. This is really something. You met when you were kids and now . . ." Her forehead furrows like she's trying to remember something. "It reminds me of this romance novel I read a long time ago."

"*Live Forever Now.*"

A small burst of a laugh comes out of your mom. "You read that terrible book too?"

"Terrible and *awesome*," I say.

"Terrible and awesome, that it was," she repeats, smiling. "Like life. Like this very moment, in fact. Whew-y." She shakes her head and there's a sharpness in her voice but when she looks my way, I see only compassion in her face. "It's okay for you to be in love with Wynton, genetically speaking. And you weren't raised together obviously so . . . Maybe Dizzy's right after all and you're the one who will bring him back to us." Wynton! The relief and joy I feel at knowing this for certain is overwhelming. But I need to know about Miles and Dizzy too.

"And the others?" I can't even look at your mother, I'm so embarrassed to ask this. I'm reading and rereading the tattoo on my wrist: *glisk, glisk, glisk, a fleeting glance at a glittering sight.* I know I'm pushing her, invading what must be a secret shameful place, but I have to know. All I want is this yes. All I've ever wanted is this yes.

Bernadette lifts my chin with her fingers. Her eyes are gentle and kind and I know. "Welcome to the family," she says.

I burst into tears, Wynton. I think of the little girl in Sadie Mae with her mother in The Silent World counting her own hairs, talking to the moon, talking to her bugs. I couldn't have dreamed a better dream for her.

Just then your mother's phone sounds. I see Dizzy's face on the screen when she pulls it out—my half sister!—as if she's heard us talking about her. Your mother takes a few steps away with the phone to her ear. She listens for several minutes in silence, until finally, she says, "Dizzy, are we awake?" before saying goodbye and ending the call.

She returns to the bench even more shaken than she was during our conversation. "They're on their way back." She meets my eyes. "With Theo. This is it." Her voice is trembling. "Will you stay with Wyn for a bit? I need to go for a quick walk, get sorted." Her face in this moment is hard to describe, somehow equal parts terror and joy.

"Of course," I say, standing, wondering how on earth Miles and Dizzy found my—our father.

After a few steps, your mother turns around. "Theo was always the one," she says. "I was just too young, dumb, and screwed up over my brother's death to realize it. It's only ever been him. It only ever will be." Then for a split second, she transforms into the young carefree girl in the photograph. "I'm glad he got to be a father to you. I know how good he was at it."

"He's the best father," I tell her, blinking so I don't cry again.

A parade of emotions traipses across her face. "I'm happy to meet you," she says, and I can tell this is true despite what it means, then she turns and walks away.

That was an hour ago.

Wynton, telling you my story in betrayals, I've realized something. Each one has brought me so much anguish, but in the end, I realize, joy as well. I didn't understand this until now. After the first betrayal, my mom started taking medication that mostly kept her out of The Silent World for years. The second betrayal brought me to Paradise Springs, to you. The third led me to my father and the best years of my life so far. I hope it will be the same for you. I do believe now that when the world tips over, joy spills out with all the sorrow.

But you have to look for it.

I have this fantasy that when you wake, we'll write the big messy saga of the Falls together. Our story. Mine, yours, Miles's, and Dizzy's. A novel. We can give Alonso Fall a voice—I was thinking I could write his story in the vein of my mother's *In the Time of Forever* tales. Sandro could have a voice too. We could make him the first dog to never ever die! And we could include bits and pieces from my father's boxes of memorabilia, from all the old journals and notebooks. Maybe even excerpts from Bernadette's diary of letters if she lets us. Anything we want to add. Anyone. A Fall family fantasia. Our unhinged love song from Paradise.

I'm hoping, together, we find the right ending.

PART
FIVE

MILES

Sandro was crashed out between Miles and Felix on the seat, snout on Miles's thigh, rump on Felix's as they raced to the hospital where a heretofore unimaginable family reunion was about to take place to save Wynton's life. With windows down and redwoods watching over them from every side, Felix said, "Okay, so what I haven't told you, haven't told anyone outside my family, is that I'm probably going to lose my eyesight at some point. Most of it anyway."

"Oh, thank God!" Miles exclaimed.

"Not the anticipated reaction."

"I thought you were dying!"

"Why?" Felix was laughing. "Why would you think that? What the fuck, Mr. Fall?"

"I don't know. I think because"—Miles didn't know how to phrase it—"because of how you're so *appreciative* of birds and stars and like *everything,* but it doesn't matter what I thought, that sucks, man."

Felix's face dimmed. He exhaled slowly. "Yeah, seriously. Had no clue about terror before this."

"Can't even imagine, Felix. I'm so sorry." Miles couldn't believe he'd been so caught up that he hadn't asked Felix outright what was going on with him. He wanted to tell him that he'd do anything for him, absolutely anything because that was the way he—Samantha effing Brooksweather incarnate—rolled.

All around them as they talked, the world glistened as sunlight stumbled into the trees, the road, into the two of them alone in a truck.

"I took so much for granted," Felix said.

"Past tense though, right?" Miles stared at Felix. "I mean, I've never met anyone like you, for real. That's what I was trying to say before. You love everything."

Felix's face broke into a smile. "I fucking do now. I love *everything*."

Miles was nodding. "You're this joy-maker, dude. It's catching."

"Is it? That's actually awesome." It seemed to genuinely uplift him. It was true too. In a day, he'd taught Miles to splendor-watch like others might bird-watch. "There's this famous chef who went blind," he told Miles. "She was on one of those reality shows. Insists she's a better chef for it because her other senses are so turned up." He sighed. "It could be ages anyway. Even fifteen years." He twirled his mustache. "It might not be total either. I read this thing online. I might see people as these shadowy figures one day. The guy describing it said it was like seeing ghosts"—he laughed—"like Dizzy. And maybe they'll find a cure by then, who knows?" He tapped the steering wheel with his fingers. "I've been on this bender since finding out—minus the booze. Felt like my life was over." Miles looked at Felix, saw something in his face he hadn't yet, a shyness maybe? "But since hanging with you," Felix said, "I feel better."

Miles crossed his arms so he didn't place his hands on Felix's face and kiss his amazing mouth at this admission. Felix went on. "I don't know how to describe it, but you're like really . . . I don't know, *stormy* or something? No, you're a total fucking mess, man." Miles laughed. "I mean it in this epic way, like the volume, the brightness, everything's cranked, I love it. You're just in it. I don't know why but it's made me less scared, like it's all some big adventure or something." Whoa. Miles couldn't believe it. Him, stormy? Him, really *in it*? Him, making someone less afraid? By being a royal mess? By being himself? Miles wanted to tell Felix that it was being with him that made Miles feel this *in it,* this glued to life, this himself, that he hadn't been this way before they met, before everything that had happened these last few days, but he didn't want to interrupt. "This weird thing happened when I got the diagnosis," Felix said. "I became obsessed with faces. My mom's, my dad's, my little brother Elvis's." He smiled. "Kid's got the best face. Looks like an elf." He took a deep breath in. "And Eddie's—especially him, my buddy. That's the problem. When I realized I might not get to see Eddie's face age, it broke me. I mean, I had a girlfriend. Thought we were happy, but I ended it because I didn't think about her face at all." He sighed. "That—plus the diagnosis obviously—is why I ran away. I just couldn't deal. With anything."

Miles bit his cheek until it bled. There it was. Felix was in love with Eddie the effing Olympic pizza-maker. Argh.

"Anyway, going to focus on the now," Felix said.

Amen. Because in the now, despite Eddie, while they yakked, their fingers kept touching as each pet the sleeping dog, and every time it happened, Miles had to close his eyes because of the full-body shudder, the way it made his breath hitch, his groan come alive. One of those times Felix lifted his shades and their eyes locked. Then Felix's gaze fell to Miles's mouth, his *lips,* and stayed there. Miles licked his bottom lip and Felix said, "Dude," in this way. They both smiled. Miles's pulse revved.

He wasn't the only one feeling it.

He wasn't the only one feeling it!

Was it Felix's unresolved feelings for Eddie or the diagnosis that had made him say he was unavailable? Or the combination? Miles wasn't sure, but Felix really didn't seem unavailable in this moment. Miles wanted to take the wheel and swerve the truck onto the shoulder of the road. What if he did? Did Felix want him too? He imagined them, the fury of *finally,* two boys colliding like planets. His fingers ached to touch Felix.

They were just a few miles away from Paradise Springs now and even with everything about to happen at the hospital, Miles didn't want to get out of the truck. His eyes traveled to Felix's chest under his black T-shirt, to his tan muscly arms, to his thighs, to the bulge in his jeans. God, it was unbearable. Desire pounded through him. He felt parched and dizzy. How do people function with this feeling? Pretend anything else matters? Miles wished they were driving to South America.

He wished they could squeeze into the glove compartment together.

When the hospital was in sight, the RV with his father and Dizzy in it, in front of them now, turned into the lot, but instead of following them, Felix drove past the hospital and parked on the fire road where their journey began with Rod the Cannibal a day and a lifetime before. What was happening?

Was *something* finally going to happen!?

Felix killed the engine and looking straight ahead, he said, "I realized from talking to you today that I have to go back to Colorado." Miles felt as if he'd been kicked in the throat. He'd not been expecting this. He'd been expecting the opposite of this! Even with the Eddie admission, he'd thought after they'd opened up so much that he'd had a shot. He wanted Samantha Brooksweather and Jericho Blane, Alonso and Sebastian, not goodbye. He couldn't make any words so just nodded.

Felix took off his sunglasses, rested them on the dashboard. He petted Sandro, who was beginning to stir. "I can't not go to Culinary School." He looked at Miles, smiled a smile that was equal parts irony and sincerity. "It's my destiny, like your great-grandfather Alonso getting on the ship."

Miles nodded again. Of course, Felix had to go. It was his dream and Miles wanted him to have it, in the now, and hopefully always. "And Eddie?" Miles asked, unable to keep it in.

Felix shrugged. He seemed like he was going to answer, but then didn't, probably to protect Miles who'd made it embarrassingly clear where he stood. Miles could see yearning in Felix's face—like a billboard for it—but as much as Miles wanted it to be, it wasn't for him. Felix was going back to Eddie. Miles had misread everything, including all the hand collisions, even the one happening this minute as they both petted Sandro. People's hands accidently touched all the time, didn't they? Meant nothing.

Even if it was making Miles feel like he had heatstroke.

Miles took his hand away, leaden with disappointment. He felt like all the birds flew away. He couldn't look at Felix anymore for fear he would throw his arms around the guy and beg him not to go or tell him that he would wait for him to finish chef school and/or forever.

He looked instead toward the hospital. What was going on in that room? Was his brother waking up? He had to get in there. For so long, he'd been running away from his family, but somehow it was running toward them that finally allowed him to begin finding himself. And his father was right, he was almost a grown-ass man. He had to stop blaming others for his life. Yes, his dad abandoned him, and his brother alienated him, but neither was responsible for who he'd be in this family, or in the world. That was on him. As Sandro said to him yesterday, his story of choice has always been a woe-is-me one. He wanted to write a new story now. A big dreamy romantic one like his great-grandfather's even.

And maybe he'd go to therapy like Dean Richards suggested, but The Gloom Room seemed light-years away. Like Felix said, he was *in* his life now and he had all these new people to turn to, if, once again, he slipped out of it. He even knew there was love somewhere somehow between him and his brother, a frail and flimsy love maybe, but love all the same. It was like lifting an impossibly heavy rock and finding some oblivious flower beneath it. How could it be alive and beautiful in that darkness, under such weight? But it was. Why couldn't two Fall brothers be brothers for once? *If the path before you is clear, you're probably on someone else's,* right? They'd forge their own uncursed path.

If he woke.

Miles turned back to Felix, whose face was still a billboard of yearning. For someone else. Miles sighed. His chest ached. This was goodbye then.

He worried his voice would break if he spoke, but he had to. "Thanks, Felix. I mean it. Thanks for everything." It was late to have made his first real friend, but better late than never. He opened the door. Sandro picked his head up, then snuggled back into Felix's leg. Miles wanted to snuggle into Felix too, wanted to do so many things with this guy. He swung his backpack over his shoulder and was looking for the leash under the seat when Felix grabbed his arm. *Felix grabbed his arm.* Grabbed it and didn't let go. "Wait," Felix said.

Miles sat up, sparks flying off every thought.

Felix was grinning. "Want to—"

"Dude, not falling for that again," Miles said. But this time, unlike last night, Felix's hand was sliding up Miles's arm, knocking the breath out of him.

Had the billboard been for him?

Felix grinned and dimpled at Miles and oh my God it was happening. "This time I mean something else." He gripped Miles's arm tighter. The air ignited. "I'm leaving, so I didn't want to . . . but I'm dying, man. I've been dying. Because the thing is, I haven't told you how it was when I saw *your* face in the hospital lobby. Or saw it when you were laughing in the woods. Or how it's been seeing it every minute over the last two days." His hand slid under the arm of Miles's T-shirt. Miles went weak. "I haven't told you how it is looking at your face right this minute."

"How is it?" The words were entirely breath, expectation.

"It's like: Who's Eddie, man?" Felix laughed. Miles couldn't believe he could be sitting in this truck and doing backflips at the same time. He was quite certain he was turning into a ball of light, like his great-grandfather. "You put it all in perspective, Miles. I've never felt like this before with anyone. I've been . . . scared though with everything going on."

"I'll be scared with you," Miles said. "I want to do it all with you, Felix."

Miles couldn't wait another second. He was velocity itself, half reeling and all hope, as he slipped his hands beneath Felix's shirt, leaving earth briefly at the sound of Felix sucking in breath as Miles's hands glided across Felix's chest, skin to skin, glided down, down, to his stomach, causing Felix to moan, which caused Miles to completely lose his mind as Felix's hands traveled to Miles's waist, to Miles's waistband, winding his finger around a belt loop, and then pulling Miles to him by it, making Miles gasp as they each leaned in and, finally, *finally,* pressed their lips together, stopping time.

They breathed in as one, holding this key-to-lock moment, this cyclone-in-a-bottle moment, this connection of bodies and way beyond bodies, Miles on the verge of tears, on the verge of *rapture,* before the glass broke, the cyclone let loose, their mouths opened, and hunger took over and they were gone, teeth banged, mustache mustaching, tongues desperate, hands everywhere, the sound of Felix's ragged breathing sending hot currents through Miles, making Miles want to say all the words in his pocket pad at once, all the words in all the books in all the world at once—because that would be the only way to describe *this,* what was happening between them, two boys in a truck falling off the world, falling in love. Miles was splashing around in happiness, and something was unfurling in his chest, something wild and free and deeply irrefutably *him.*

As if all the atoms in his body had been spinning at 1,000 mph for billions of years (which they had!) just to get to this moment.

What had he been thinking, keeping this most joyful side of himself a secret?

"Miles," Felix said, smiling, their foreheads touching, their breath mingling. "We're Alonso and Sebastian. We're in the air."

Then too, too soon, Miles was outside the truck and leaning in the driver's-side window, his hand on Felix's arm. He felt made of dreams.

You did it! Sandro was doing figure eights around his feet. *Lucky duck! Lucky devil! Lucky dog!*

I know! Miles made eye contact with the dog. It was time to forgive his eternal companion. *You too, Sandro. You found Beauty.*

His tail wagged. *I know!*

Felix grinned, looking at them. "Are you guys talking right now?"

I wish he could hear me!

Miles was untethered, so very far from perfect where happy seemed to be. And this was a goodbye that felt jam-packed with hello. He said to Felix, "If you get a letter one day with just a blank page inside, you'll know what it means, right?"

Felix's face configured into the deadliest half-smile yet.

Nice one, Sandro said to Miles. *Maybe you do have some game after all.*

Thank you.

Miles and Sandro began walking toward the hospital, toward the most improbable family gathering, when Miles heard Felix. "Hey!"

Miles turned. This guy was terrible at goodbyes. "You could come to Denver later in the summer? We have bigger mountains. At least I think we do."

Miles had the money for a ticket, but would Felix be with Eddie later in the summer? Or back with his girlfriend? Who knew? Who knew anything? Miles said, "That'd be cool."

Then he started for the hospital once more, hoping to be stopped again.

"Hey!" he heard, and Miles spun around. Felix was laughing. "Dude, this is your mother's truck!"

DIZZY

Dizzy left her father to park the RV and ran across the parking lot and through the hospital doors. She couldn't wait another second. She was careening down the hall to Wynton's room when she heard her name.

It was Lizard. Right there in the hallway with his hair gelled but nerd glasses back on like in the pre-divorce days. Dizzy had the same feeling she got right before she started crying. There were moments in life, she understood, seeing her best friend smile big at her again, when souls bloomed like flowers.

"You got my texts?" he asked.

She nodded. "We hurried." She wanted to burst out of herself like a jack-in-the-box and hug him. She wanted to tell him every single thing that had happened since their breakup. But then she remembered Melinda, remembered what he'd written on the bathroom mirror the last time she'd seen him: *Leave Me Alone*. "You said there was a reason for our divorce," she said. "What was it?"

He smiled, shyly this time, then straightened his glasses, which were already straight. Dizzy did the same to her pair. Her stomach was churning, and her skin felt prickly. "Okay," he said. "What I have to tell you . . ." He took a big dramatic breath. "The reason I . . . I mean . . . So, okay, Dizzy, when we . . . for me . . . There were, you know . . . I lied—"

She was impatient to get in the hospital room where everything was happening, but equally as impatient to know what was going on here. Lizard never acted shy like this, never ever stammered—she had no idea what he was trying to say. And he'd lied to her? "Just say it, Tristan." She'd call him this if that was what he wanted, but in the privacy of her mind, he'd always be Lizard.

"Okay, okay." He smiled sheepishly. His cheeks were flushing. "All right. Here goes. When we kissed that time, I felt them."

"Them?"

"The endorphins! And the spontaneous internal explosions from your stupid romance book too! I said I didn't because you said you didn't first, but *I* did!"

"Did you feel endorphins and spontaneous internal explosions with Melinda?" Dizzy asked.

He shook his head.

Okay. Okay. There was only one thing for her to do then. She walked over to him, put her hands on Lizard's shoulders, closed her eyes, and for the second time, she kissed her best friend. It felt like lips touching, nothing else. She was about to pull away, to break it to him that she felt no endorphins or internal explosions when his thumb brushed her cheek. Had he done that the last time? She didn't think so. Then his hands were in her hair. He definitely hadn't done this before. He parted his lips—nope, not this either—and so did she. Then they were wrapping their arms around each other, and she was buzzing, buzzing, buzzing, and not just in her soul but *in her fiery furnace.*

The doors of her wild femininity were swinging open just like Samantha Brooksweather's!

Two weeks' worth of this would definitely not be enough for *her* lifetime. It took all her strength to disentangle from him. "I felt it this time, Lizard." The words came out more like breaths. Whoa was Dizzy dizzy.

His glasses were crooked, as was his smile. She straightened her own. "That was dope," he said.

"So dope," she said. "Now come on. Everything's about to happen!"

Dizzy and Lizard blew into Wynton's hospital room.

By the window, in a row, looking out over the parking lot were her mother, her uncle Clive, and Cassidy, who was with a man she'd seen playing chess with Wynton on the square. But that wasn't all. At Wynton's bedside were Dizzy's favorite mute ghosts. Her ancestors, she now knew for sure. Alonso Fall and Sebastian Ortega were holding hands, their feet a few inches above the ground. On the other side of Wynton was Maria Guerrero, her fire-red hair tumbling with buttercups and orange roses, filling the hospital room with a magenta smell. But there was another ghost next to her, holding her hand, a new one Dizzy had never seen before, a younger man with a sad face and red hair like Maria. Was it Bazzy from Cassidy's story? Dizzy's grandfather's ghost? Had he been with his son Theo all these years? And had now followed him home to Paradise Springs? Yes, she thought, he must have.

Dizzy went to Wynton, placed her hand on his chest, nodded at the ghosts who all ignored her like always, and then she and Lizard joined the rest by the window. Cassidy met Dizzy's eyes, then bopped her nose and Dizzy did it back, happiness overtaking Dizzy, toes to head. She had a sister now, what on earth could be better than that? Except that Wynton was about to wake! Then Dizzy hugged her mother and could smell sweat on her—green with rust speckles. Her mother's body was shaking and even as they embraced, her mother didn't take her eyes off the purple RV out of which Dizzy's father had not yet emerged.

Dizzy then turned her attention to what was going on outside the window too. The sun was setting over the mountain, flooding the valley with golden light. By the entrance to the hospital was Miles telling Sandro something, to wait probably, then he opened the door to enter, but Sandro darted in anyway, and moments later, Miles walked in with the dog, who was definitely not allowed in the hospital, but no one seemed to care.

To her surprise, Miles walked to the side of the hospital bed and placed his hand on Wynton's chest, on his heart like she had done. Dizzy wasn't sure she'd ever seen her brothers touch. Miles bent over and whispered something in Wynton's ear. She couldn't hear what. Then he approached the rest of them at the window bank, and he and Cassidy welled up looking at each other. Dizzy thought they might be mind-talking like shamans. Miles hugged his mother and nodded at Uncle Clive. Dizzy reached for Miles's hand. Miles smiled and took it and reached for Cassidy's. Below the window, people were gathering in front of the hospital. "Word's out," Cassidy whispered.

Every gaze was on the RV called Purple Rain as the door opened and Theo Fall emerged in his cowboy hat. Even through the window, Dizzy could hear the *thwap*, *thwap*, *thwap* of his boots on the pavement as he strode across the lot. Tears were rolling down her mother's face and she didn't bother to wipe them away. Her uncle Clive was smiling, and Dizzy realized she'd never seen him do that before, not once in her life. All these firsts were happening in this room now, a good omen.

She remembered the atheist hospital administrator Cynthia explaining to her on the night of the accident that she could pray by trying to wrap her arms around the whole world. This was Dizzy's whole world, she thought, her personal people-pile. And the only safety in the world was that. She couldn't really permanently lock everyone in a house together, but she could close her eyes and imagine wrapping her arms around this newly expanded family, her best friend (first boyfriend?), even the dumb dog. Cynthia was right, it was a good way to pray, to hope, to wring sacredness out of life.

There was so much, Dizzy thought, so much muchness to it all.

Then she opened her eyes and set them on her father, who was going to wake Wynton. Her father, who'd finally come home.

However, when he was halfway across the lot, he stopped, pivoted, and headed back toward the RV at a fast, purposeful clip.

"No!" the row of them shouted in unison, all banging on the window with their palms.

Her mom said, "Not again, Theo," and was out the hospital room door so she didn't see that he'd only gone back to the RV because he'd forgotten his trumpet.

WYNTON

The first note calls to you like it used to when you had a body, had a violin, had a wonderful screwed-up life, like it used to when your father's ghost-music would take you from room to river to roof to meadow.

And now, it's brought you back to the hospital room.

Except something's wrong. Terribly wrong.

This can't be him because this musician can't play. You shudder inside at the tone, cringe at how shrill the sound. You recoil at the braying notes slapped together haphazardly, anemically. Who is this awful musician? And why is he so close to you, blaring each atrocious riff right at your head. This is not the trumpet-playing you've been hearing your whole life!

If only you could move so you could cover your ears!

You beg whoever is playing to stop already, to just stop, but they don't. You have to get away. You're on your way back to the meadow, to wait for death, anywhere where that noise pretending to be jazz isn't, when . . .

It's Miles talking to you, whispering about the day on the swings. You can't believe it. He remembers that afternoon too! And once again you're running across that field hand in hand and he's your little brother, your monkey, your banana, your little guy.

You want to tell him sorry for everything, that you are done done done being an ogre like Hector. You want to tell him that this moment, like every moment, is a first, is the beginning again, so you two can start over. You try with all your might to move your mouth so you can say the words *little brother,* when . . .

You're face down in a pile of leaves. You try to lift your head.

Can it be?

And then you hear his voice for the first time in twelve years. It *is* him. *He's come back for you,* you cry in your head at the same time he says, *Wynton please come back to us.*

Oh, you have to see him! You don't care anymore that he's not your father by blood, he's still the father in your memory, in your heart. You use all your strength to open one eyelid, but you can't do it.

You are so infinitesimally close to returning to your family, to the crappy amazing world, to all the glorious noise, but you can't make your eyes open, as much as you try, until you're overwhelmed by the scent of flowers—Cassidy!

You hear her cry out, "Wynton and I are not related!"

And then what is this?

What is it?

A hand—*her* hand!—tenderly grazes your forehead, your cheek, then lands on your fingers, and you know this because you can *feel* it which means you are back. You are back! If you open your eyes, you will see Cassidy—that waterfall of beauty—and you will see your brother who forgives you and your mother and little sister who love you completely, effortlessly. You will see your father Theo who left and your father Clive who didn't—someone whose horn-playing you very well may have been hearing all these years, for it's just occurred to you, it was him and not the other man who gave you the greatest gift of your life: the ability to make music.

You've now watched the world walk away from you without a thought, until these people, *your* people, dragged it back. For you. Is that the actual divine frequency then?

You know right on the other side of your eyelids are tremendous days that will ring out clear as bells and nights that will escort you through songs with only sad parts. You are here for every last bit of it, every last note.

Except not yet.

Cassidy's holding your hand and you know she's leaning over you because tumbles of hair are tickling your face and neck. You summon all your strength, all your *life*, and squeeze her hand to tell her yes and yes and still more yes, then with eyes still shut, you whisper only for her to hear, "Closer," and she understands, because your lips have found each other's—your mouths!—and kissing her is Beethoven's freaking Fifth and you never want to stop, never want to, never will stop loving this girl. This girl who has planted a sun in your chest. This girl who has brought you back to life, word by word, with the full orchestra of her being, her story, and now with this kiss that is turning you into brightness, into music, into yourself.

You realize you can lift your right arm even though it's heavy and likely in a cast and when you do to gently place it on Cassidy's back to bring her still closer, to pull her in in in, the room explodes with cries, and the world that you're all in together tips over, and for once, it's joy, and only joy that spills out.

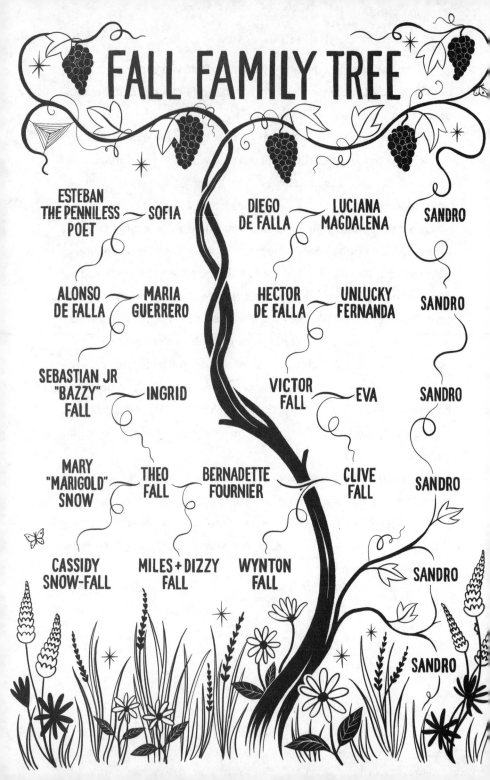

The First Meal Theo Fall Eats at The Blue Spoonful:

AMUSE-BOUCHE: OYSTERS WITH SEA URCHIN, LEMON PEARLS, AND BLACK PEPPER

STARTER: A TOWER OF SCALLOPS, CUCUMBERS, NECTARINES, TOPPED WITH A CARDAMOM AND HORSERADISH SAUCE

MAIN: TENDER ROAST CHICKEN SMOTHERED IN ELDERBERRY JUICE, OLIVES, AND CAPERS

DESSERT #1: ANNIE'S CHOCOLATE VINEGAR CAKE

DESSERT #2: DIZZY'S PANSY PETAL CRÊPES WITH LAVENDER CREAM

PAIRING: A PINOT NOIR FROM A LOCAL WINERY CALLED SECOND CHANCE

ACKNOWLEDGMENTS

Years ago, an author friend said to me that writing a novel is like trying to fit a quilt the size of a football field into a tiny envelope. With *When the World Tips Over*, it often felt like that quilt was the size of a continent. I never would have finished without the insightful, passionate, and enthusiastic help I received from so many. I want to thank the readers at Pippin Properties, Inc.: Holly McGhee, Marissa Brown, Julia Ermi, Jason Ajas Steiner, Morgan Hughes, who read and reread, who moved into the work with me, whose insights were genius, spot-on, and always honest, no matter the timing. I also want to thank all the Pippins—adding in Elena Giovinazzo, Ashley Valentine, and the awesome interns—for everything else on earth they do with such expertise, enthusiasm, ferocity, competence, joy. Especially my funny, fierce, indomitable literary agent and dear friend, Holly McGhee, with her heart-and-soul devotion to art and life. She is her own horizon.

I'm overflowing with gratitude for my spectacular editor Jessica Dandino Garrison, my trench-mate, whom I adore and trust wholeheartedly. She lived in this story with me, bringing to the editing process brilliance, enthusiasm, openness, stamina, kindness, and a delight for words and story that is regenerative and inspiring. I want to thank everyone else at Penguin Young Readers too, for support and patience during the writing years as well as mad passion and attack when the novel was finally delivered. You are an extraordinary team, and I am thrilled and honored to be a part of it. You always make me feel like I'm home. So much gratitude goes to absolutely everyone there, including: Jen Loja,

Jen Klonsky, Nancy Mercado, Felicity Vallence, Lizzie Goodell, Emily Romero, Jocelyn Schmidt, Christina Colangelo, Carmela Iaria, Venessa Carson, Shanta Newlin, Lauri Hornik, Lindsay Boggs, Squish Pruitt, Lathea Mondesir, Alex Garber, James Akinaka, Jayne Ziemba, Regina Castillo, Kenny Young, Jenn Ridgway, Tabitha Dulla, Shannon Spann, Jenny Kelly, who put her heart into designing these stunning pages, and Theresa Evangelista, who designed this cover I love so much, I want to eat it. Thanks also go to Jessica Cruickshank for her gorgeous artwork, which brings so much to the story.

So much gratitude goes to the incredible team at Rights People in the UK for bringing my stories to so many readers worldwide. You are peerless and I am so lucky to work with you. Thank you: Alex Devlin, Harim Yim, Claudia Galluzzi, Amy Threadgold, Charlotte Bodman, Hannah Whitaker, Annie Blombach. Thanks also go to the entire fantastic crew at Walker Books in the UK and Australia/New Zealand for their support, enthusiasm, and ingenuity. Particularly my wonderful UK editors: Jane Winterbotham, Frances Taffinder, and my former editor Annalie Grainger. Thanks also to my German editor Birte Hecker, who's become a friend, as well as all my editors, translators, and publishers across the globe. I can't tell you how much it means to me that my characters get to live in your languages. Much appreciation also goes to my audio book publishers at Brilliance and Listening Library as well as the gifted actors who narrate them.

I want to thank the fabulous team of Diane Golden and Sarah Lerner for their savvy, expertise, and friendship, and my wonderful film agent Dana Spector at CAA for the same.

For their astute early reads when this novel was still a continent-size quilt, I thank Tim Wynne-Jones, Brent Hartinger, and later: Patricia Nelson, Carol Nelson, Marianna Baer, Nina LaCour, and my amazing mother, Edie Block.

Thanks especially to my friend, the incredible author and editor Marianna Baer, who talked about this story with me for years, offering brilliance and belly laughs. I couldn't bear writing and publishing without you.

Thanks to doctors Anne and Maggie for help with my coma patient, and to Dr. Bautista for help with eye conditions.

Enormous heartfelt appreciation to all the booksellers, librarians, and educators across the country who are so dedicated in these years of terrible book bannings to getting the right books into the hands of young people. You are heroes.

This was not an easy novel to write, and it was also a difficult bunch of years to write in for many reasons. I want to thank my family for all the love, support, and revelry, for the martini dinners, for making life a celebration, no matter what else is going on. Thank you to my huge-hearted and hilarious mother, whom I cherish beyond words and who is the heart outside my body. My father died while I was writing this book and he is forever in me and my words, and I'm pretty sure, the bouquet of dried yellow roses that I seem to talk to when I miss him most. So much love goes to my stepmother, Carol, who is a blazing meteor lighting up the sky, to the best brothers and pals on earth, my ballasts: Bruce and Bobby, whom I love immeasurably, who always make me laugh, and for whom I'm grateful every day—how are we so fortunate that we get to go through it all together? To Pat and Monica, my beloved, kickass sisters in this life, to my joyful dynamo of a niece Lena, to my sweet and compassionate nephew Jake, the bravest person I know, to clever Adam with his kind heart whom I miss. Great appreciation to Rick and Patricia, to Andy, Sarah, Alyssa, and Lindsay, to Jeff and Deborah and always and forever Michele. Huge love to Paul, who somehow is both always in the moment and sublimely in the clouds, for incomparable joie de vivre, conversation, celebration. To Mark for bringing the joy, the tender heart to days past and to come. Also, love to the extended families: the Greens, the Blocks, the Shumans, the Routhiers, the Feuerwerkers.

I think the luckiest part of my life is that I have a second family of decades-old friends, who plant the sun in my chest, whom I couldn't live without, who fill my life with life, joy, hope, hilarity, safety, continuity. I think maybe we're all trees at this point whose roots have joined under the earth. All my love forever to Anne, Ami, Becky, Emily, Jeremy, Julie, Larry, James, Maggie, Mo, Simone, Sarah, Alex, Zoe, Tim, Jeff, Dave, Matt, and the kids: Ila, Jo, Lucas, Sora, Siena, Sam, Jules, Prudence.

And for eternity: Barbie, Stacy, and James.

I also want to thank my cherished house family: Nina, Kristyn, Juju, Luka, and Mazie. I am so happy to live in The Magic Circle with you, to share the days, the flowers, the dinners, the whist games, the cocktails, the howlings into the wind, even the busted pipes. You are all in my heart forever.

So much gratitude to so many friends and faculty at VCFA for changing the course of my life. Same goes to my English teachers and literature professors over the years. And to all my writer friends.

Deep thanks to MacDowell for a fellowship where I spent a magical, timeless six weeks walking the woods in moonlight, finishing this novel. I had such an enchanted time with everyone I met there, wish I could name all the names but there's too many of you amazing people, so just a special shout-out to Ingrid and Victor.

For everyone I've mentioned and so many I haven't because of space, I'm so grateful that we get to spend this life together, that when the world tips over, because of you, for me, joy always spills out.

It's ridiculous how much I love you all.

JANDY NELSON is the *New York Times* bestselling author of *I'll Give You the Sun*, which received the Printz Award, was a Stonewall Honor Book, and was named one of TIME's 100 Best Young Adult Books of all Time. Her critically acclaimed debut, *The Sky Is Everywhere*, is now an AppleTV+ and A24 original film starring Jason Segel and Cherry Jones, for which Jandy wrote the screenplay. Together, *Sun* and *Sky* have sold well over a million copies worldwide and have been translated into more than thirty-eight languages. Both have been YALSA Best Fiction for Young Adults picks and on multiple best of the year lists, have earned many starred reviews, and continue to enjoy great international success. Currently a full-time writer, Jandy lives and writes in San Francisco, California, not far from the settings of her novels.

Visit Jandy at jandynelson.com, on Instagram @jandy.nelson, on Twitter @jandynelson, and on Facebook at Jandy Nelson.